PHILIP PULLMAN

THE ADVENTURES OF
JOHN BLAKE
· MYSTERY OF THE GHOST SHIP ·
ILLUSTRATED BY FRED FORDHAM

graphix   d·b
           David Fickling Books   the PHOENIX

SCHOLASTIC

To the spirit of *The Phoenix* – P. P.
For Goosey. With special thanks to Camille – F. F.

First published in the United Kingdom in 2017 by David Fickling Books, 31 Beaumont Street,
Oxford OX1 2NP, and The Phoenix Comic, 29 Beaumont Street, Oxford OX1 2NP.
www.davidficklingbooks.com
www.thephoenixcomic.co.uk

Library of Congress Cataloging-in-Publication Data available

ISBN 978-1-338-14912-8
ISBN 978-1-338-14911-1

10 9 8 7 6 5 4 3 2 1   17 18 19 20 21

Printed and bound in China by Toppan Leefung
First edition, June 2017

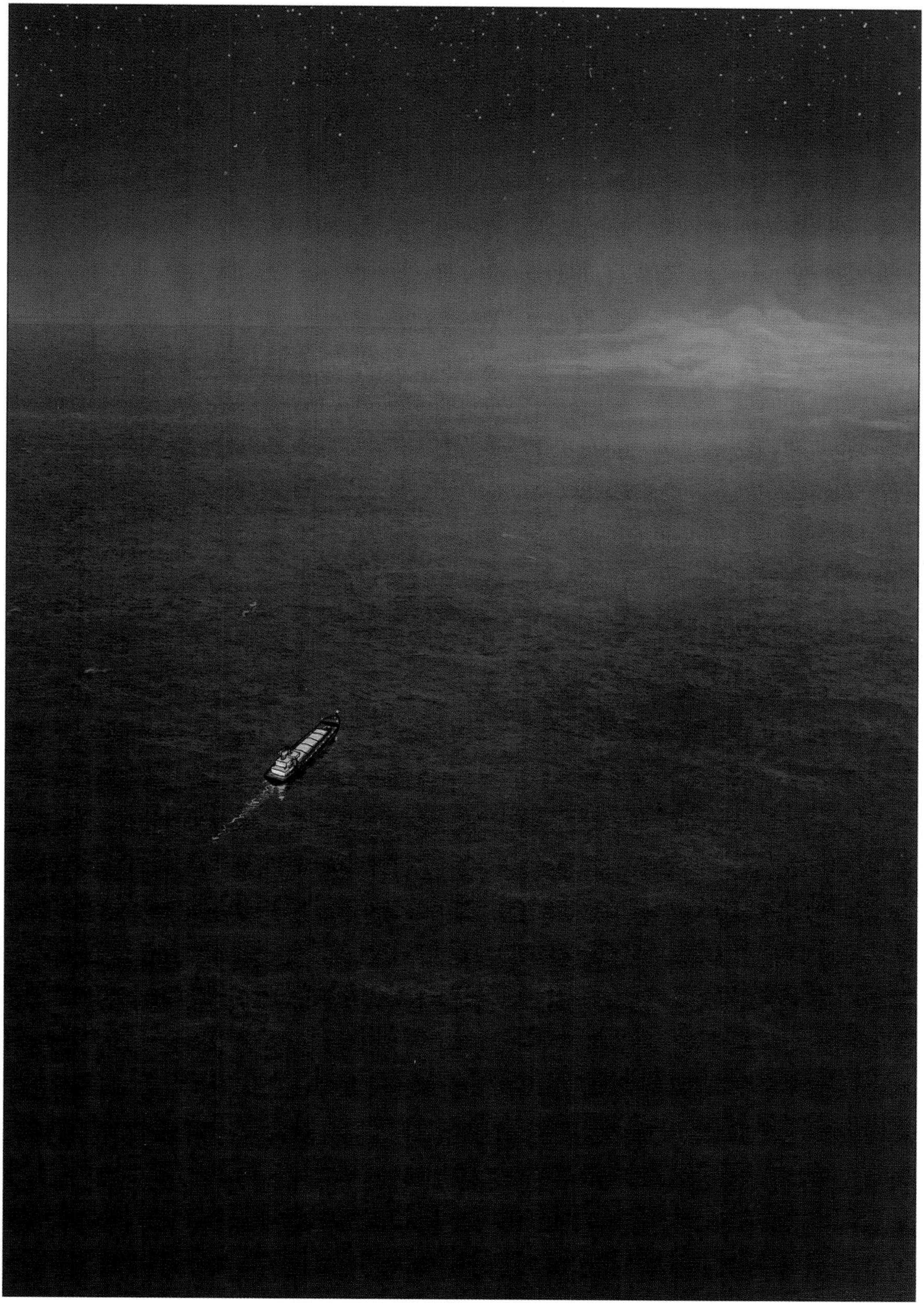

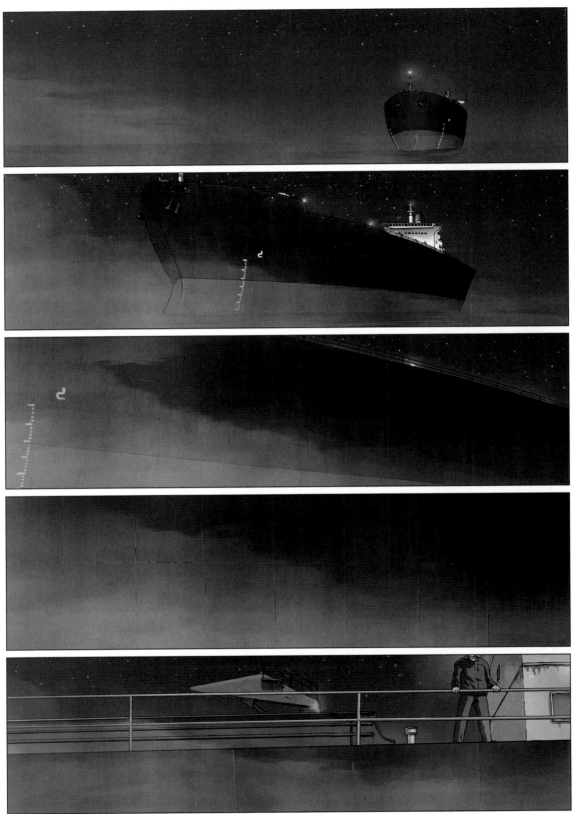

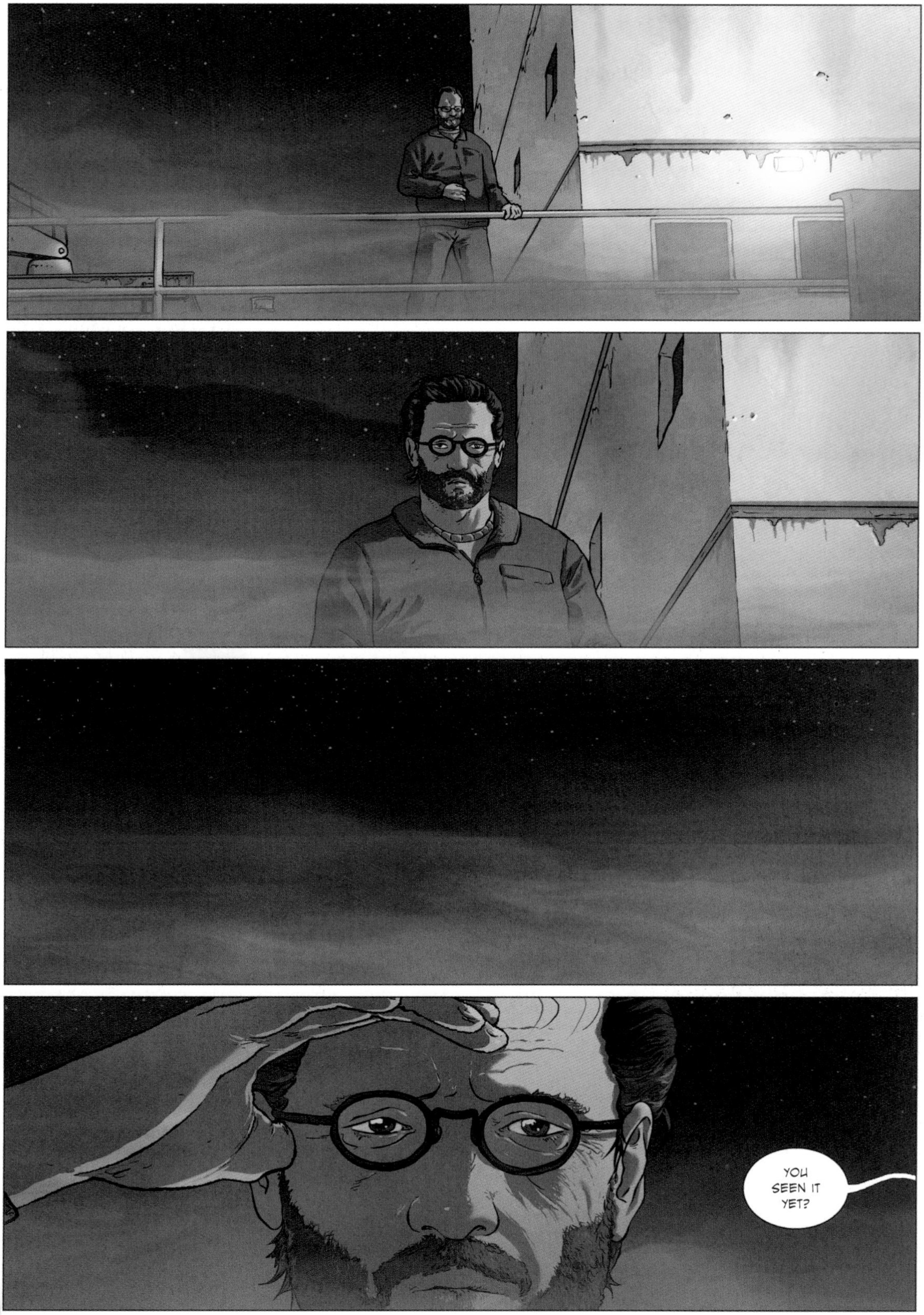
YOU SEEN IT YET?

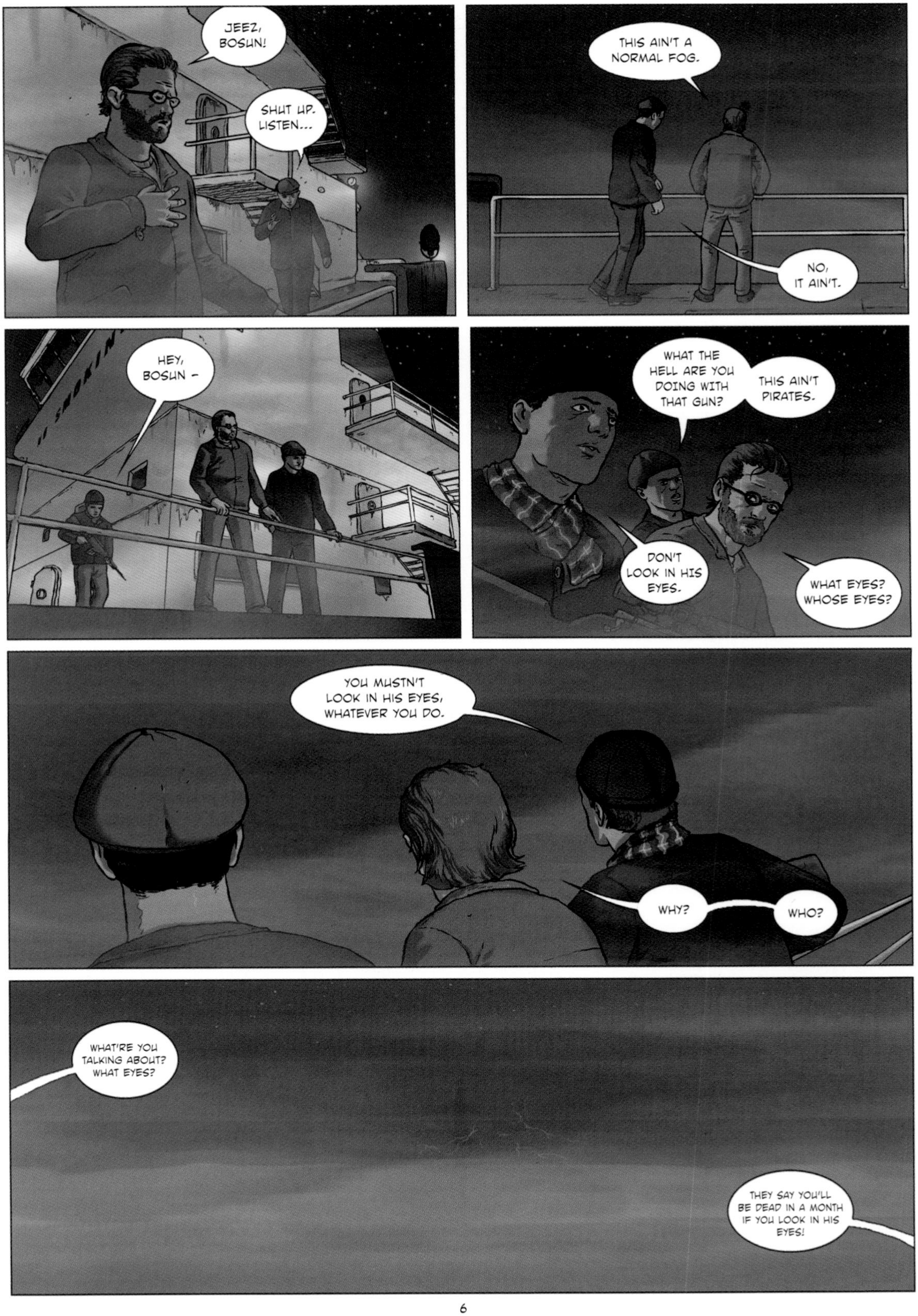
JEEZ, BOSUN!
SHUT UP. LISTEN...
THIS AIN'T A NORMAL FOG.
NO, IT AIN'T.
HEY, BOSUN –
WHAT THE HELL ARE YOU DOING WITH THAT GUN?
THIS AIN'T PIRATES.
DON'T LOOK IN HIS EYES.
WHAT EYES? WHOSE EYES?
YOU MUSTN'T LOOK IN HIS EYES, WHATEVER YOU DO.
WHY?
WHO?
WHAT'RE YOU TALKING ABOUT? WHAT EYES?
THEY SAY YOU'LL BE DEAD IN A MONTH IF YOU LOOK IN HIS EYES!

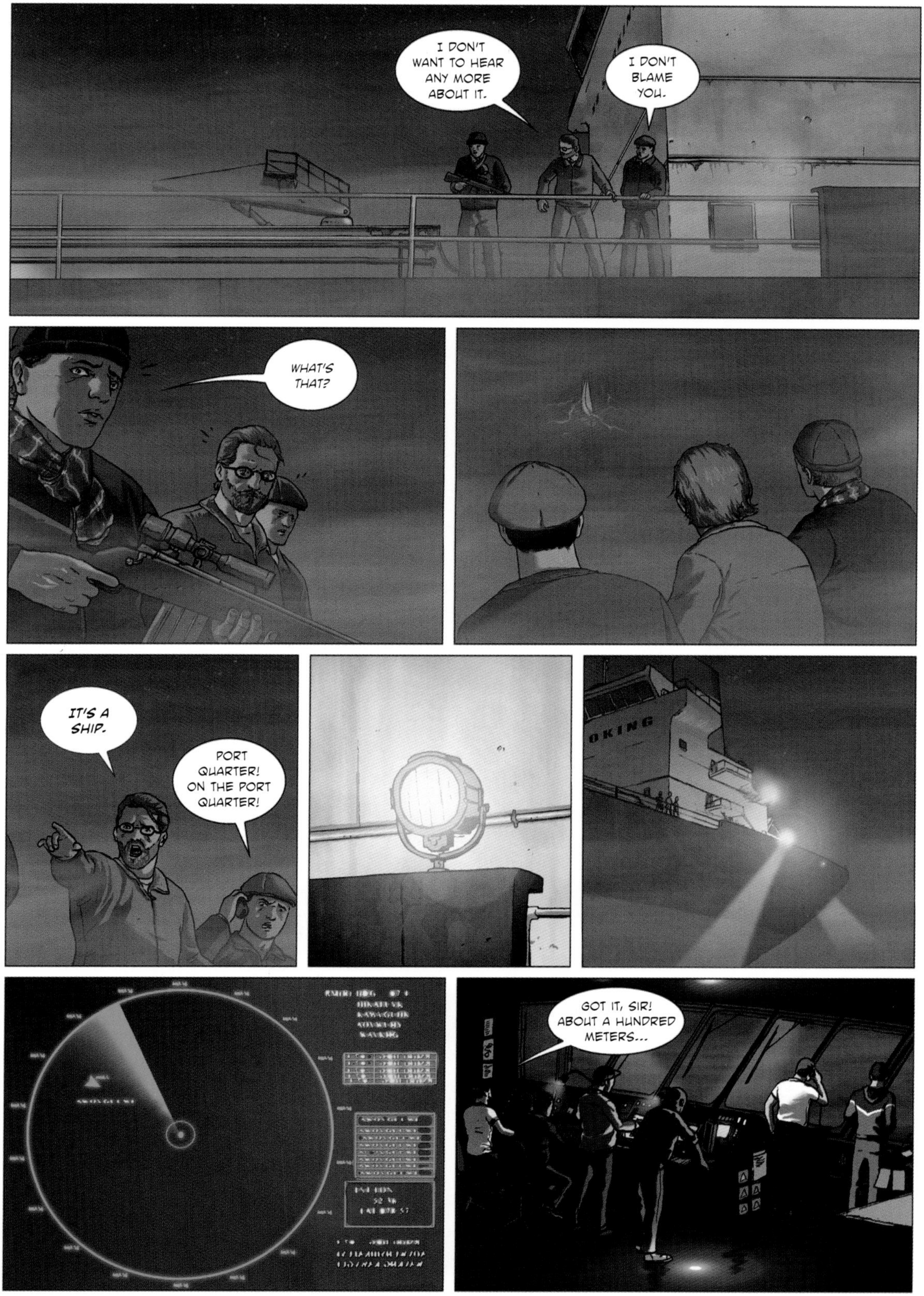
I DON'T WANT TO HEAR ANY MORE ABOUT IT.
I DON'T BLAME YOU.
WHAT'S THAT?
IT'S A SHIP.
PORT QUARTER! ON THE PORT QUARTER!
GOT IT, SIR! ABOUT A HUNDRED METERS...

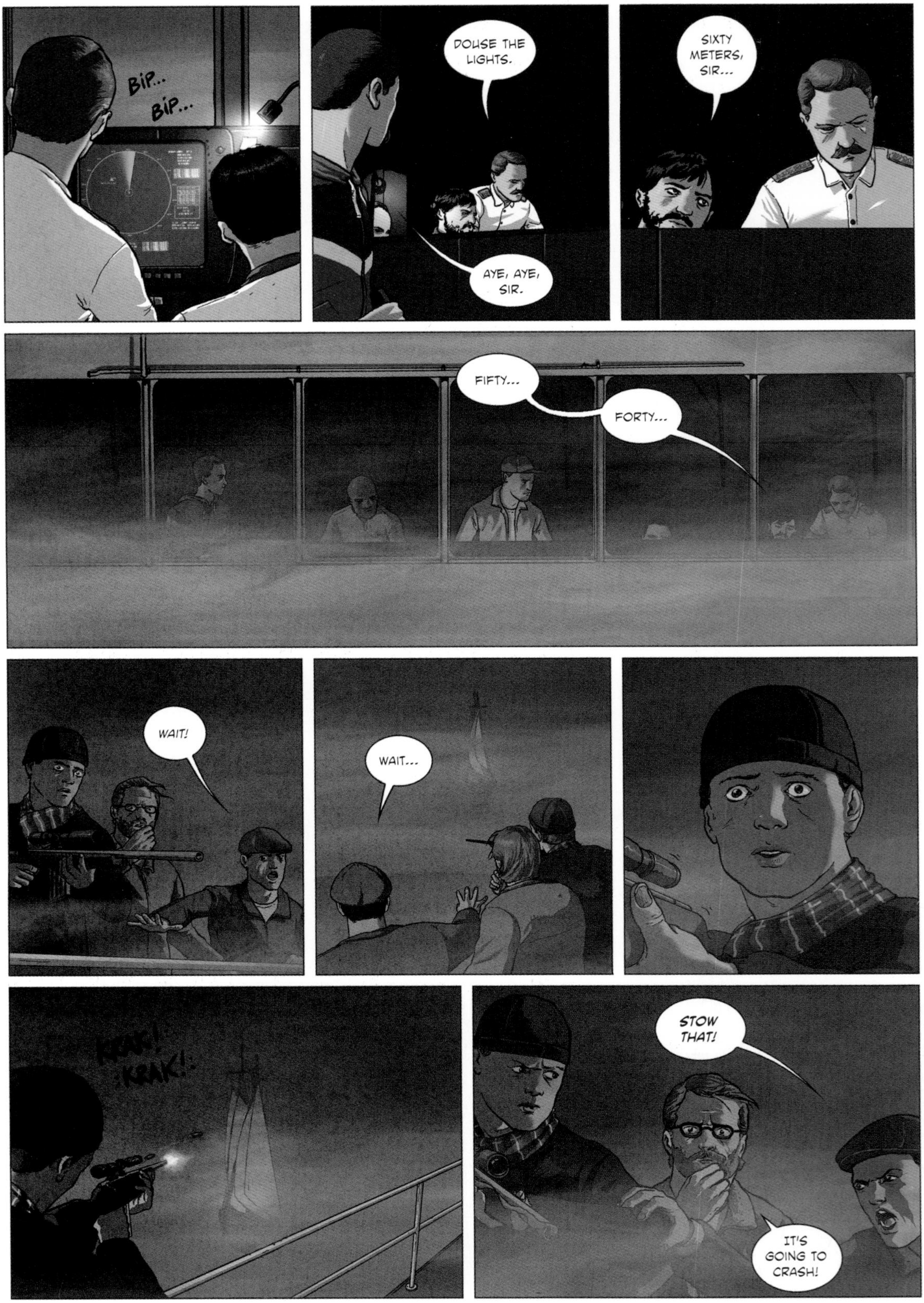
BIP...
BIP...
DOUSE THE LIGHTS.
AYE, AYE, SIR.
SIXTY METERS, SIR...
FIFTY...
FORTY...
WAIT!
WAIT...
KRAK!
KRAK!
STOW THAT!
IT'S GOING TO CRASH!

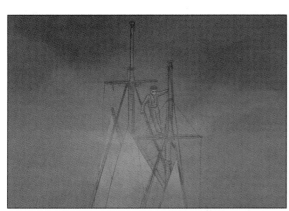

OH, MOTHER OF GOD, PROTECT US...

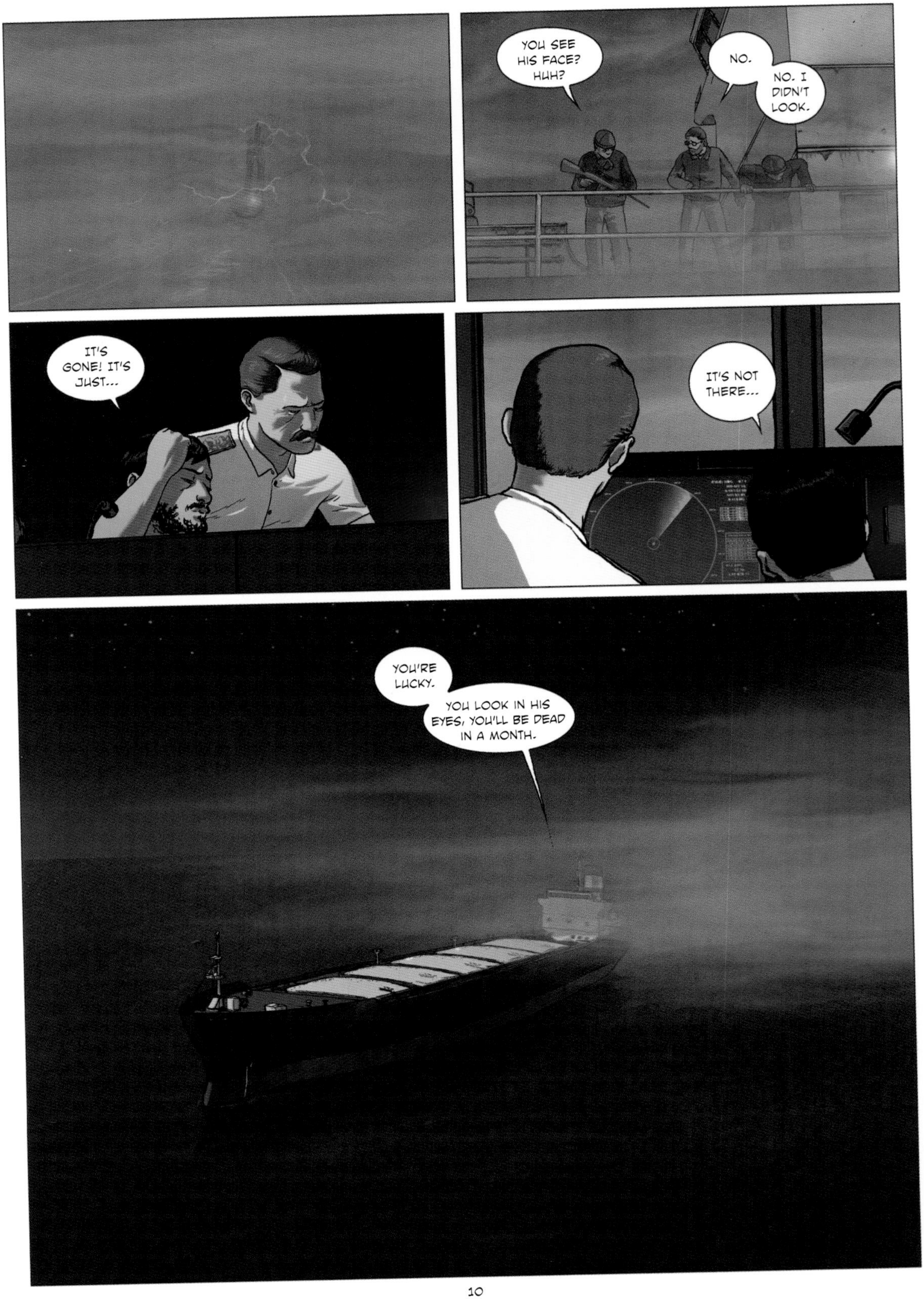
YOU SEE HIS FACE? HUH?
NO.
NO. I DIDN'T LOOK.
IT'S GONE! IT'S JUST...
IT'S NOT THERE...
YOU'RE LUCKY.
YOU LOOK IN HIS EYES, YOU'LL BE DEAD IN A MONTH.

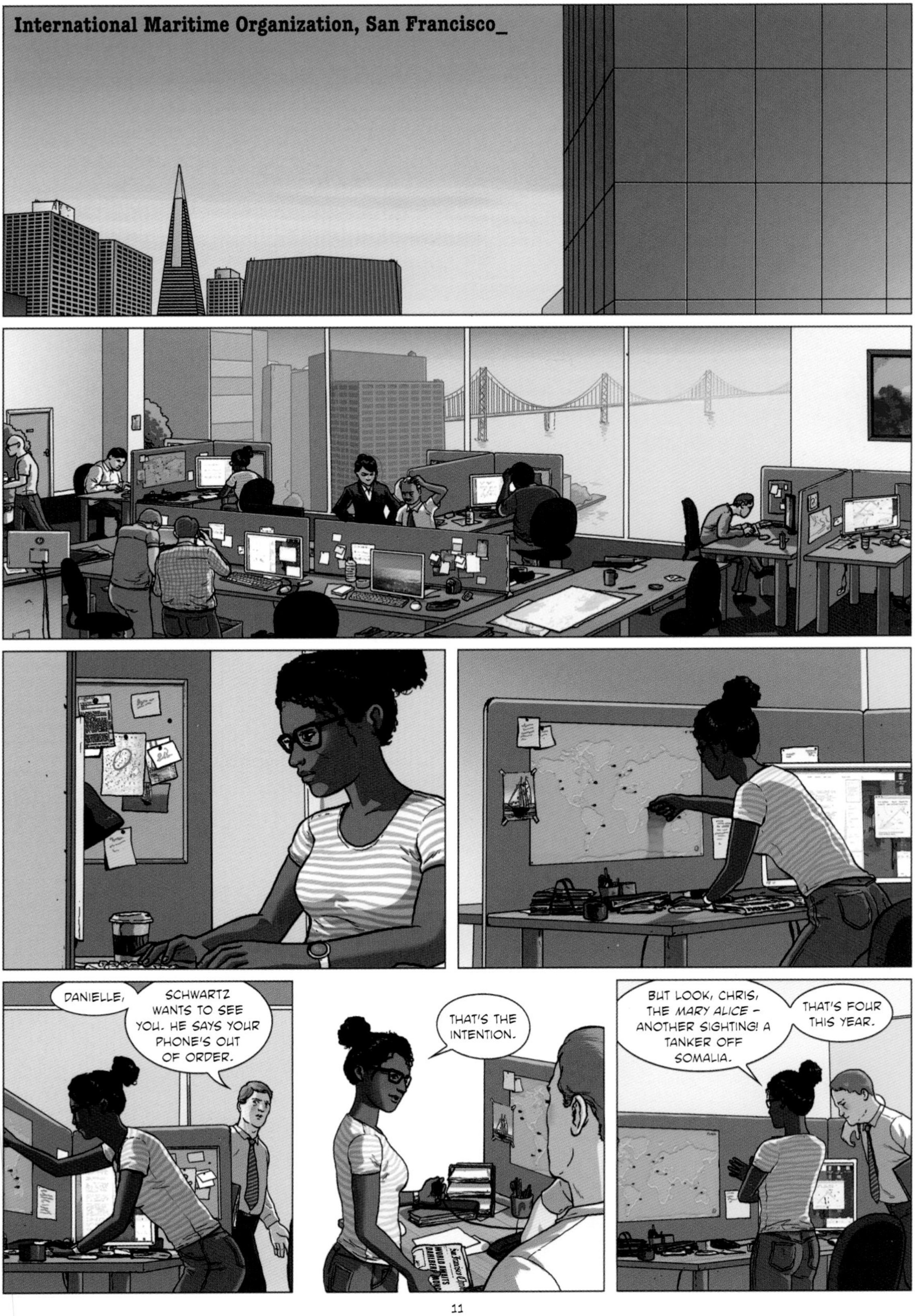
International Maritime Organization, San Francisco_
DANIELLE,
SCHWARTZ WANTS TO SEE YOU. HE SAYS YOUR PHONE'S OUT OF ORDER.
THAT'S THE INTENTION.
BUT LOOK, CHRIS, THE MARY ALICE – ANOTHER SIGHTING! A TANKER OFF SOMALIA.
THAT'S FOUR THIS YEAR.

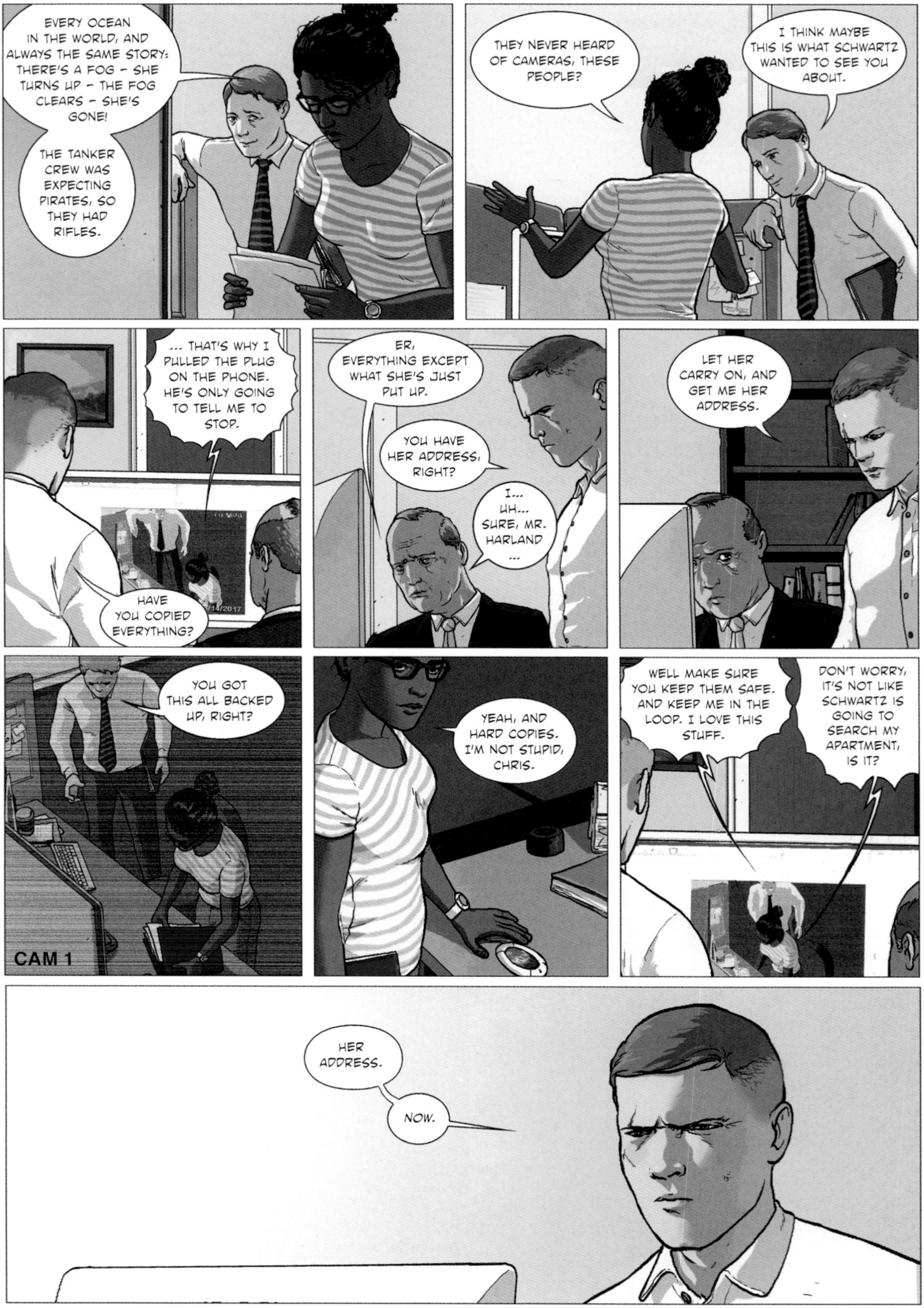
EVERY OCEAN IN THE WORLD, AND ALWAYS THE SAME STORY: THERE'S A FOG – SHE TURNS UP – THE FOG CLEARS – SHE'S GONE!
THE TANKER CREW WAS EXPECTING PIRATES, SO THEY HAD RIFLES.
THEY NEVER HEARD OF CAMERAS, THESE PEOPLE?
I THINK MAYBE THIS IS WHAT SCHWARTZ WANTED TO SEE YOU ABOUT.
... THAT'S WHY I PULLED THE PLUG ON THE PHONE. HE'S ONLY GOING TO TELL ME TO STOP.
HAVE YOU COPIED EVERYTHING?
ER, EVERYTHING EXCEPT WHAT SHE'S JUST PUT UP.
YOU HAVE HER ADDRESS, RIGHT?
I... UH... SURE, MR. HARLAND ...
LET HER CARRY ON, AND GET ME HER ADDRESS.
YOU GOT THIS ALL BACKED UP, RIGHT?
CAM 1
YEAH, AND HARD COPIES. I'M NOT STUPID, CHRIS.
WELL MAKE SURE YOU KEEP THEM SAFE. AND KEEP ME IN THE LOOP. I LOVE THIS STUFF.
DON'T WORRY, IT'S NOT LIKE SCHWARTZ IS GOING TO SEARCH MY APARTMENT, IS IT?
HER ADDRESS.
NOW.

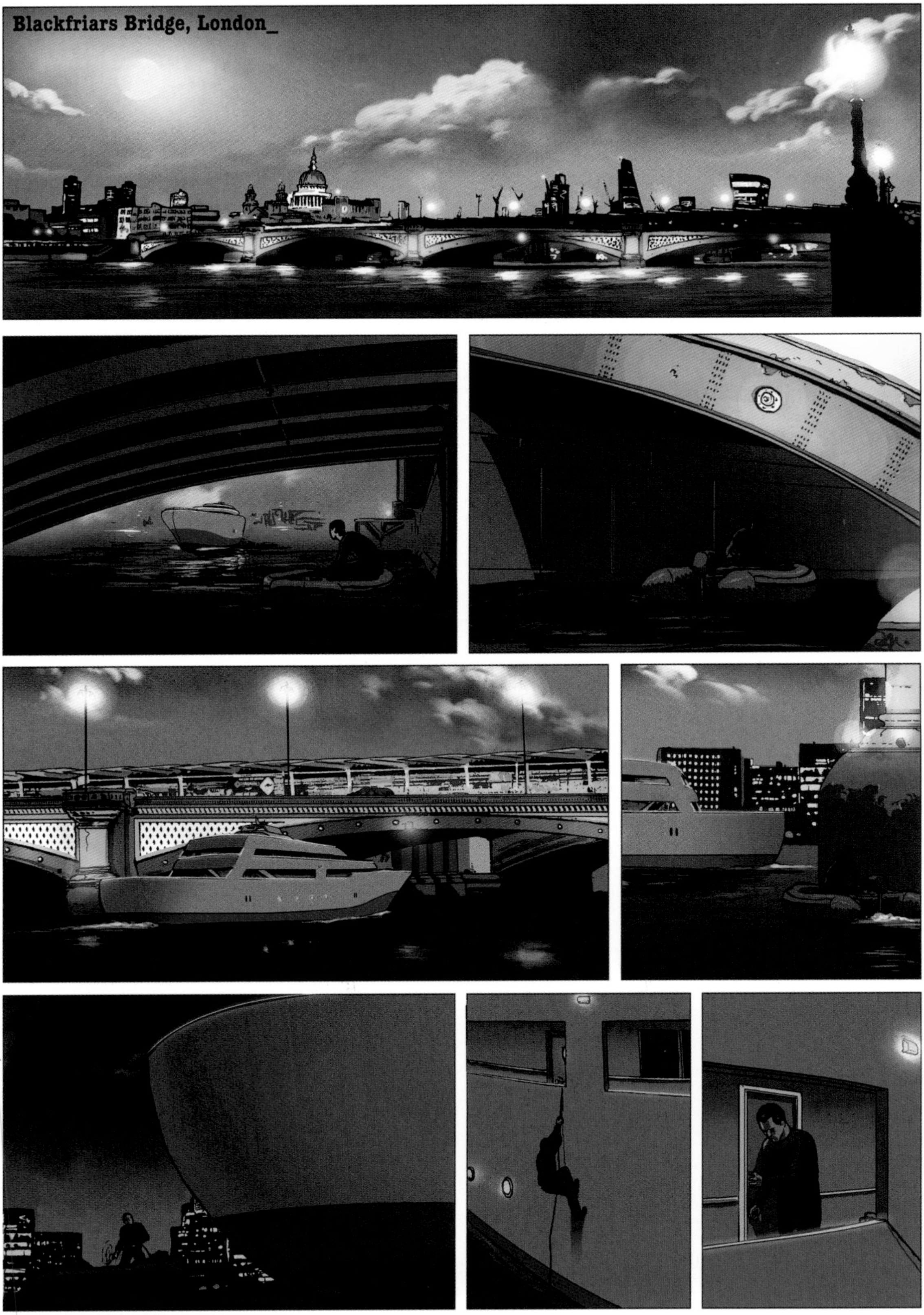
Blackfriars Bridge, London_

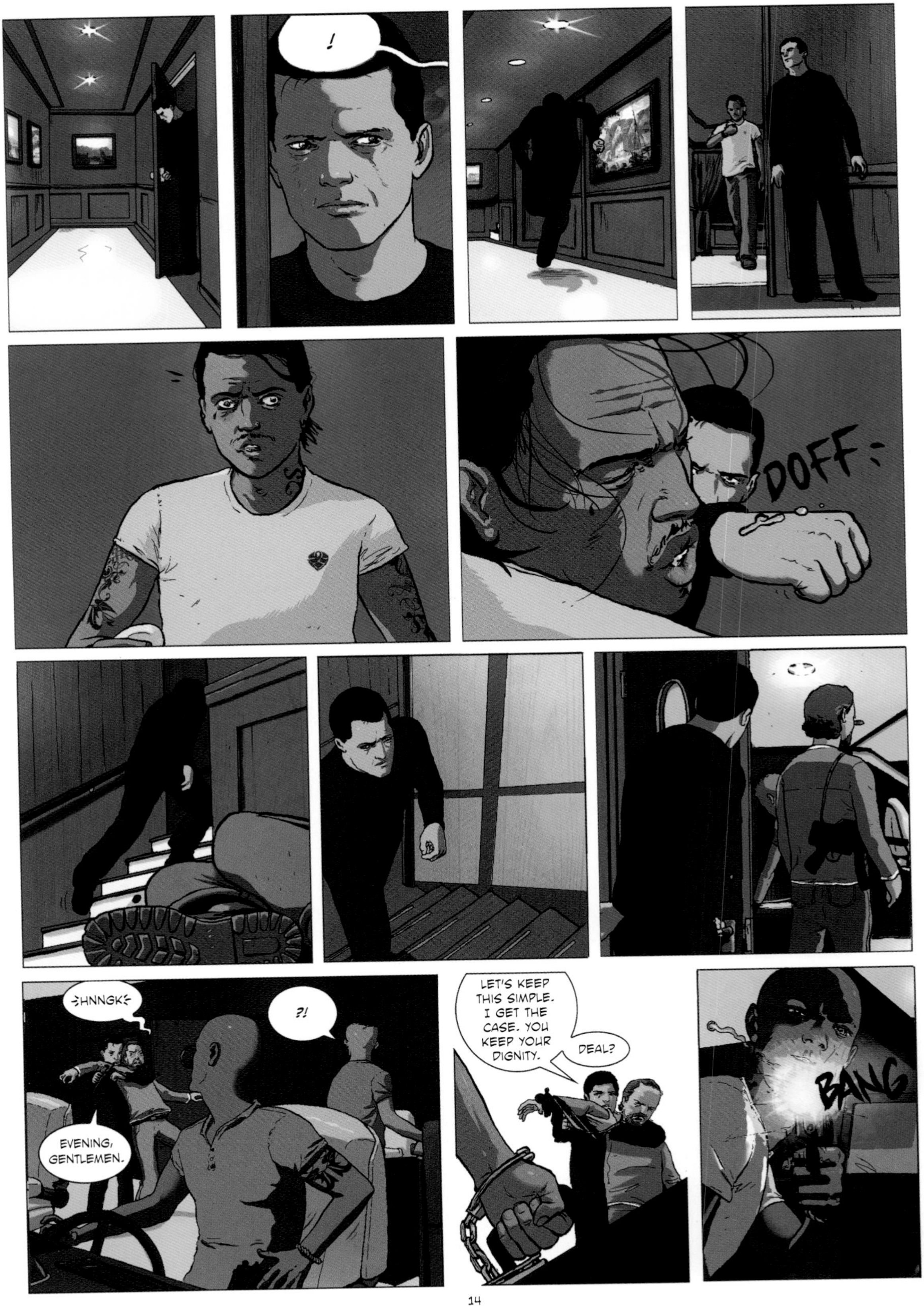
!
DOFF
HNNGK
?!
EVENING, GENTLEMEN.
LET'S KEEP THIS SIMPLE. I GET THE CASE. YOU KEEP YOUR DIGNITY.
DEAL?
BANG

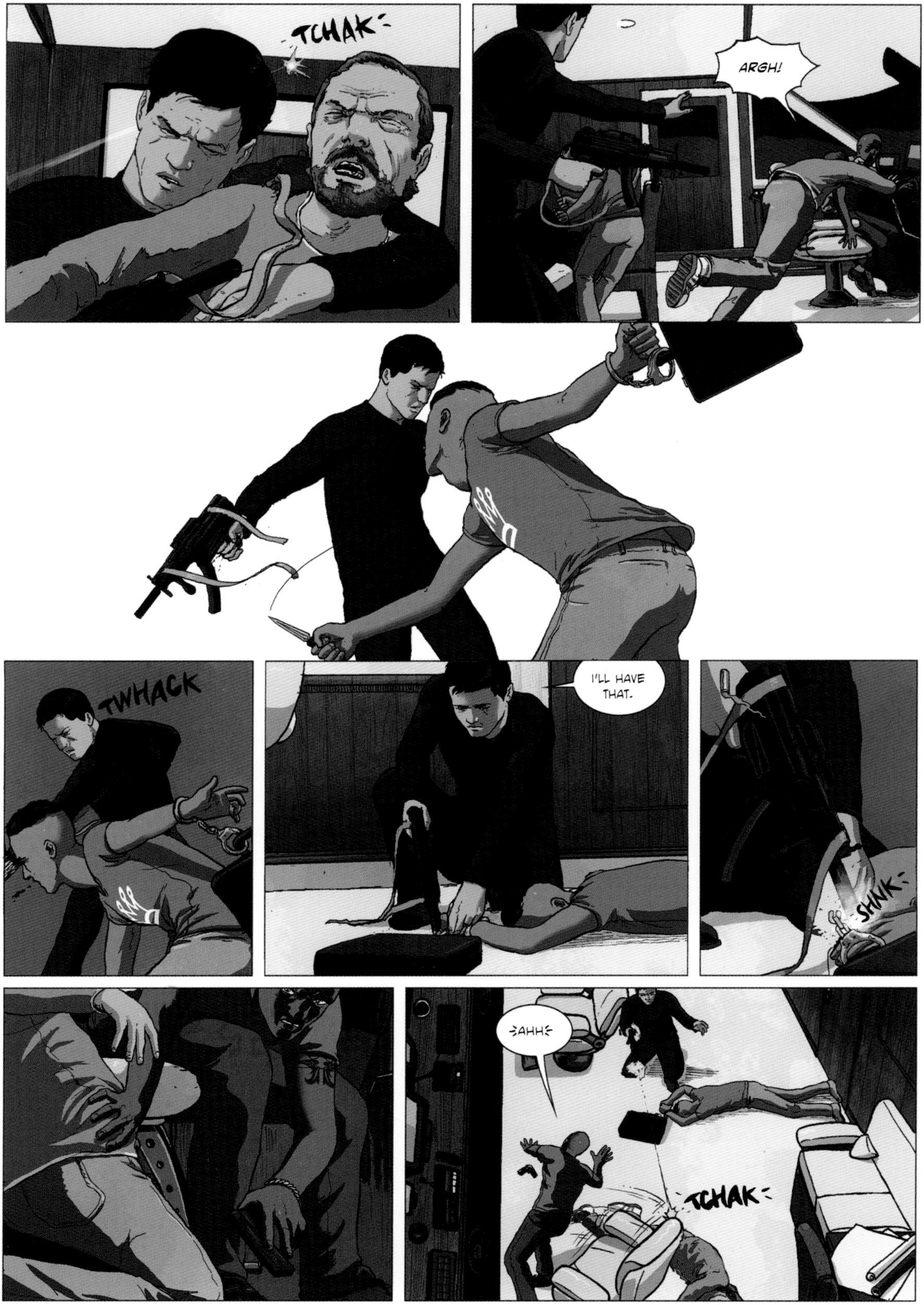
TCHAK
ARGH!
TWHACK
I'LL HAVE THAT.
SHNK
AHH
TCHAK

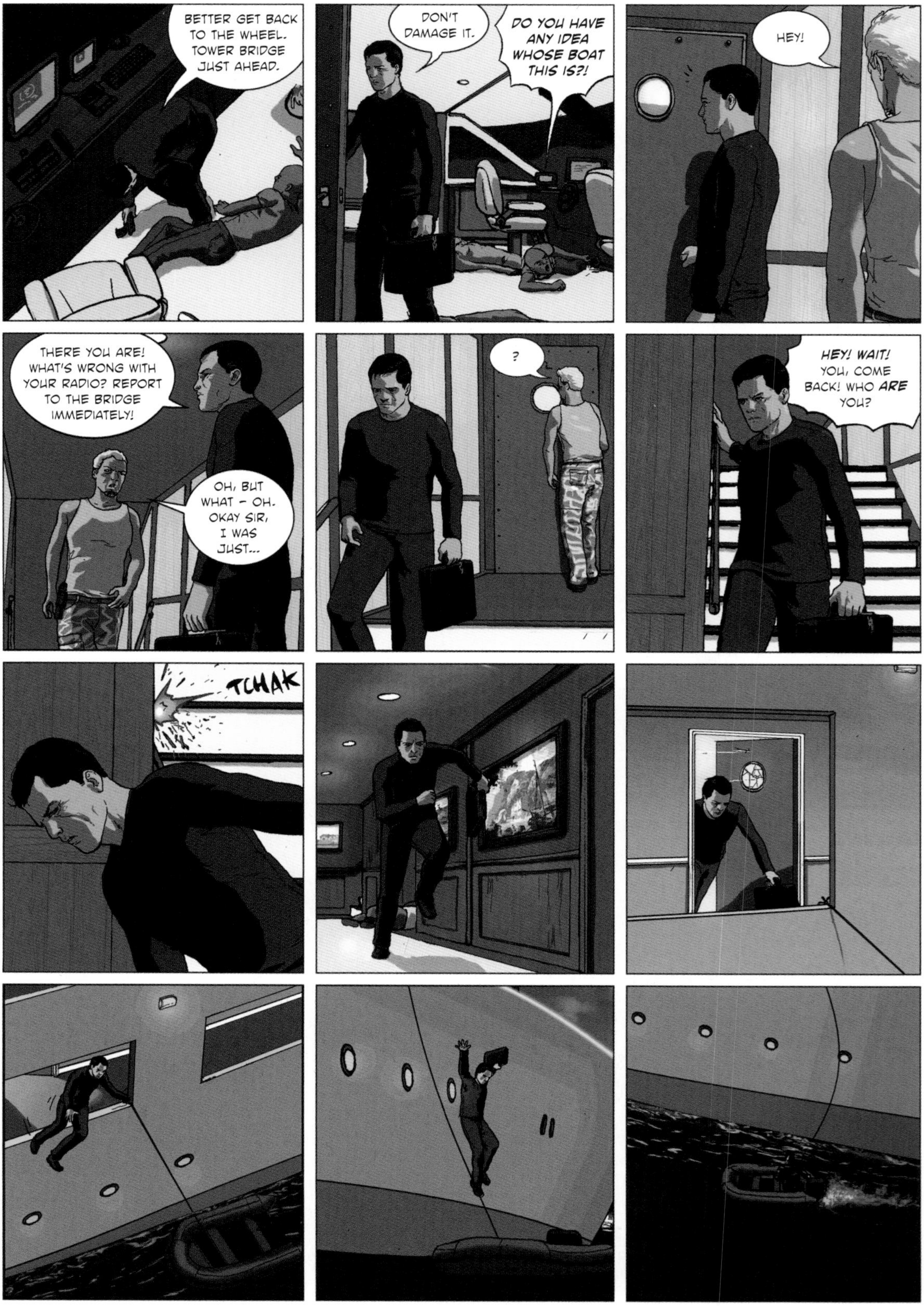
BETTER GET BACK TO THE WHEEL. TOWER BRIDGE JUST AHEAD.
DON'T DAMAGE IT.
DO YOU HAVE ANY IDEA WHOSE BOAT THIS IS?!
HEY!
THERE YOU ARE! WHAT'S WRONG WITH YOUR RADIO? REPORT TO THE BRIDGE IMMEDIATELY!
OH, BUT WHAT – OH. OKAY SIR, I WAS JUST...
?
HEY! WAIT! YOU, COME BACK! WHO ARE YOU?
TCHAK

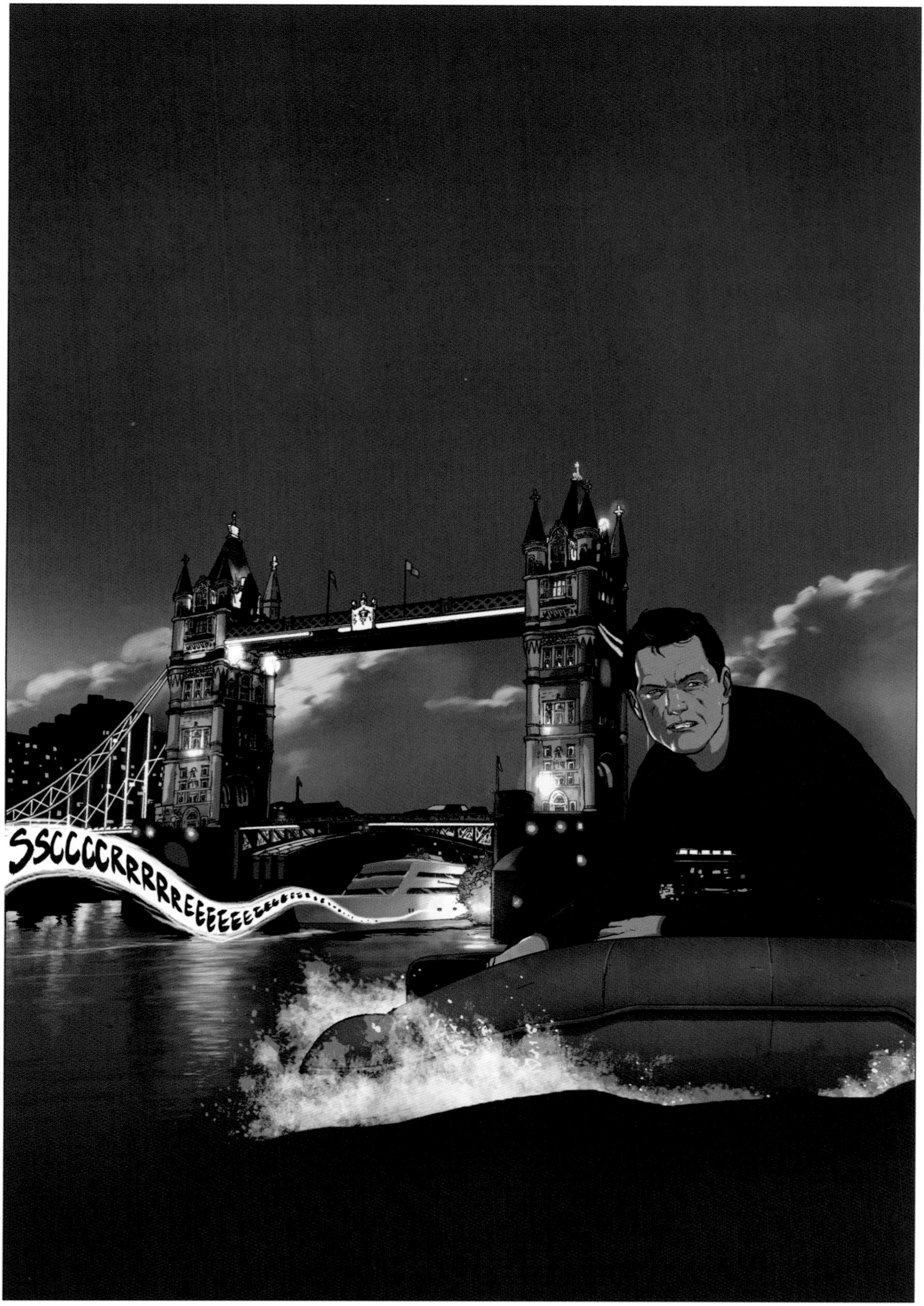
SSCCCCRRRRRREEEEEEE

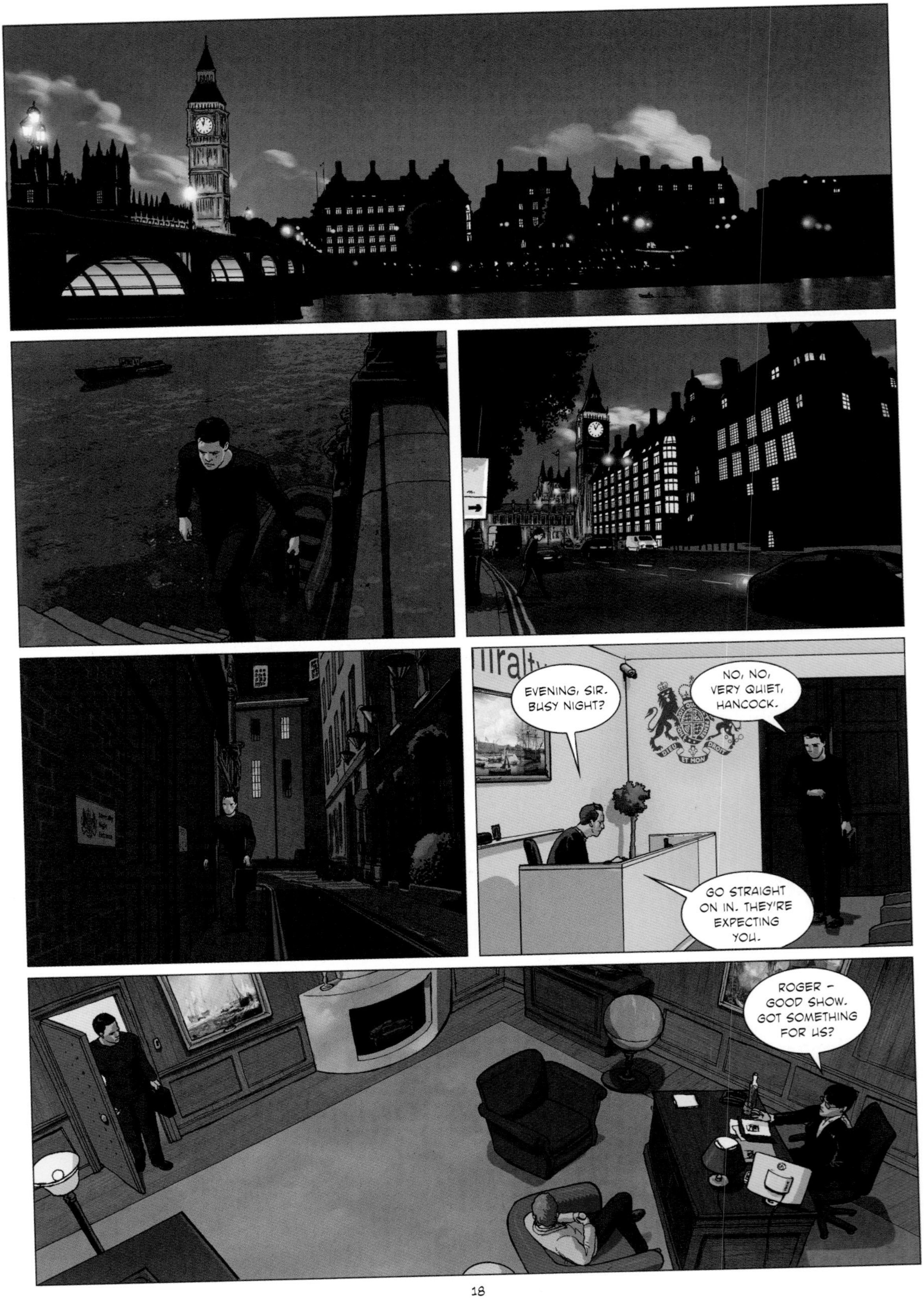
EVENING, SIR. BUSY NIGHT?
NO, NO, VERY QUIET, HANCOCK.
GO STRAIGHT ON IN. THEY'RE EXPECTING YOU.
ROGER – GOOD SHOW. GOT SOMETHING FOR US?

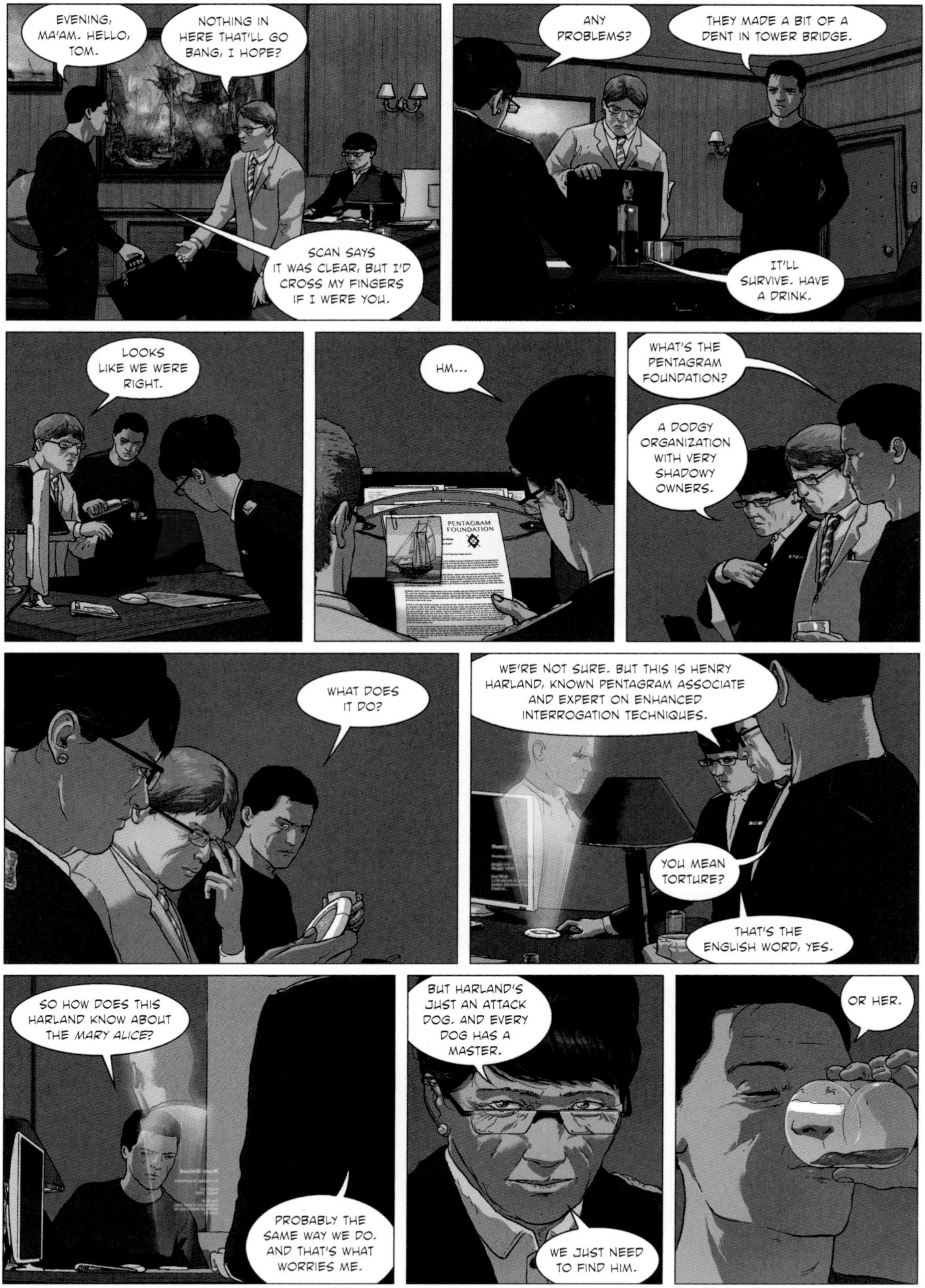
EVENING, MA'AM. HELLO, TOM.
NOTHING IN HERE THAT'LL GO BANG, I HOPE?
SCAN SAYS IT WAS CLEAR, BUT I'D CROSS MY FINGERS IF I WERE YOU.
ANY PROBLEMS?
THEY MADE A BIT OF A DENT IN TOWER BRIDGE.
IT'LL SURVIVE. HAVE A DRINK.
LOOKS LIKE WE WERE RIGHT.
HM...
PENTAGRAM FOUNDATION
WHAT'S THE PENTAGRAM FOUNDATION?
A DODGY ORGANIZATION WITH VERY SHADOWY OWNERS.
WHAT DOES IT DO?
WE'RE NOT SURE. BUT THIS IS HENRY HARLAND, KNOWN PENTAGRAM ASSOCIATE AND EXPERT ON ENHANCED INTERROGATION TECHNIQUES.
YOU MEAN TORTURE?
THAT'S THE ENGLISH WORD, YES.
SO HOW DOES THIS HARLAND KNOW ABOUT THE *MARY ALICE*?
PROBABLY THE SAME WAY WE DO. AND THAT'S WHAT WORRIES ME.
BUT HARLAND'S JUST AN ATTACK DOG. AND EVERY DOG HAS A MASTER.
WE JUST NEED TO FIND HIM.
OR HER.

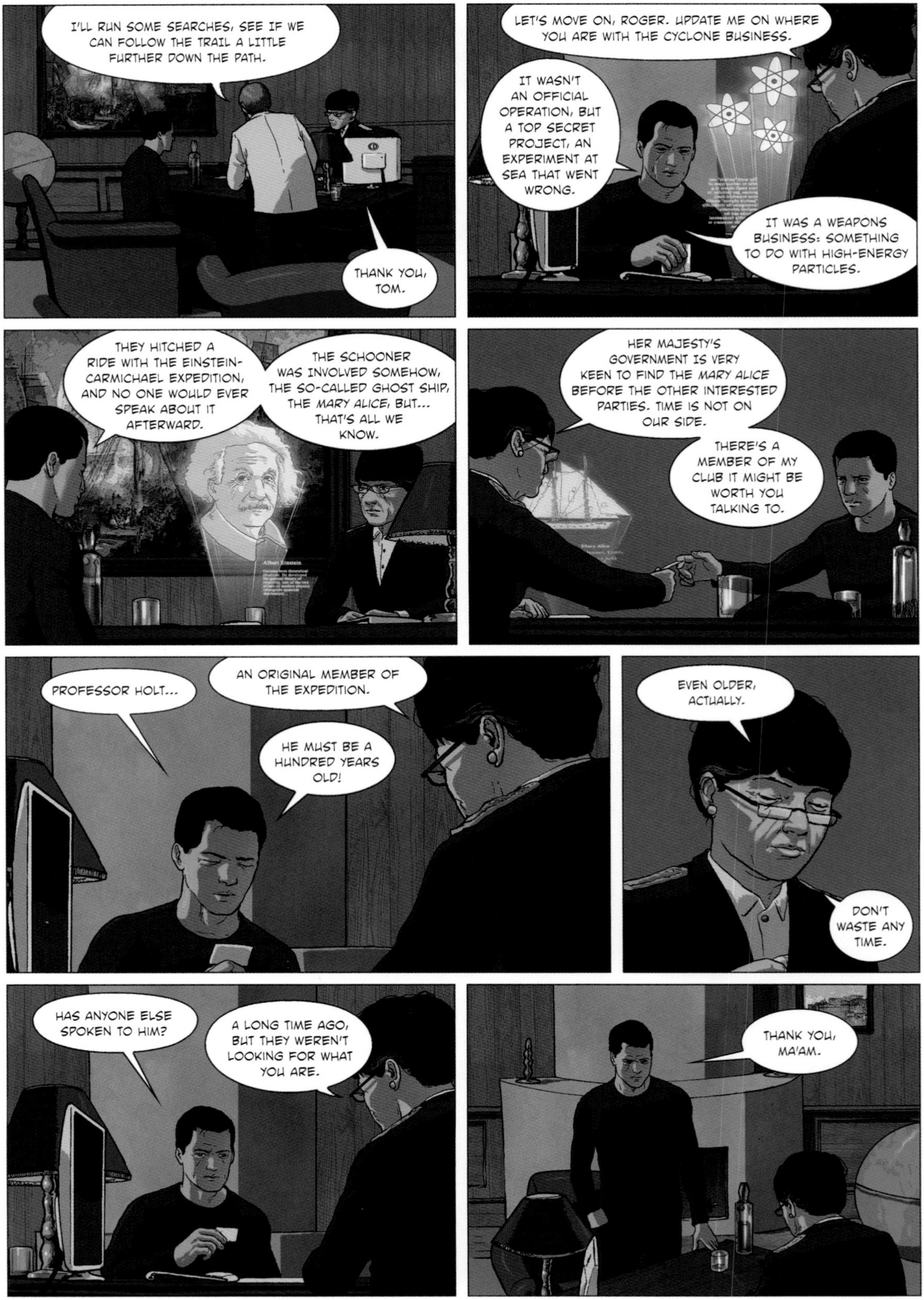
I'LL RUN SOME SEARCHES, SEE IF WE CAN FOLLOW THE TRAIL A LITTLE FURTHER DOWN THE PATH.
THANK YOU, TOM.
LET'S MOVE ON, ROGER. UPDATE ME ON WHERE YOU ARE WITH THE CYCLONE BUSINESS.
IT WASN'T AN OFFICIAL OPERATION, BUT A TOP SECRET PROJECT, AN EXPERIMENT AT SEA THAT WENT WRONG.
IT WAS A WEAPONS BUSINESS: SOMETHING TO DO WITH HIGH-ENERGY PARTICLES.
THEY HITCHED A RIDE WITH THE EINSTEIN-CARMICHAEL EXPEDITION, AND NO ONE WOULD EVER SPEAK ABOUT IT AFTERWARD.
THE SCHOONER WAS INVOLVED SOMEHOW, THE SO-CALLED GHOST SHIP, THE *MARY ALICE*, BUT... THAT'S ALL WE KNOW.
Albert Einstein
HER MAJESTY'S GOVERNMENT IS VERY KEEN TO FIND THE *MARY ALICE* BEFORE THE OTHER INTERESTED PARTIES. TIME IS NOT ON OUR SIDE.
THERE'S A MEMBER OF MY CLUB IT MIGHT BE WORTH YOU TALKING TO.
Mary Alice
PROFESSOR HOLT...
AN ORIGINAL MEMBER OF THE EXPEDITION.
HE MUST BE A HUNDRED YEARS OLD!
EVEN OLDER, ACTUALLY.
DON'T WASTE ANY TIME.
HAS ANYONE ELSE SPOKEN TO HIM?
A LONG TIME AGO, BUT THEY WEREN'T LOOKING FOR WHAT YOU ARE.
THANK YOU, MA'AM.

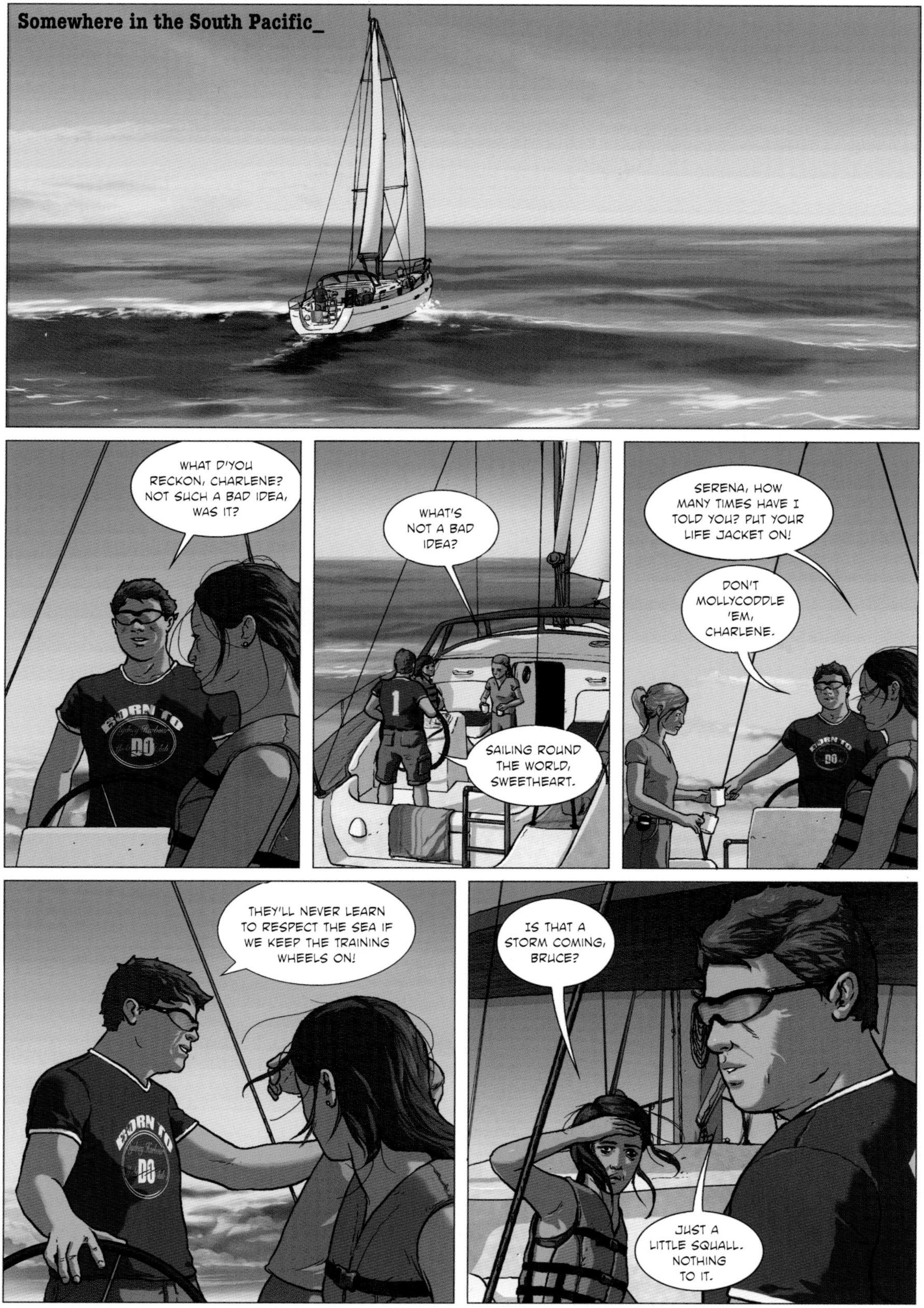
Somewhere in the South Pacific_
WHAT D'YOU RECKON, CHARLENE? NOT SUCH A BAD IDEA, WAS IT?
WHAT'S NOT A BAD IDEA?
SAILING ROUND THE WORLD, SWEETHEART.
SERENA, HOW MANY TIMES HAVE I TOLD YOU? PUT YOUR LIFE JACKET ON!
DON'T MOLLYCODDLE 'EM, CHARLENE.
THEY'LL NEVER LEARN TO RESPECT THE SEA IF WE KEEP THE TRAINING WHEELS ON!
IS THAT A STORM COMING, BRUCE?
JUST A LITTLE SQUALL. NOTHING TO IT.

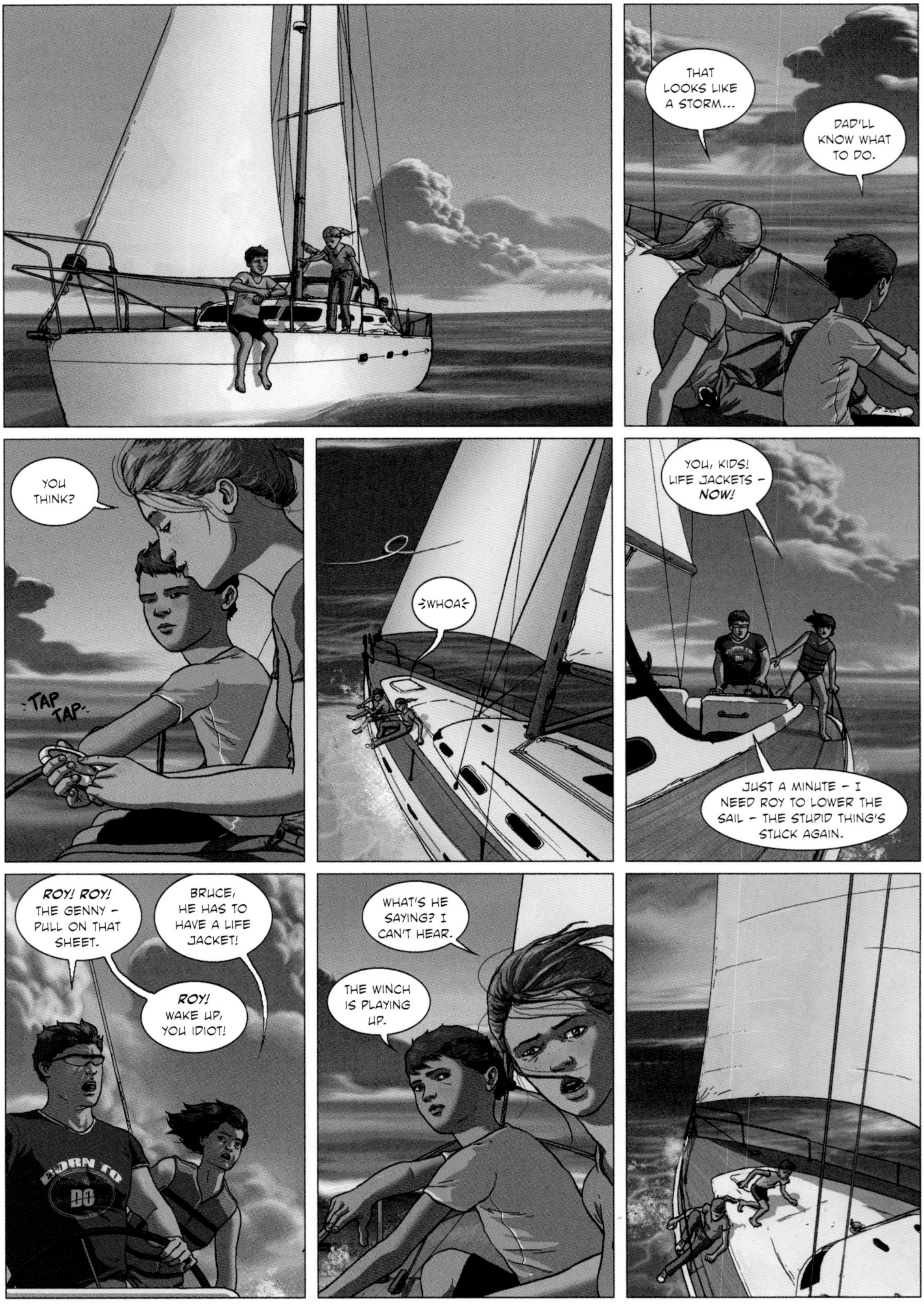
THAT LOOKS LIKE A STORM...
DAD'LL KNOW WHAT TO DO.
YOU THINK?
TAP TAP
WHOA
YOU, KIDS! LIFE JACKETS - NOW!
JUST A MINUTE - I NEED ROY TO LOWER THE SAIL - THE STUPID THING'S STUCK AGAIN.
ROY! ROY! THE GENNY - PULL ON THAT SHEET.
BRUCE, HE HAS TO HAVE A LIFE JACKET!
ROY! WAKE UP, YOU IDIOT!
BORN TO
DO
WHAT'S HE SAYING? I CAN'T HEAR.
THE WINCH IS PLAYING UP.

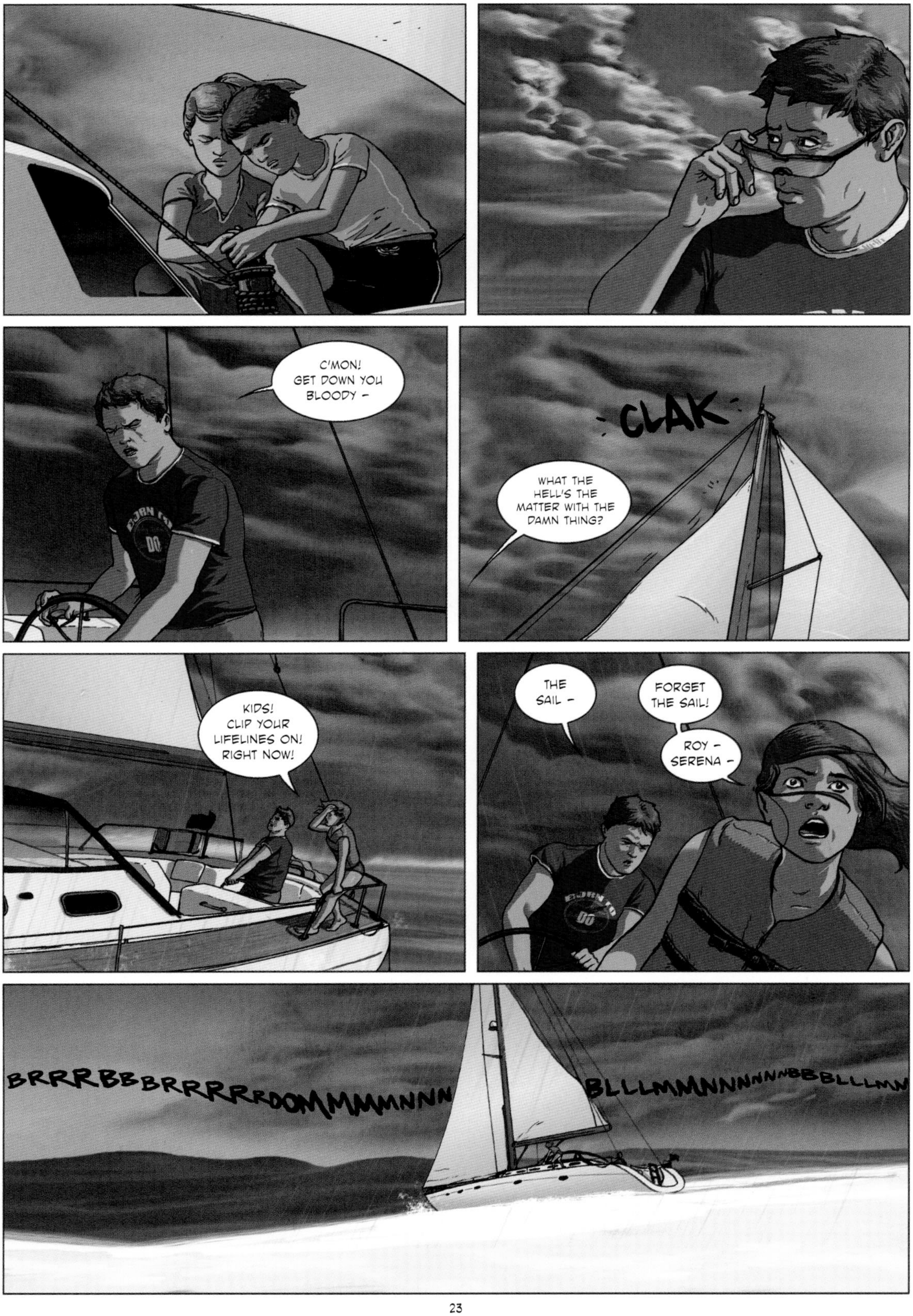
C'MON! GET DOWN YOU BLOODY -
CLAK
WHAT THE HELL'S THE MATTER WITH THE DAMN THING?
KIDS! CLIP YOUR LIFELINES ON! RIGHT NOW!
THE SAIL -
FORGET THE SAIL!
ROY - SERENA -
BRRRBBBRRRRRROOMMMMMNNN
BLLLMMNNNNNNNBBBLLLMM

SNAP

KRAK!

ROY! WHAT THE HELL HAVE YOU DONE, YOU MORON?

ROY! SERENA!

ARE YOU...

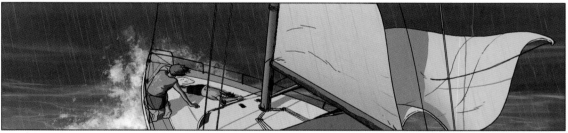

SERENA!

OH GOD –

I TRIED TO HOLD ON TO HER, MOM – BUT SHE SLIPPED OUT OF MY HAND –

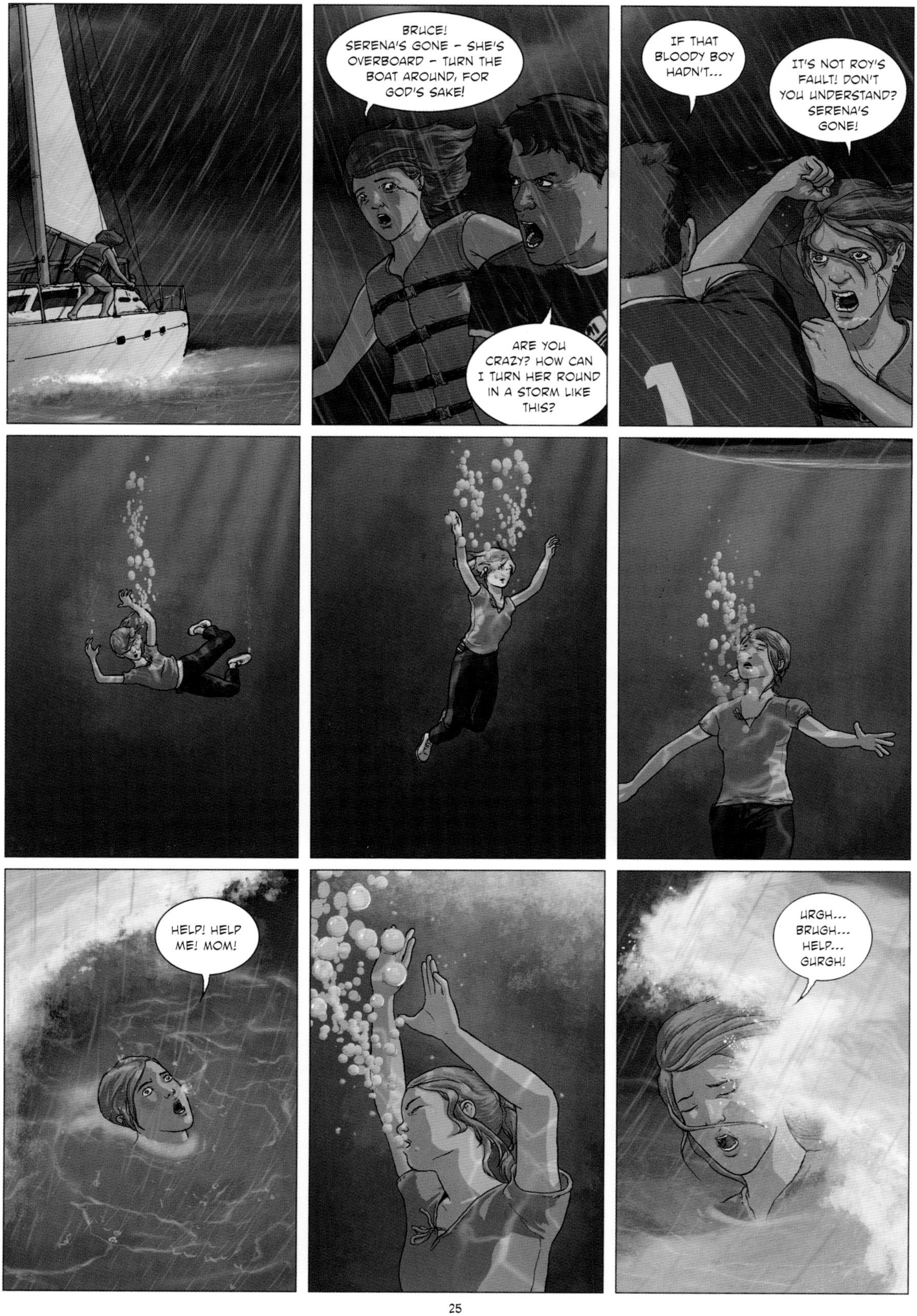
BRUCE! SERENA'S GONE – SHE'S OVERBOARD – TURN THE BOAT AROUND, FOR GOD'S SAKE!
ARE YOU CRAZY? HOW CAN I TURN HER ROUND IN A STORM LIKE THIS?
IF THAT BLOODY BOY HADN'T...
IT'S NOT ROY'S FAULT! DON'T YOU UNDERSTAND? SERENA'S GONE!
HELP! HELP ME! MOM!
URGH... BRUGH... HELP... GURGH!

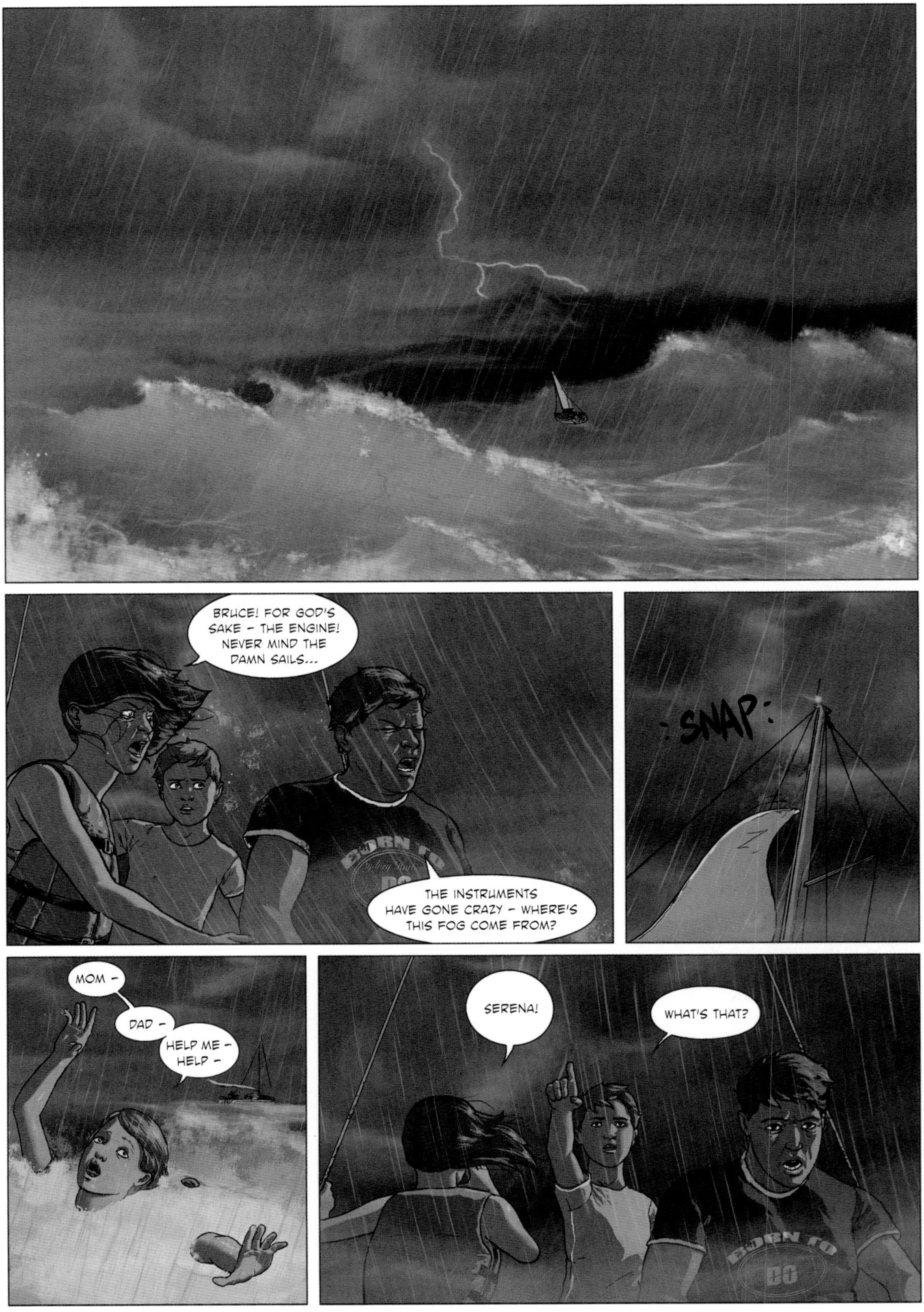
BRUCE! FOR GOD'S SAKE – THE ENGINE! NEVER MIND THE DAMN SAILS...
THE INSTRUMENTS HAVE GONE CRAZY – WHERE'S THIS FOG COME FROM?
SNAP
MOM –
DAD –
HELP ME – HELP –
SERENA!
WHAT'S THAT?

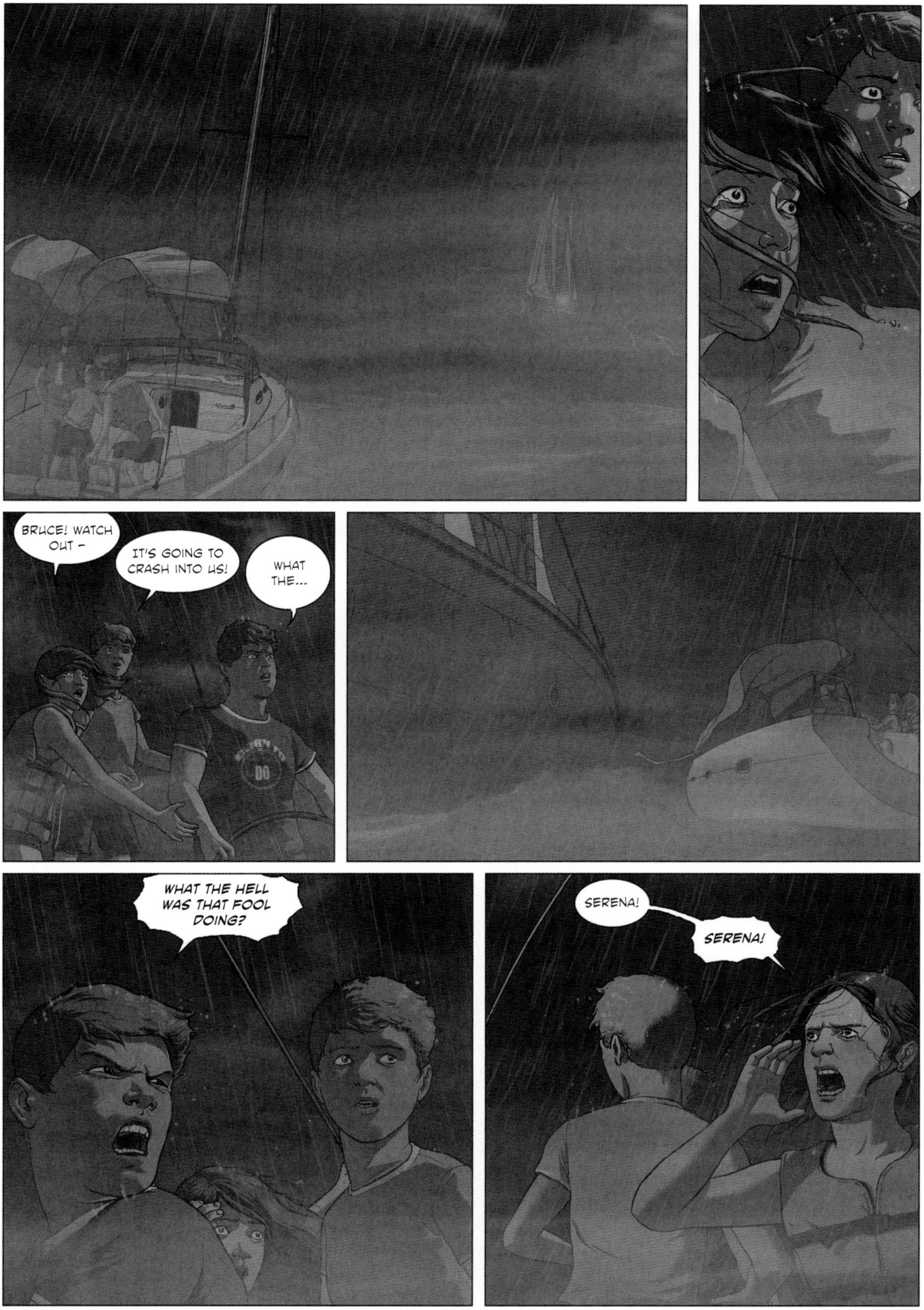
BRUCE! WATCH OUT –
IT'S GOING TO CRASH INTO US!
WHAT THE...
WHAT THE HELL WAS THAT FOOL DOING?
SERENA!
SERENA!

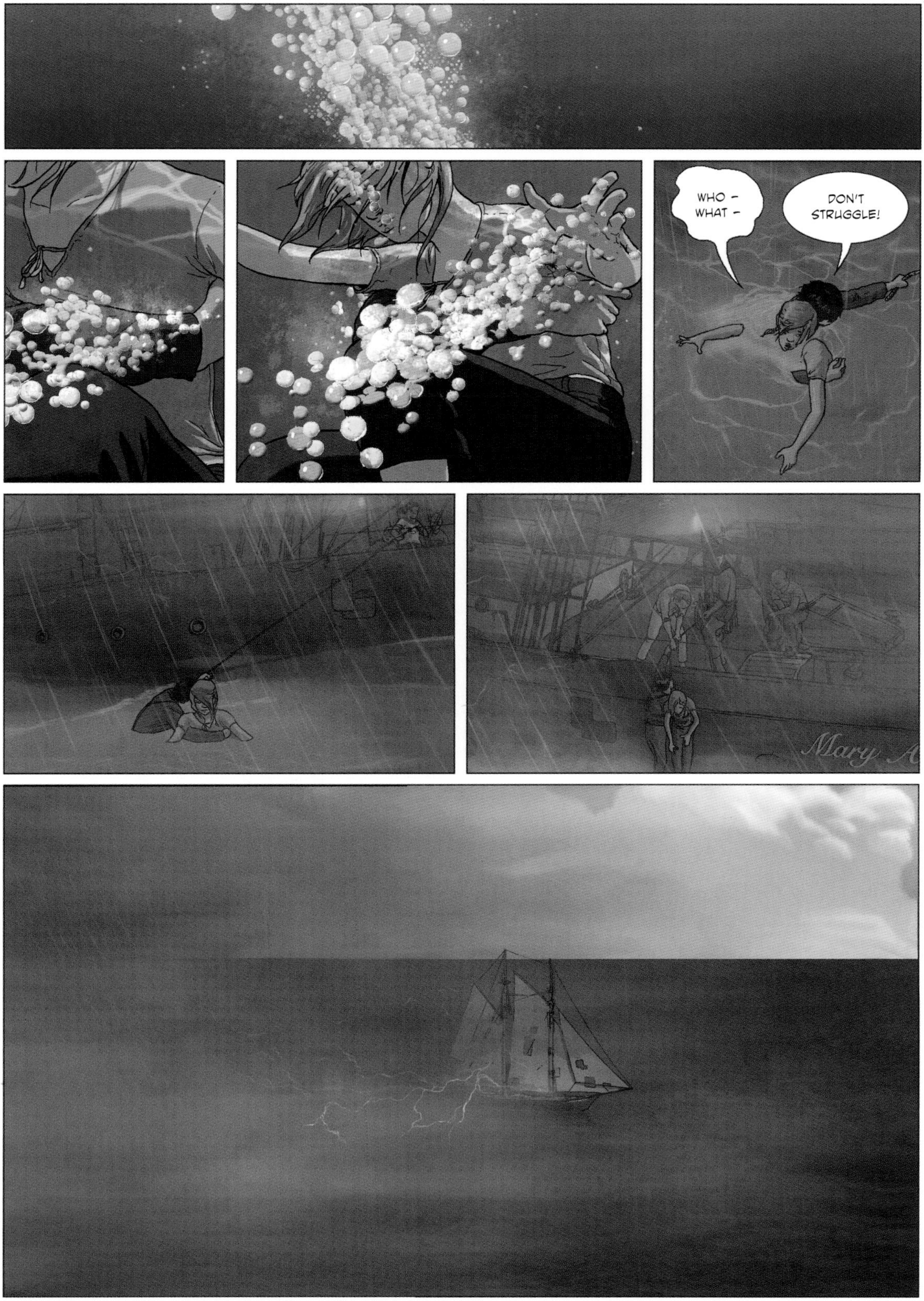
WHO –
WHAT –
DON'T STRUGGLE!
Mary A

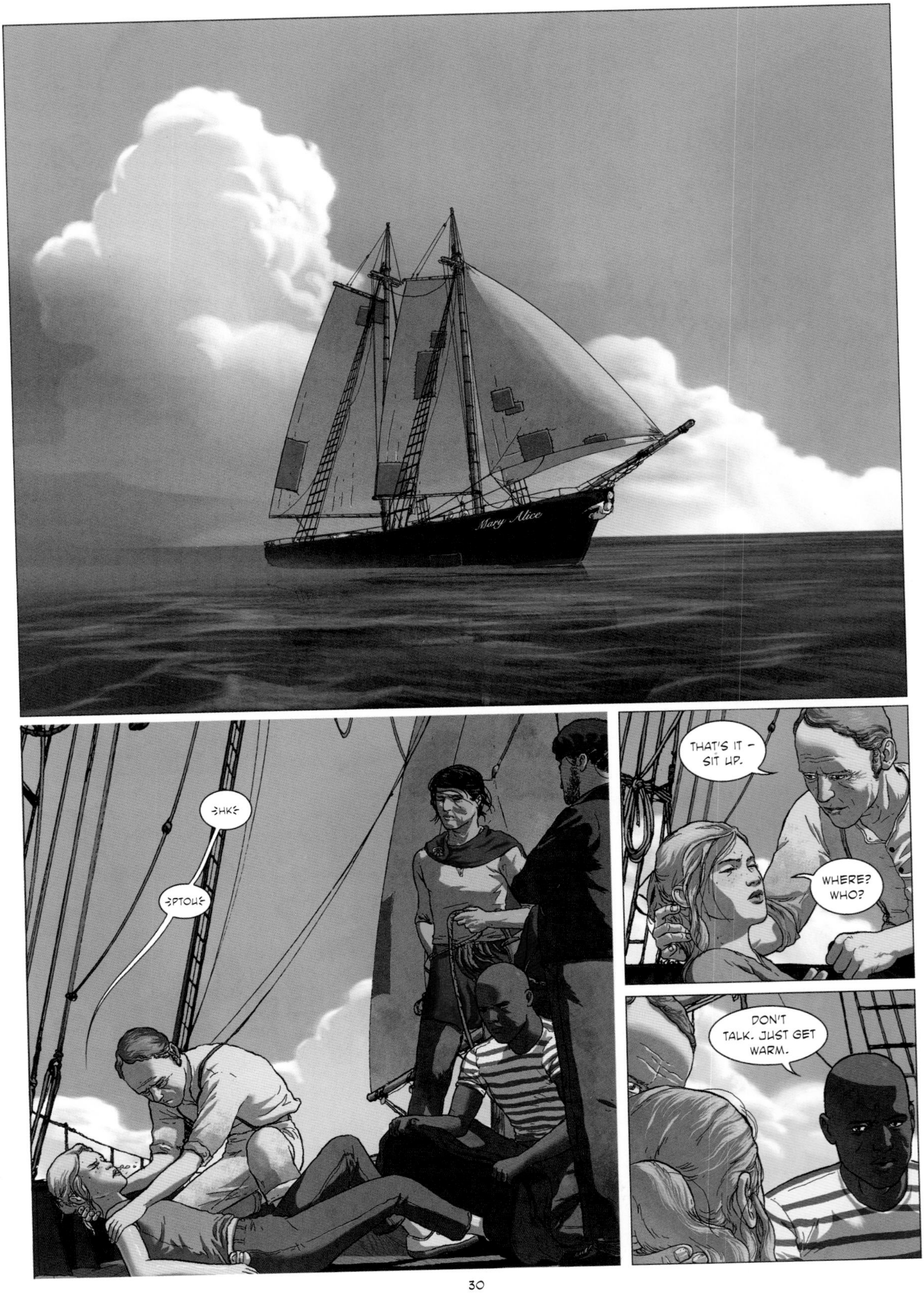
Mary Alice
HK
PTOU
THAT'S IT – SIT UP.
WHERE? WHO?
DON'T TALK. JUST GET WARM.

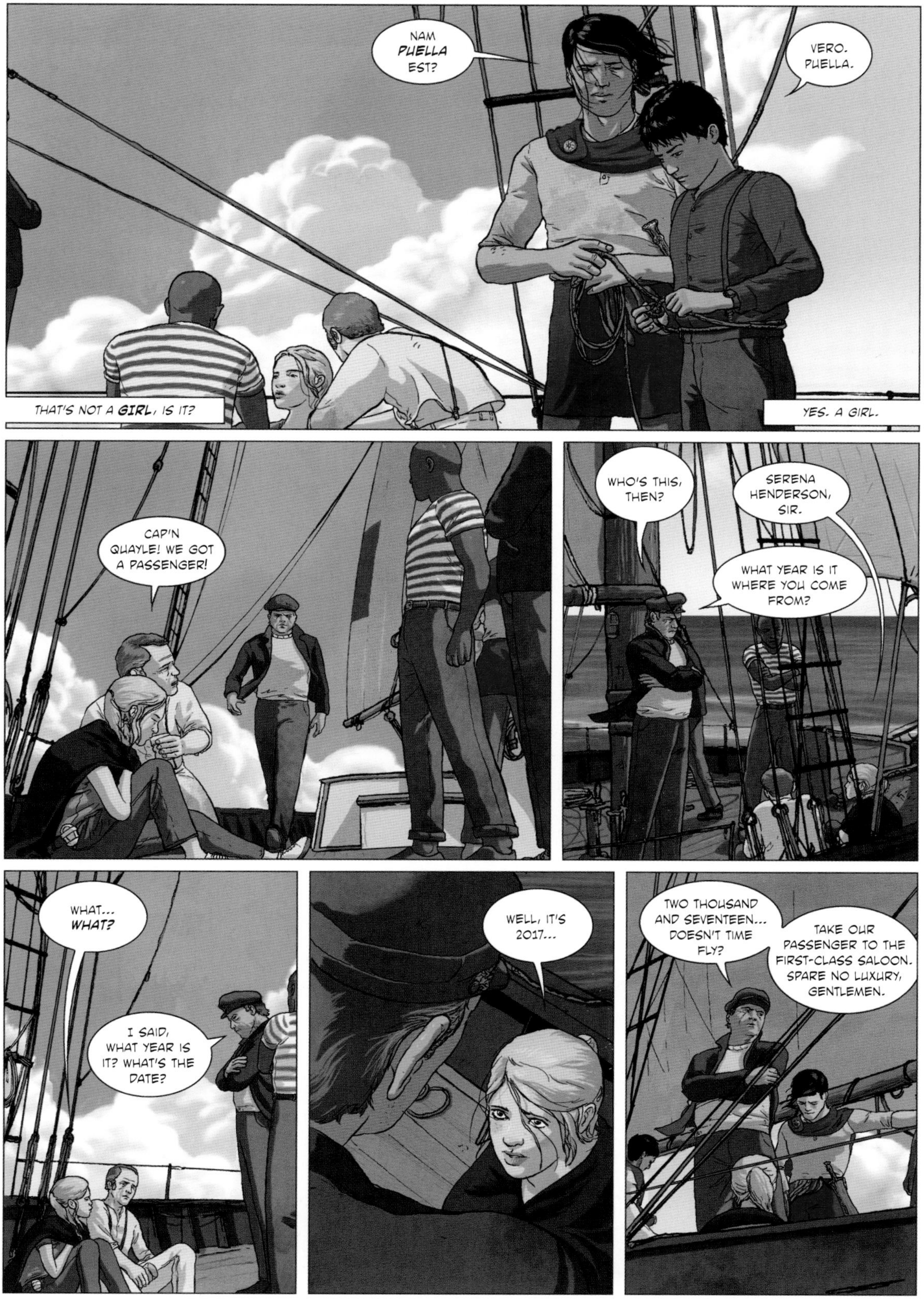
NAM PUELLA EST?
THAT'S NOT A GIRL, IS IT?
VERO. PUELLA.
YES. A GIRL.
CAP'N QUAYLE! WE GOT A PASSENGER!
WHO'S THIS, THEN?
SERENA HENDERSON, SIR.
WHAT YEAR IS IT WHERE YOU COME FROM?
WHAT... WHAT?
I SAID, WHAT YEAR IS IT? WHAT'S THE DATE?
WELL, IT'S 2017...
TWO THOUSAND AND SEVENTEEN... DOESN'T TIME FLY?
TAKE OUR PASSENGER TO THE FIRST-CLASS SALOON. SPARE NO LUXURY, GENTLEMEN.

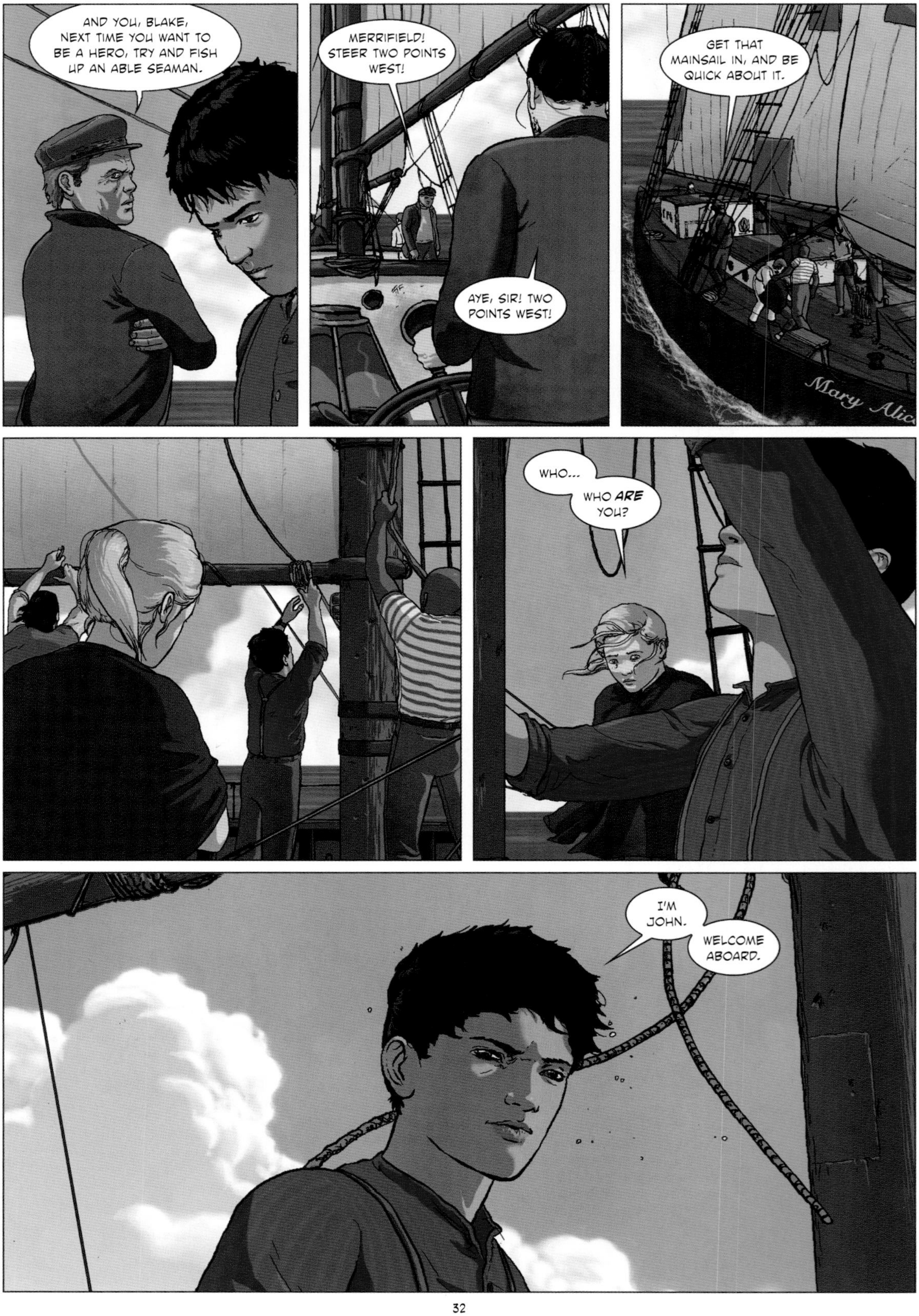
AND YOU, BLAKE, NEXT TIME YOU WANT TO BE A HERO, TRY AND FISH UP AN ABLE SEAMAN.
MERRIFIELD! STEER TWO POINTS WEST!
AYE, SIR! TWO POINTS WEST!
GET THAT MAINSAIL IN, AND BE QUICK ABOUT IT.
Mary Alic
WHO...
WHO ARE YOU?
I'M JOHN.
WELCOME ABOARD.

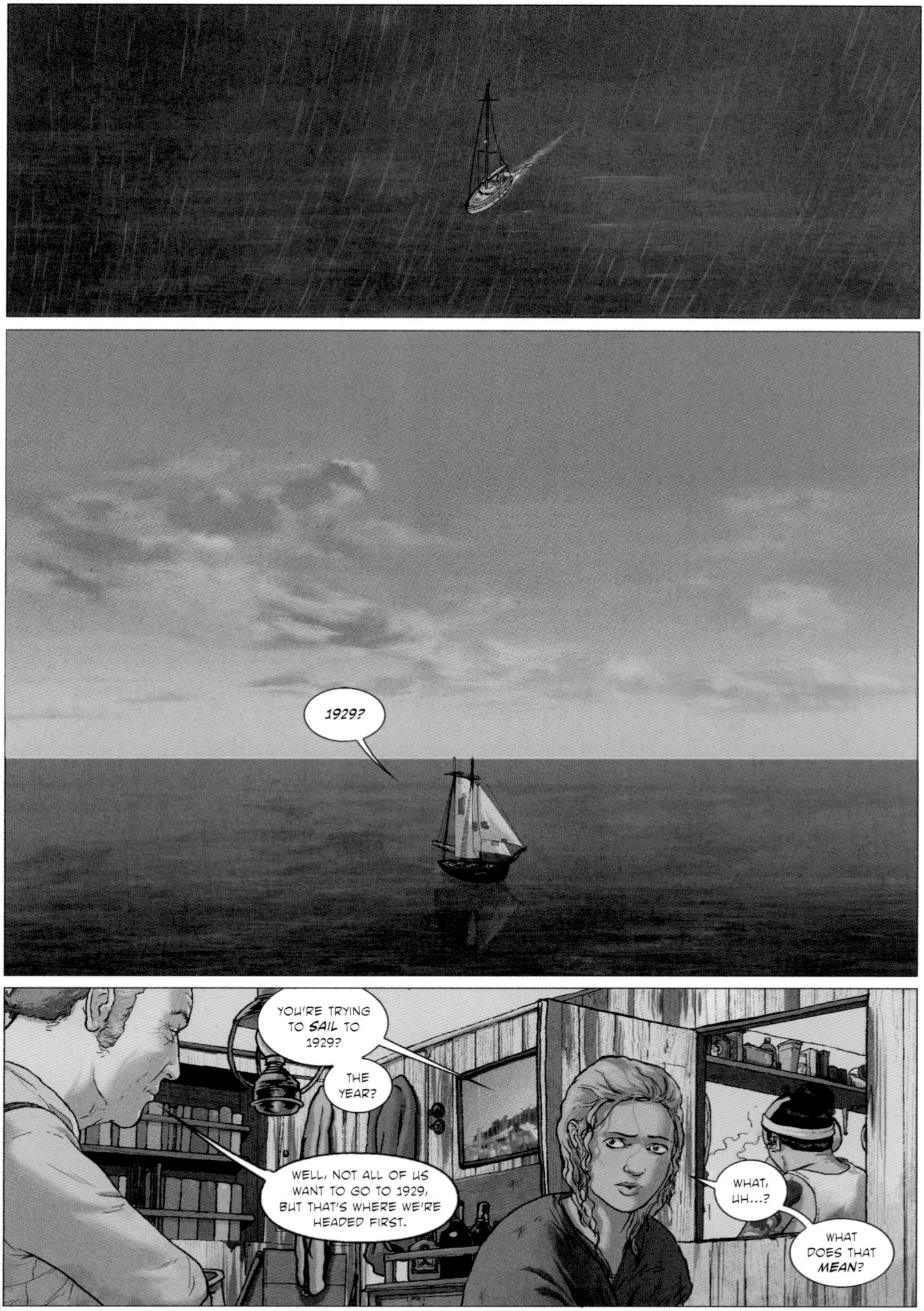
1929?
YOU'RE TRYING TO SAIL TO 1929?
THE YEAR?
WELL, NOT ALL OF US WANT TO GO TO 1929, BUT THAT'S WHERE WE'RE HEADED FIRST.
WHAT, UH...?
WHAT DOES THAT MEAN?

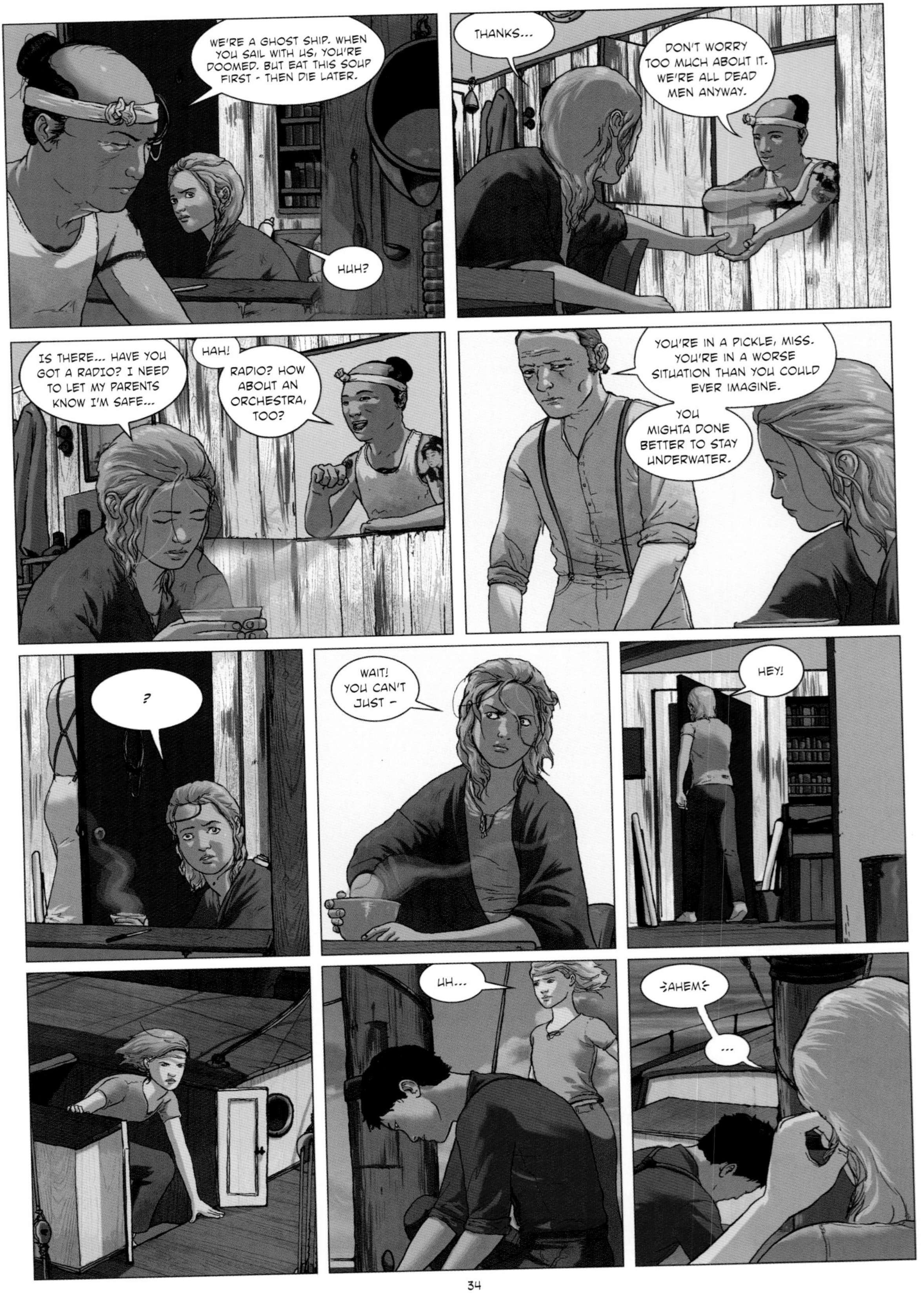
WE'RE A GHOST SHIP. WHEN YOU SAIL WITH US, YOU'RE DOOMED. BUT EAT THIS SOUP FIRST - THEN DIE LATER.
HUH?
THANKS...
DON'T WORRY TOO MUCH ABOUT IT. WE'RE ALL DEAD MEN ANYWAY.
IS THERE... HAVE YOU GOT A RADIO? I NEED TO LET MY PARENTS KNOW I'M SAFE...
HAH!
RADIO? HOW ABOUT AN ORCHESTRA, TOO?
YOU'RE IN A PICKLE, MISS. YOU'RE IN A WORSE SITUATION THAN YOU COULD EVER IMAGINE.
YOU MIGHTA DONE BETTER TO STAY UNDERWATER.
?
WAIT! YOU CAN'T JUST -
HEY!
UH...
AHEM
...

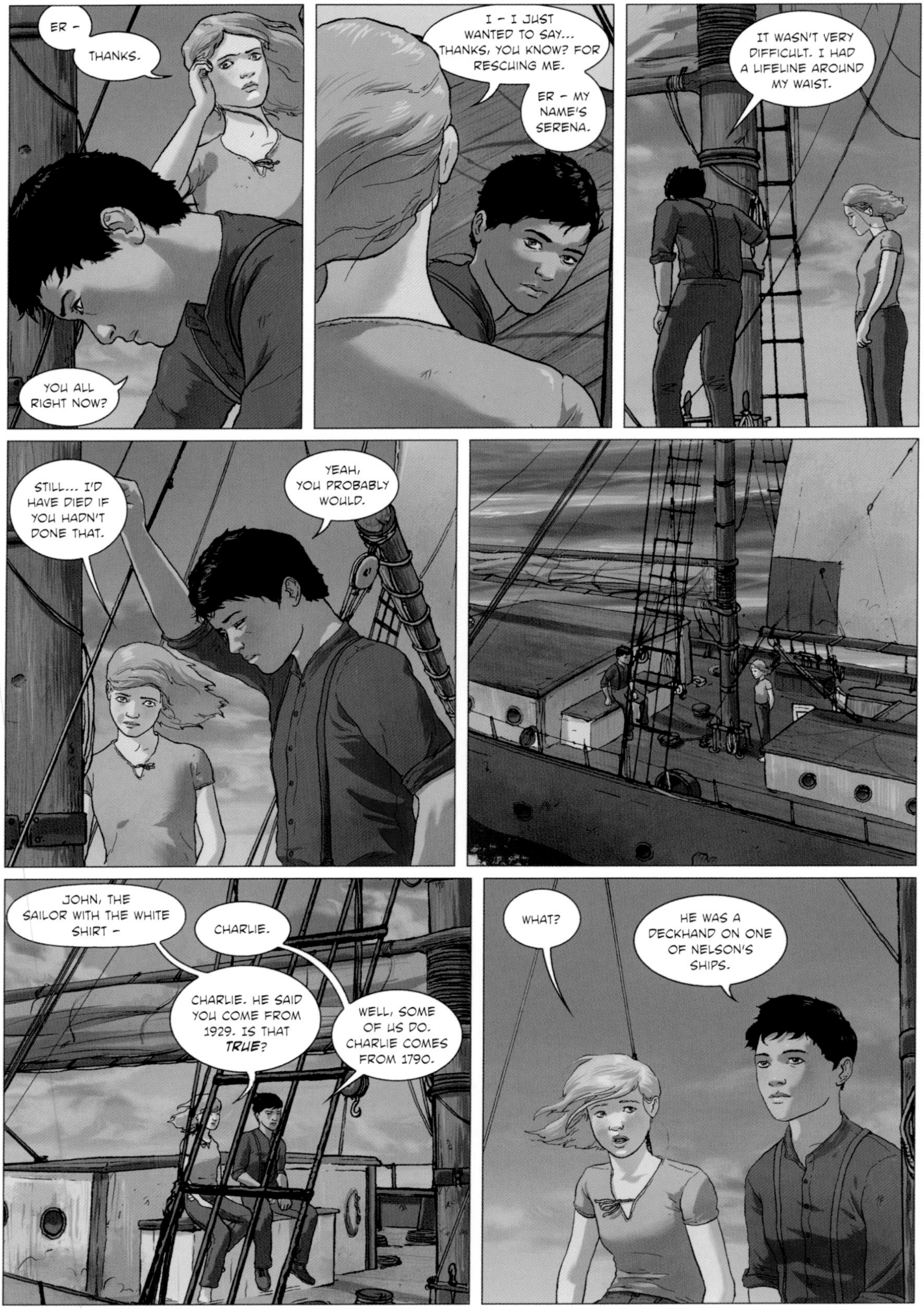
ER –
THANKS.
YOU ALL RIGHT NOW?
I – I JUST WANTED TO SAY... THANKS, YOU KNOW? FOR RESCUING ME.
ER – MY NAME'S SERENA.
IT WASN'T VERY DIFFICULT. I HAD A LIFELINE AROUND MY WAIST.
STILL... I'D HAVE DIED IF YOU HADN'T DONE THAT.
YEAH, YOU PROBABLY WOULD.
JOHN, THE SAILOR WITH THE WHITE SHIRT –
CHARLIE.
CHARLIE. HE SAID YOU COME FROM 1929. IS THAT *TRUE*?
WELL, SOME OF US DO. CHARLIE COMES FROM 1790.
WHAT?
HE WAS A DECKHAND ON ONE OF NELSON'S SHIPS.

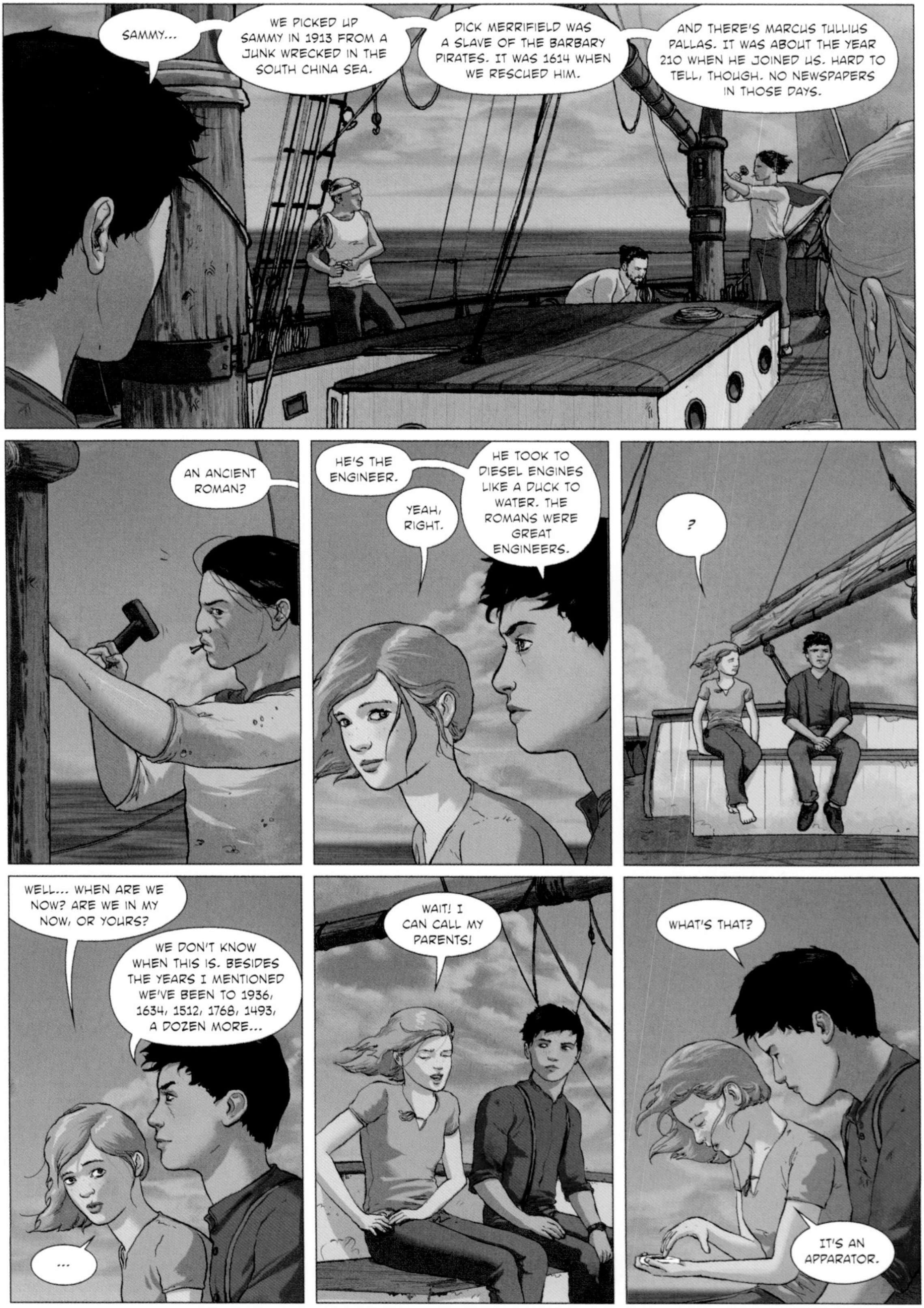
SAMMY...
WE PICKED UP SAMMY IN 1913 FROM A JUNK WRECKED IN THE SOUTH CHINA SEA.
DICK MERRIFIELD WAS A SLAVE OF THE BARBARY PIRATES. IT WAS 1614 WHEN WE RESCUED HIM.
AND THERE'S MARCUS TULLIUS PALLAS. IT WAS ABOUT THE YEAR 210 WHEN HE JOINED US. HARD TO TELL, THOUGH. NO NEWSPAPERS IN THOSE DAYS.
AN ANCIENT ROMAN?
HE'S THE ENGINEER.
YEAH, RIGHT.
HE TOOK TO DIESEL ENGINES LIKE A DUCK TO WATER. THE ROMANS WERE GREAT ENGINEERS.
?
WELL... WHEN ARE WE NOW? ARE WE IN MY NOW, OR YOURS?
WE DON'T KNOW WHEN THIS IS. BESIDES THE YEARS I MENTIONED WE'VE BEEN TO 1936, 1634, 1512, 1768, 1493, A DOZEN MORE...
...
WAIT! I CAN CALL MY PARENTS!
WHAT'S THAT?
IT'S AN APPARATOR.

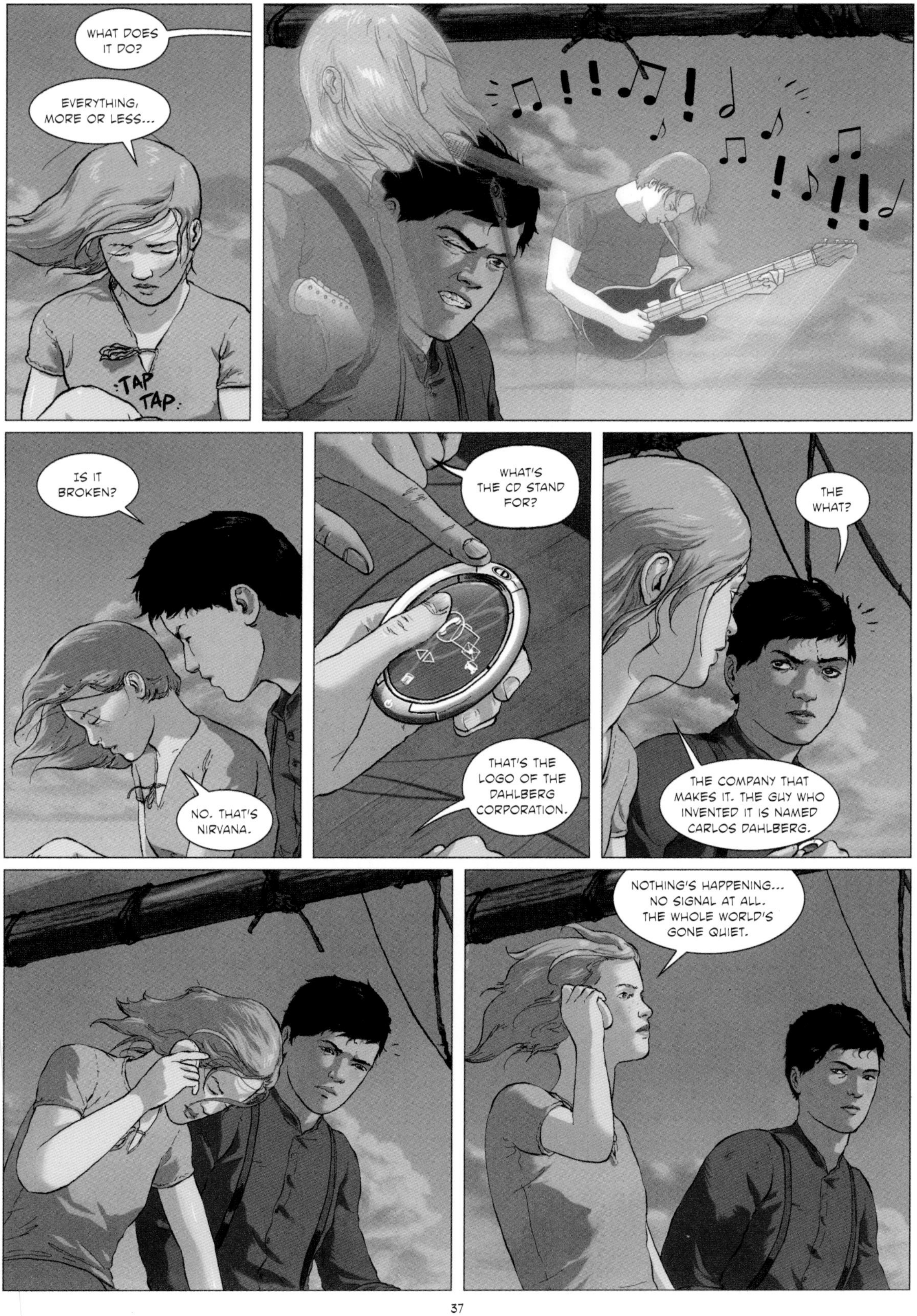
WHAT DOES IT DO?
EVERYTHING, MORE OR LESS...
TAP TAP
IS IT BROKEN?
NO. THAT'S NIRVANA.
WHAT'S THE CD STAND FOR?
THAT'S THE LOGO OF THE DAHLBERG CORPORATION.
THE WHAT?
THE COMPANY THAT MAKES IT. THE GUY WHO INVENTED IT IS NAMED CARLOS DAHLBERG.
NOTHING'S HAPPENING... NO SIGNAL AT ALL. THE WHOLE WORLD'S GONE QUIET.

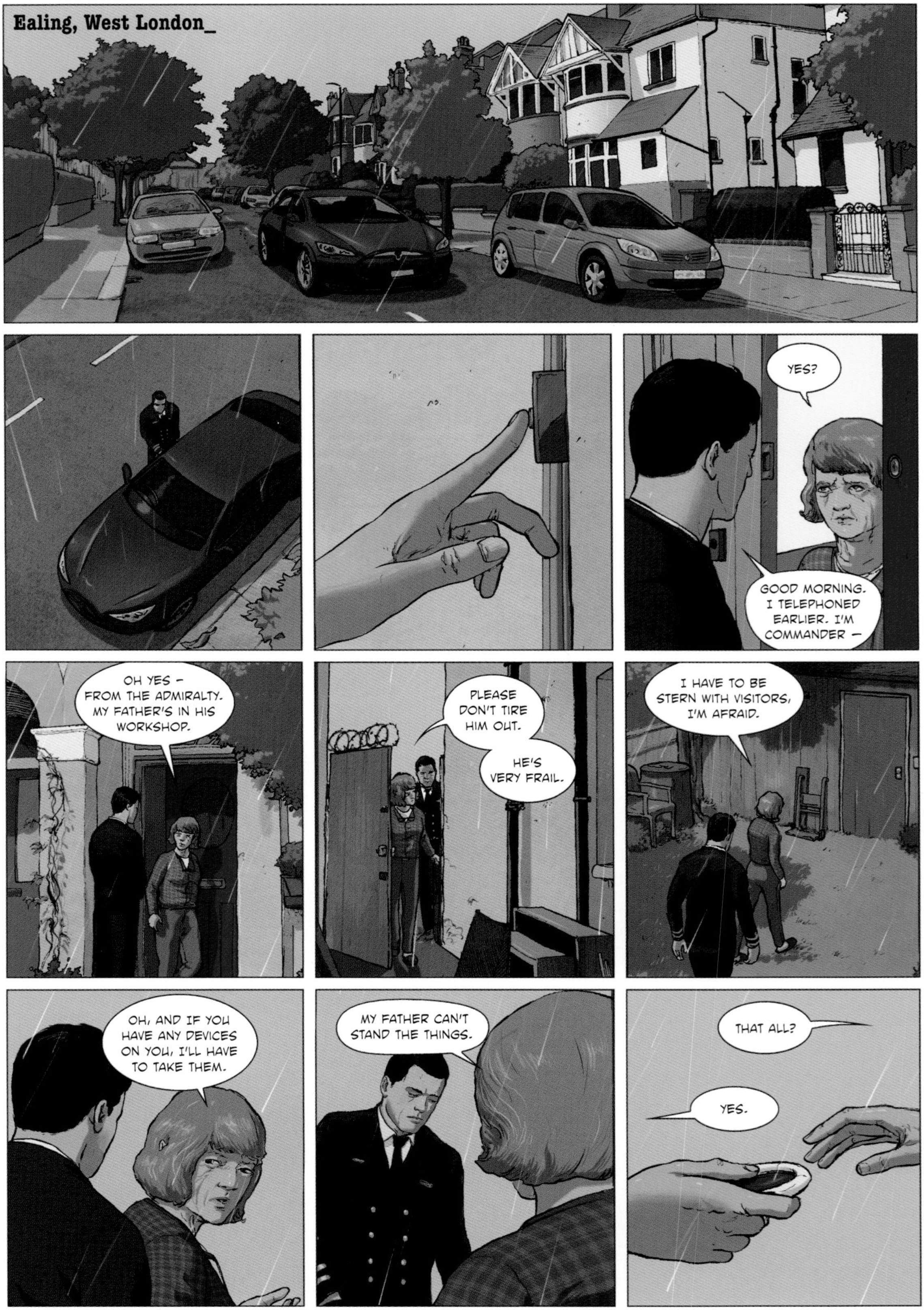
Ealing, West London_
YES?
GOOD MORNING. I TELEPHONED EARLIER. I'M COMMANDER —
OH YES – FROM THE ADMIRALTY. MY FATHER'S IN HIS WORKSHOP.
PLEASE DON'T TIRE HIM OUT.
HE'S VERY FRAIL.
I HAVE TO BE STERN WITH VISITORS, I'M AFRAID.
OH, AND IF YOU HAVE ANY DEVICES ON YOU, I'LL HAVE TO TAKE THEM.
MY FATHER CAN'T STAND THE THINGS.
THAT ALL?
YES.

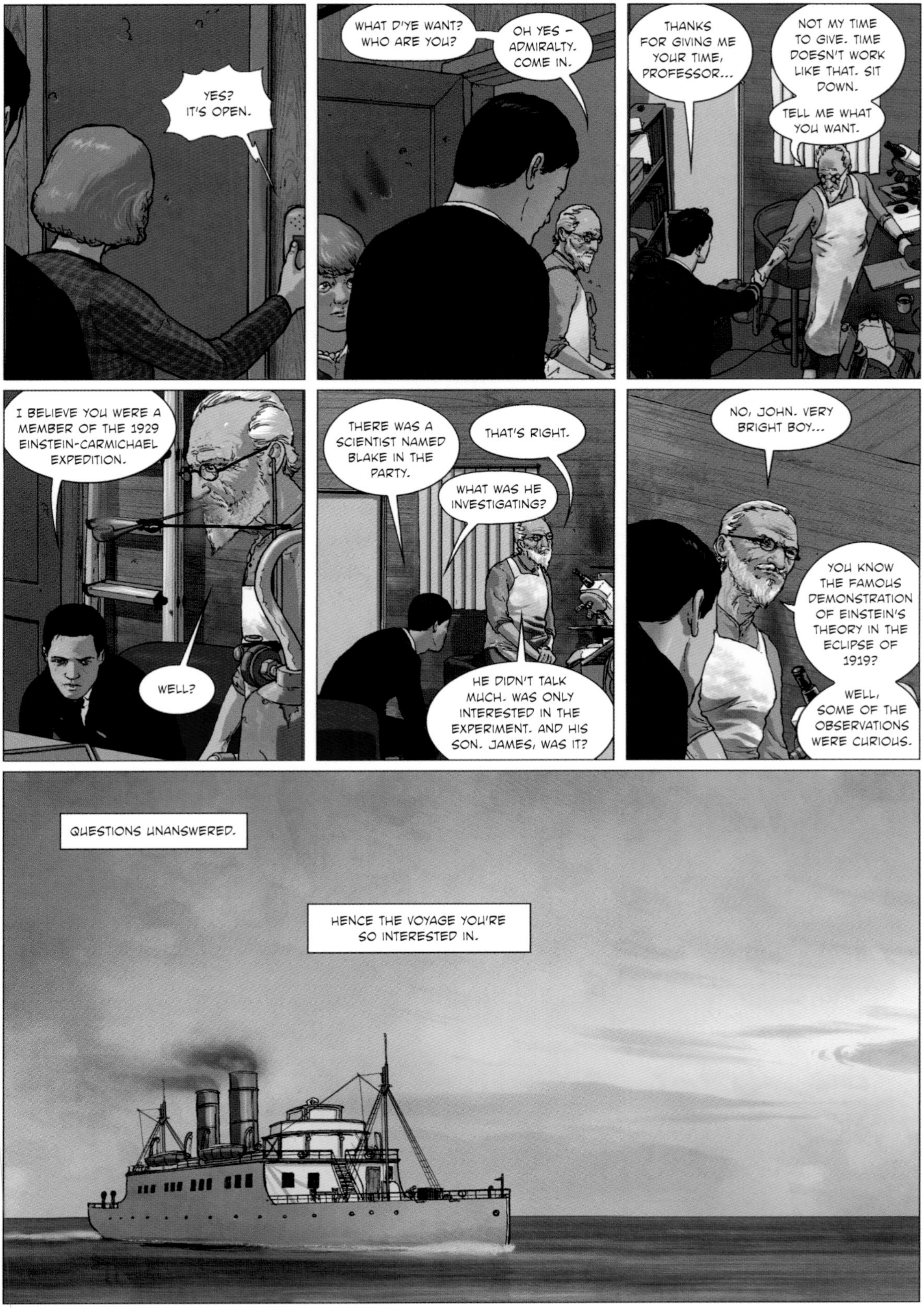
YES? IT'S OPEN.
WHAT D'YE WANT? WHO ARE YOU?
OH YES – ADMIRALTY. COME IN.
THANKS FOR GIVING ME YOUR TIME, PROFESSOR...
NOT MY TIME TO GIVE. TIME DOESN'T WORK LIKE THAT. SIT DOWN.
TELL ME WHAT YOU WANT.
I BELIEVE YOU WERE A MEMBER OF THE 1929 EINSTEIN-CARMICHAEL EXPEDITION.
WELL?
THERE WAS A SCIENTIST NAMED BLAKE IN THE PARTY.
THAT'S RIGHT.
WHAT WAS HE INVESTIGATING?
HE DIDN'T TALK MUCH. WAS ONLY INTERESTED IN THE EXPERIMENT. AND HIS SON. JAMES, WAS IT?
NO, JOHN. VERY BRIGHT BOY...
YOU KNOW THE FAMOUS DEMONSTRATION OF EINSTEIN'S THEORY IN THE ECLIPSE OF 1919?
WELL, SOME OF THE OBSERVATIONS WERE CURIOUS.
QUESTIONS UNANSWERED.
HENCE THE VOYAGE YOU'RE SO INTERESTED IN.

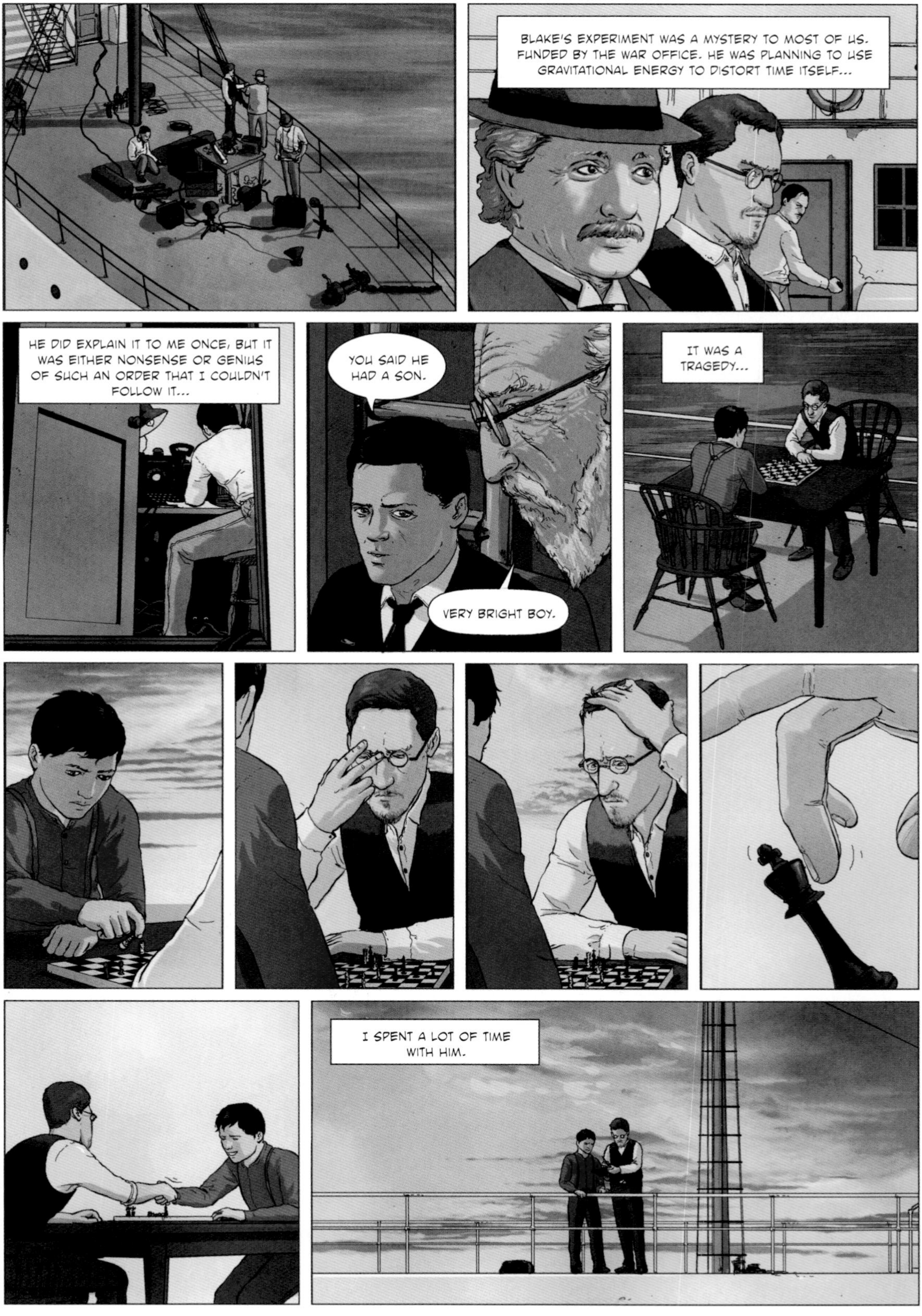

BLAKE'S EXPERIMENT WAS A MYSTERY TO MOST OF US. FUNDED BY THE WAR OFFICE. HE WAS PLANNING TO USE GRAVITATIONAL ENERGY TO DISTORT TIME ITSELF...
HE DID EXPLAIN IT TO ME ONCE, BUT IT WAS EITHER NONSENSE OR GENIUS OF SUCH AN ORDER THAT I COULDN'T FOLLOW IT...
YOU SAID HE HAD A SON.
VERY BRIGHT BOY.
IT WAS A TRAGEDY...
I SPENT A LOT OF TIME WITH HIM.

I TAUGHT HIM SOME MATHEMATICS AT, OH, GRADUATE DEGREE LEVEL.

HE WAS BRILLIANT.

I THINK HE WOULD RATHER HAVE SPENT THE TIME WITH HIS FATHER.

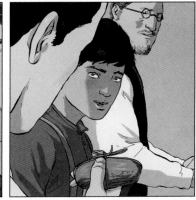

BUT THINGS WERE NOT HAPPY...

EINSTEIN THOUGHT BLAKE'S EXPERIMENT WAS AN IRRESPONSIBLE COMPROMISE WITH POLITICS...

BUT BLAKE WAS A PROFOUNDLY STUBBORN MAN. AND ON THE DAY OF THE ECLIPSE...

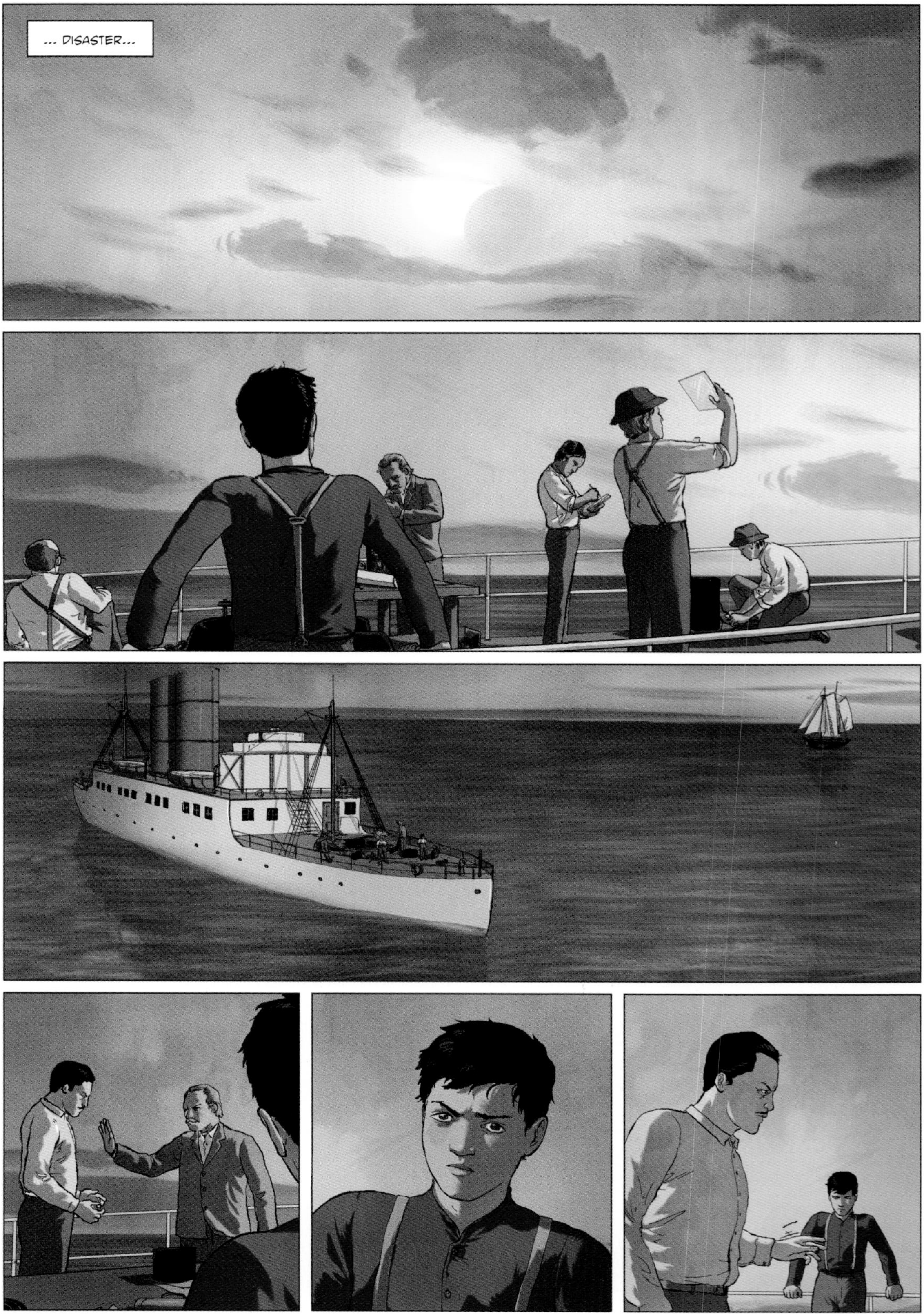
... DISASTER...

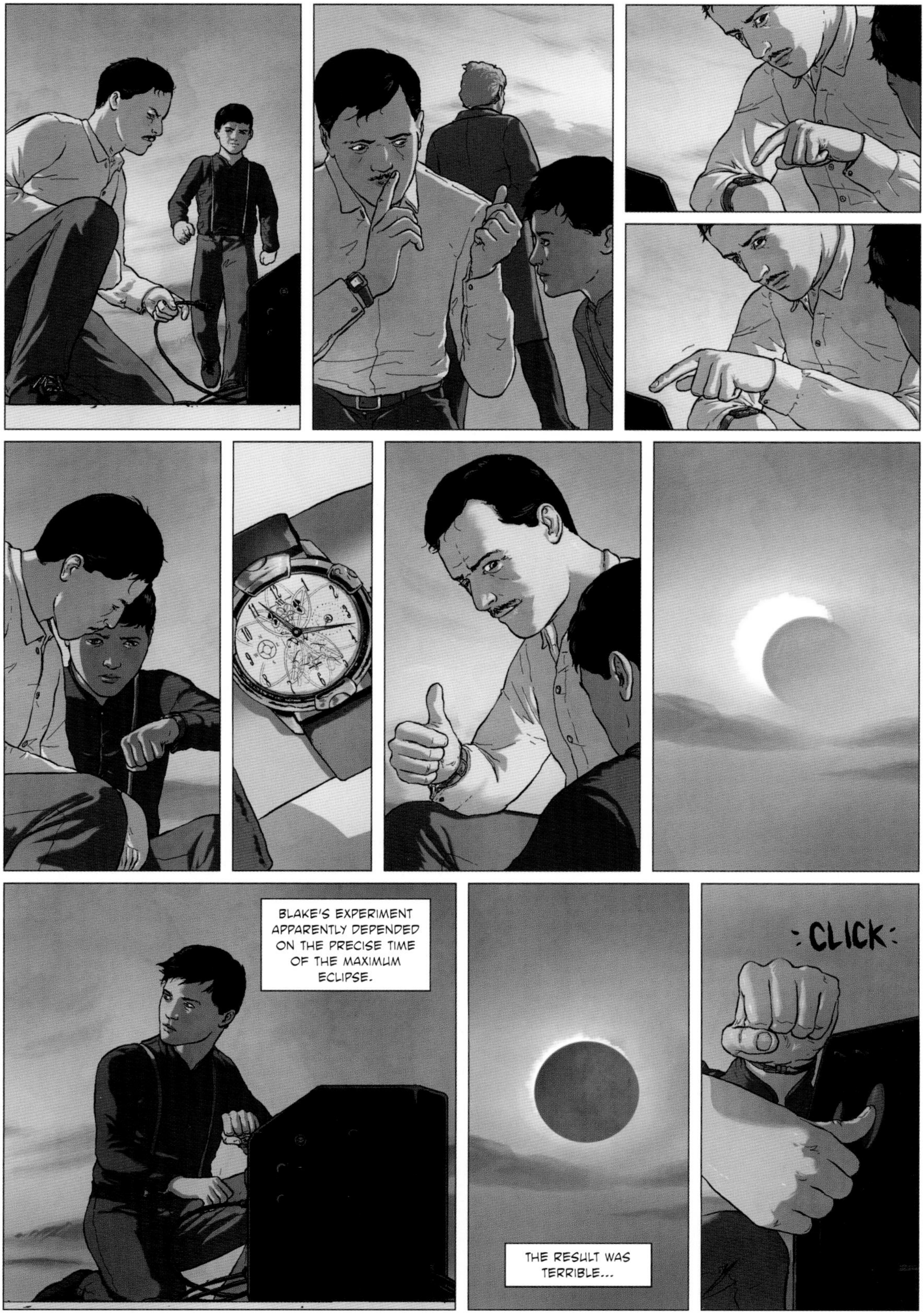
BLAKE'S EXPERIMENT APPARENTLY DEPENDED ON THE PRECISE TIME OF THE MAXIMUM ECLIPSE.
THE RESULT WAS TERRIBLE...
CLICK

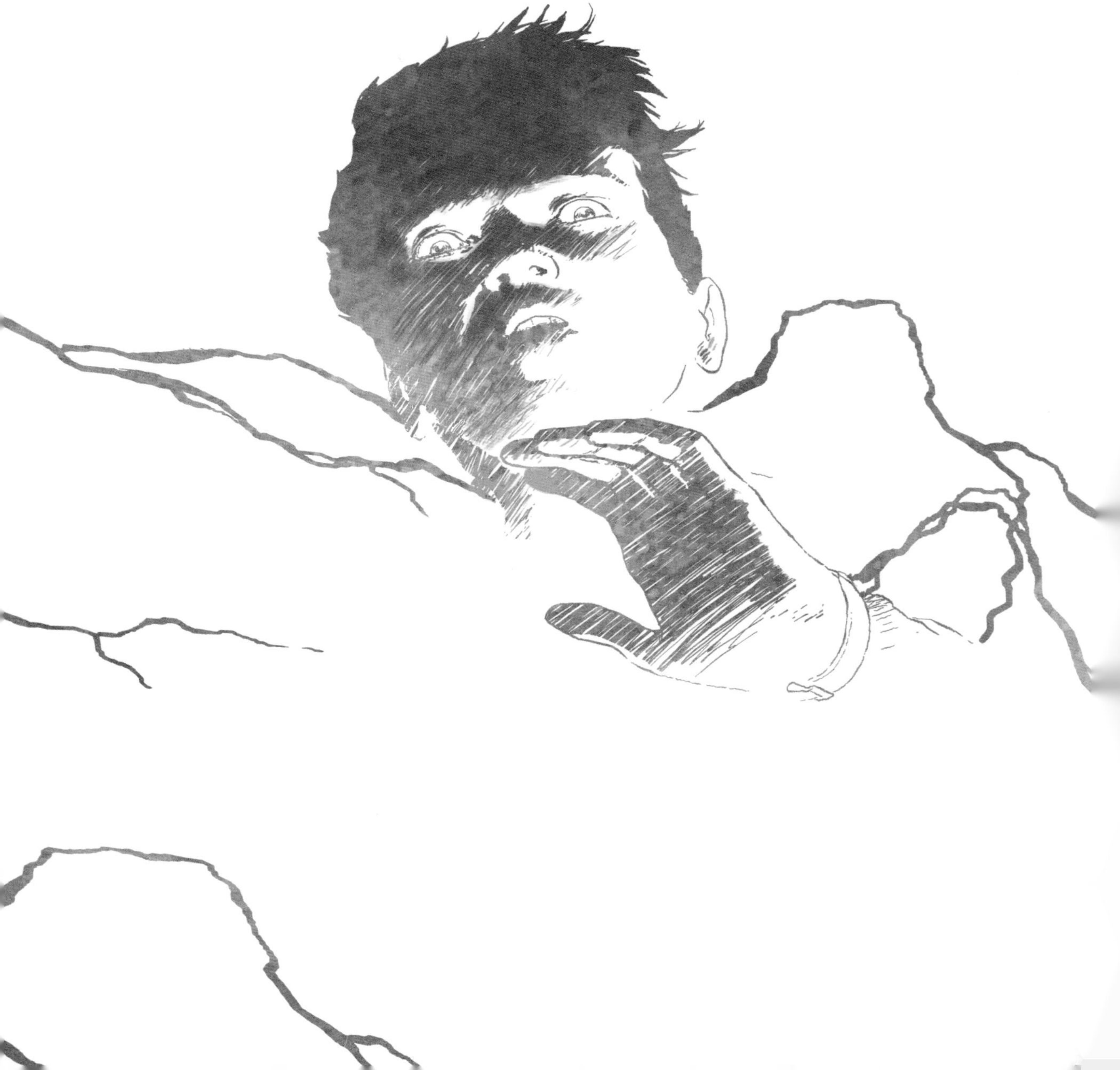

WHAT HAPPENED?

THERE WAS AN EXPLOSION — PERFECTLY SILENT — THE LIGHT SEEMED TO SHINE THROUGH US ALL LIKE X-RAYS...

A MOMENT LATER, WHEN OUR EYES ADJUSTED, WE FOUND OURSELVES IN THE MIDDLE OF THE DENSEST FOG I'D EVER KNOWN.

AND THE BOY WAS... GONE...

THEY SENT A BOAT OUT, IN CASE HE'D FALLEN IN THE WATER, BUT...

NO LUCK.

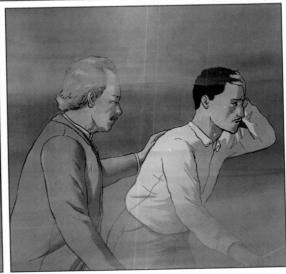

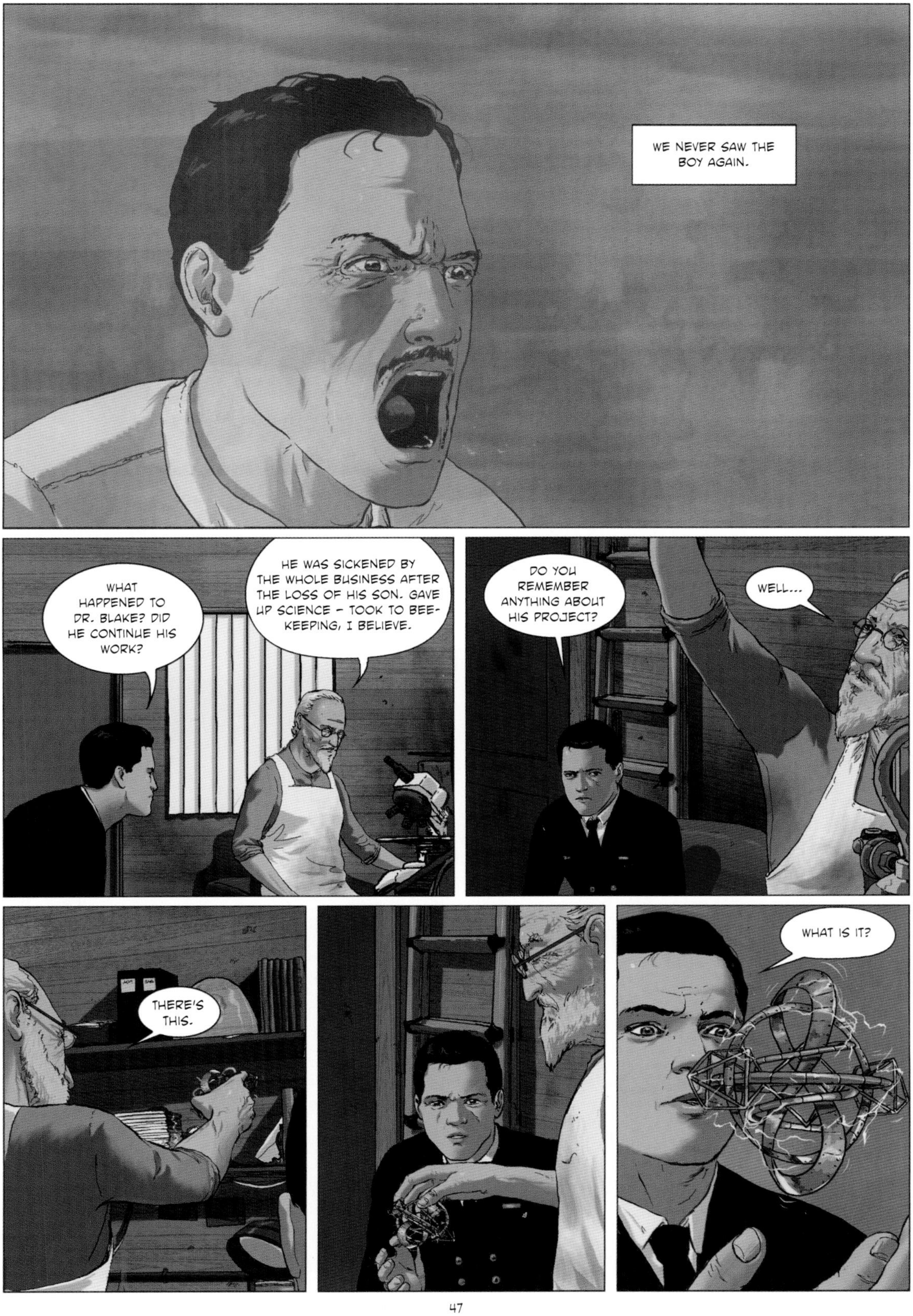
WE NEVER SAW THE BOY AGAIN.
WHAT HAPPENED TO DR. BLAKE? DID HE CONTINUE HIS WORK?
HE WAS SICKENED BY THE WHOLE BUSINESS AFTER THE LOSS OF HIS SON. GAVE UP SCIENCE – TOOK TO BEE-KEEPING, I BELIEVE.
DO YOU REMEMBER ANYTHING ABOUT HIS PROJECT?
WELL...
THERE'S THIS.
WHAT IS IT?

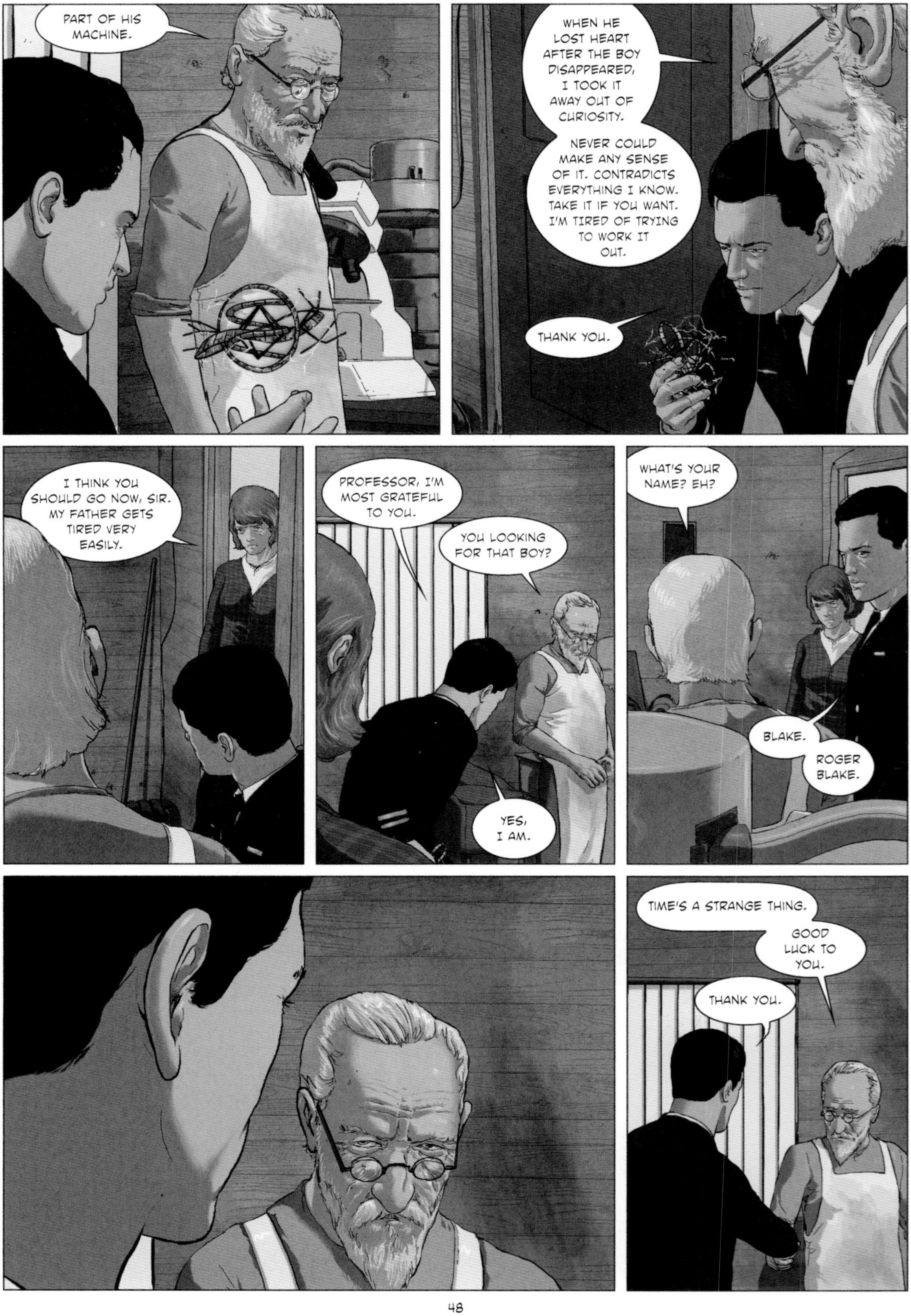
PART OF HIS MACHINE.
WHEN HE LOST HEART AFTER THE BOY DISAPPEARED, I TOOK IT AWAY OUT OF CURIOSITY.
NEVER COULD MAKE ANY SENSE OF IT. CONTRADICTS EVERYTHING I KNOW. TAKE IT IF YOU WANT. I'M TIRED OF TRYING TO WORK IT OUT.
THANK YOU.
I THINK YOU SHOULD GO NOW, SIR. MY FATHER GETS TIRED VERY EASILY.
PROFESSOR, I'M MOST GRATEFUL TO YOU.
YOU LOOKING FOR THAT BOY?
YES, I AM.
WHAT'S YOUR NAME? EH?
BLAKE.
ROGER BLAKE.
TIME'S A STRANGE THING.
GOOD LUCK TO YOU.
THANK YOU.

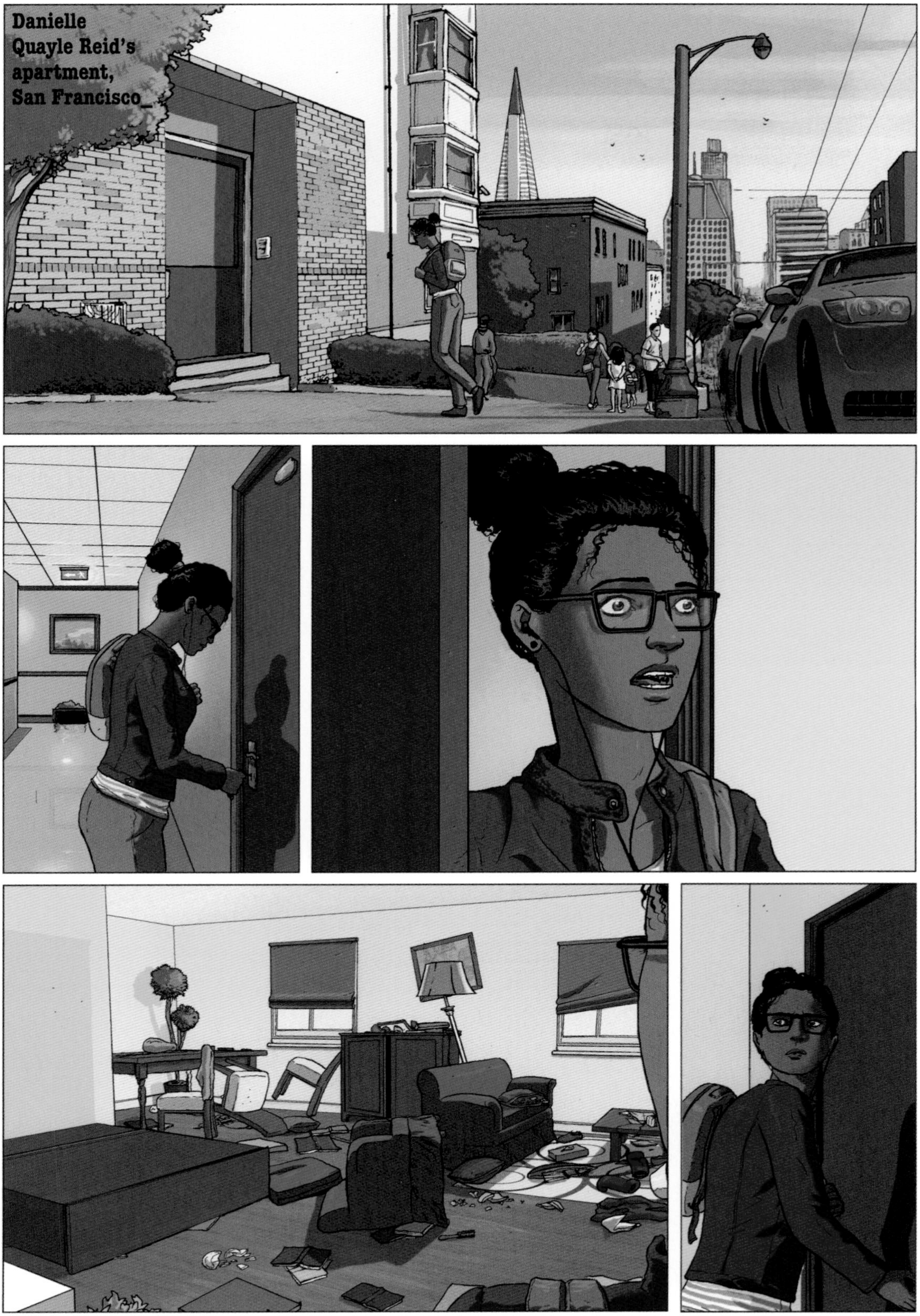
Danielle Quayle Reid's apartment, San Francisco_

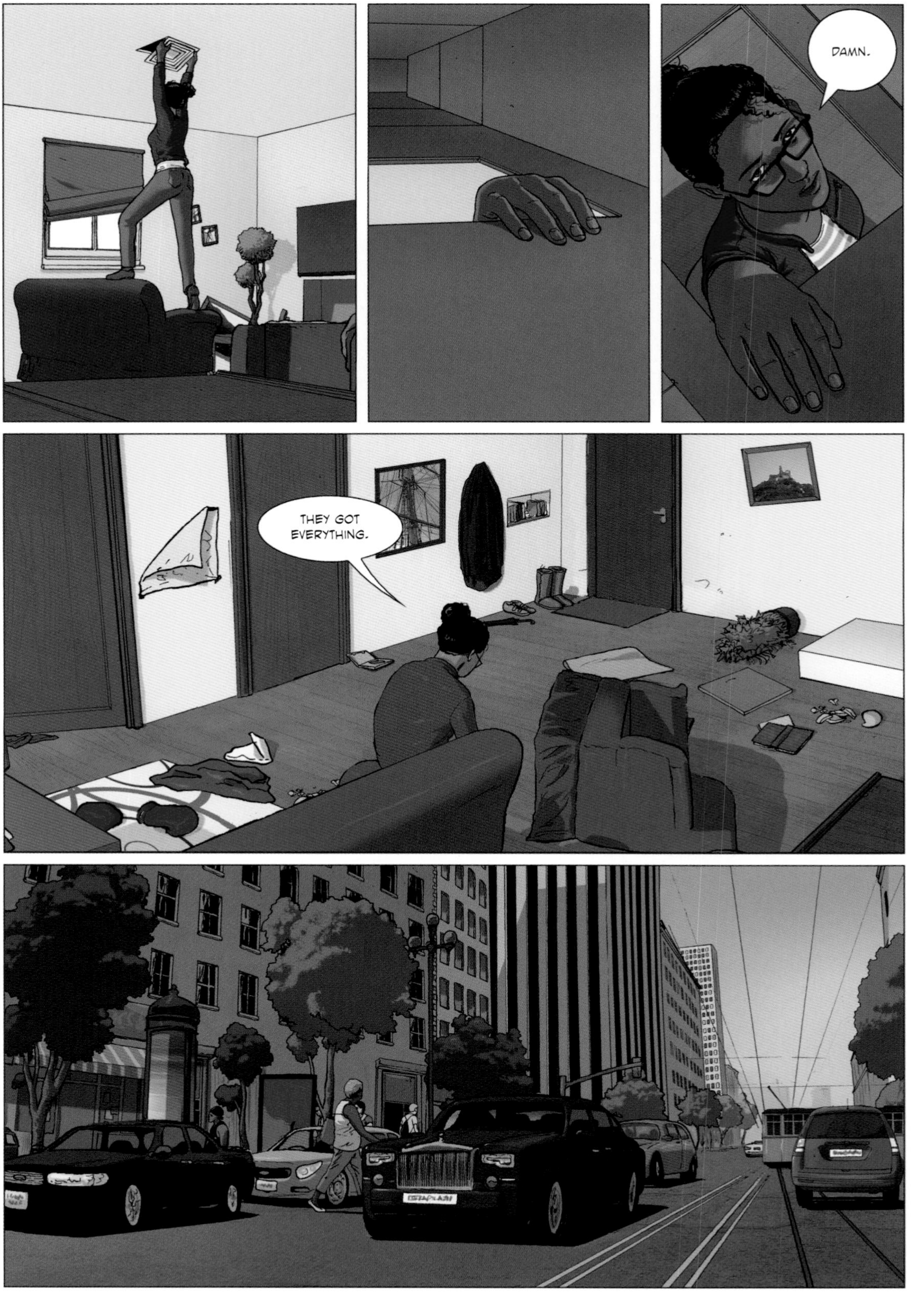
DAMN.
THEY GOT EVERYTHING.

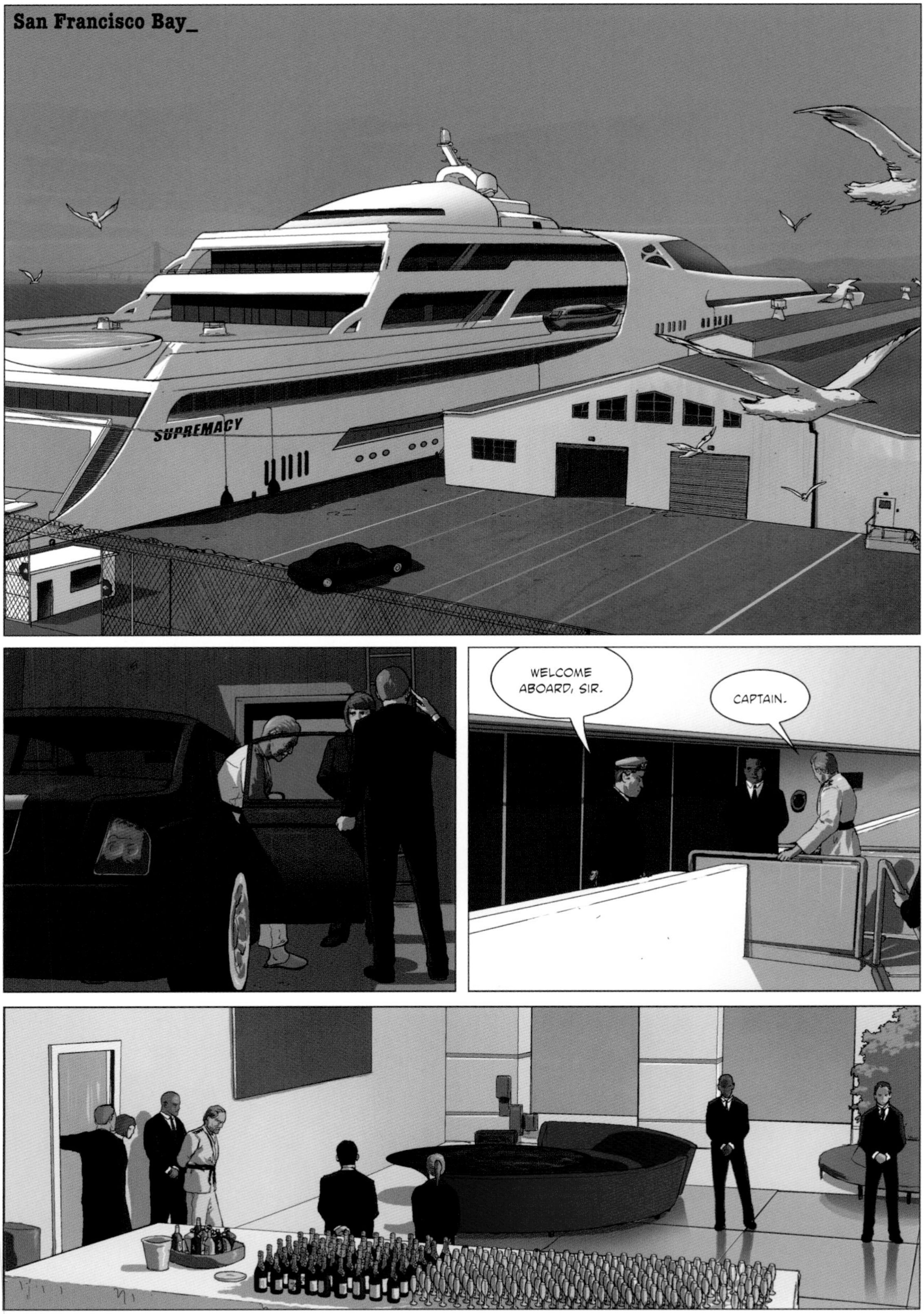
San Francisco Bay_
SUPREMACY
WELCOME ABOARD, SIR.
CAPTAIN.

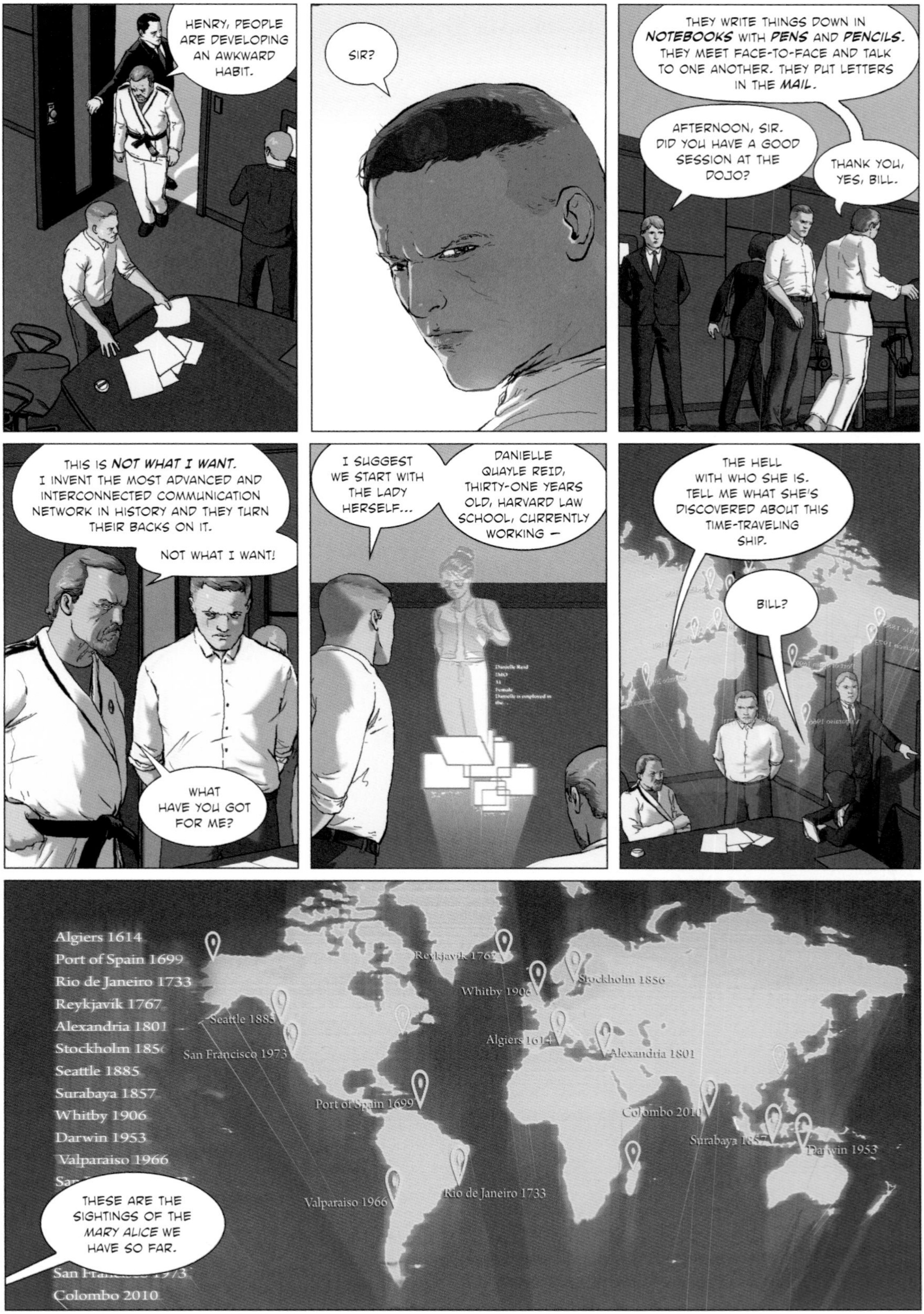
HENRY, PEOPLE ARE DEVELOPING AN AWKWARD HABIT.
SIR?
THEY WRITE THINGS DOWN IN NOTEBOOKS WITH PENS AND PENCILS. THEY MEET FACE-TO-FACE AND TALK TO ONE ANOTHER. THEY PUT LETTERS IN THE MAIL.
AFTERNOON, SIR. DID YOU HAVE A GOOD SESSION AT THE DOJO?
THANK YOU, YES, BILL.
THIS IS NOT WHAT I WANT. I INVENT THE MOST ADVANCED AND INTERCONNECTED COMMUNICATION NETWORK IN HISTORY AND THEY TURN THEIR BACKS ON IT.
NOT WHAT I WANT!
WHAT HAVE YOU GOT FOR ME?
I SUGGEST WE START WITH THE LADY HERSELF...
DANIELLE QUAYLE REID, THIRTY-ONE YEARS OLD, HARVARD LAW SCHOOL, CURRENTLY WORKING —
THE HELL WITH WHO SHE IS. TELL ME WHAT SHE'S DISCOVERED ABOUT THIS TIME-TRAVELING SHIP.
BILL?
Algiers 1614
Port of Spain 1699
Rio de Janeiro 1733
Reykjavik 1767
Seattle 1885
Surabaya 1857
Whitby 1906
Darwin 1953
Valparaiso 1966
Colombo 2010
Reykjavik 1767
Whitby 1906
Stockholm 1856
Seattle 1885
San Francisco 1973
Algiers 1614
Alexandria 1801
Port of Spain 1699
Colombo 2010
Surabaya 1857
Darwin 1953
Valparaiso 1966
Rio de Janeiro 1733
THESE ARE THE SIGHTINGS OF THE MARY ALICE WE HAVE SO FAR.

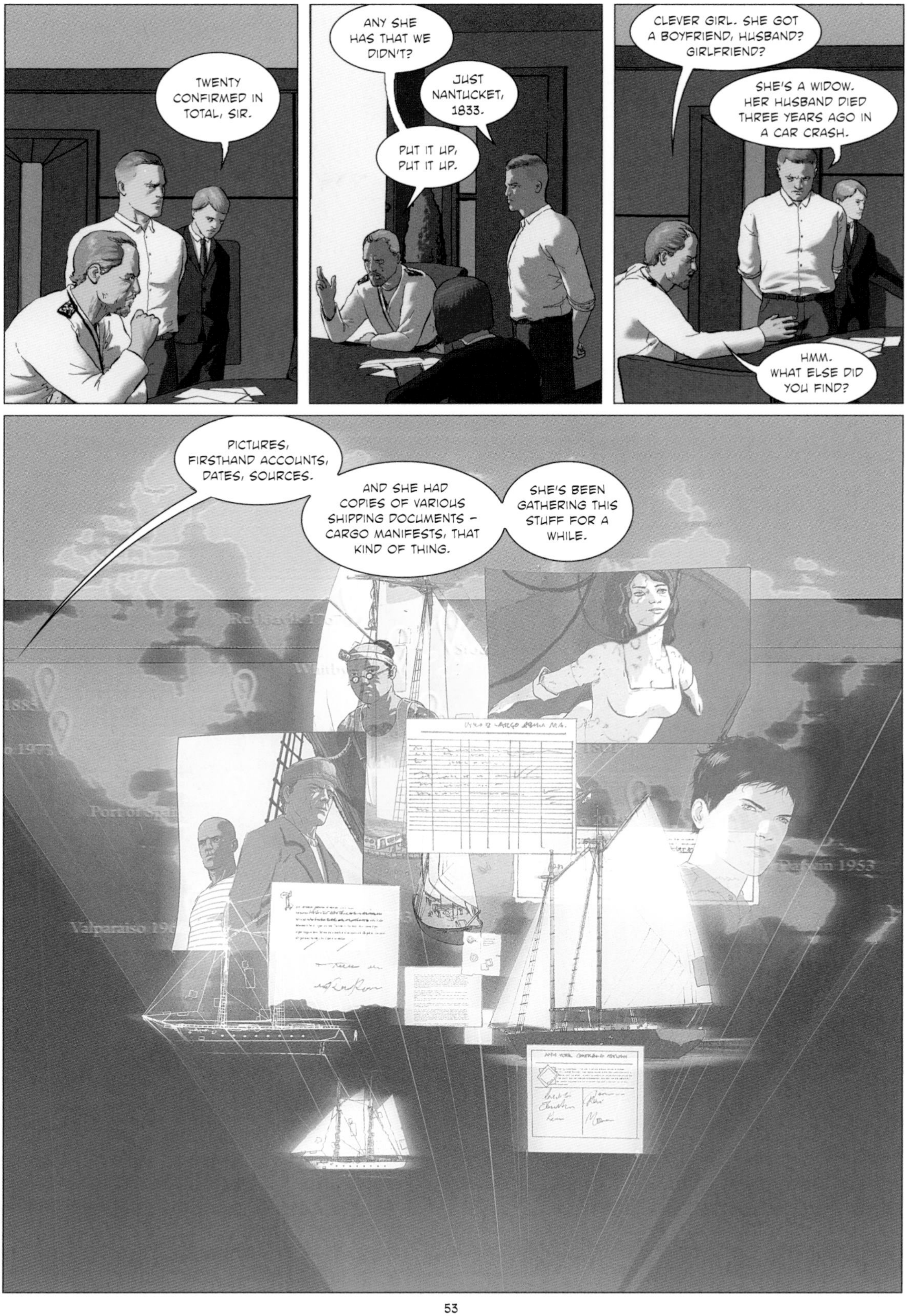
TWENTY CONFIRMED IN TOTAL, SIR.
ANY SHE HAS THAT WE DIDN'T?
JUST NANTUCKET, 1833.
PUT IT UP, PUT IT UP.
CLEVER GIRL. SHE GOT A BOYFRIEND, HUSBAND? GIRLFRIEND?
SHE'S A WIDOW. HER HUSBAND DIED THREE YEARS AGO IN A CAR CRASH.
HMM. WHAT ELSE DID YOU FIND?
PICTURES, FIRSTHAND ACCOUNTS, DATES, SOURCES.
AND SHE HAD COPIES OF VARIOUS SHIPPING DOCUMENTS – CARGO MANIFESTS, THAT KIND OF THING.
SHE'S BEEN GATHERING THIS STUFF FOR A WHILE.
Port of Spai
Valparaiso 19
Darwin 1953

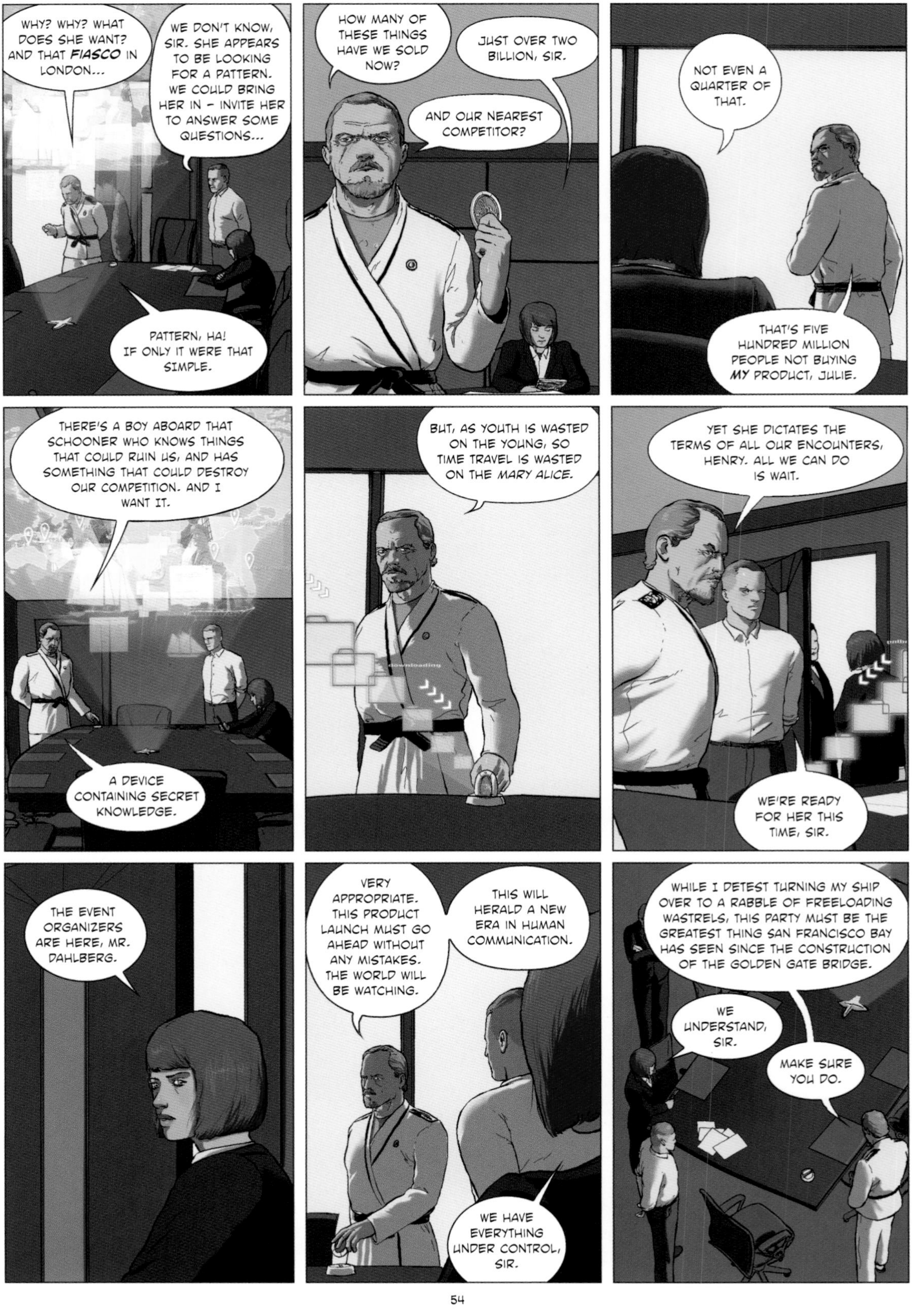
WHY? WHY? WHAT DOES SHE WANT? AND THAT FIASCO IN LONDON...
WE DON'T KNOW, SIR. SHE APPEARS TO BE LOOKING FOR A PATTERN. WE COULD BRING HER IN – INVITE HER TO ANSWER SOME QUESTIONS...
PATTERN, HA! IF ONLY IT WERE THAT SIMPLE.
HOW MANY OF THESE THINGS HAVE WE SOLD NOW?
JUST OVER TWO BILLION, SIR.
AND OUR NEAREST COMPETITOR?
NOT EVEN A QUARTER OF THAT.
THAT'S FIVE HUNDRED MILLION PEOPLE NOT BUYING MY PRODUCT, JULIE.
THERE'S A BOY ABOARD THAT SCHOONER WHO KNOWS THINGS THAT COULD RUIN US, AND HAS SOMETHING THAT COULD DESTROY OUR COMPETITION. AND I WANT IT.
A DEVICE CONTAINING SECRET KNOWLEDGE.
BUT, AS YOUTH IS WASTED ON THE YOUNG, SO TIME TRAVEL IS WASTED ON THE MARY ALICE.
downloading
YET SHE DICTATES THE TERMS OF ALL OUR ENCOUNTERS, HENRY. ALL WE CAN DO IS WAIT.
WE'RE READY FOR HER THIS TIME, SIR.
THE EVENT ORGANIZERS ARE HERE, MR. DAHLBERG.
VERY APPROPRIATE. THIS PRODUCT LAUNCH MUST GO AHEAD WITHOUT ANY MISTAKES. THE WORLD WILL BE WATCHING.
THIS WILL HERALD A NEW ERA IN HUMAN COMMUNICATION.
WE HAVE EVERYTHING UNDER CONTROL, SIR.
WHILE I DETEST TURNING MY SHIP OVER TO A RABBLE OF FREELOADING WASTRELS, THIS PARTY MUST BE THE GREATEST THING SAN FRANCISCO BAY HAS SEEN SINCE THE CONSTRUCTION OF THE GOLDEN GATE BRIDGE.
WE UNDERSTAND, SIR.
MAKE SURE YOU DO.

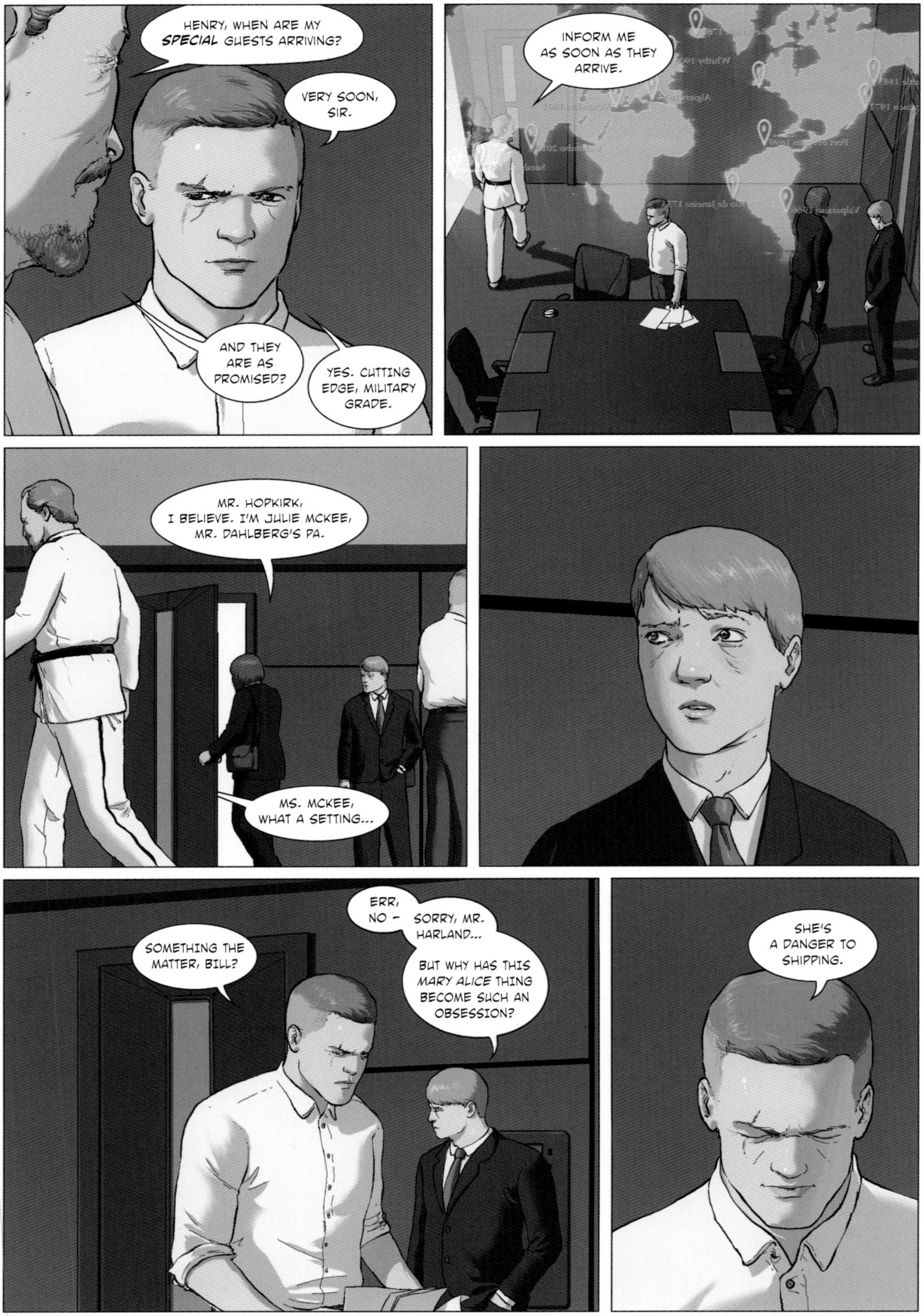
HENRY, WHEN ARE MY *SPECIAL* GUESTS ARRIVING?
VERY SOON, SIR.
AND THEY ARE AS PROMISED?
YES. CUTTING EDGE, MILITARY GRADE.
INFORM ME AS SOON AS THEY ARRIVE.
MR. HOPKIRK, I BELIEVE. I'M JULIE MCKEE, MR. DAHLBERG'S PA.
MS. MCKEE, WHAT A SETTING...
SOMETHING THE MATTER, BILL?
ERR, NO –
SORRY, MR. HARLAND...
BUT WHY HAS THIS *MARY ALICE* THING BECOME SUCH AN OBSESSION?
SHE'S A DANGER TO SHIPPING.

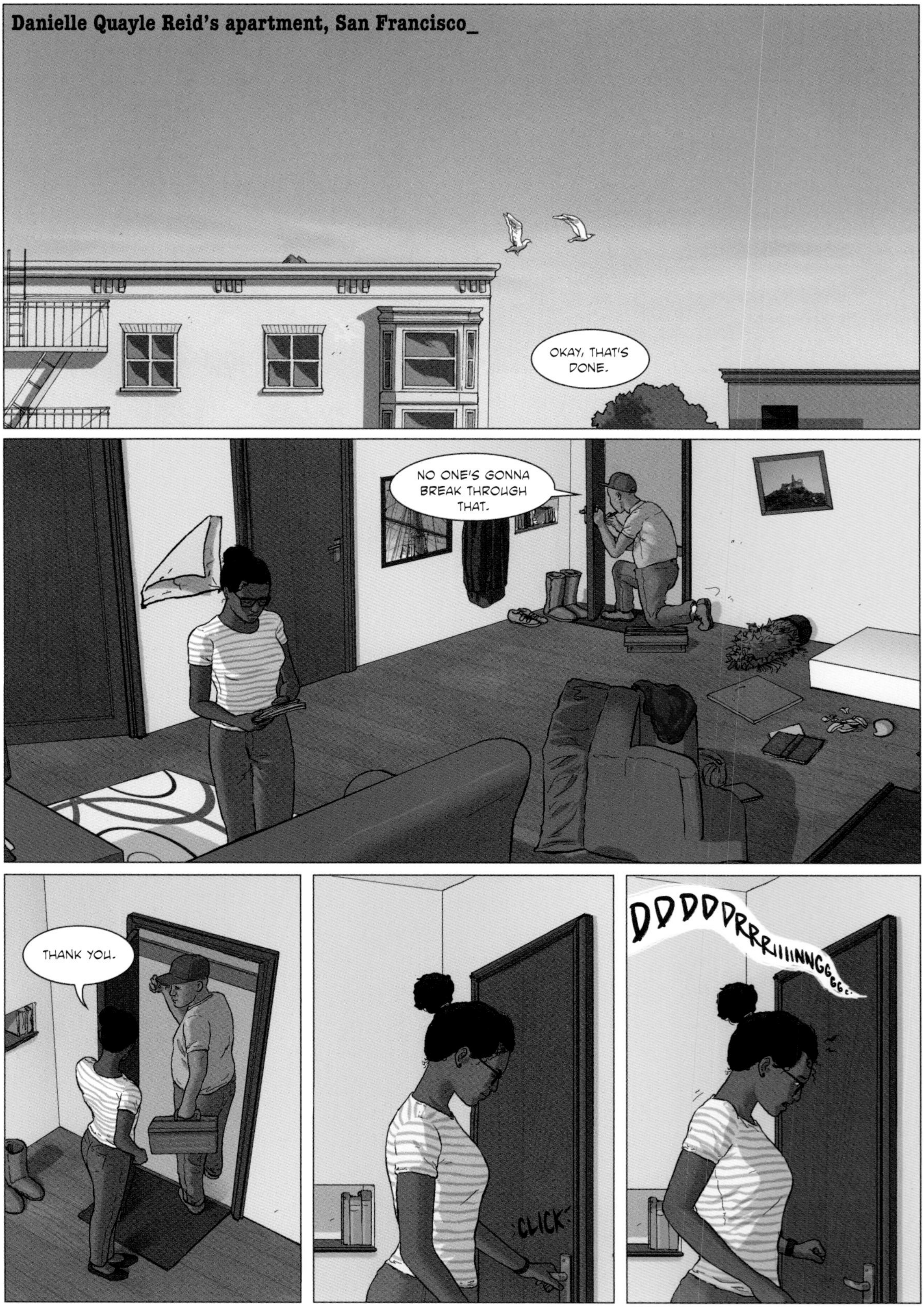
Danielle Quayle Reid's apartment, San Francisco_
OKAY, THAT'S DONE.
NO ONE'S GONNA BREAK THROUGH THAT.
THANK YOU.
:CLICK:
DDDDDRRRRIIIINNNGGGGG

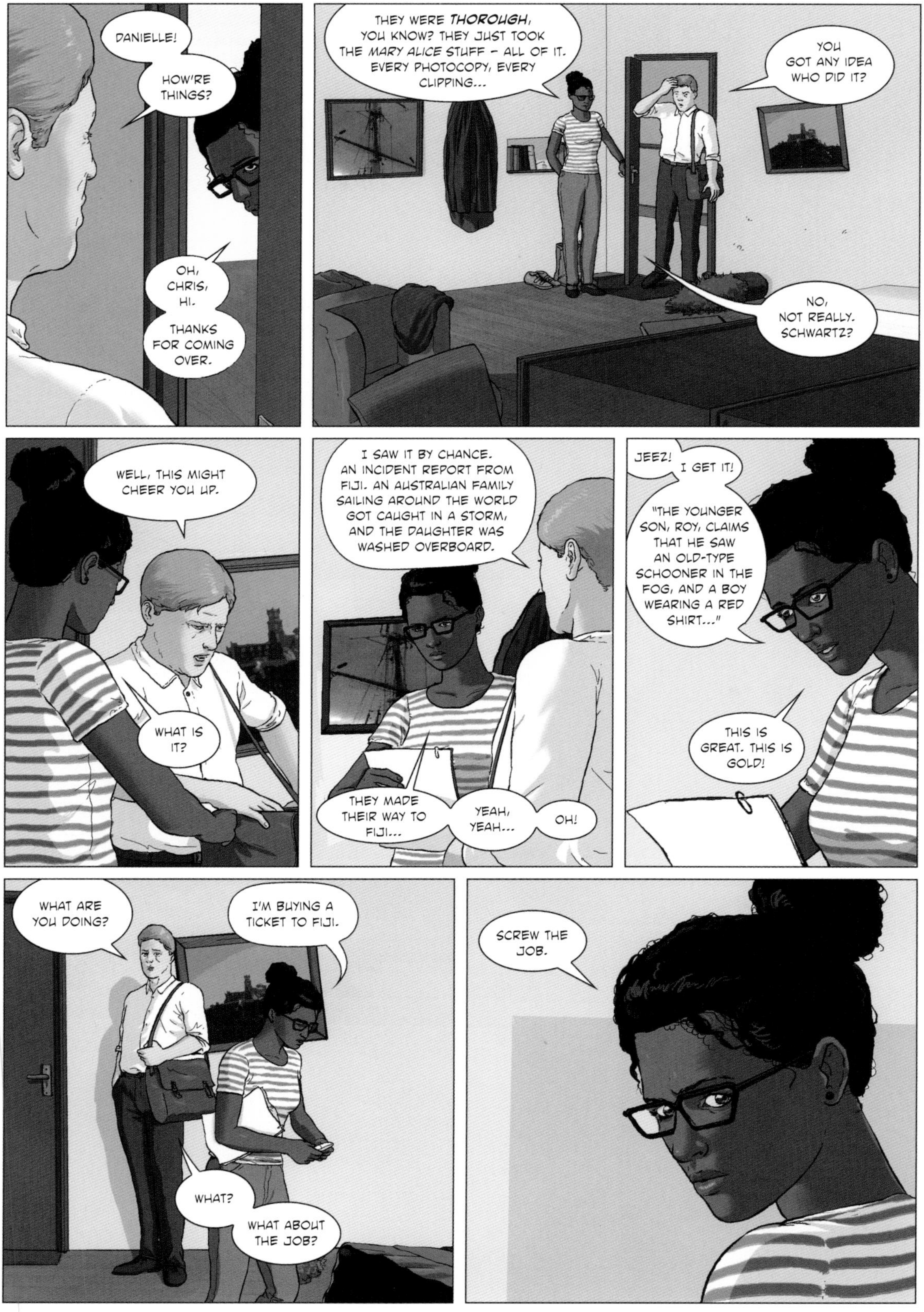
DANIELLE!
HOW'RE THINGS?
OH, CHRIS, HI.
THANKS FOR COMING OVER.
THEY WERE *THOROUGH*, YOU KNOW? THEY JUST TOOK THE *MARY ALICE* STUFF – ALL OF IT. EVERY PHOTOCOPY, EVERY CLIPPING...
YOU GOT ANY IDEA WHO DID IT?
NO, NOT REALLY. SCHWARTZ?
WELL, THIS MIGHT CHEER YOU UP.
WHAT IS IT?
I SAW IT BY CHANCE. AN INCIDENT REPORT FROM FIJI. AN AUSTRALIAN FAMILY SAILING AROUND THE WORLD GOT CAUGHT IN A STORM, AND THE DAUGHTER WAS WASHED OVERBOARD.
THEY MADE THEIR WAY TO FIJI...
YEAH, YEAH...
OH!
JEEZ!
I GET IT!
"THE YOUNGER SON, ROY, CLAIMS THAT HE SAW AN OLD-TYPE SCHOONER IN THE FOG, AND A BOY WEARING A RED SHIRT..."
THIS IS GREAT. THIS IS GOLD!
WHAT ARE YOU DOING?
I'M BUYING A TICKET TO FIJI.
WHAT?
WHAT ABOUT THE JOB?
SCREW THE JOB.

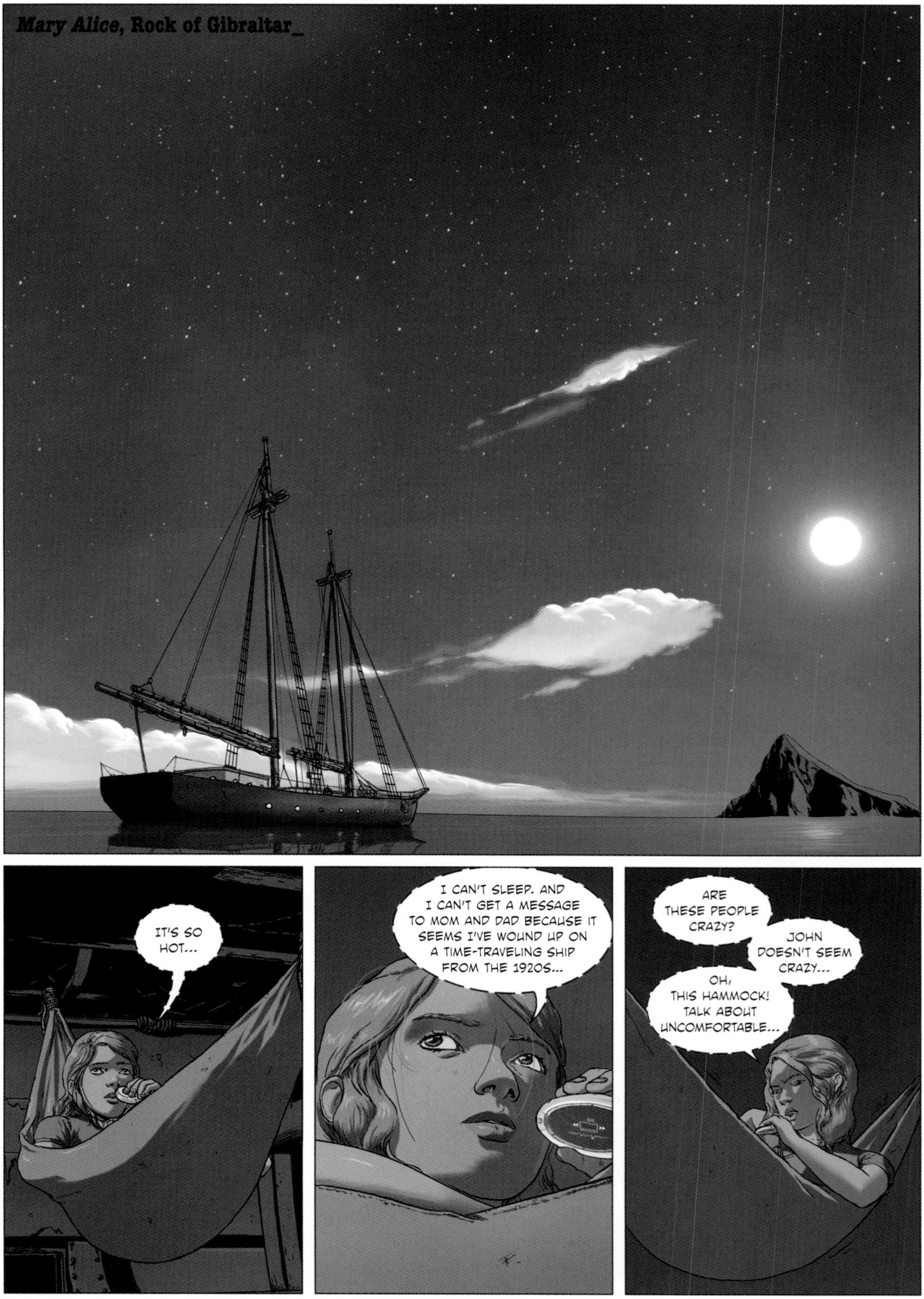
Mary Alice, Rock of Gibraltar_
IT'S SO HOT...
I CAN'T SLEEP. AND I CAN'T GET A MESSAGE TO MOM AND DAD BECAUSE IT SEEMS I'VE WOUND UP ON A TIME-TRAVELING SHIP FROM THE 1920S...
ARE THESE PEOPLE CRAZY?
JOHN DOESN'T SEEM CRAZY...
OH, THIS HAMMOCK! TALK ABOUT UNCOMFORTABLE...

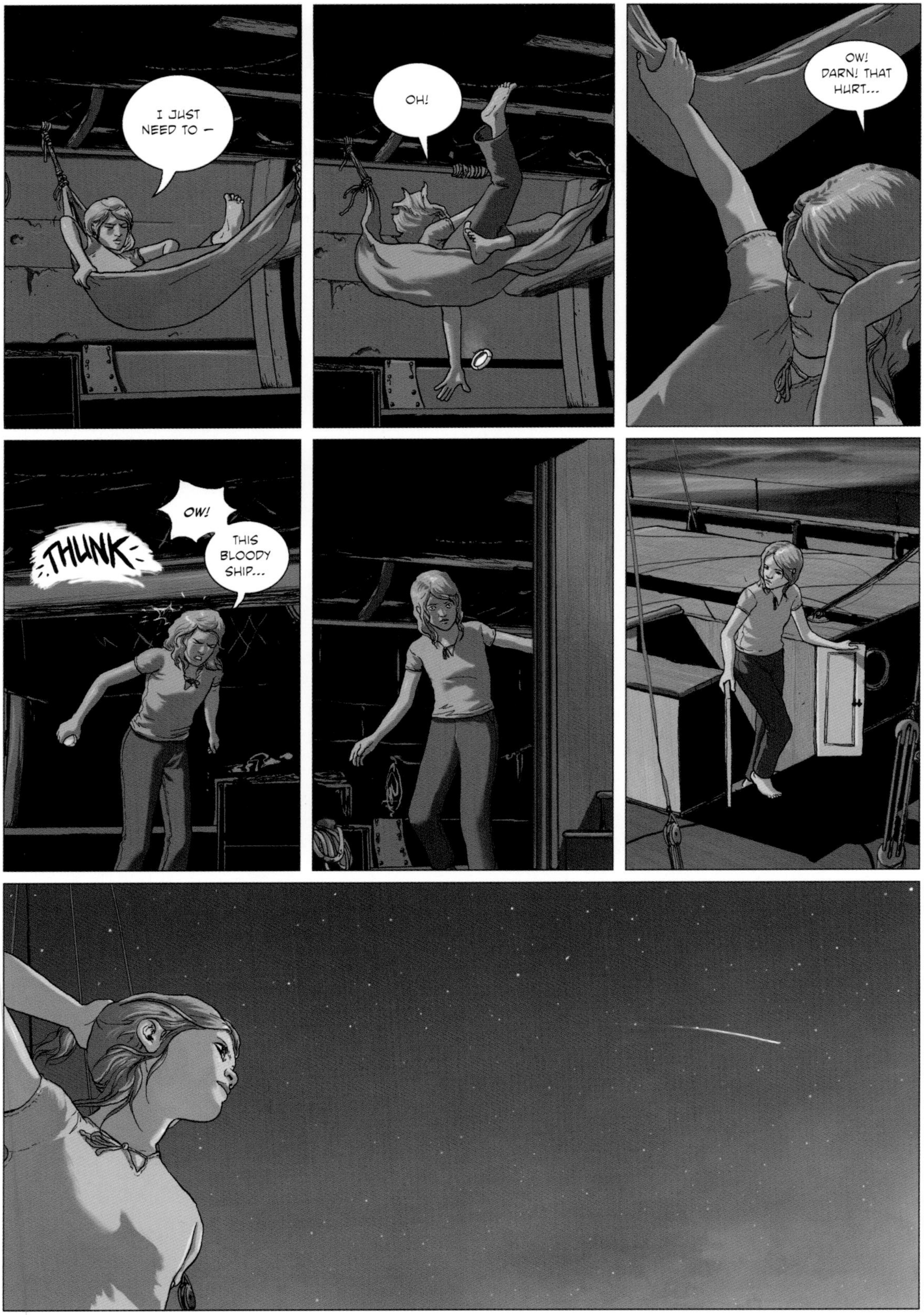
I JUST NEED TO —
OH!
OW! DARN! THAT HURT...
THUNK
OW!
THIS BLOODY SHIP...

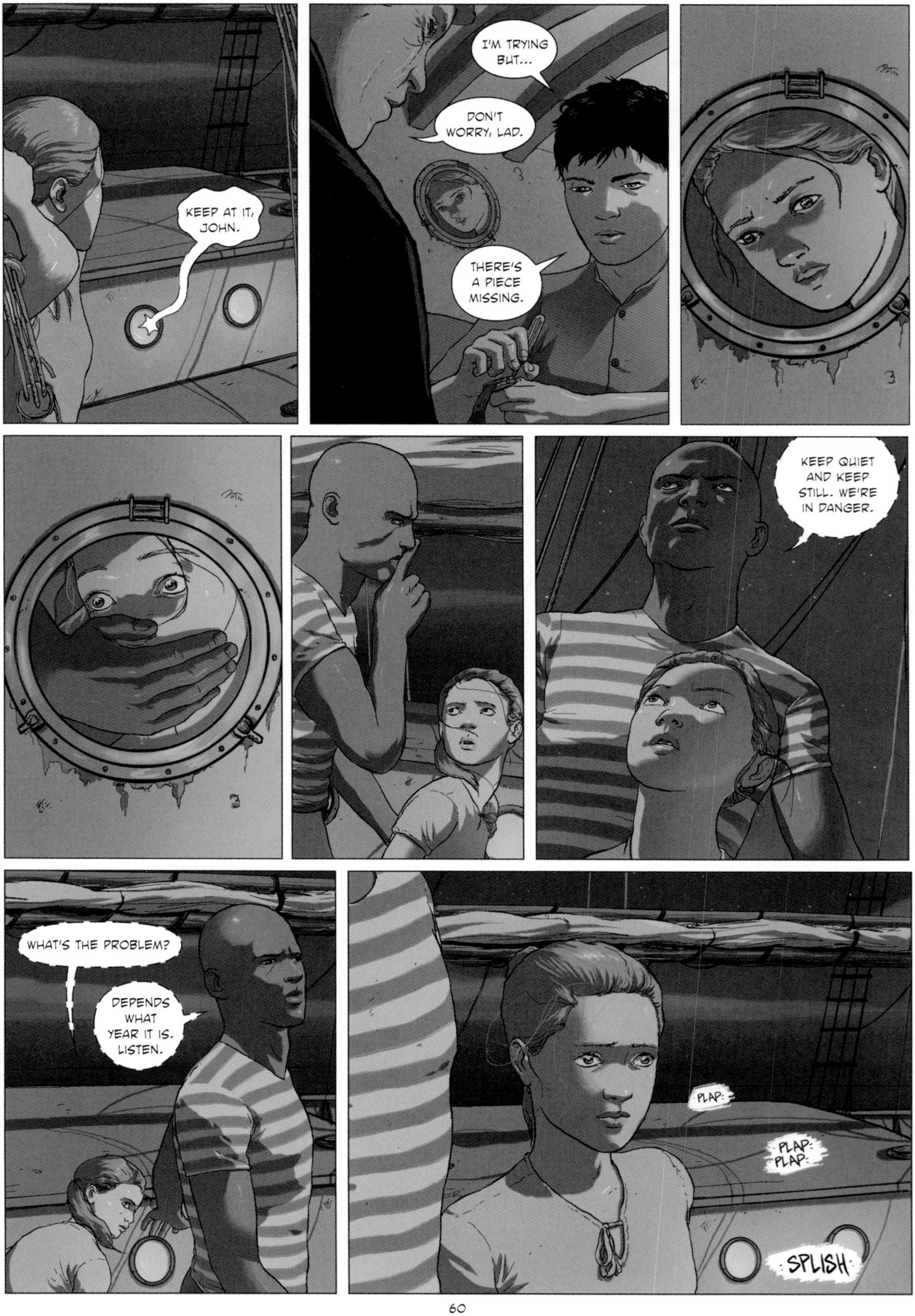
KEEP AT IT, JOHN.
I'M TRYING BUT...
DON'T WORRY, LAD.
THERE'S A PIECE MISSING.
KEEP QUIET AND KEEP STILL. WE'RE IN DANGER.
WHAT'S THE PROBLEM?
DEPENDS WHAT YEAR IT IS. LISTEN.
PLAP
PLAP PLAP
SPLISH

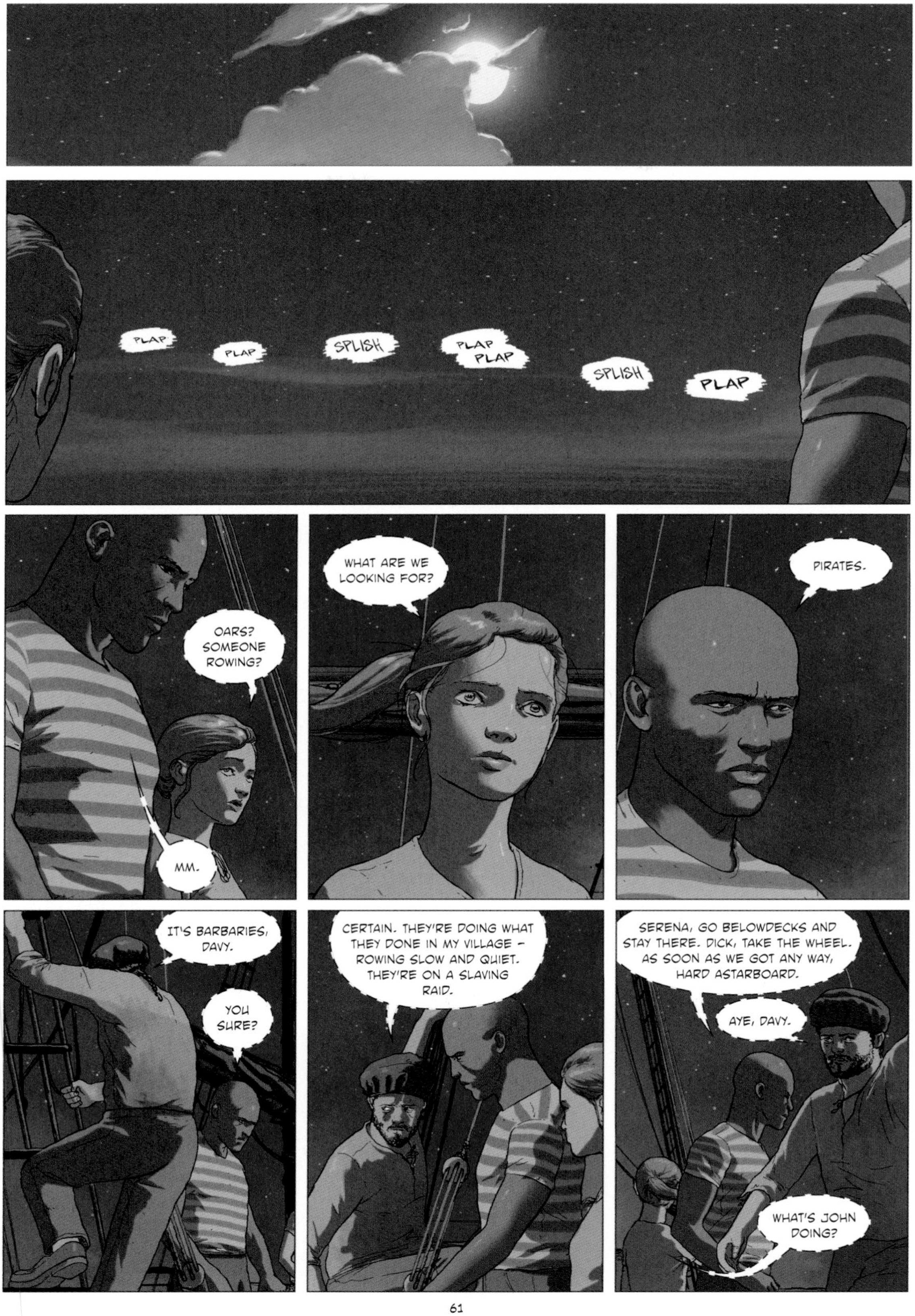
PLAP
PLAP
SPLISH
PLAP PLAP
SPLISH
PLAP
OARS? SOMEONE ROWING?
MM.
WHAT ARE WE LOOKING FOR?
PIRATES.
IT'S BARBARIES, DAVY.
YOU SURE?
CERTAIN. THEY'RE DOING WHAT THEY DONE IN MY VILLAGE - ROWING SLOW AND QUIET. THEY'RE ON A SLAVING RAID.
SERENA, GO BELOWDECKS AND STAY THERE. DICK, TAKE THE WHEEL. AS SOON AS WE GOT ANY WAY, HARD ASTARBOARD.
AYE, DAVY.
WHAT'S JOHN DOING?

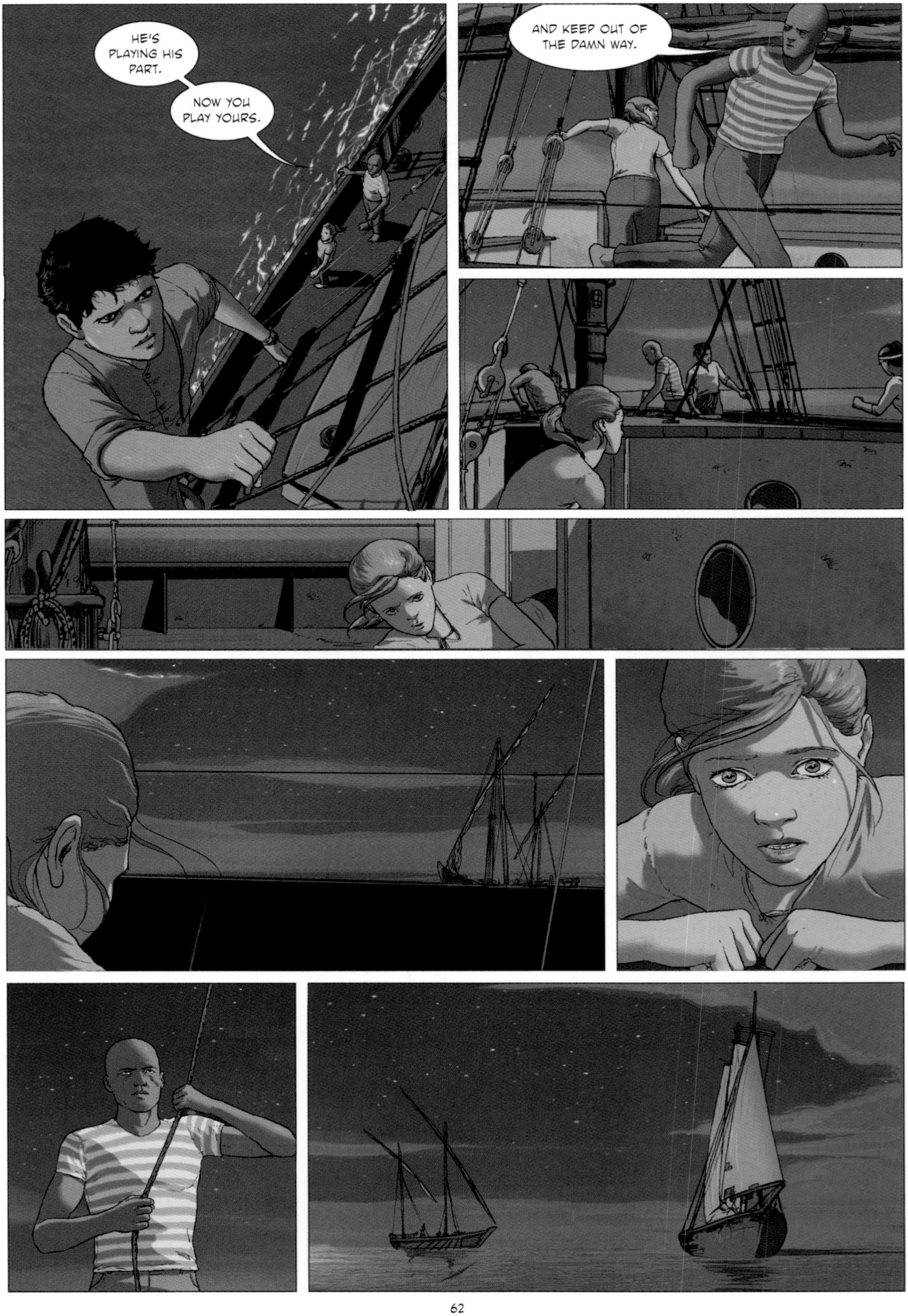
HE'S PLAYING HIS PART.
NOW YOU PLAY YOURS.
AND KEEP OUT OF THE DAMN WAY.

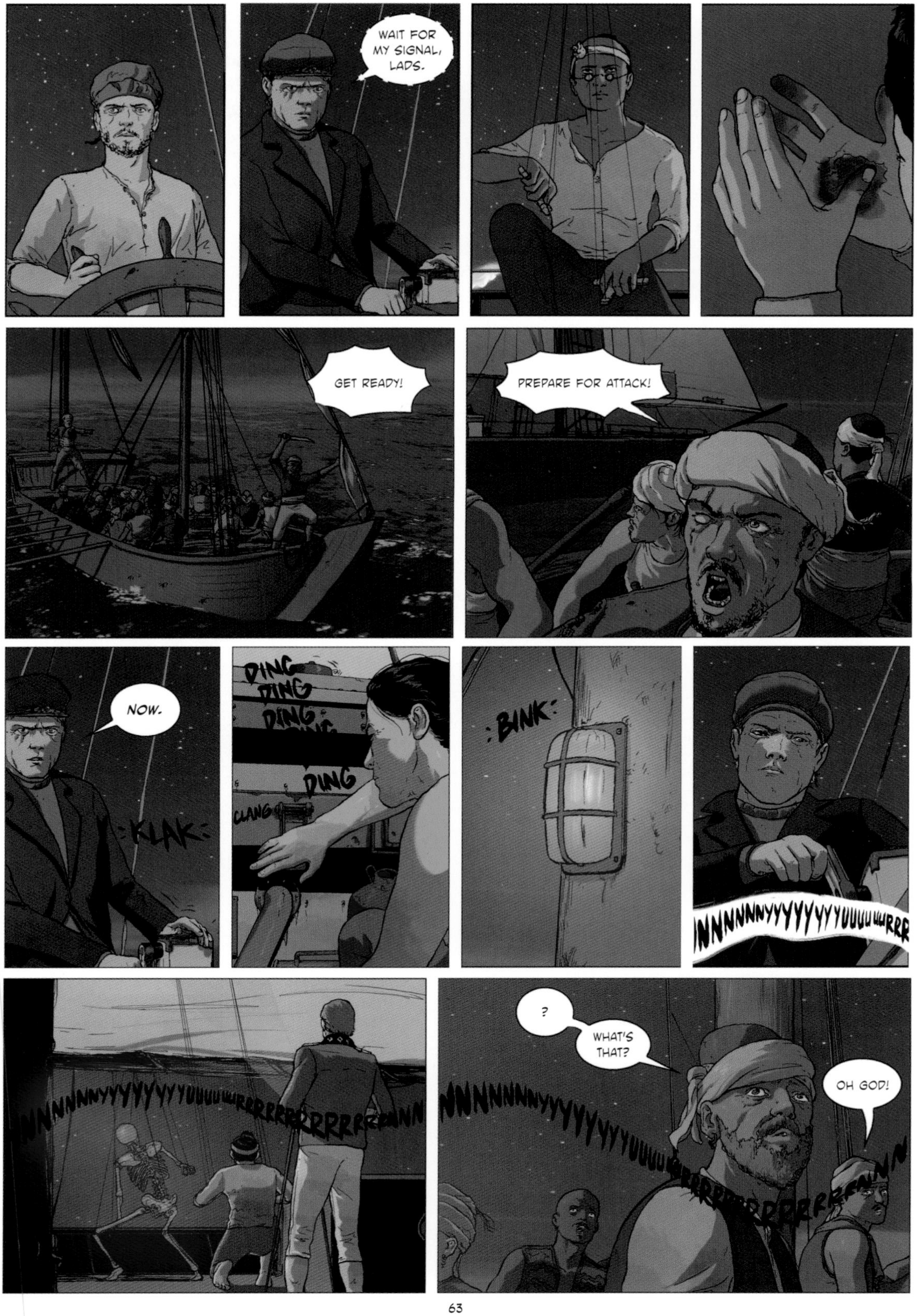
WAIT FOR MY SIGNAL, LADS.
GET READY!
PREPARE FOR ATTACK!
NOW.
KLAK
DING DING DING DING
DING
CLANG
BINK
NNNNNNYYYYYYYYUUUUUURRR
NNNNNNYYYYYYYYUUUUUURRRRRRRRRRRRRNNN
?
WHAT'S THAT?
OH GOD!

HA
HA HA
HA
HA
HA HA
HA HA
HA HA
HA
HA
NNNNNNYYYYYYYYUUUUU
RRRRRNNN
AAAAAHHHHH!!
NNNNNNYYYY YYYUUUUWRRRRRRRRRRRRRNNNNNNN
YYYYUUUUWRRRRRRRRRRRRRRN
HA, HA!
AWESOME.
NNNNNNNYYYYYYYUUUUUWRRRRRRRRRRRRRNN
LOOK!
LOOK!
WHAT IS IT?
NNYYYYYYYYUUUUWRRRRRRRRRRRRRNNN
YYYUUUUWRRR
NNNNNNYYVV
RR

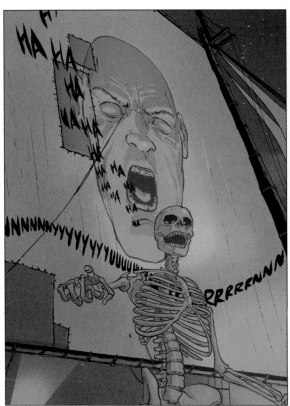

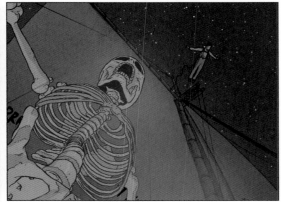

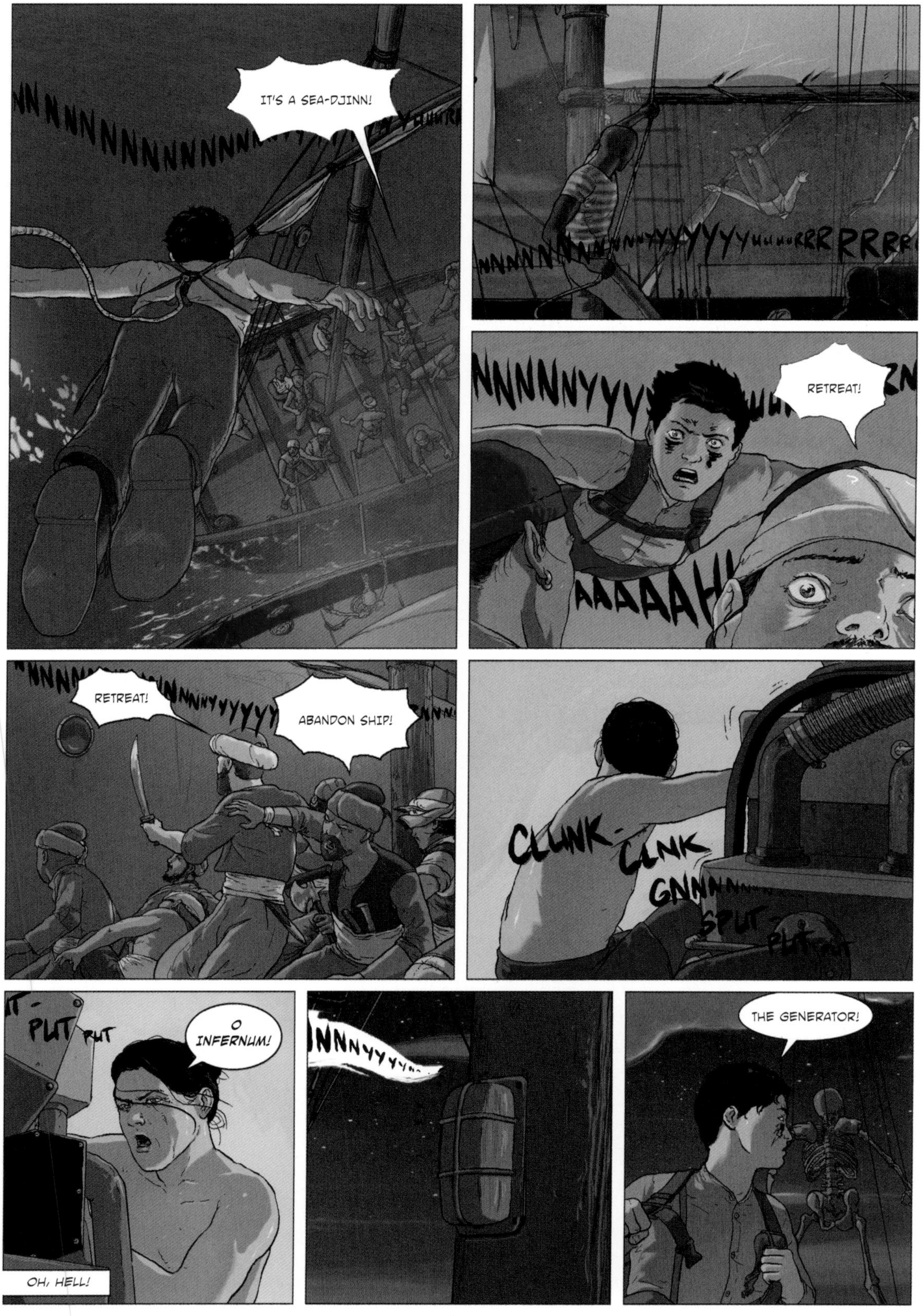
IT'S A SEA-DJINN!
RETREAT!
AAAAAH!
RETREAT!
ABANDON SHIP!
CLUNK-
CLNK
O INFERNUM!
OH, HELL!
THE GENERATOR!

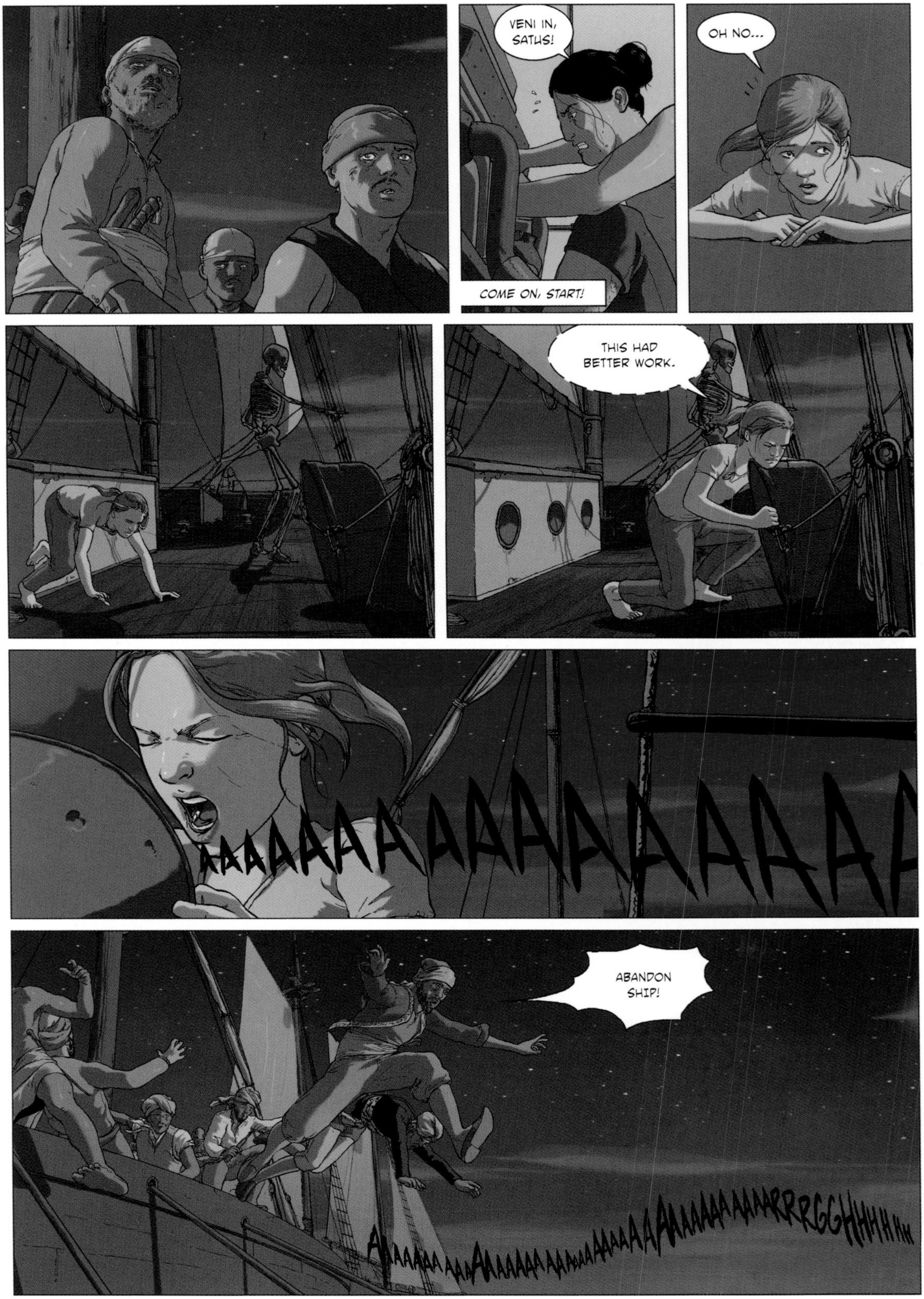
VENI IN, SATUS!
COME ON, START!
OH NO...
THIS HAD BETTER WORK.
AAAAAAAAAAAAAAAAAAA
ABANDON SHIP!
AAAAAAAAAAAAAAAAAAAAAAAAAAAAAAAAAAAAAAAAARRRGGHHHHHH

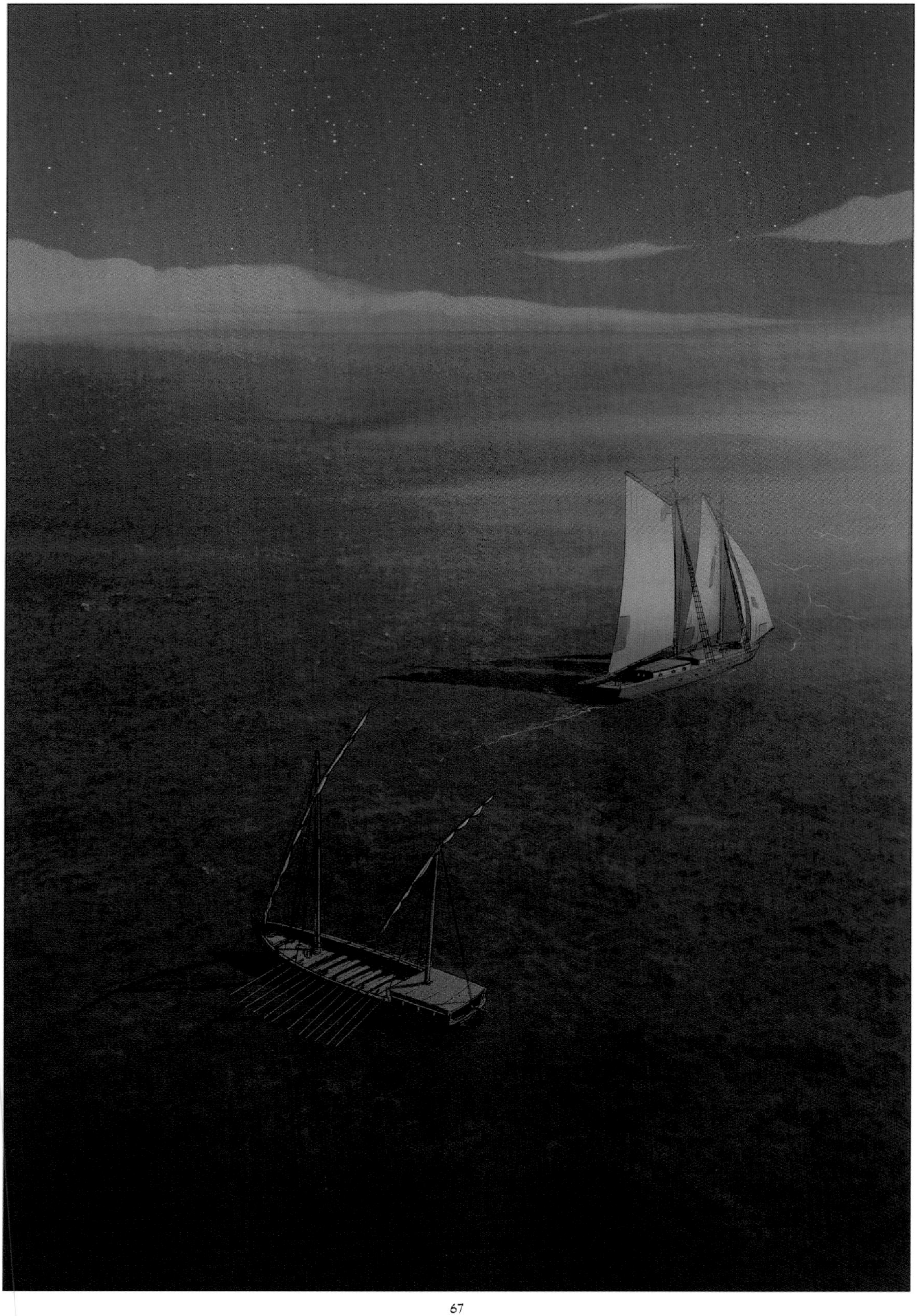

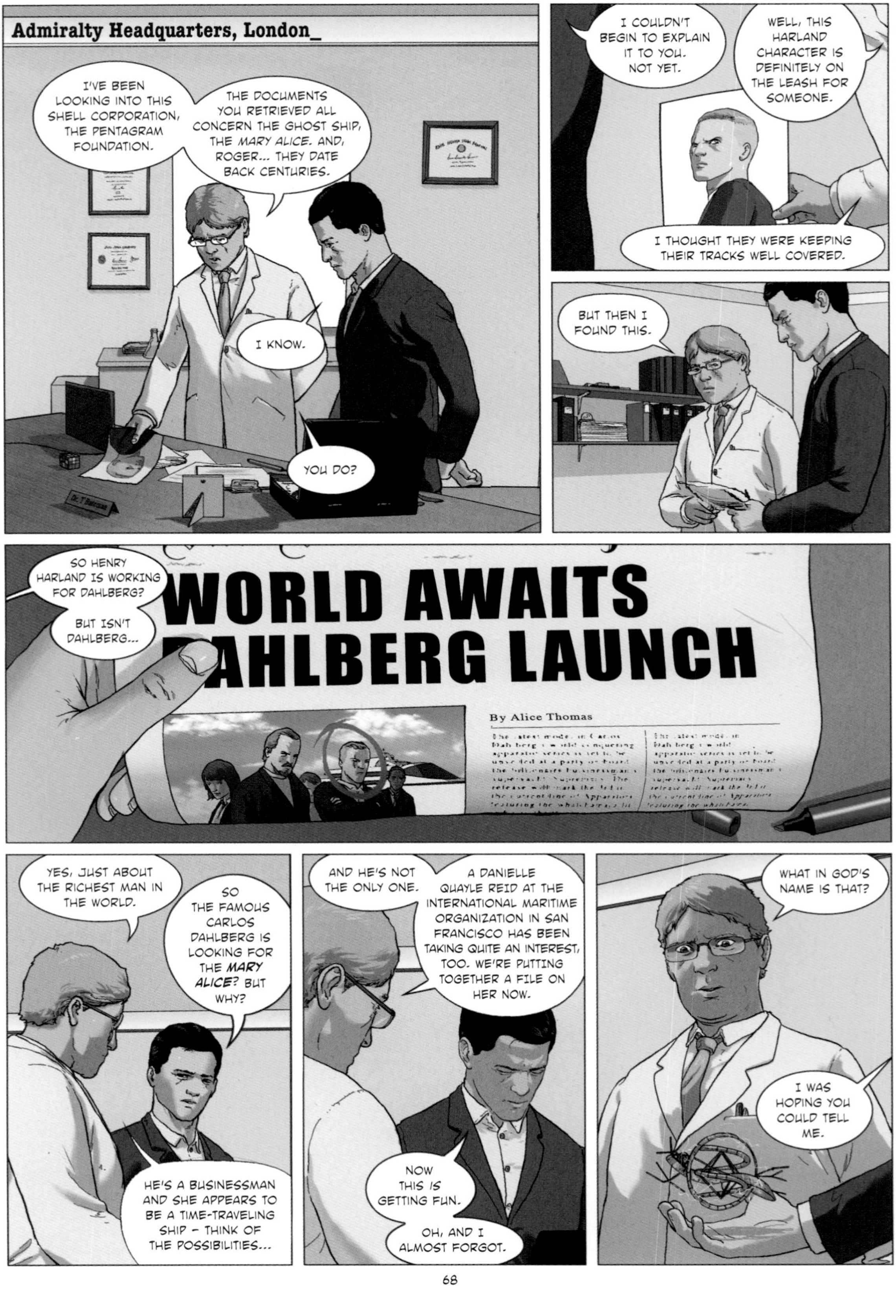
Admiralty Headquarters, London_
I'VE BEEN LOOKING INTO THIS SHELL CORPORATION, THE PENTAGRAM FOUNDATION.
THE DOCUMENTS YOU RETRIEVED ALL CONCERN THE GHOST SHIP, THE MARY ALICE. AND, ROGER... THEY DATE BACK CENTURIES.
I KNOW.
YOU DO?
I COULDN'T BEGIN TO EXPLAIN IT TO YOU. NOT YET.
WELL, THIS HARLAND CHARACTER IS DEFINITELY ON THE LEASH FOR SOMEONE.
I THOUGHT THEY WERE KEEPING THEIR TRACKS WELL COVERED.
BUT THEN I FOUND THIS.
SO HENRY HARLAND IS WORKING FOR DAHLBERG?
BUT ISN'T DAHLBERG...
WORLD AWAITS DAHLBERG LAUNCH
By Alice Thomas
YES, JUST ABOUT THE RICHEST MAN IN THE WORLD.
SO THE FAMOUS CARLOS DAHLBERG IS LOOKING FOR THE MARY ALICE? BUT WHY?
HE'S A BUSINESSMAN AND SHE APPEARS TO BE A TIME-TRAVELING SHIP - THINK OF THE POSSIBILITIES...
AND HE'S NOT THE ONLY ONE.
A DANIELLE QUAYLE REID AT THE INTERNATIONAL MARITIME ORGANIZATION IN SAN FRANCISCO HAS BEEN TAKING QUITE AN INTEREST, TOO. WE'RE PUTTING TOGETHER A FILE ON HER NOW.
NOW THIS IS GETTING FUN.
OH, AND I ALMOST FORGOT.
WHAT IN GOD'S NAME IS THAT?
I WAS HOPING YOU COULD TELL ME.

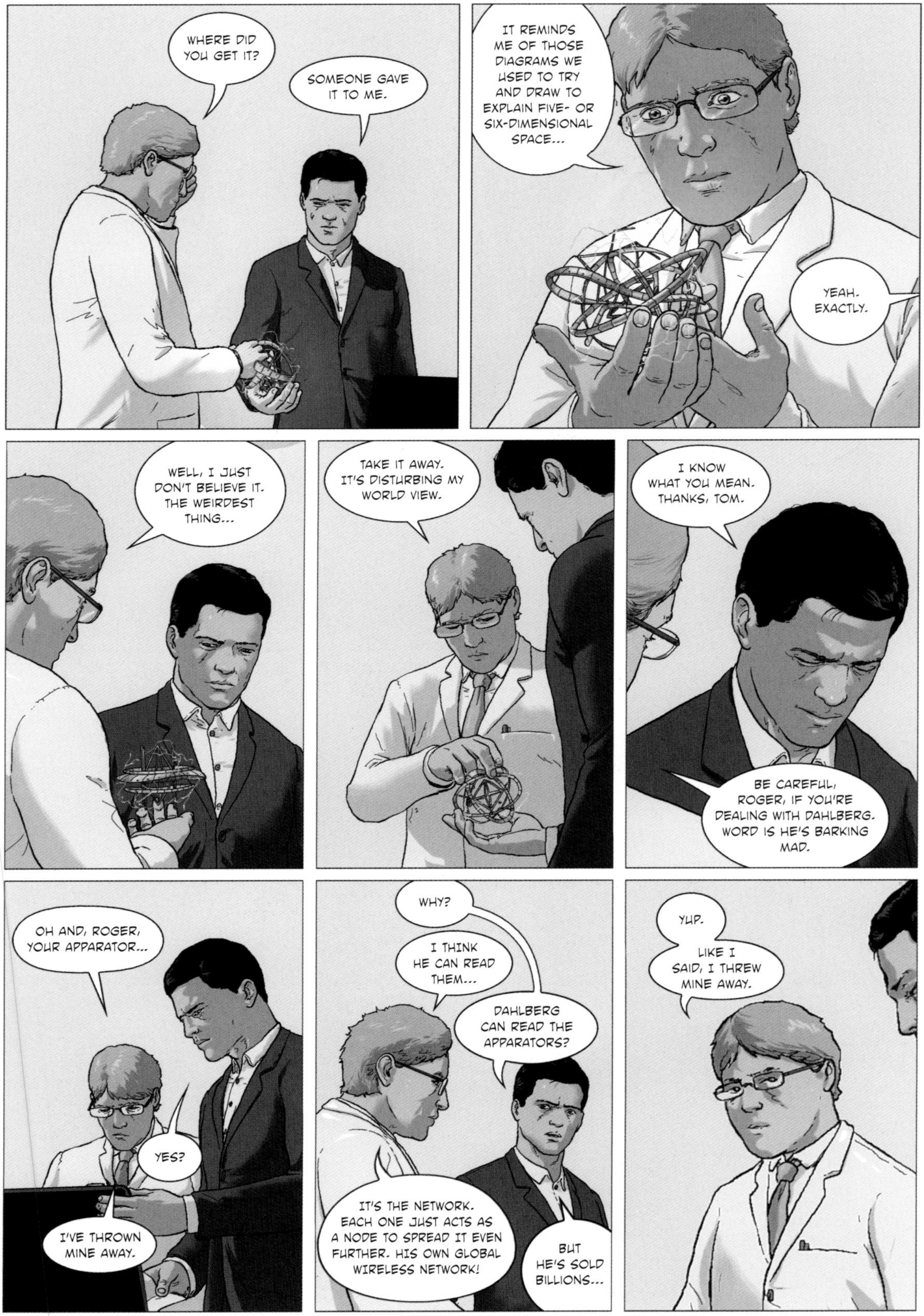
WHERE DID YOU GET IT?
SOMEONE GAVE IT TO ME.
IT REMINDS ME OF THOSE DIAGRAMS WE USED TO TRY AND DRAW TO EXPLAIN FIVE- OR SIX-DIMENSIONAL SPACE...
YEAH. EXACTLY.
WELL, I JUST DON'T BELIEVE IT. THE WEIRDEST THING...
TAKE IT AWAY. IT'S DISTURBING MY WORLD VIEW.
I KNOW WHAT YOU MEAN. THANKS, TOM.
BE CAREFUL, ROGER, IF YOU'RE DEALING WITH DAHLBERG. WORD IS HE'S BARKING MAD.
OH AND, ROGER, YOUR APPARATOR...
YES?
I'VE THROWN MINE AWAY.
WHY?
I THINK HE CAN READ THEM...
DAHLBERG CAN READ THE APPARATORS?
IT'S THE NETWORK. EACH ONE JUST ACTS AS A NODE TO SPREAD IT EVEN FURTHER. HIS OWN GLOBAL WIRELESS NETWORK!
BUT HE'S SOLD BILLIONS...
YUP.
LIKE I SAID, I THREW MINE AWAY.

Australian High Commission, Fiji_

DDRRRRIIIIINNNGGG DDRRRRIIIIINNNG

ROGER?

JIM CASEY HERE.

JIM! HOW'RE YOU DOING?

D'YOU REMEMBER THAT YARN YOU TOLD ME IN AUCKLAND A COUPLE OF YEARS AGO?

THE MYSTERIOUS SCHOONER, AND THE BOY IN THE RED SHIRT?

I REMEMBER... WHAT ABOUT IT?

THEY'VE JUST TURNED UP IN FIJI, MATE. WELL, NOT THEM EXACTLY, BUT A REPORT.

YOU'RE KIDDING.

THERE'S AN AUSSIE FAMILY WASHED UP HERE IN A SMASHED-UP YACHT. TRYING TO SAIL ROUND THE WORLD, AND I WOULDN'T TRUST THE IDIOT OF A FATHER TO SAIL A RUBBER TUBE ACROSS A SWIMMING POOL.

ANYWAY, THEY GOT CAUGHT IN A STORM, AND THE DAUGHTER – YOUNG KID – GETS SWEPT OVERBOARD.

NOW THERE'S A BROTHER – COUPLE YEARS YOUNGER – STEADY, CLEARHEADED BOY, A GOOD DEAL SHARPER THAN HIS DAD. HE SWEARS HE SAW A BEATEN-UP OLD SCHOONER APPEAR OUT OF A FOG, AND A BOY IN A RED SHIRT DIVED IN THE WATER AND PICKED UP HIS SISTER.

THEN THEY VANISHED.

ARE THEY STILL IN FIJI, THIS FAMILY?

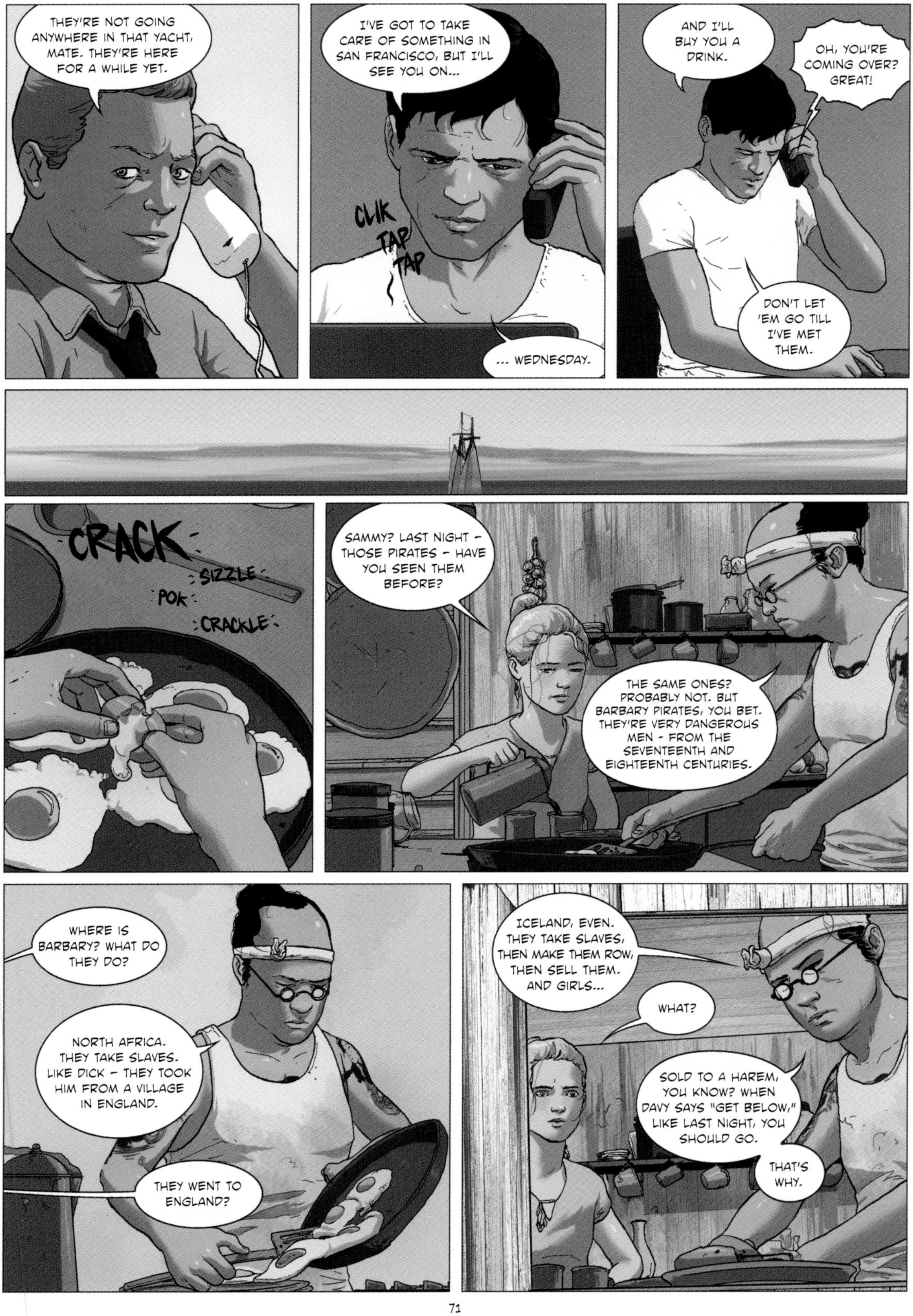
THEY'RE NOT GOING ANYWHERE IN THAT YACHT, MATE. THEY'RE HERE FOR A WHILE YET.
I'VE GOT TO TAKE CARE OF SOMETHING IN SAN FRANCISCO, BUT I'LL SEE YOU ON...
CLIK
TAP
TAP
... WEDNESDAY.
AND I'LL BUY YOU A DRINK.
OH, YOU'RE COMING OVER? GREAT!
DON'T LET 'EM GO TILL I'VE MET THEM.
CRACK
SIZZLE
POK
CRACKLE
SAMMY? LAST NIGHT – THOSE PIRATES – HAVE YOU SEEN THEM BEFORE?
THE SAME ONES? PROBABLY NOT. BUT BARBARY PIRATES, YOU BET. THEY'RE VERY DANGEROUS MEN - FROM THE SEVENTEENTH AND EIGHTEENTH CENTURIES.
WHERE IS BARBARY? WHAT DO THEY DO?
NORTH AFRICA. THEY TAKE SLAVES. LIKE DICK – THEY TOOK HIM FROM A VILLAGE IN ENGLAND.
THEY WENT TO ENGLAND?
ICELAND, EVEN. THEY TAKE SLAVES, THEN MAKE THEM ROW, THEN SELL THEM. AND GIRLS...
WHAT?
SOLD TO A HAREM, YOU KNOW? WHEN DAVY SAYS "GET BELOW," LIKE LAST NIGHT, YOU SHOULD GO.
THAT'S WHY.

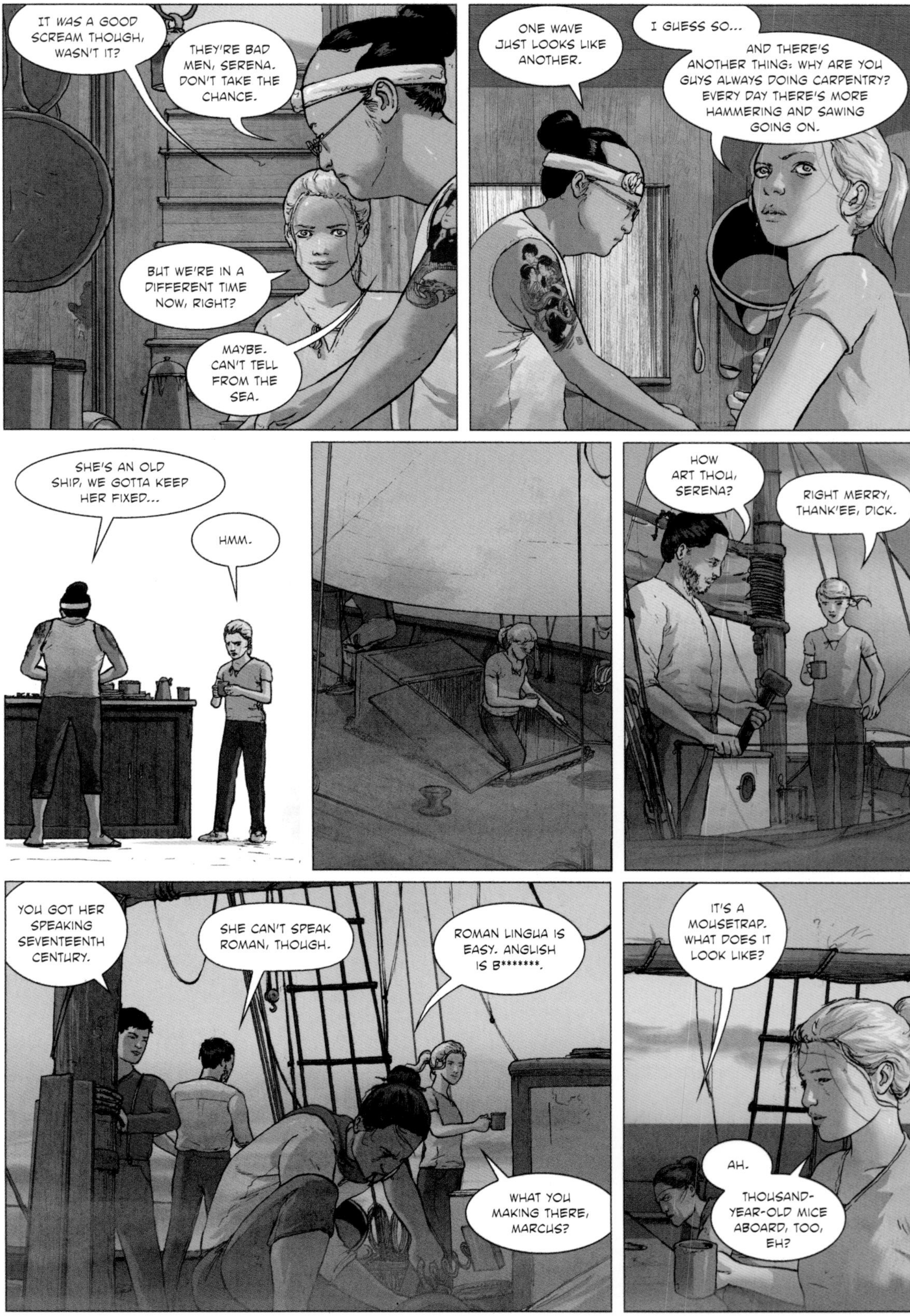
IT WAS A GOOD SCREAM THOUGH, WASN'T IT?
THEY'RE BAD MEN, SERENA. DON'T TAKE THE CHANCE.
BUT WE'RE IN A DIFFERENT TIME NOW, RIGHT?
MAYBE. CAN'T TELL FROM THE SEA.
ONE WAVE JUST LOOKS LIKE ANOTHER.
I GUESS SO...
AND THERE'S ANOTHER THING: WHY ARE YOU GUYS ALWAYS DOING CARPENTRY? EVERY DAY THERE'S MORE HAMMERING AND SAWING GOING ON.
SHE'S AN OLD SHIP, WE GOTTA KEEP HER FIXED...
HMM.
HOW ART THOU, SERENA?
RIGHT MERRY, THANK'EE, DICK.
YOU GOT HER SPEAKING SEVENTEENTH CENTURY.
SHE CAN'T SPEAK ROMAN, THOUGH.
ROMAN LINGUA IS EASY. ANGLISH IS B*******.
WHAT YOU MAKING THERE, MARCUS?
IT'S A MOUSETRAP. WHAT DOES IT LOOK LIKE?
AH.
THOUSAND-YEAR-OLD MICE ABOARD, TOO, EH?

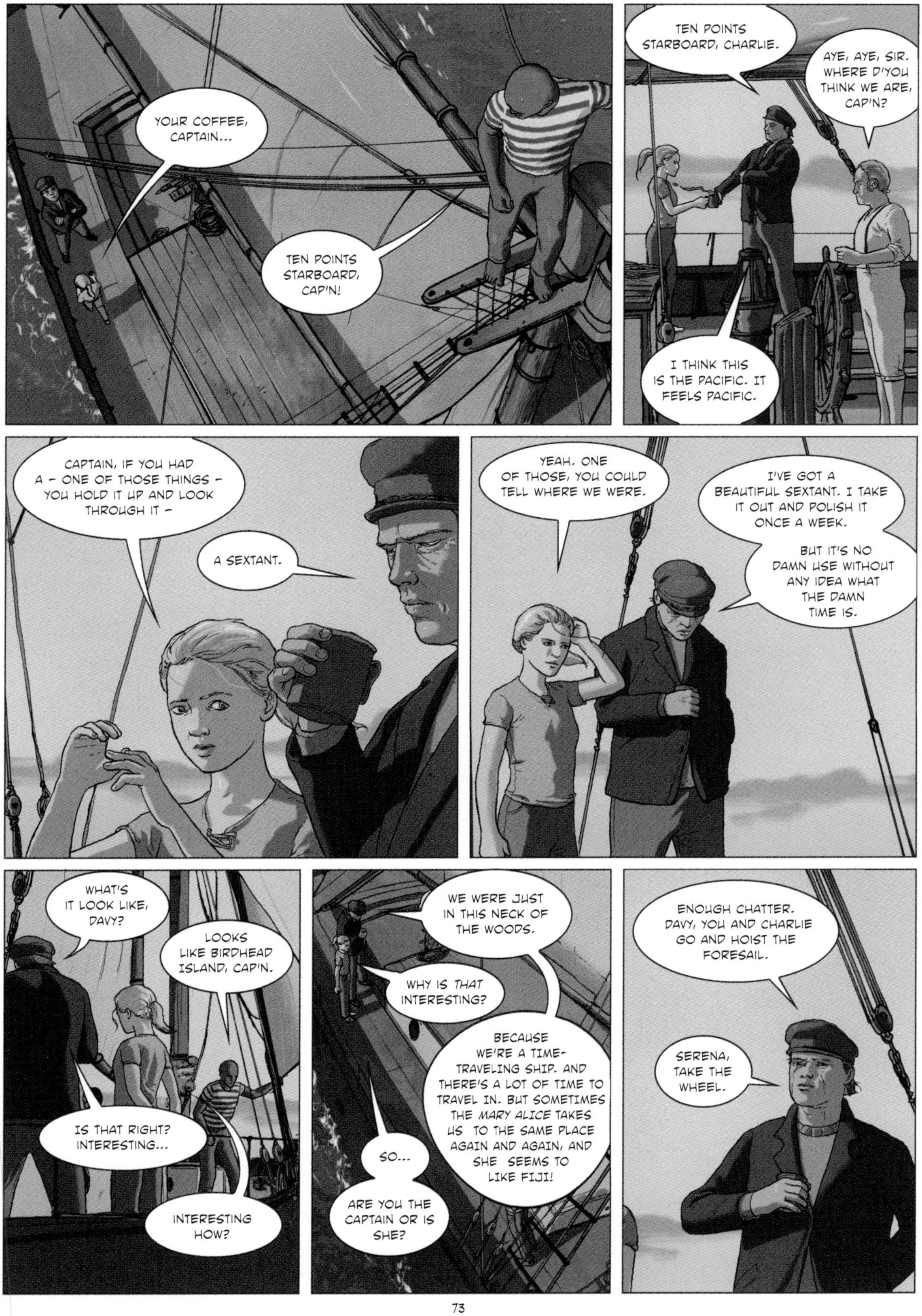
YOUR COFFEE, CAPTAIN...
TEN POINTS STARBOARD, CAP'N!
TEN POINTS STARBOARD, CHARLIE.
AYE, AYE, SIR. WHERE D'YOU THINK WE ARE, CAP'N?
I THINK THIS IS THE PACIFIC. IT FEELS PACIFIC.
CAPTAIN, IF YOU HAD A – ONE OF THOSE THINGS – YOU HOLD IT UP AND LOOK THROUGH IT –
A SEXTANT.
YEAH. ONE OF THOSE, YOU COULD TELL WHERE WE WERE.
I'VE GOT A BEAUTIFUL SEXTANT. I TAKE IT OUT AND POLISH IT ONCE A WEEK.
BUT IT'S NO DAMN USE WITHOUT ANY IDEA WHAT THE DAMN TIME IS.
WHAT'S IT LOOK LIKE, DAVY?
LOOKS LIKE BIRDHEAD ISLAND, CAP'N.
IS THAT RIGHT? INTERESTING...
INTERESTING HOW?
WE WERE JUST IN THIS NECK OF THE WOODS.
WHY IS *THAT* INTERESTING?
BECAUSE WE'RE A TIME-TRAVELING SHIP. AND THERE'S A LOT OF TIME TO TRAVEL IN. BUT SOMETIMES THE *MARY ALICE* TAKES US TO THE SAME PLACE AGAIN AND AGAIN, AND SHE SEEMS TO LIKE FIJI!
SO...
ARE YOU THE CAPTAIN OR IS SHE?
ENOUGH CHATTER. DAVY, YOU AND CHARLIE GO AND HOIST THE FORESAIL.
SERENA, TAKE THE WHEEL.

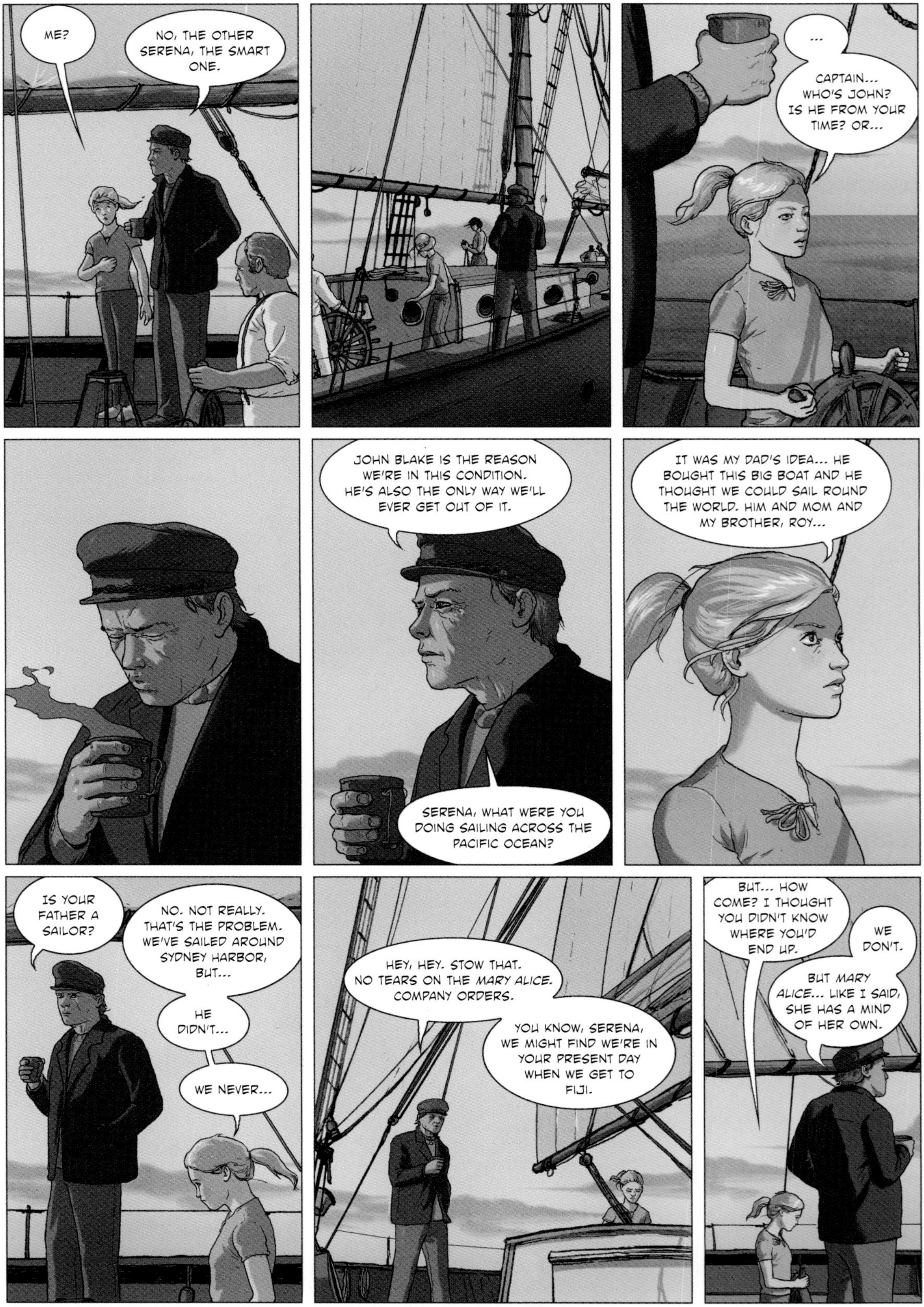
ME?
NO, THE OTHER SERENA, THE SMART ONE.
...
CAPTAIN... WHO'S JOHN? IS HE FROM YOUR TIME? OR...
JOHN BLAKE IS THE REASON WE'RE IN THIS CONDITION. HE'S ALSO THE ONLY WAY WE'LL EVER GET OUT OF IT.
SERENA, WHAT WERE YOU DOING SAILING ACROSS THE PACIFIC OCEAN?
IT WAS MY DAD'S IDEA... HE BOUGHT THIS BIG BOAT AND HE THOUGHT WE COULD SAIL ROUND THE WORLD. HIM AND MOM AND MY BROTHER, ROY...
IS YOUR FATHER A SAILOR?
NO. NOT REALLY. THAT'S THE PROBLEM. WE'VE SAILED AROUND SYDNEY HARBOR, BUT...
HE DIDN'T...
WE NEVER...
HEY, HEY. STOW THAT. NO TEARS ON THE *MARY ALICE*. COMPANY ORDERS.
YOU KNOW, SERENA, WE MIGHT FIND WE'RE IN YOUR PRESENT DAY WHEN WE GET TO FIJI.
BUT... HOW COME? I THOUGHT YOU DIDN'T KNOW WHERE YOU'D END UP.
WE DON'T.
BUT *MARY ALICE*... LIKE I SAID, SHE HAS A MIND OF HER OWN.

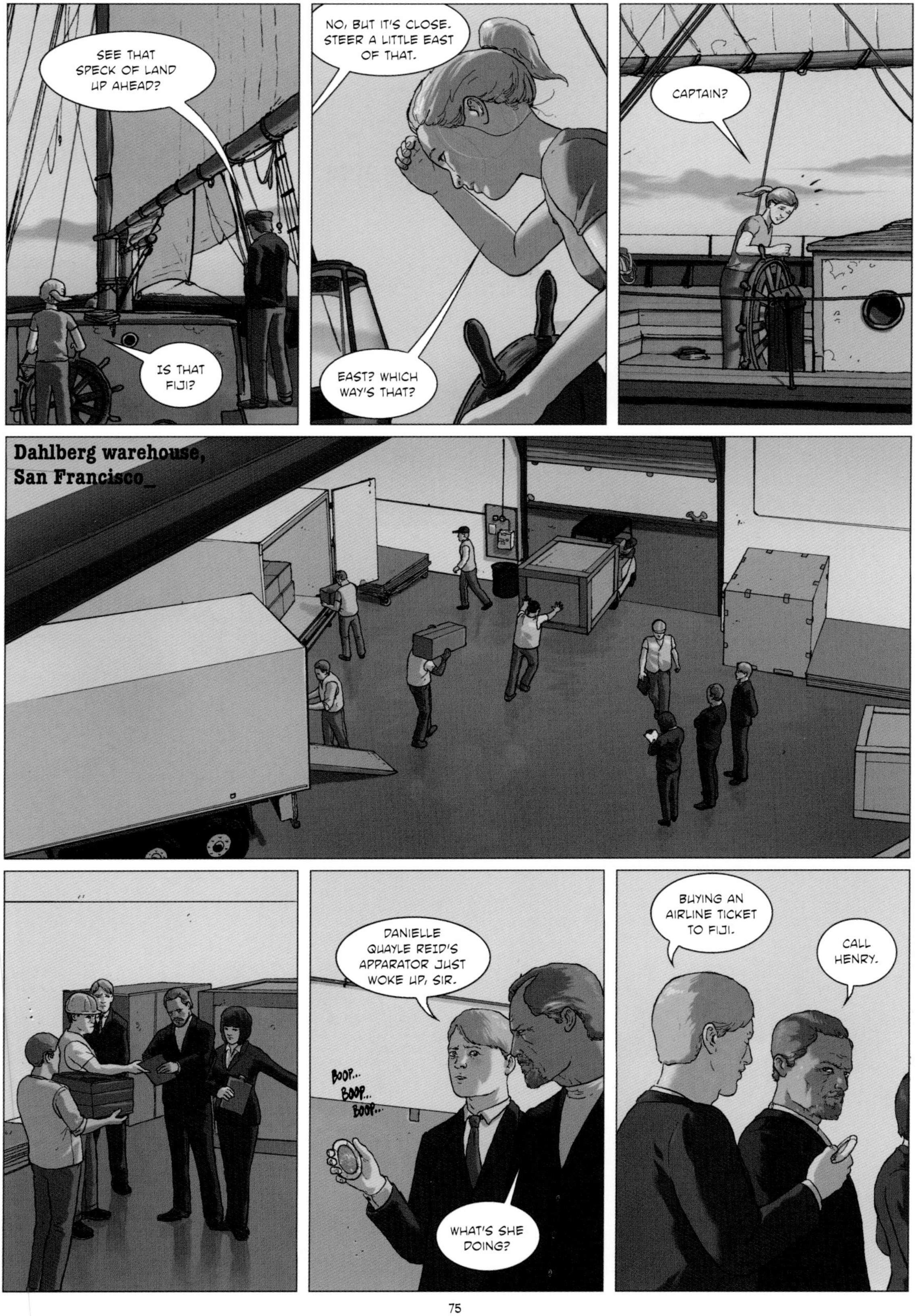
SEE THAT SPECK OF LAND UP AHEAD?
IS THAT FIJI?
NO, BUT IT'S CLOSE. STEER A LITTLE EAST OF THAT.
EAST? WHICH WAY'S THAT?
CAPTAIN?
Dahlberg warehouse, San Francisco_
DANIELLE QUAYLE REID'S APPARATOR JUST WOKE UP, SIR.
BOOP... BOOP... BOOP...
WHAT'S SHE DOING?
BUYING AN AIRLINE TICKET TO FIJI.
CALL HENRY.

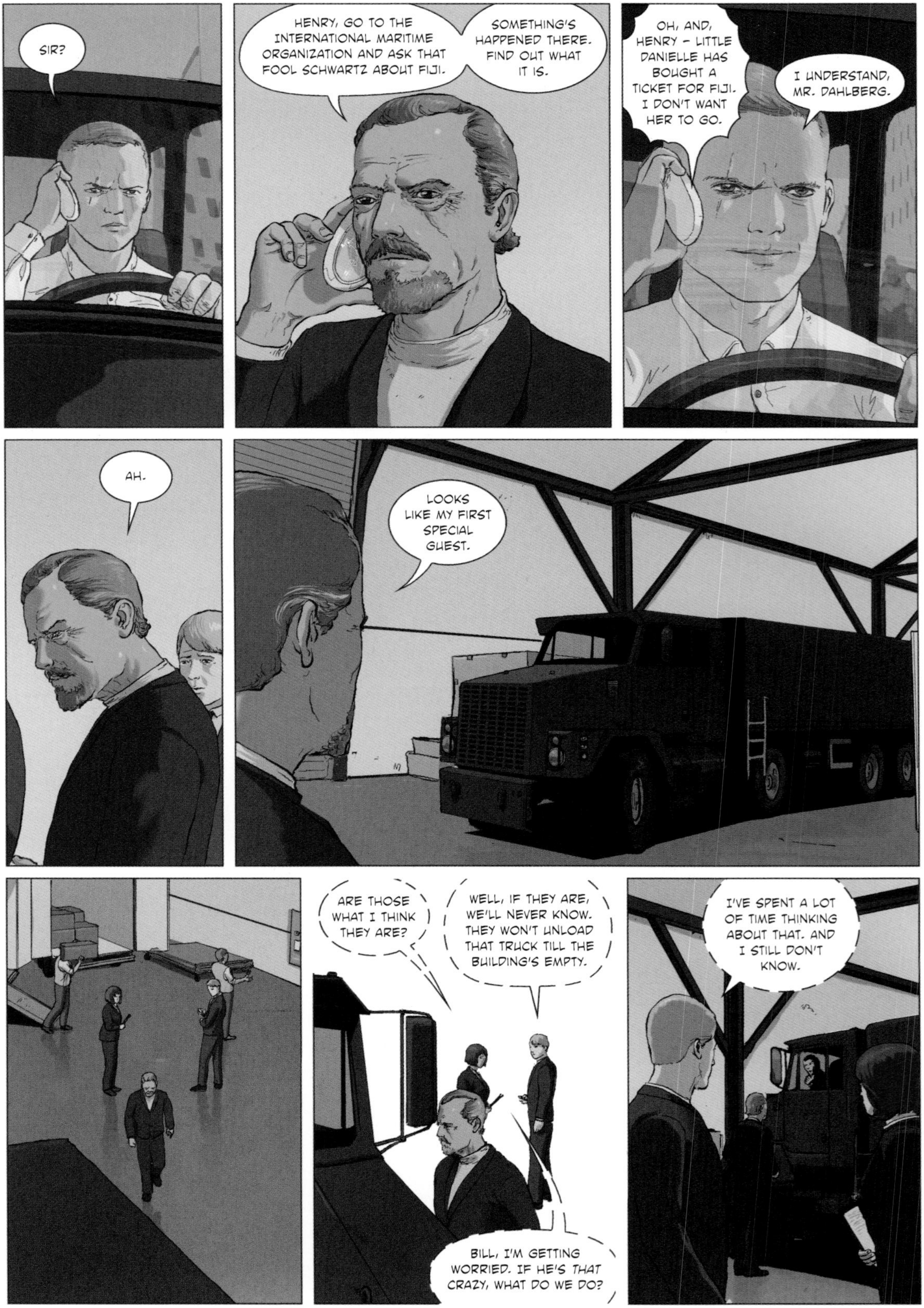
SIR?
HENRY, GO TO THE INTERNATIONAL MARITIME ORGANIZATION AND ASK THAT FOOL SCHWARTZ ABOUT FIJI.
SOMETHING'S HAPPENED THERE. FIND OUT WHAT IT IS.
OH, AND, HENRY – LITTLE DANIELLE HAS BOUGHT A TICKET FOR FIJI. I DON'T WANT HER TO GO.
I UNDERSTAND, MR. DAHLBERG.
AH.
LOOKS LIKE MY FIRST SPECIAL GUEST.
ARE THOSE WHAT I THINK THEY ARE?
WELL, IF THEY ARE, WE'LL NEVER KNOW. THEY WON'T UNLOAD THAT TRUCK TILL THE BUILDING'S EMPTY.
BILL, I'M GETTING WORRIED. IF HE'S *THAT* CRAZY, WHAT DO WE DO?
I'VE SPENT A LOT OF TIME THINKING ABOUT THAT. AND I STILL DON'T KNOW.

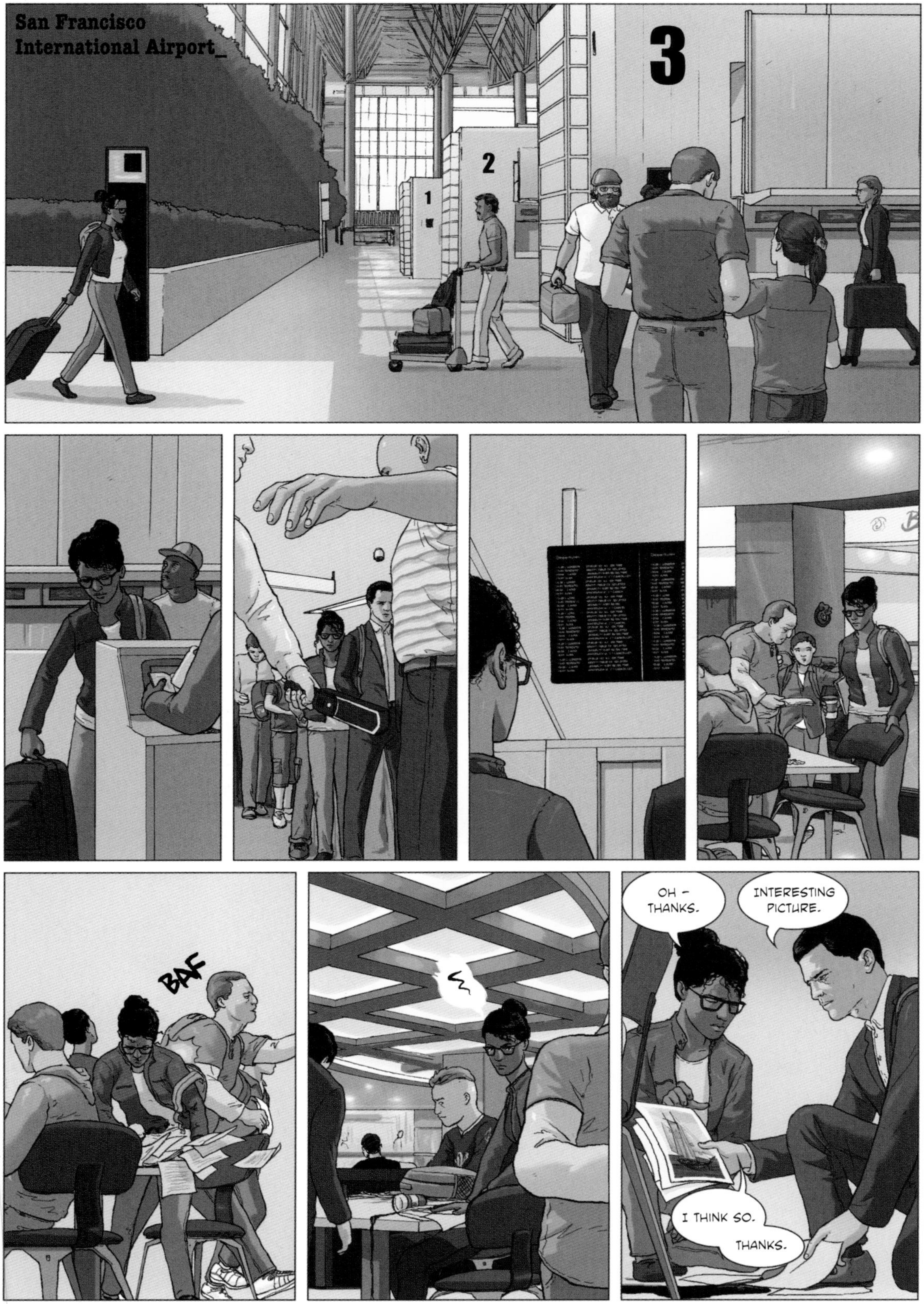
San Francisco International Airport_
3
2
1
BAF
OH - THANKS.
INTERESTING PICTURE.
I THINK SO.
THANKS.

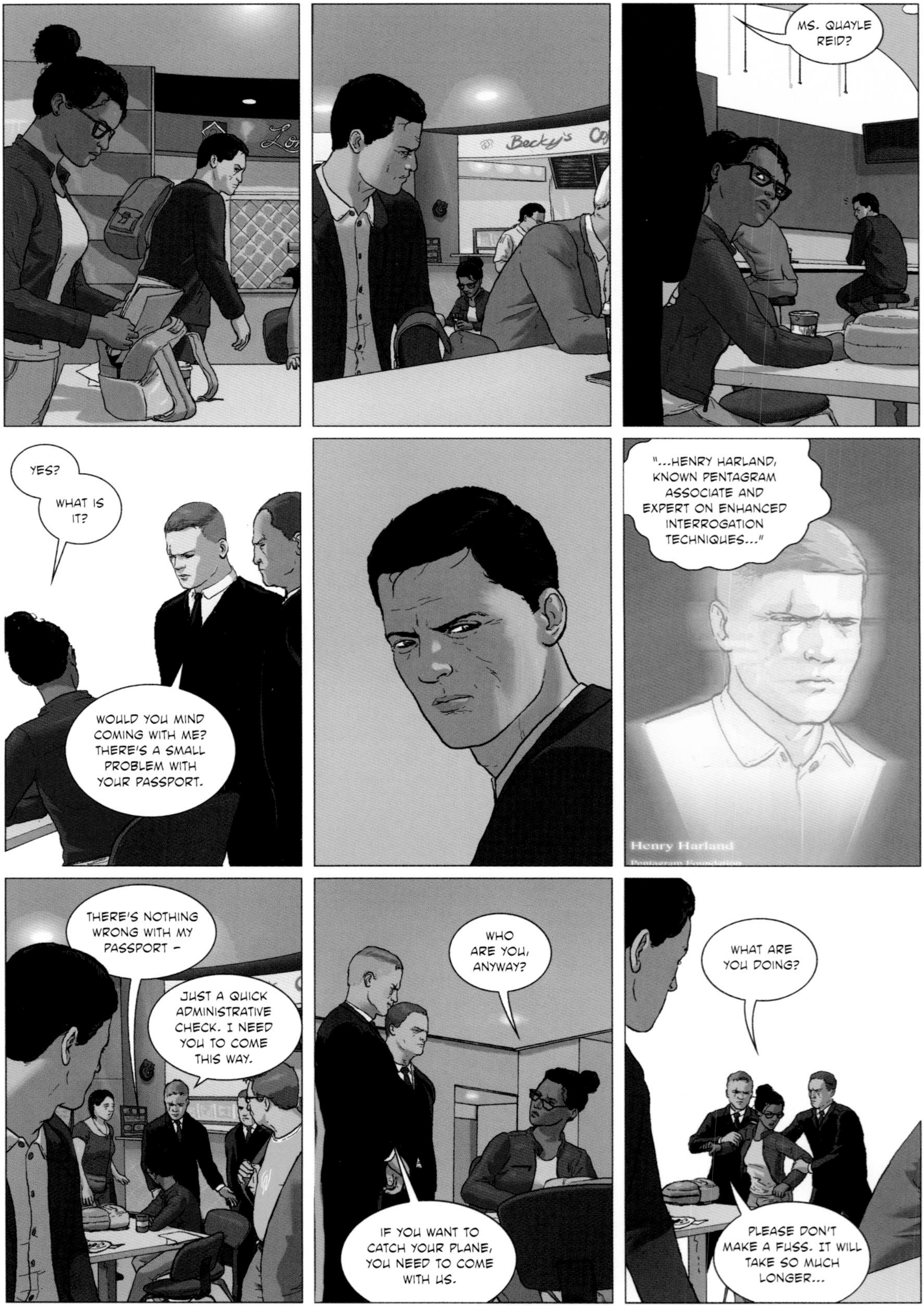

MS. QUAYLE REID?
YES?
WHAT IS IT?
WOULD YOU MIND COMING WITH ME? THERE'S A SMALL PROBLEM WITH YOUR PASSPORT.
"...HENRY HARLAND, KNOWN PENTAGRAM ASSOCIATE AND EXPERT ON ENHANCED INTERROGATION TECHNIQUES..."
Henry Harland
THERE'S NOTHING WRONG WITH MY PASSPORT –
JUST A QUICK ADMINISTRATIVE CHECK. I NEED YOU TO COME THIS WAY.
WHO ARE YOU, ANYWAY?
IF YOU WANT TO CATCH YOUR PLANE, YOU NEED TO COME WITH US.
WHAT ARE YOU DOING?
PLEASE DON'T MAKE A FUSS. IT WILL TAKE SO MUCH LONGER...

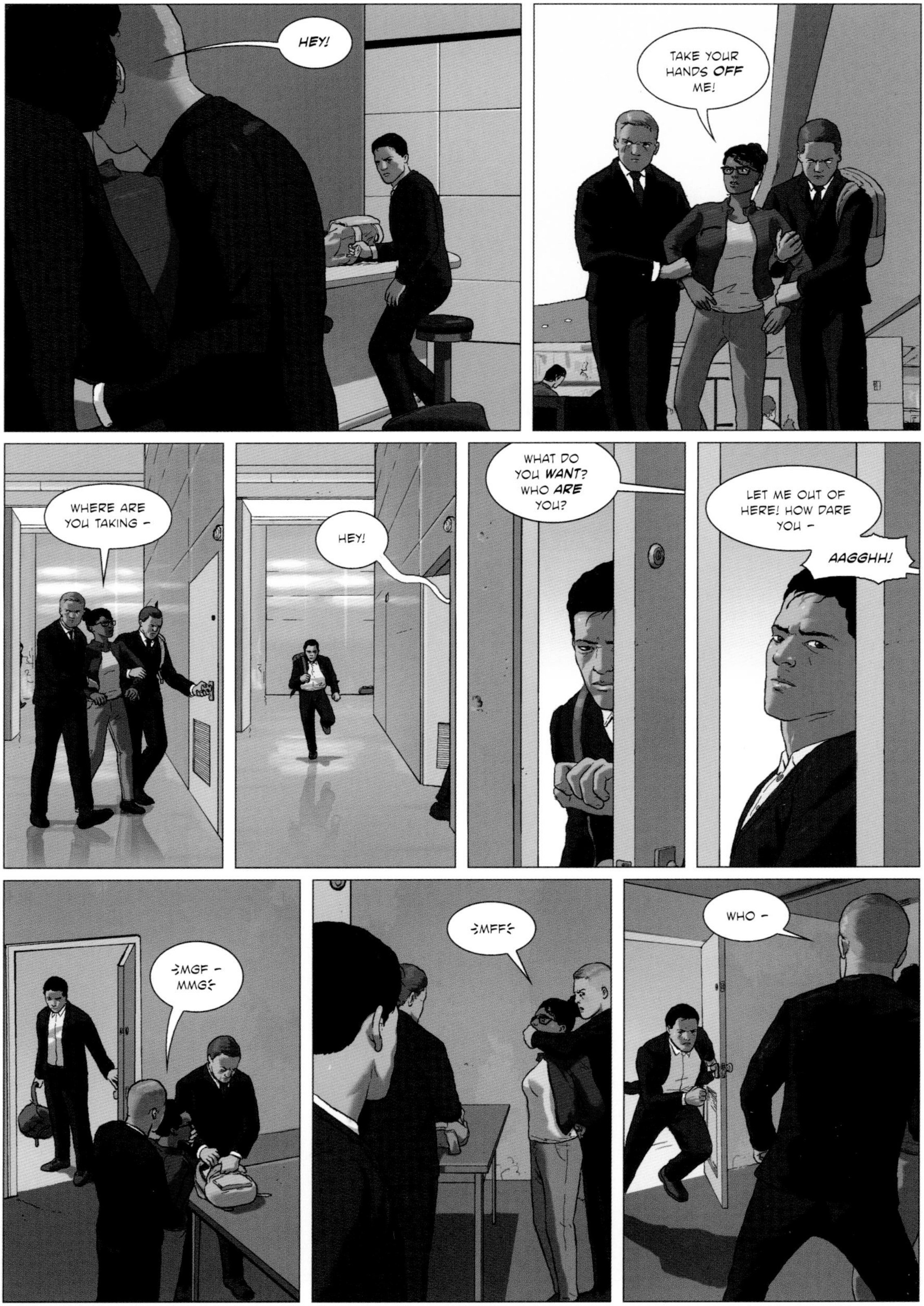
HEY!
TAKE YOUR HANDS OFF ME!
WHERE ARE YOU TAKING –
HEY!
WHAT DO YOU WANT? WHO ARE YOU?
LET ME OUT OF HERE! HOW DARE YOU –
AAGGHH!
MGF – MMG
MFF
WHO –

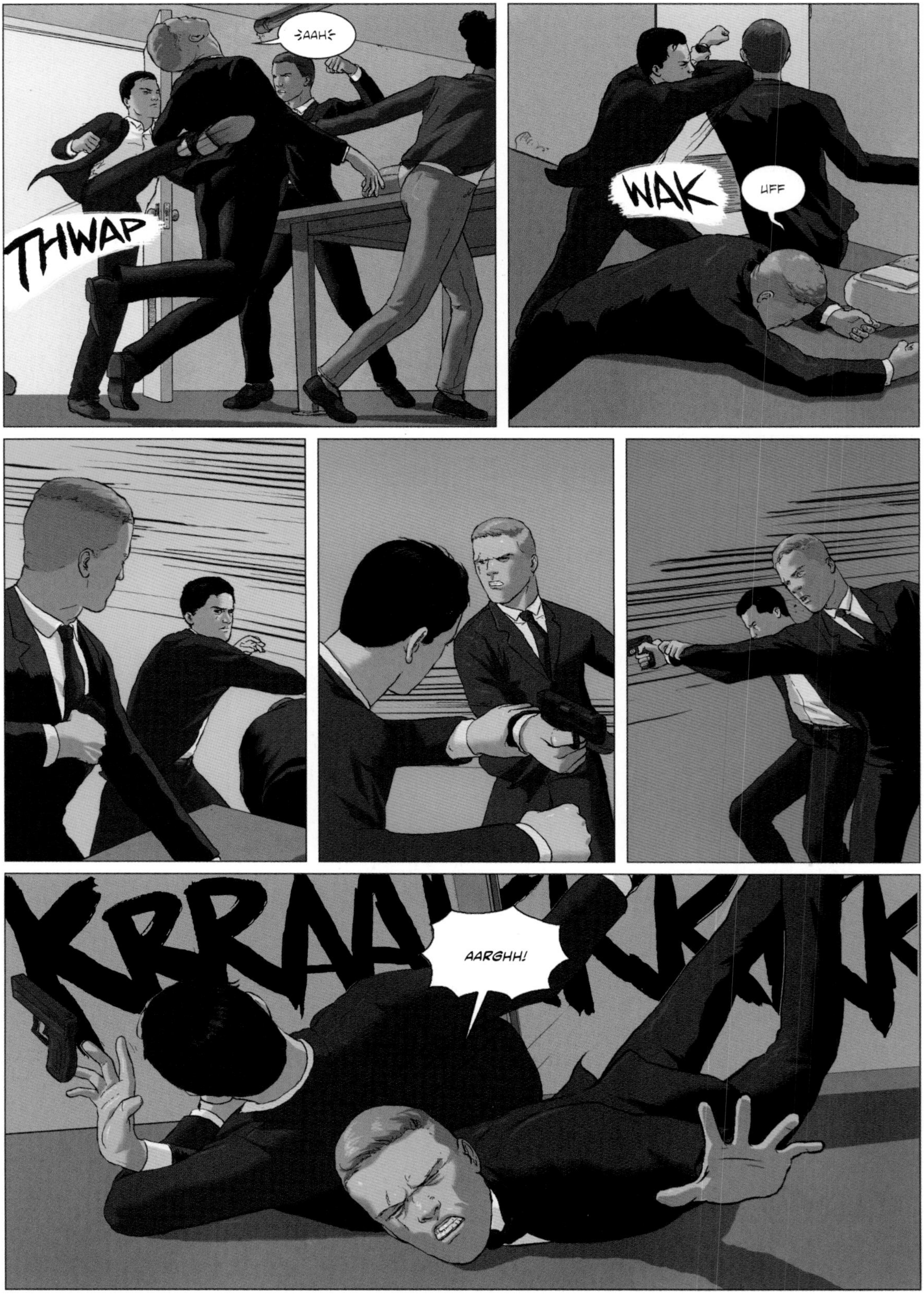
AAH
THWAP
WAK
UFF
KRRAAKK
AARGHH!

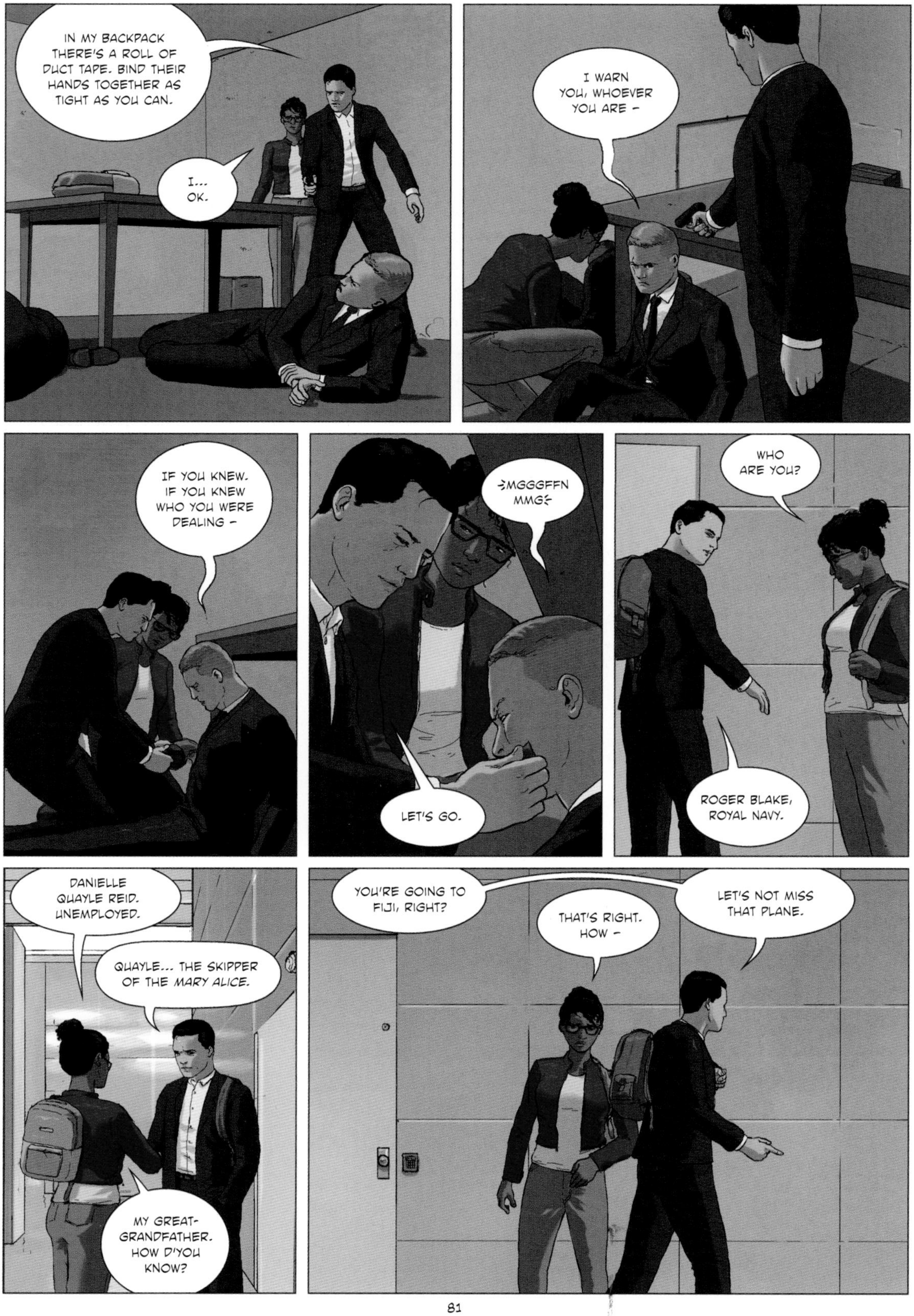
IN MY BACKPACK THERE'S A ROLL OF DUCT TAPE. BIND THEIR HANDS TOGETHER AS TIGHT AS YOU CAN.
I... OK.
I WARN YOU, WHOEVER YOU ARE –
IF YOU KNEW. IF YOU KNEW WHO YOU WERE DEALING –
MGGGFFN MMG
LET'S GO.
WHO ARE YOU?
ROGER BLAKE, ROYAL NAVY.
DANIELLE QUAYLE REID. UNEMPLOYED.
QUAYLE... THE SKIPPER OF THE *MARY ALICE*.
MY GREAT-GRANDFATHER. HOW D'YOU KNOW?
YOU'RE GOING TO FIJI, RIGHT?
THAT'S RIGHT. HOW –
LET'S NOT MISS THAT PLANE.

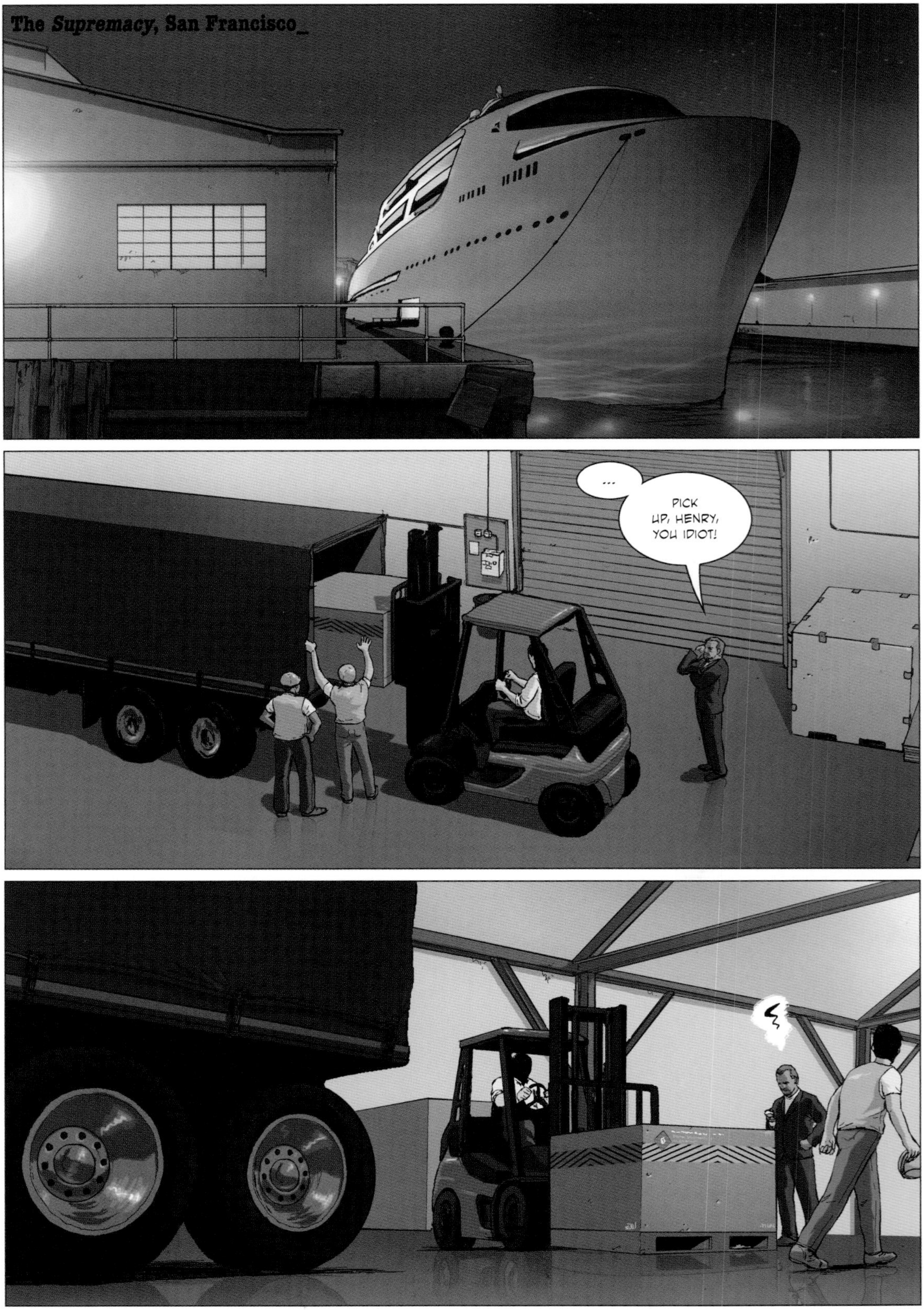

The *Supremacy*, San Francisco_
...
PICK UP, HENRY, YOU IDIOT!

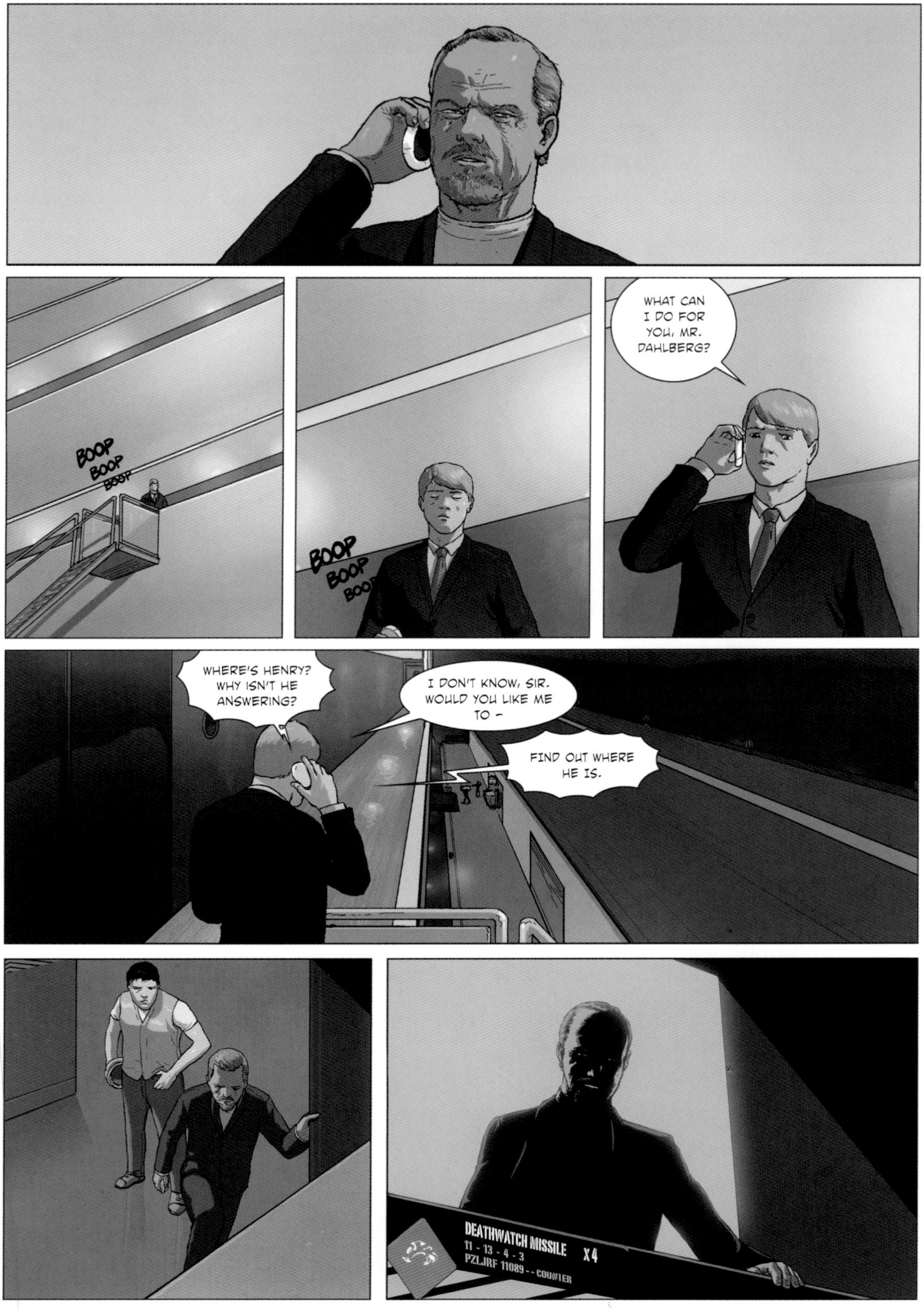
BOOP
BOOP
BOOP
BOOP
BOOP
WHAT CAN I DO FOR YOU, MR. DAHLBERG?
WHERE'S HENRY? WHY ISN'T HE ANSWERING?
I DON'T KNOW, SIR. WOULD YOU LIKE ME TO –
FIND OUT WHERE HE IS.
DEATHWATCH MISSILE
X4
11 - 13 - 4 - 3
PZLJRF 11089 - - COUNTER

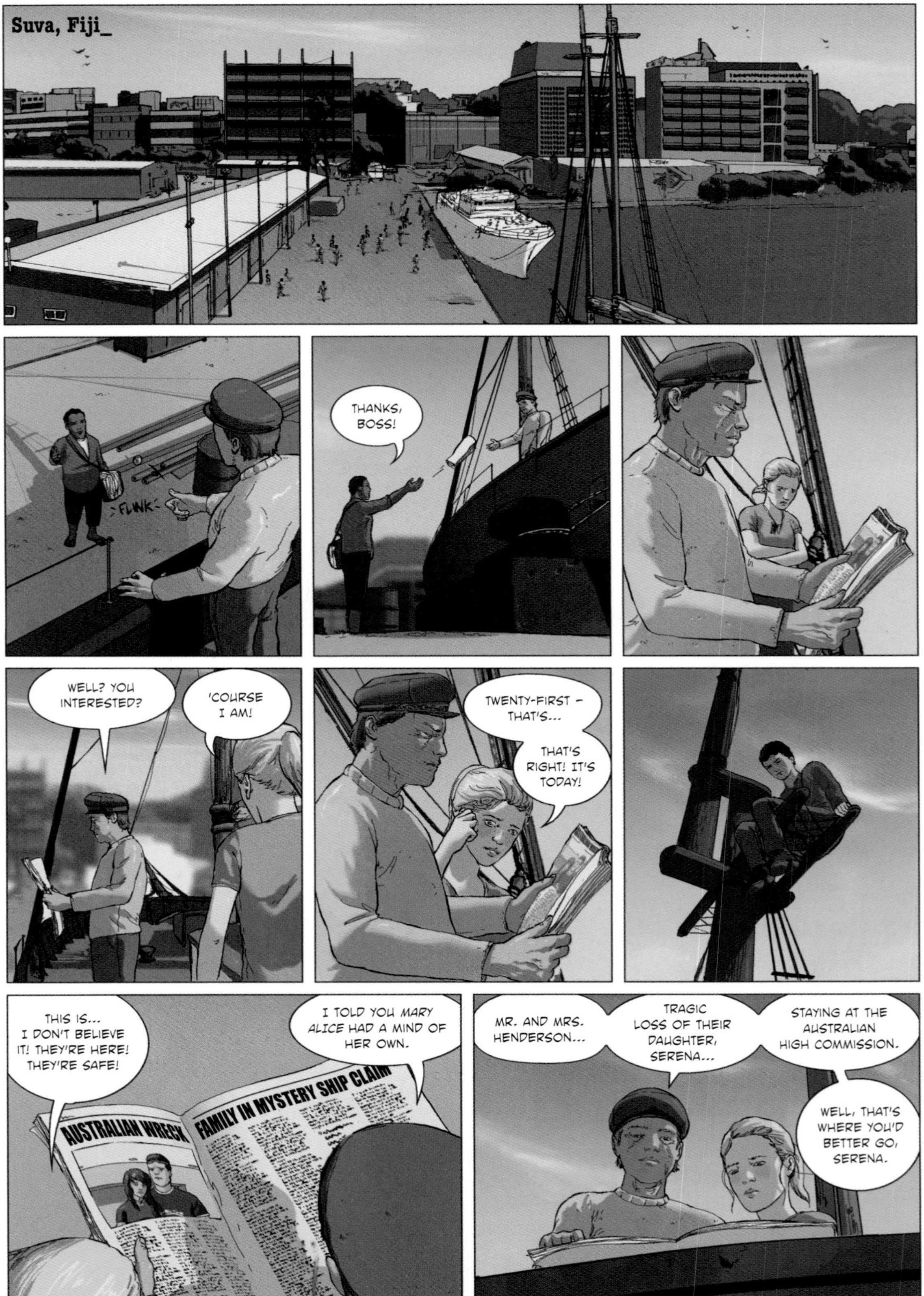
Suva, Fiji_
FLUNK
THANKS, BOSS!
WELL? YOU INTERESTED?
'COURSE I AM!
TWENTY-FIRST – THAT'S...
THAT'S RIGHT! IT'S TODAY!
THIS IS... I DON'T BELIEVE IT! THEY'RE HERE! THEY'RE SAFE!
I TOLD YOU *MARY ALICE* HAD A MIND OF HER OWN.
AUSTRALIAN WRECK
FAMILY IN MYSTERY SHIP CLAIM
MR. AND MRS. HENDERSON...
TRAGIC LOSS OF THEIR DAUGHTER, SERENA...
STAYING AT THE AUSTRALIAN HIGH COMMISSION.
WELL, THAT'S WHERE YOU'D BETTER GO, SERENA.

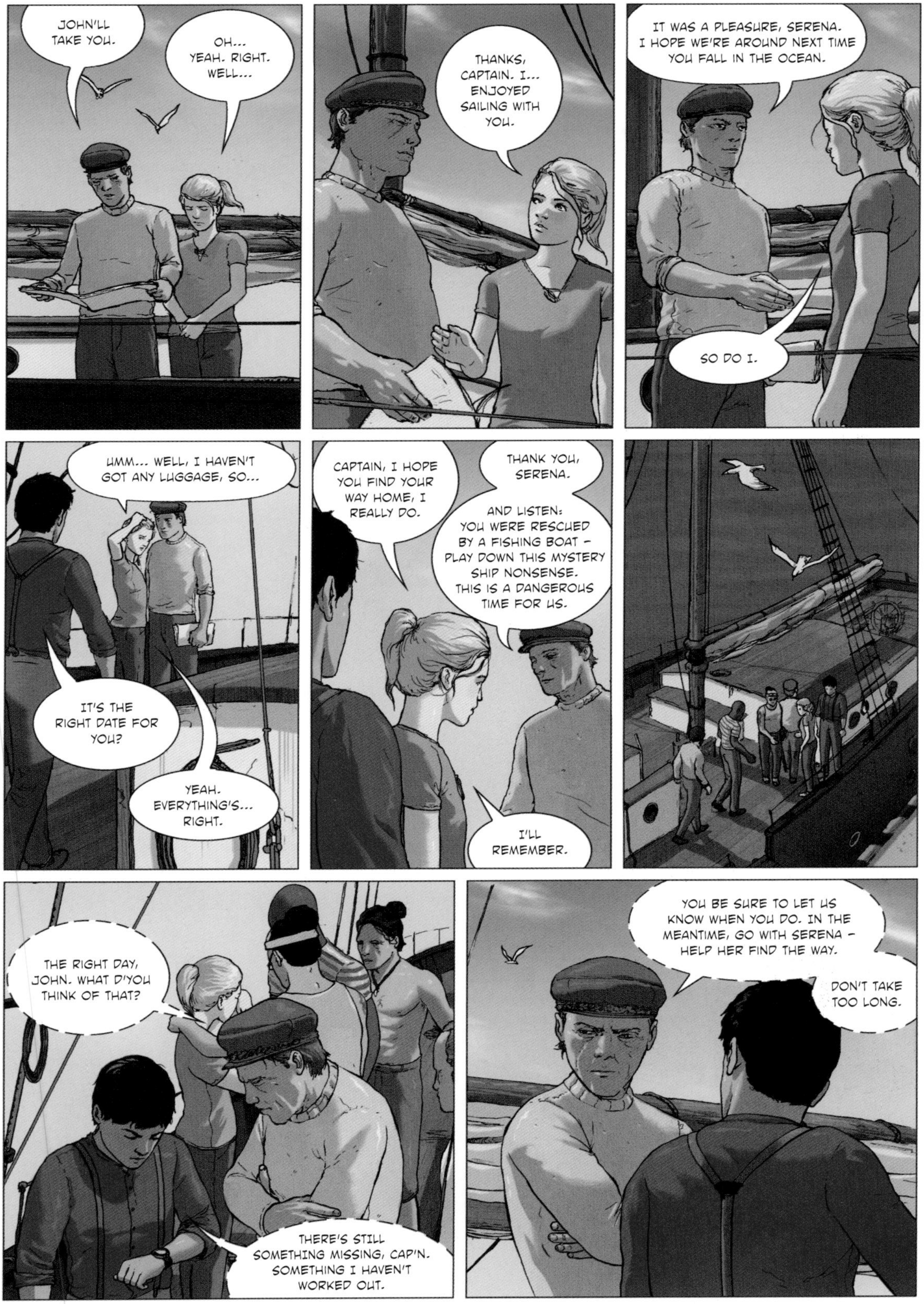
JOHN'LL TAKE YOU.
OH... YEAH. RIGHT. WELL...
THANKS, CAPTAIN. I... ENJOYED SAILING WITH YOU.
IT WAS A PLEASURE, SERENA. I HOPE WE'RE AROUND NEXT TIME YOU FALL IN THE OCEAN.
SO DO I.
UMM... WELL, I HAVEN'T GOT ANY LUGGAGE, SO...
IT'S THE RIGHT DATE FOR YOU?
YEAH. EVERYTHING'S... RIGHT.
CAPTAIN, I HOPE YOU FIND YOUR WAY HOME, I REALLY DO.
THANK YOU, SERENA.
AND LISTEN: YOU WERE RESCUED BY A FISHING BOAT - PLAY DOWN THIS MYSTERY SHIP NONSENSE. THIS IS A DANGEROUS TIME FOR US.
I'LL REMEMBER.
THE RIGHT DAY, JOHN. WHAT D'YOU THINK OF THAT?
THERE'S STILL SOMETHING MISSING, CAP'N. SOMETHING I HAVEN'T WORKED OUT.
YOU BE SURE TO LET US KNOW WHEN YOU DO. IN THE MEANTIME, GO WITH SERENA - HELP HER FIND THE WAY.
DON'T TAKE TOO LONG.

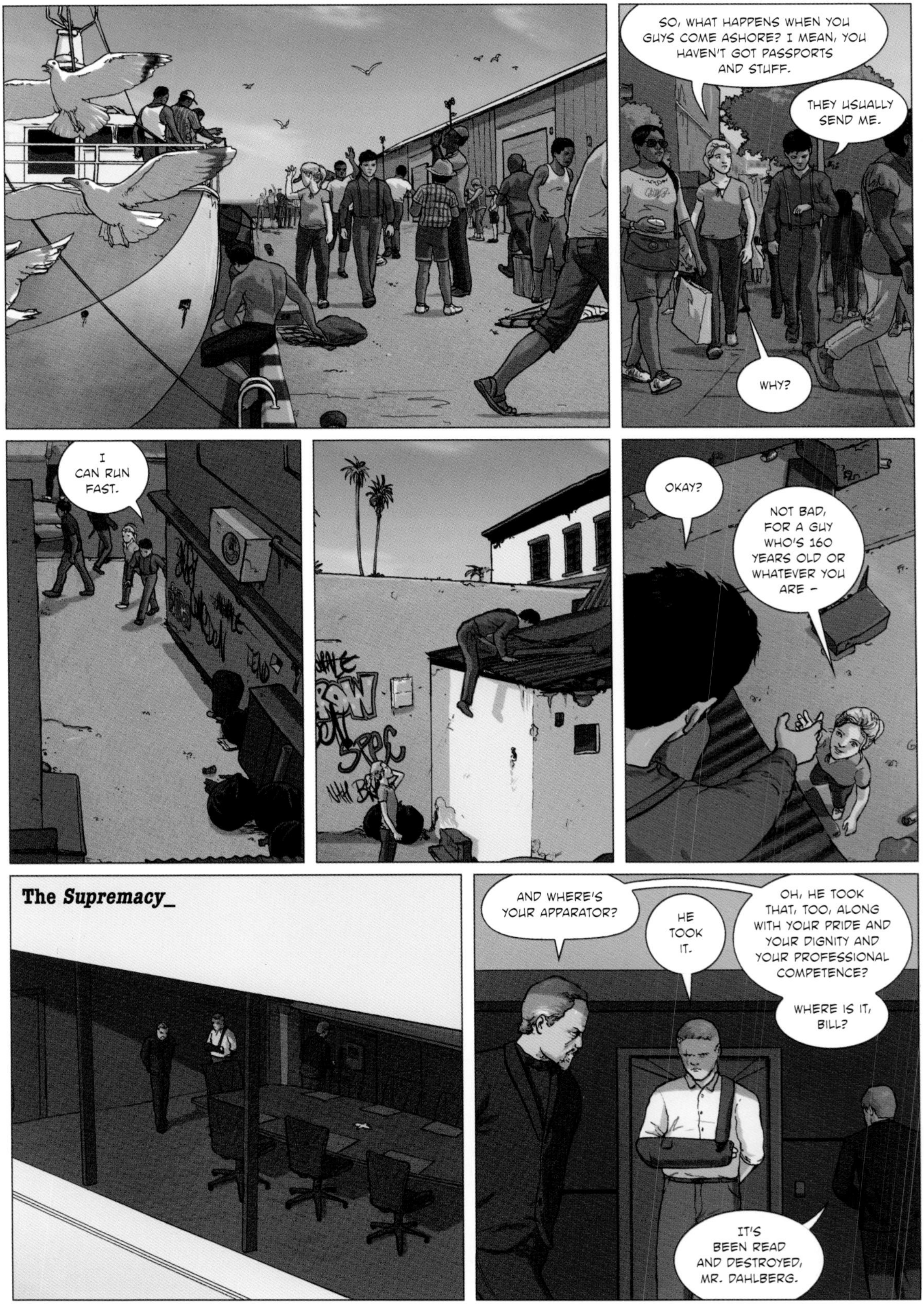
SO, WHAT HAPPENS WHEN YOU GUYS COME ASHORE? I MEAN, YOU HAVEN'T GOT PASSPORTS AND STUFF.
THEY USUALLY SEND ME.
WHY?
I CAN RUN FAST.
OKAY?
NOT BAD, FOR A GUY WHO'S 160 YEARS OLD OR WHATEVER YOU ARE –
The Supremacy_
AND WHERE'S YOUR APPARATOR?
HE TOOK IT.
OH, HE TOOK THAT, TOO, ALONG WITH YOUR PRIDE AND YOUR DIGNITY AND YOUR PROFESSIONAL COMPETENCE?
WHERE IS IT, BILL?
IT'S BEEN READ AND DESTROYED, MR. DAHLBERG.

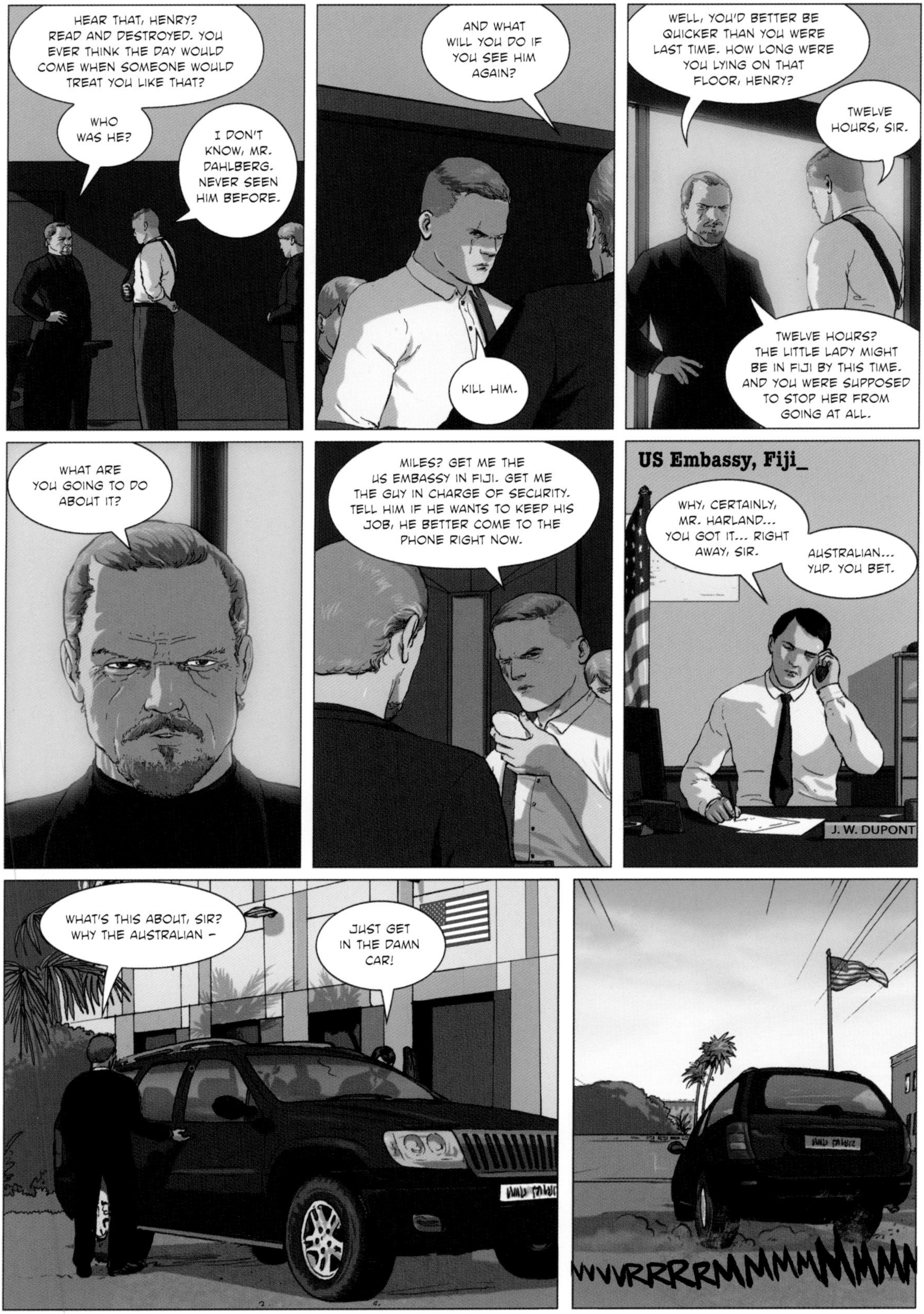
HEAR THAT, HENRY? READ AND DESTROYED. YOU EVER THINK THE DAY WOULD COME WHEN SOMEONE WOULD TREAT YOU LIKE THAT?
WHO WAS HE?
I DON'T KNOW, MR. DAHLBERG. NEVER SEEN HIM BEFORE.
AND WHAT WILL YOU DO IF YOU SEE HIM AGAIN?
KILL HIM.
WELL, YOU'D BETTER BE QUICKER THAN YOU WERE LAST TIME. HOW LONG WERE YOU LYING ON THAT FLOOR, HENRY?
TWELVE HOURS, SIR.
TWELVE HOURS? THE LITTLE LADY MIGHT BE IN FIJI BY THIS TIME. AND YOU WERE SUPPOSED TO STOP HER FROM GOING AT ALL.
WHAT ARE YOU GOING TO DO ABOUT IT?
MILES? GET ME THE US EMBASSY IN FIJI. GET ME THE GUY IN CHARGE OF SECURITY. TELL HIM IF HE WANTS TO KEEP HIS JOB, HE BETTER COME TO THE PHONE RIGHT NOW.
US Embassy, Fiji_
WHY, CERTAINLY, MR. HARLAND... YOU GOT IT... RIGHT AWAY, SIR.
AUSTRALIAN... YUP. YOU BET.
J. W. DUPONT
WHAT'S THIS ABOUT, SIR? WHY THE AUSTRALIAN –
JUST GET IN THE DAMN CAR!
VVVVRRRRMMMMMMMM

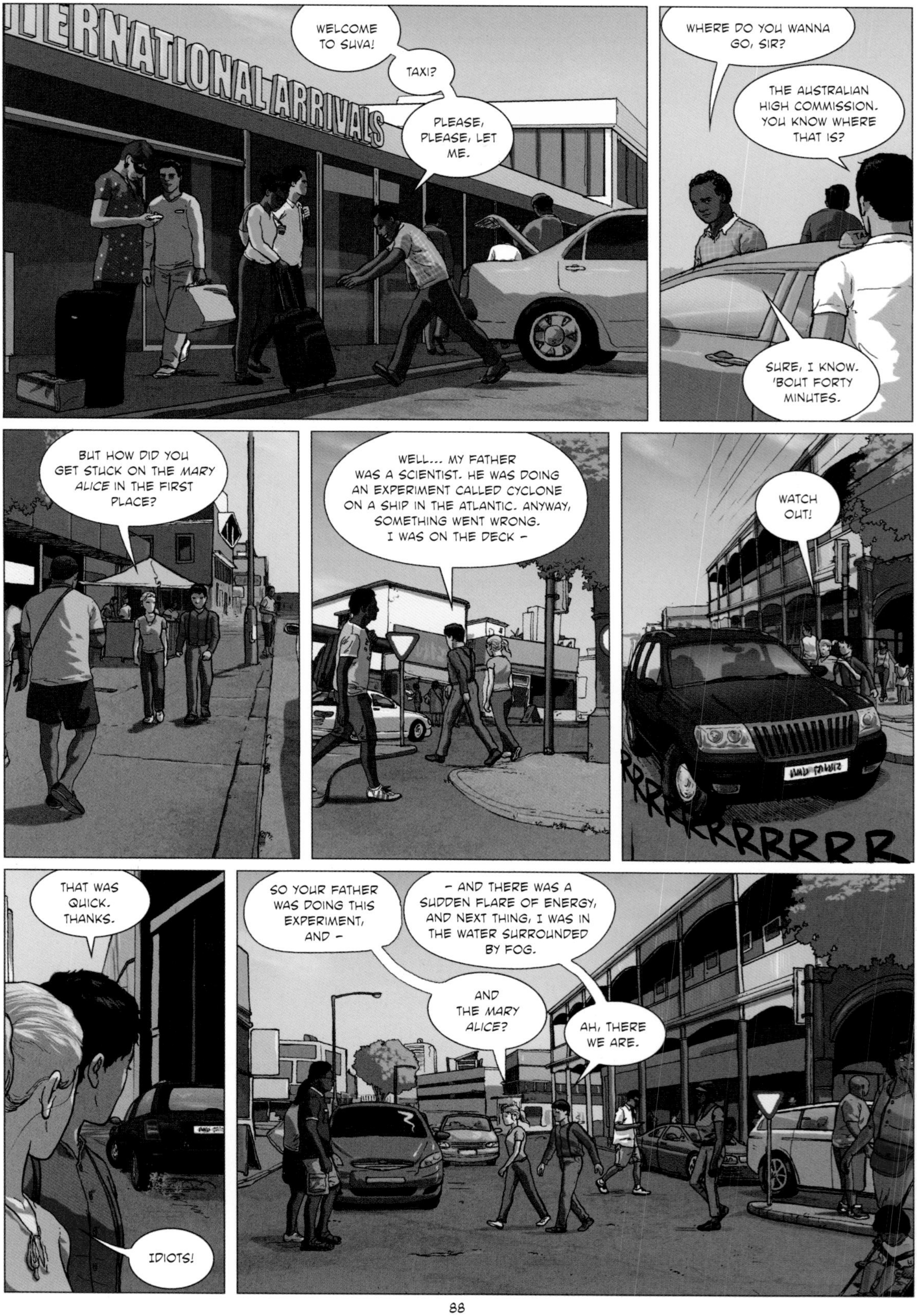
ERNATIONAL ARRIVALS
WELCOME TO SUVA!
TAXI?
PLEASE, PLEASE, LET ME.
WHERE DO YOU WANNA GO, SIR?
THE AUSTRALIAN HIGH COMMISSION. YOU KNOW WHERE THAT IS?
SURE, I KNOW. 'BOUT FORTY MINUTES.
BUT HOW DID YOU GET STUCK ON THE *MARY ALICE* IN THE FIRST PLACE?
WELL... MY FATHER WAS A SCIENTIST. HE WAS DOING AN EXPERIMENT CALLED CYCLONE ON A SHIP IN THE ATLANTIC. ANYWAY, SOMETHING WENT WRONG. I WAS ON THE DECK –
WATCH OUT!
RRRRRRRRRRRRR
THAT WAS QUICK. THANKS.
IDIOTS!
SO YOUR FATHER WAS DOING THIS EXPERIMENT, AND –
– AND THERE WAS A SUDDEN FLARE OF ENERGY, AND NEXT THING, I WAS IN THE WATER SURROUNDED BY FOG.
AND THE *MARY ALICE*?
AH, THERE WE ARE.

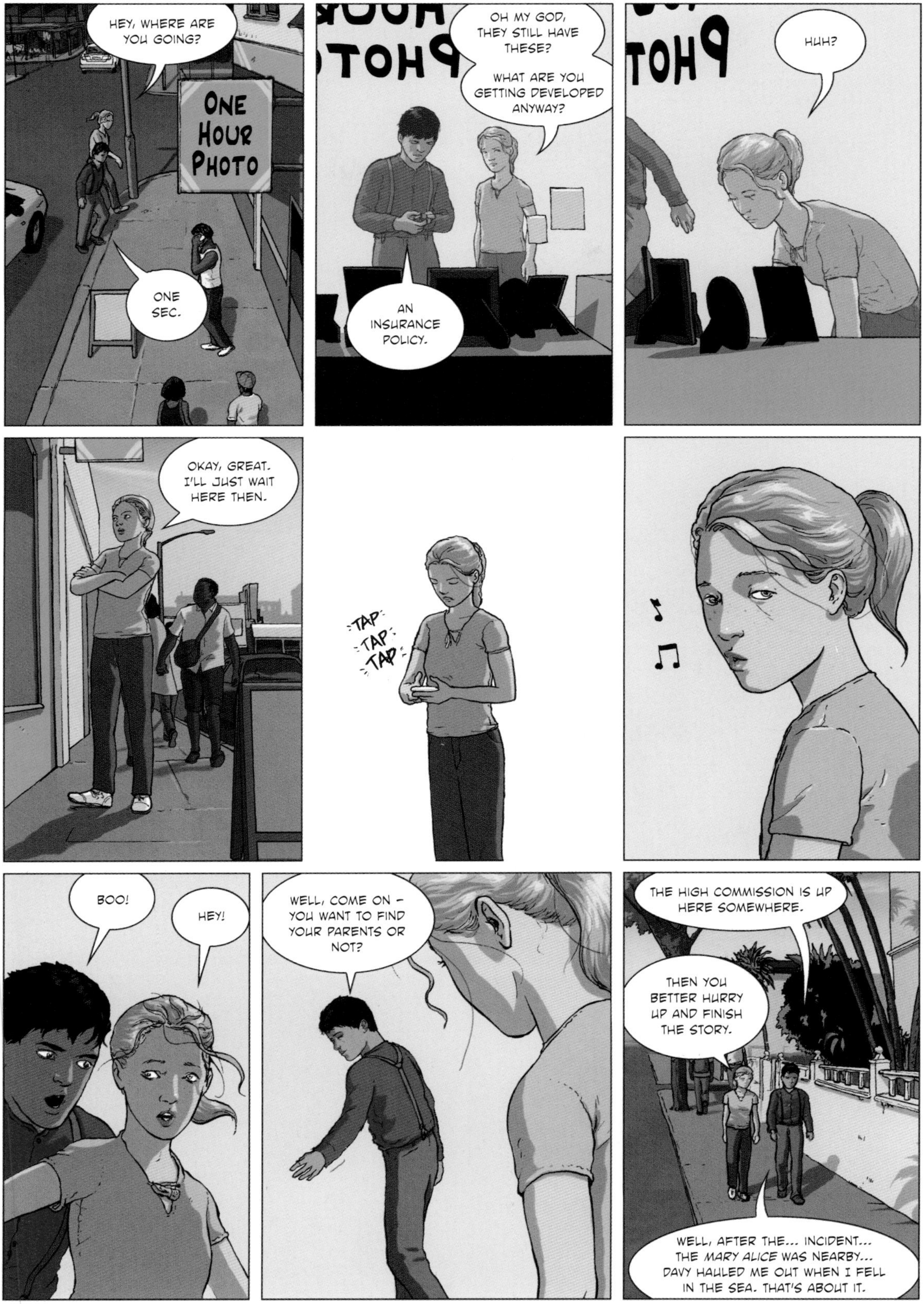
HEY, WHERE ARE YOU GOING?
ONE HOUR PHOTO
ONE SEC.
OH MY GOD, THEY STILL HAVE THESE?
WHAT ARE YOU GETTING DEVELOPED ANYWAY?
AN INSURANCE POLICY.
HUH?
OKAY, GREAT. I'LL JUST WAIT HERE THEN.
TAP TAP TAP
BOO!
HEY!
WELL, COME ON – YOU WANT TO FIND YOUR PARENTS OR NOT?
THE HIGH COMMISSION IS UP HERE SOMEWHERE.
THEN YOU BETTER HURRY UP AND FINISH THE STORY.
WELL, AFTER THE... INCIDENT... THE *MARY ALICE* WAS NEARBY... DAVY HAULED ME OUT WHEN I FELL IN THE SEA. THAT'S ABOUT IT.

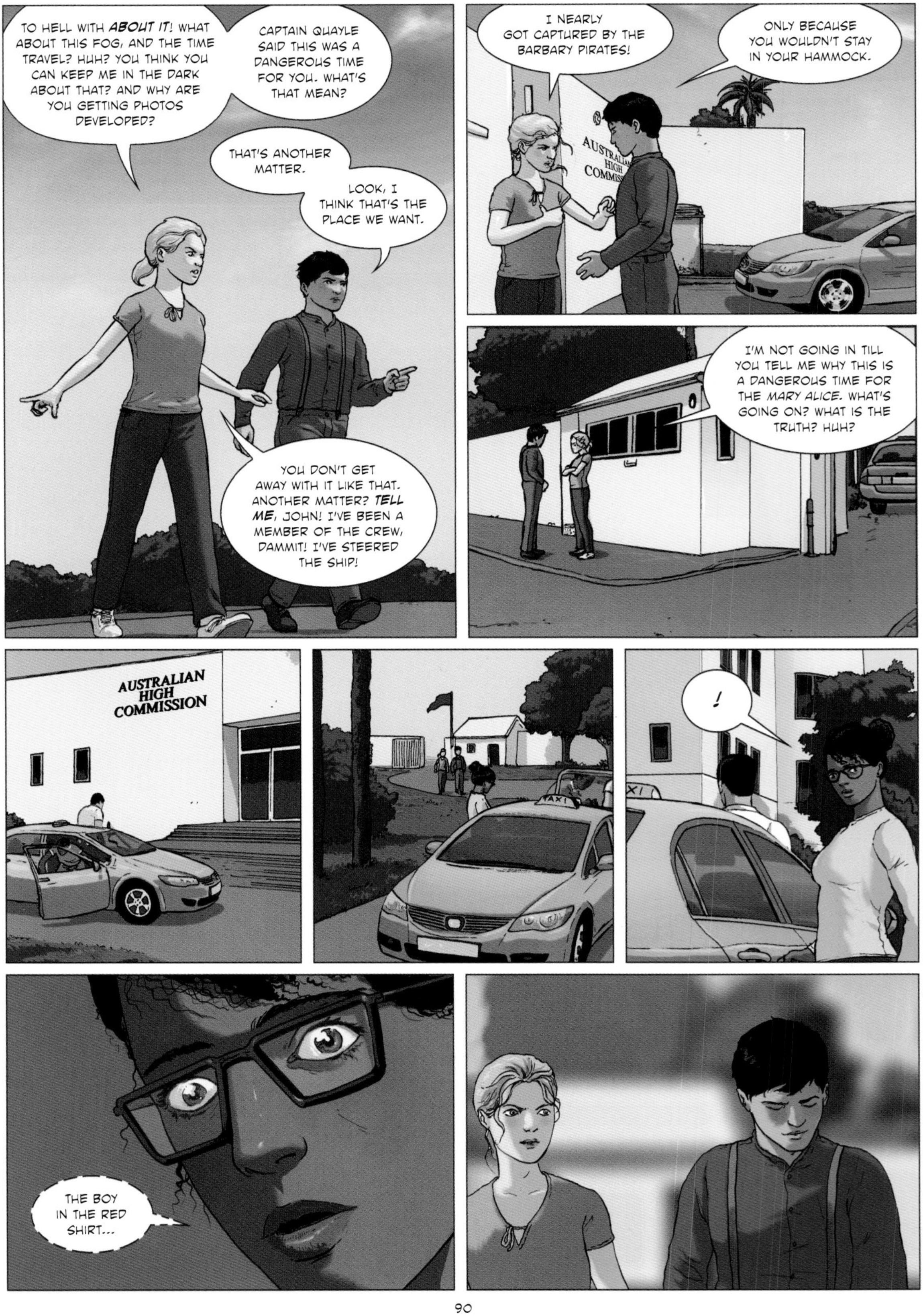
TO HELL WITH ABOUT IT! WHAT ABOUT THIS FOG, AND THE TIME TRAVEL? HUH? YOU THINK YOU CAN KEEP ME IN THE DARK ABOUT THAT? AND WHY ARE YOU GETTING PHOTOS DEVELOPED?
CAPTAIN QUAYLE SAID THIS WAS A DANGEROUS TIME FOR YOU. WHAT'S THAT MEAN?
THAT'S ANOTHER MATTER.
LOOK, I THINK THAT'S THE PLACE WE WANT.
YOU DON'T GET AWAY WITH IT LIKE THAT. ANOTHER MATTER? TELL ME, JOHN! I'VE BEEN A MEMBER OF THE CREW, DAMMIT! I'VE STEERED THE SHIP!
I NEARLY GOT CAPTURED BY THE BARBARY PIRATES!
ONLY BECAUSE YOU WOULDN'T STAY IN YOUR HAMMOCK.
I'M NOT GOING IN TILL YOU TELL ME WHY THIS IS A DANGEROUS TIME FOR THE MARY ALICE. WHAT'S GOING ON? WHAT IS THE TRUTH? HUH?
AUSTRALIAN HIGH COMMISSION
TAXI
!
THE BOY IN THE RED SHIRT...

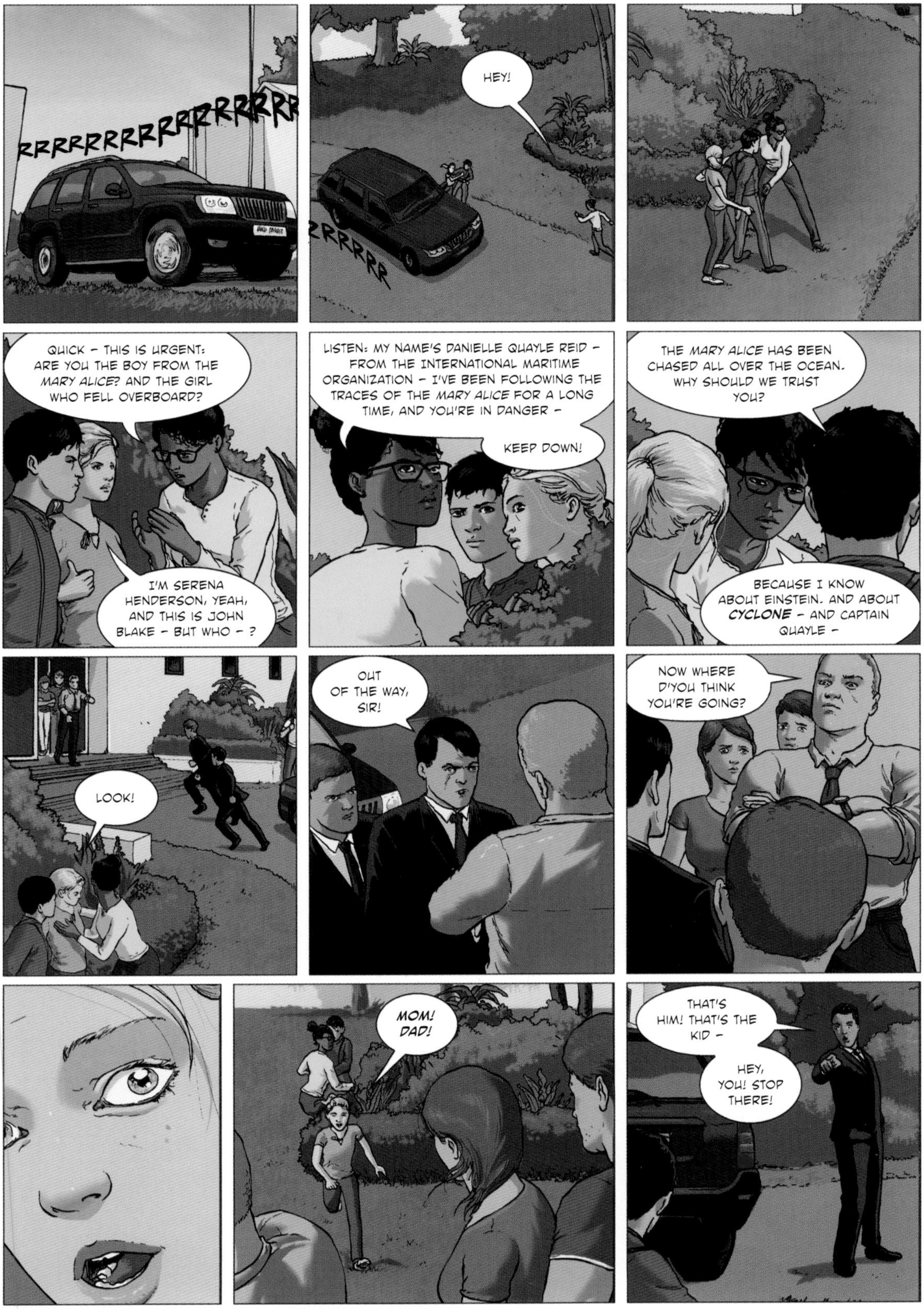
RRRRRRRRRRRRRRRRR
HEY!
RRRRRRR
QUICK – THIS IS URGENT: ARE YOU THE BOY FROM THE MARY ALICE? AND THE GIRL WHO FELL OVERBOARD?
I'M SERENA HENDERSON, YEAH, AND THIS IS JOHN BLAKE – BUT WHO – ?
LISTEN: MY NAME'S DANIELLE QUAYLE REID – FROM THE INTERNATIONAL MARITIME ORGANIZATION – I'VE BEEN FOLLOWING THE TRACES OF THE MARY ALICE FOR A LONG TIME, AND YOU'RE IN DANGER –
KEEP DOWN!
THE MARY ALICE HAS BEEN CHASED ALL OVER THE OCEAN. WHY SHOULD WE TRUST YOU?
BECAUSE I KNOW ABOUT EINSTEIN. AND ABOUT CYCLONE – AND CAPTAIN QUAYLE –
LOOK!
OUT OF THE WAY, SIR!
NOW WHERE D'YOU THINK YOU'RE GOING?
MOM! DAD!
THAT'S HIM! THAT'S THE KID –
HEY, YOU! STOP THERE!

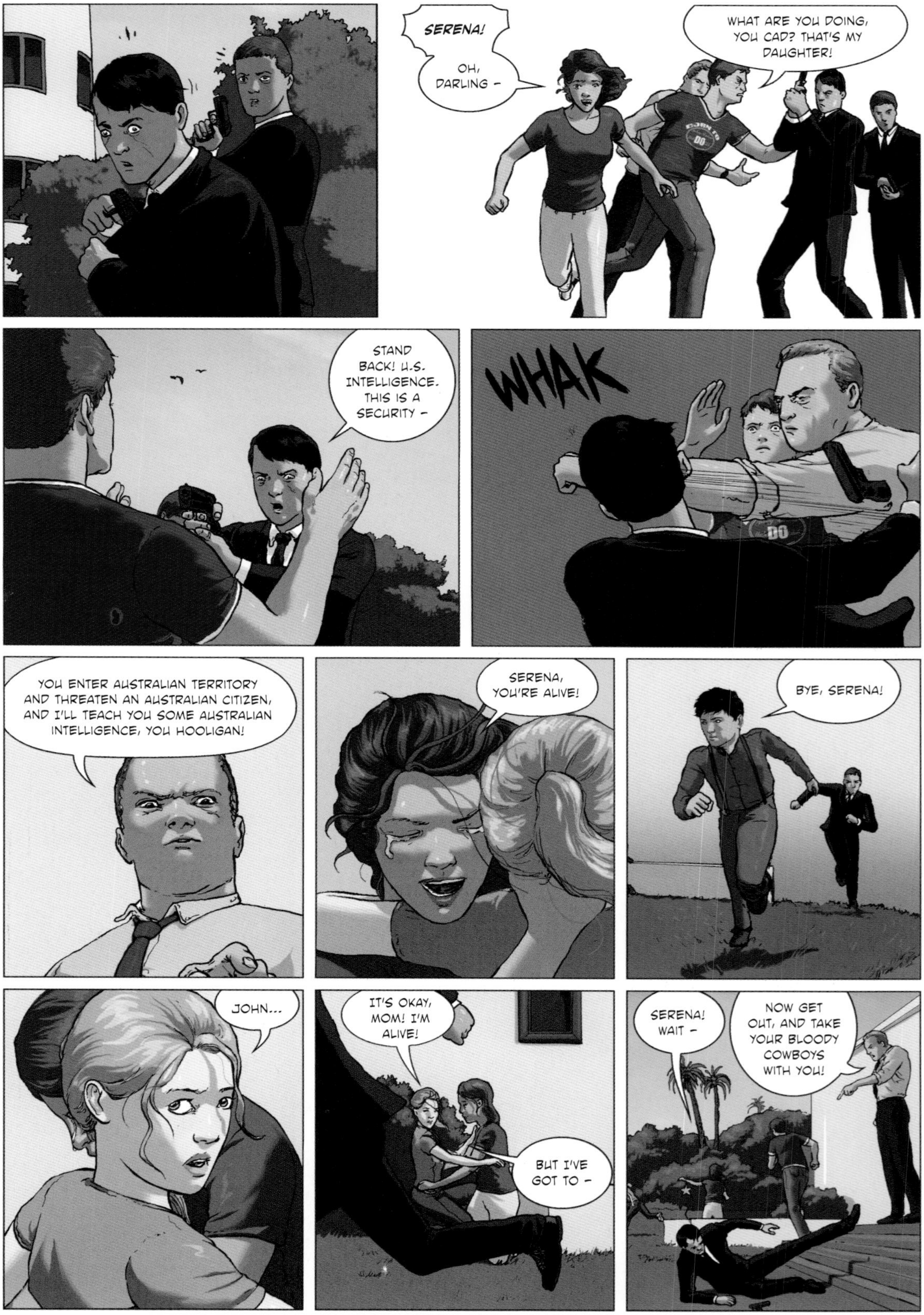
SERENA!
OH, DARLING –
WHAT ARE YOU DOING, YOU CAD? THAT'S MY DAUGHTER!
STAND BACK! U.S. INTELLIGENCE. THIS IS A SECURITY –
WHAK
YOU ENTER AUSTRALIAN TERRITORY AND THREATEN AN AUSTRALIAN CITIZEN, AND I'LL TEACH YOU SOME AUSTRALIAN INTELLIGENCE, YOU HOOLIGAN!
SERENA, YOU'RE ALIVE!
BYE, SERENA!
JOHN...
IT'S OKAY, MOM! I'M ALIVE!
BUT I'VE GOT TO –
SERENA! WAIT –
NOW GET OUT, AND TAKE YOUR BLOODY COWBOYS WITH YOU!

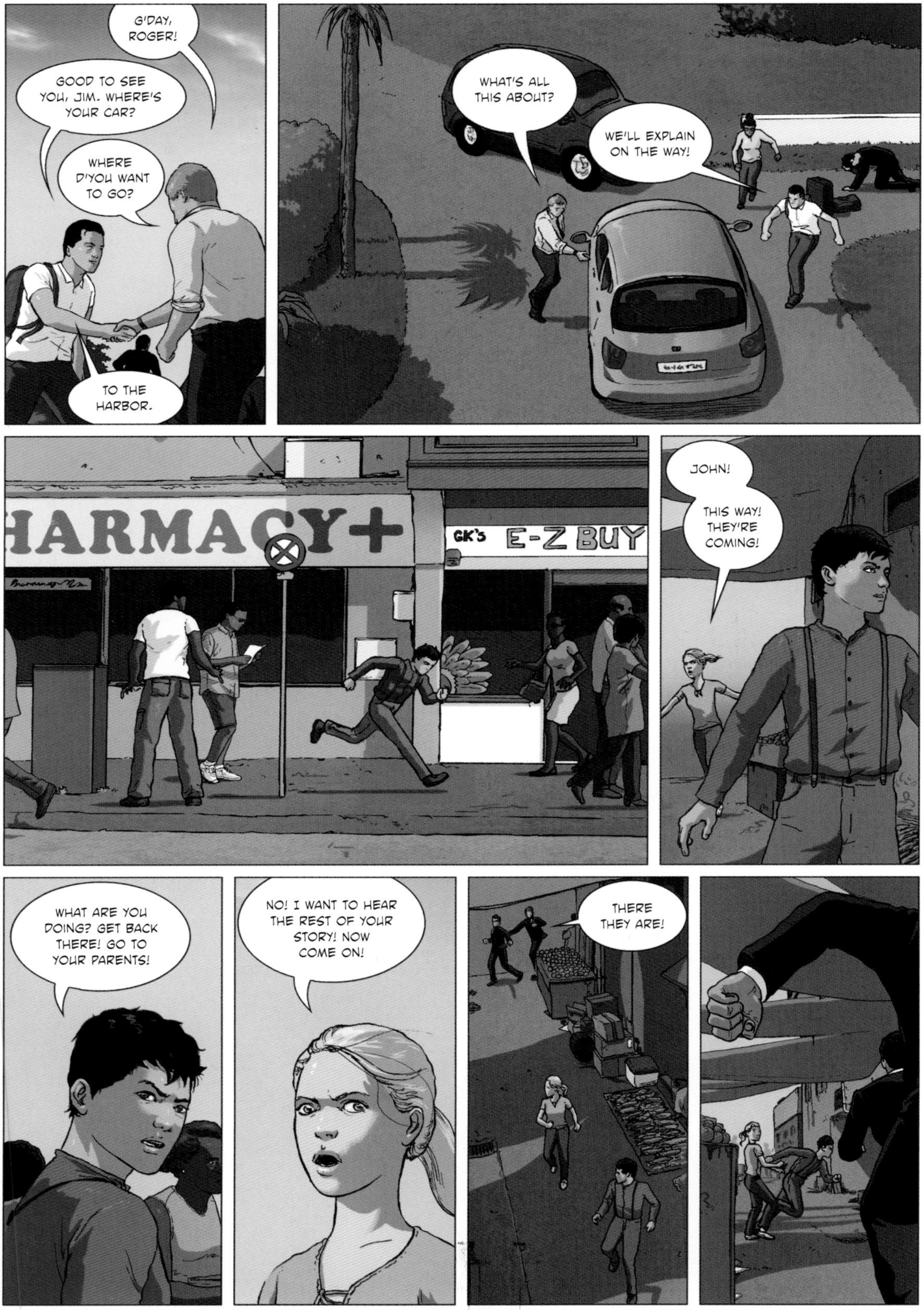
G'DAY, ROGER!
GOOD TO SEE YOU, JIM. WHERE'S YOUR CAR?
WHERE D'YOU WANT TO GO?
TO THE HARBOR.
WHAT'S ALL THIS ABOUT?
WE'LL EXPLAIN ON THE WAY!
HARMACY+
GK'S E-Z BUY
JOHN!
THIS WAY! THEY'RE COMING!
WHAT ARE YOU DOING? GET BACK THERE! GO TO YOUR PARENTS!
NO! I WANT TO HEAR THE REST OF YOUR STORY! NOW COME ON!
THERE THEY ARE!

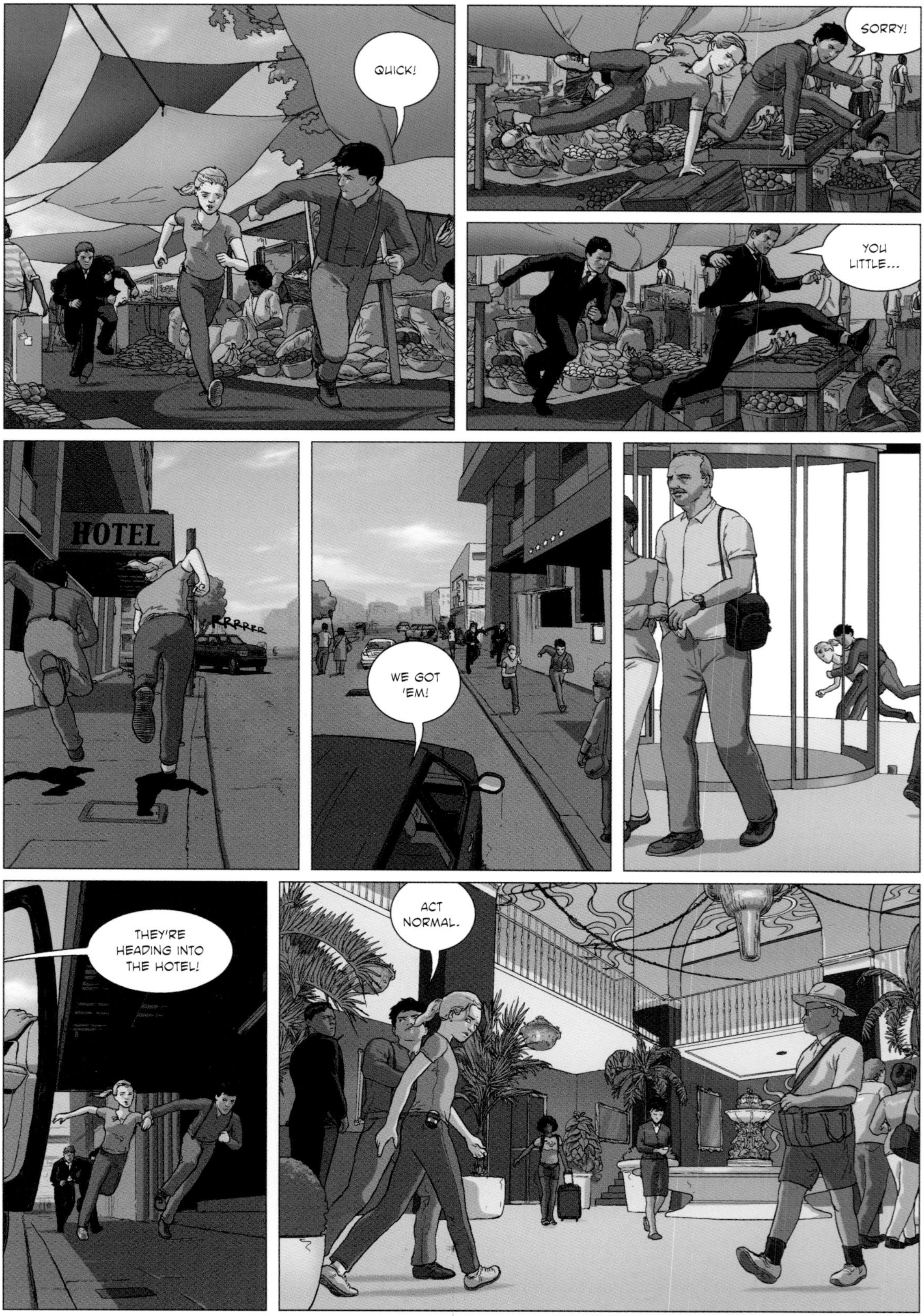
QUICK!
SORRY!
YOU LITTLE...
HOTEL
RRRRRR
WE GOT 'EM!
THEY'RE HEADING INTO THE HOTEL!
ACT NORMAL.

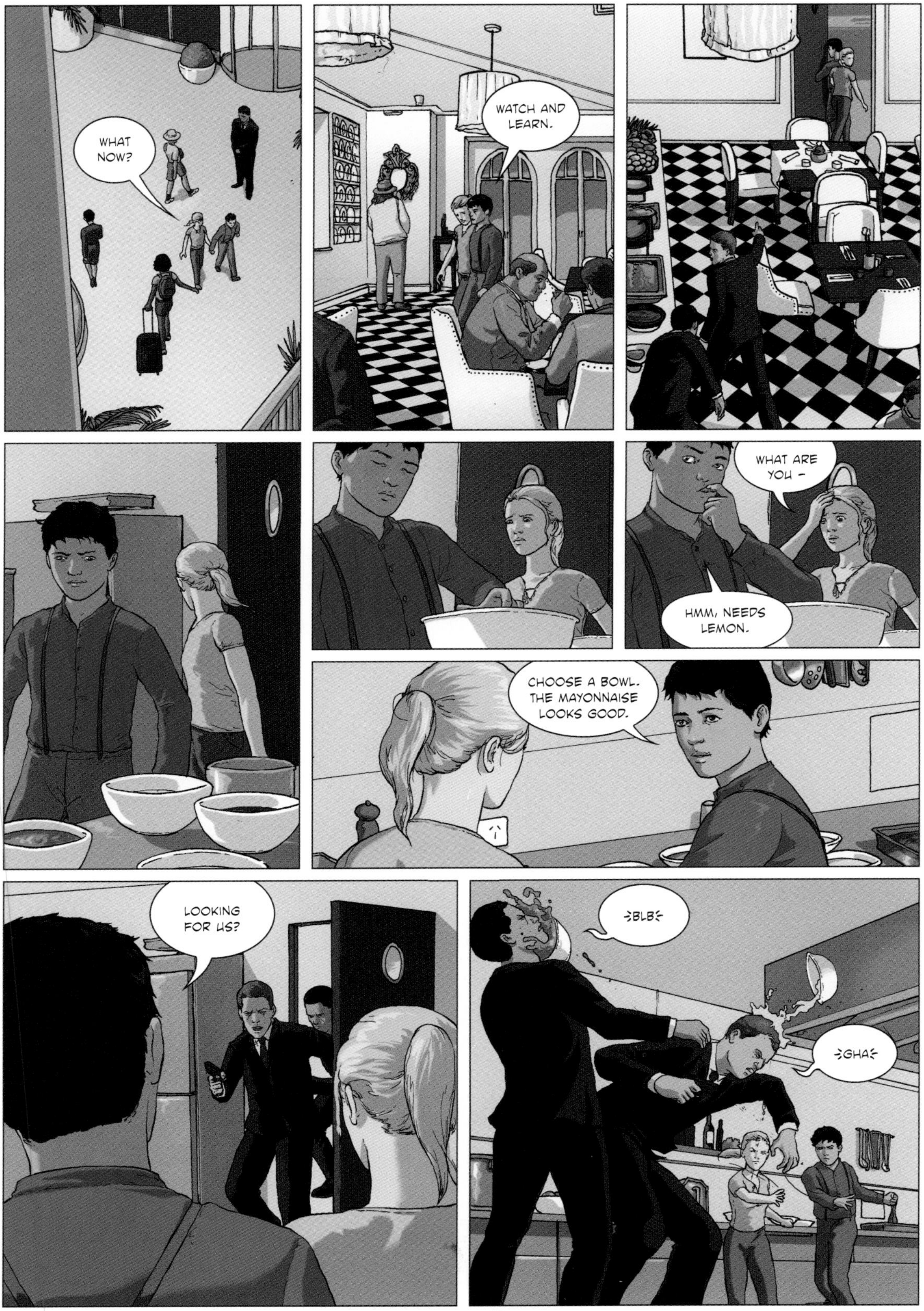
WHAT NOW?
WATCH AND LEARN.
WHAT ARE YOU –
HMM, NEEDS LEMON.
CHOOSE A BOWL. THE MAYONNAISE LOOKS GOOD.
LOOKING FOR US?
BLB
GHA

BAF

SPLAT!

BACK TO THE KITCHEN.

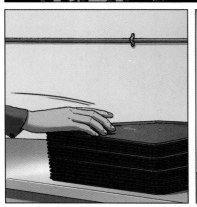

THAT SHOULD DO IT.

SERIOUSLY?!

COME ON!

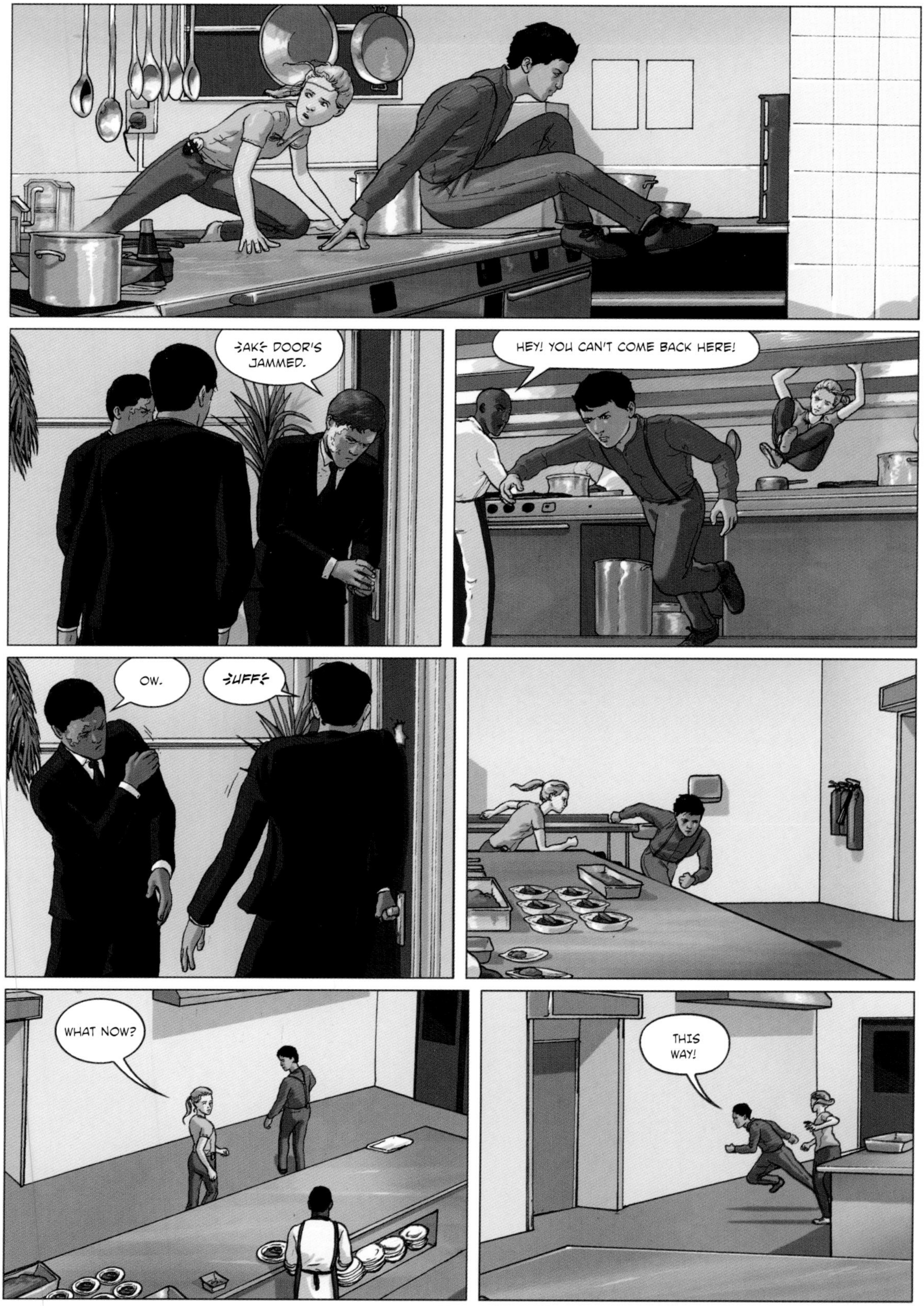

-AK- DOOR'S JAMMED.
HEY! YOU CAN'T COME BACK HERE!
OW.
-UFF-
WHAT NOW?
THIS WAY!

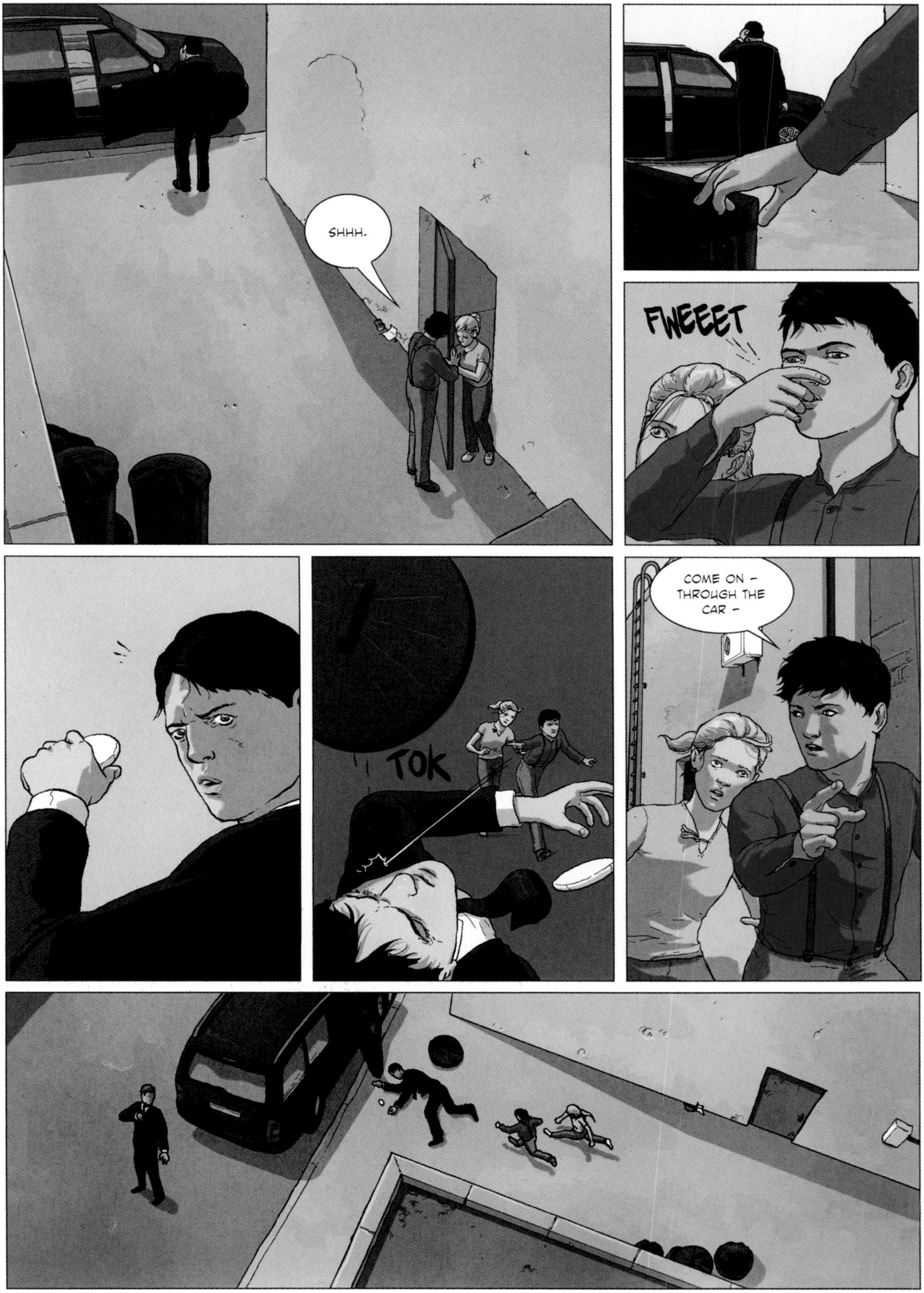
SHHH.
FWEEET
TOK
COME ON - THROUGH THE CAR -

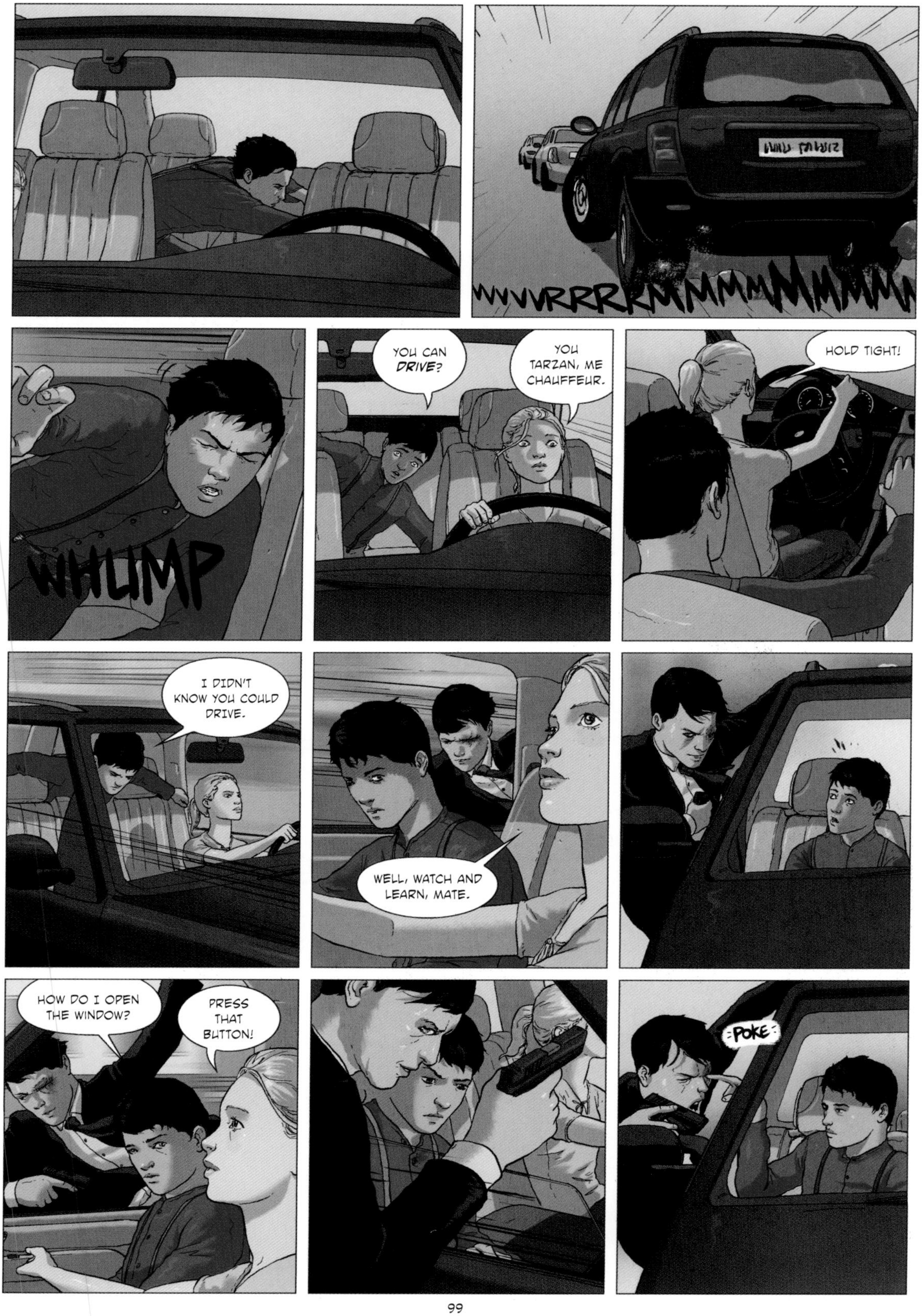
WVVVRRRRMMMMMMMMM
WHUMP
YOU CAN *DRIVE*?
YOU TARZAN, ME CHAUFFEUR.
HOLD TIGHT!
I DIDN'T KNOW YOU COULD DRIVE.
WELL, WATCH AND LEARN, MATE.
HOW DO I OPEN THE WINDOW?
PRESS THAT BUTTON!
POKE

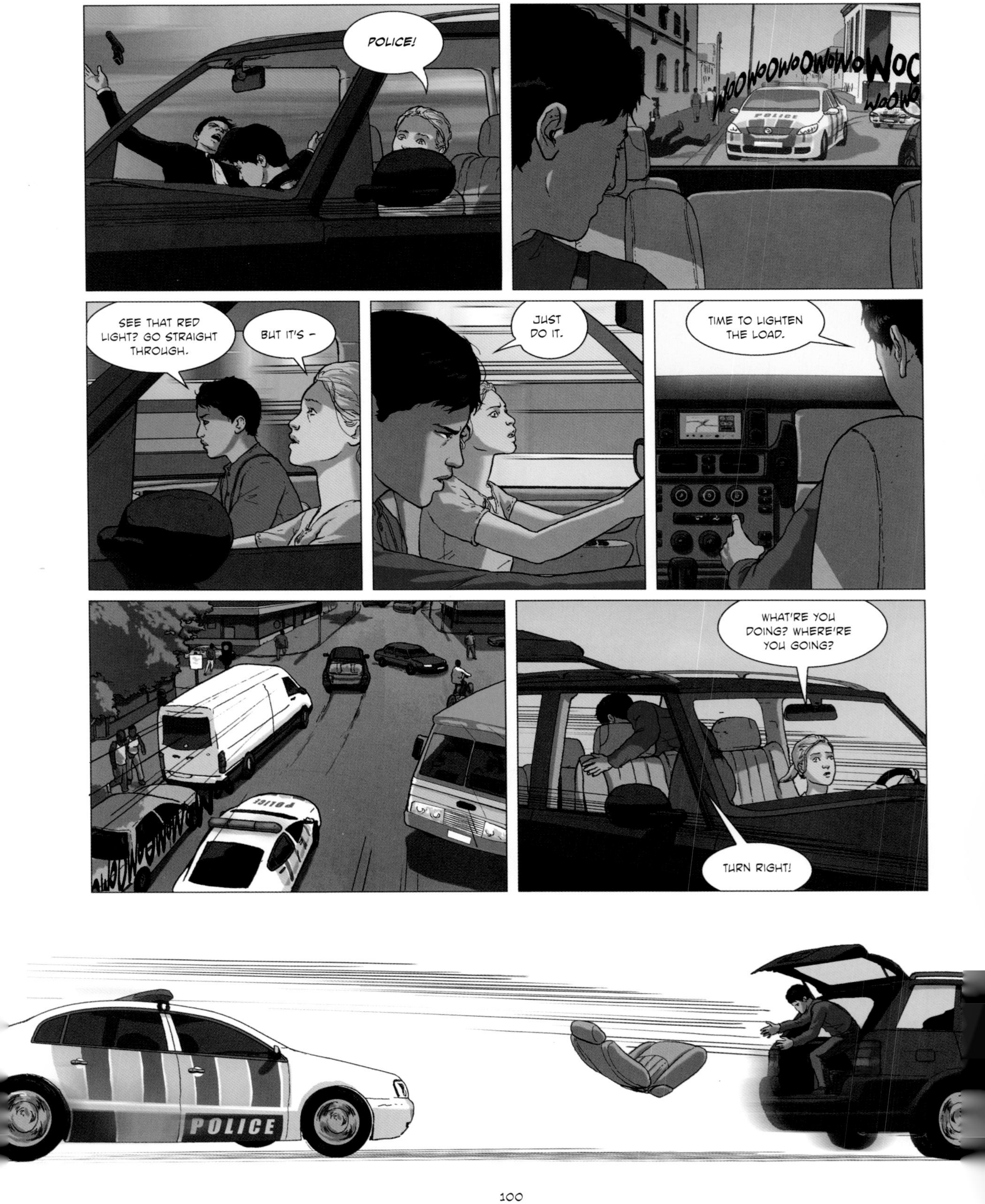
POLICE!
SEE THAT RED LIGHT? GO STRAIGHT THROUGH.
BUT IT'S –
JUST DO IT.
TIME TO LIGHTEN THE LOAD.
WHAT'RE YOU DOING? WHERE'RE YOU GOING?
TURN RIGHT!
POLICE

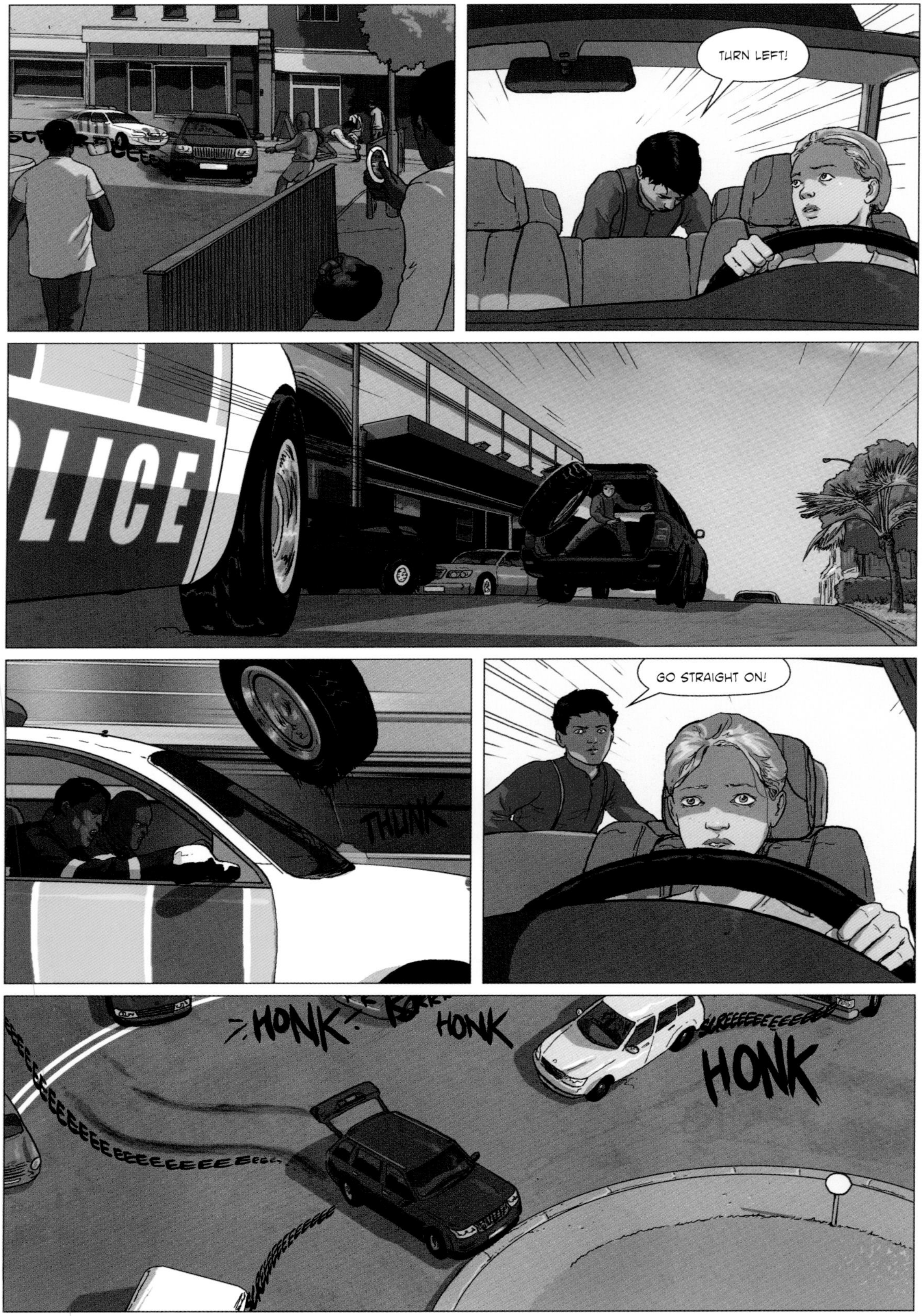
TURN LEFT!
THUNK
GO STRAIGHT ON!
HONK
HONK
HONK

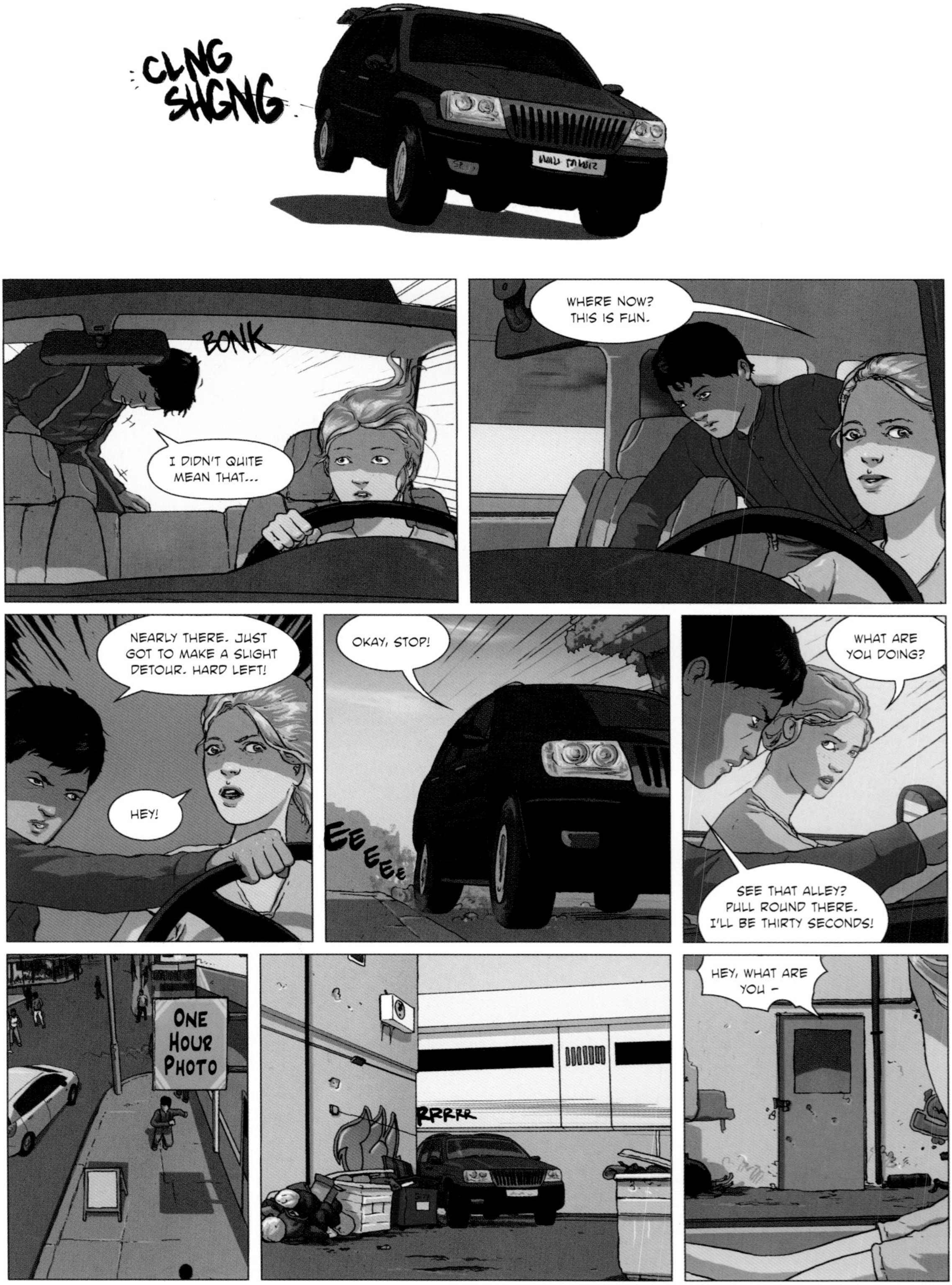

CLNG SHGNG
BONK
I DIDN'T QUITE MEAN THAT...
WHERE NOW? THIS IS FUN.
NEARLY THERE. JUST GOT TO MAKE A SLIGHT DETOUR. HARD LEFT!
HEY!
OKAY, STOP!
EEEEEE
WHAT ARE YOU DOING?
SEE THAT ALLEY? PULL ROUND THERE. I'LL BE THIRTY SECONDS!
ONE HOUR PHOTO
RRRRR
HEY, WHAT ARE YOU –

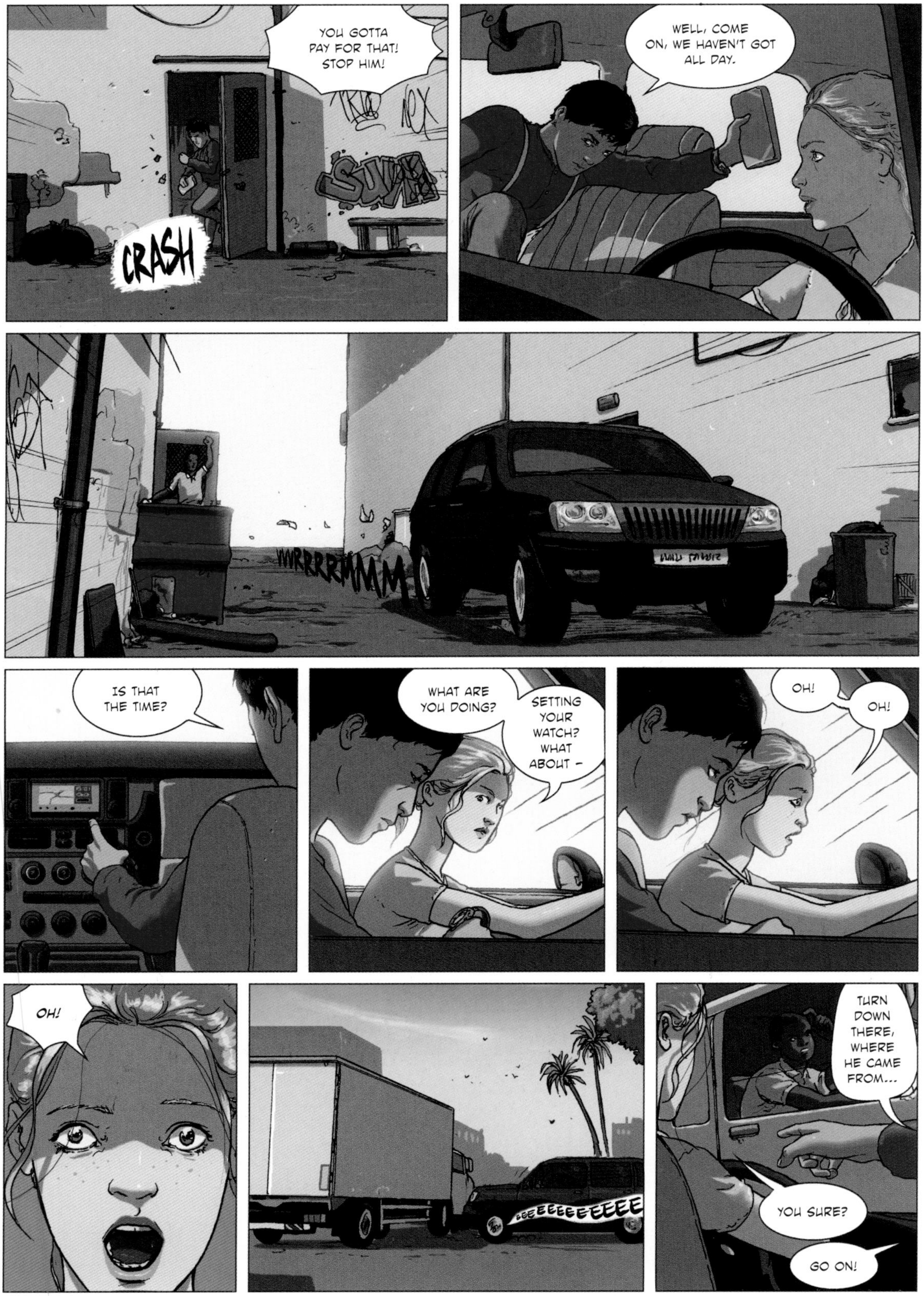
YOU GOTTA PAY FOR THAT! STOP HIM!
CRASH
WELL, COME ON, WE HAVEN'T GOT ALL DAY.
WWRRRRMMM
IS THAT THE TIME?
WHAT ARE YOU DOING?
SETTING YOUR WATCH? WHAT ABOUT –
OH!
OH!
OH!
EEEEEEEEEEEE
TURN DOWN THERE, WHERE HE CAME FROM...
YOU SURE?
GO ON!

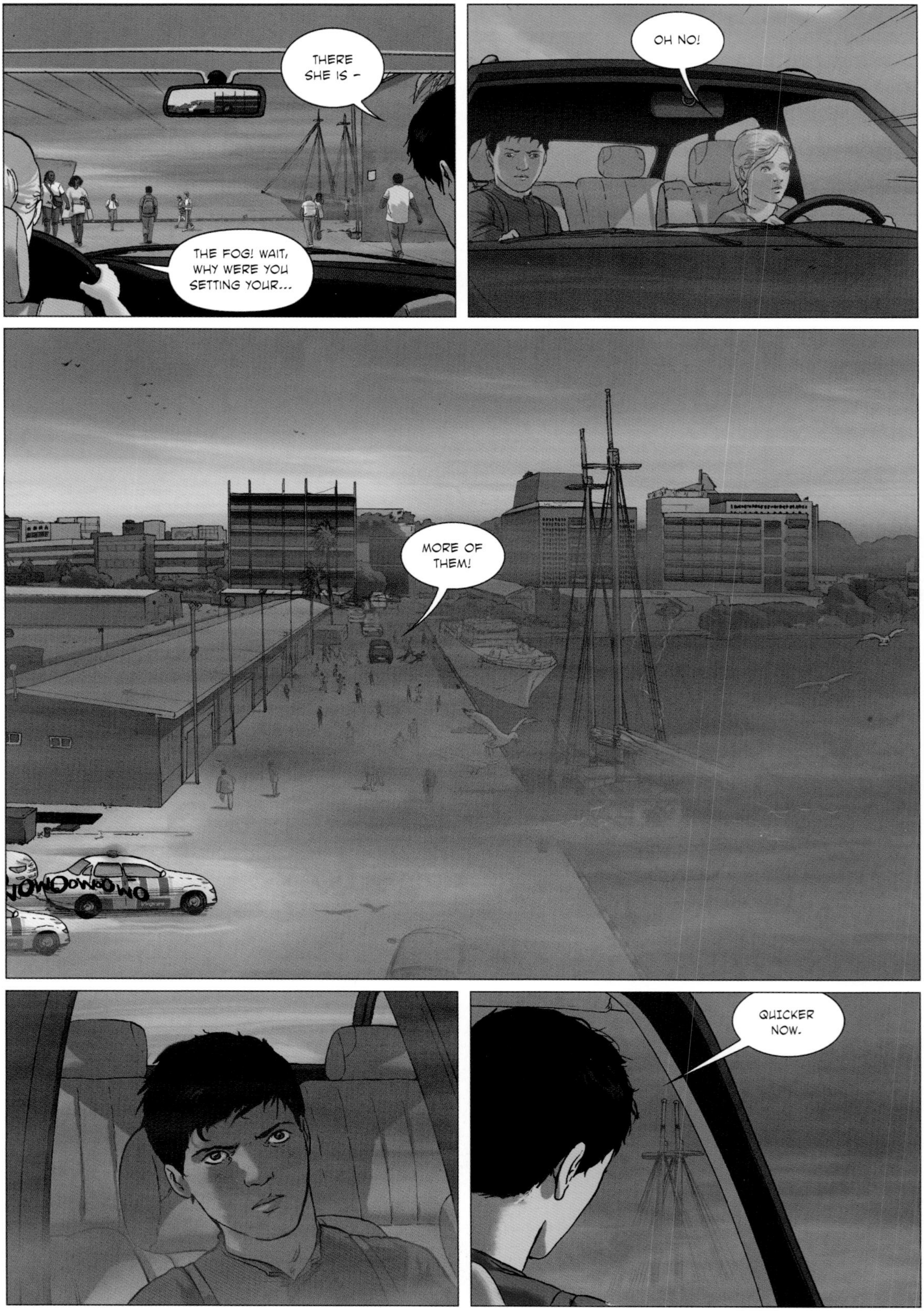
THERE SHE IS –
THE FOG! WAIT, WHY WERE YOU SETTING YOUR...
OH NO!
MORE OF THEM!
WOWOOWOOWO
QUICKER NOW.

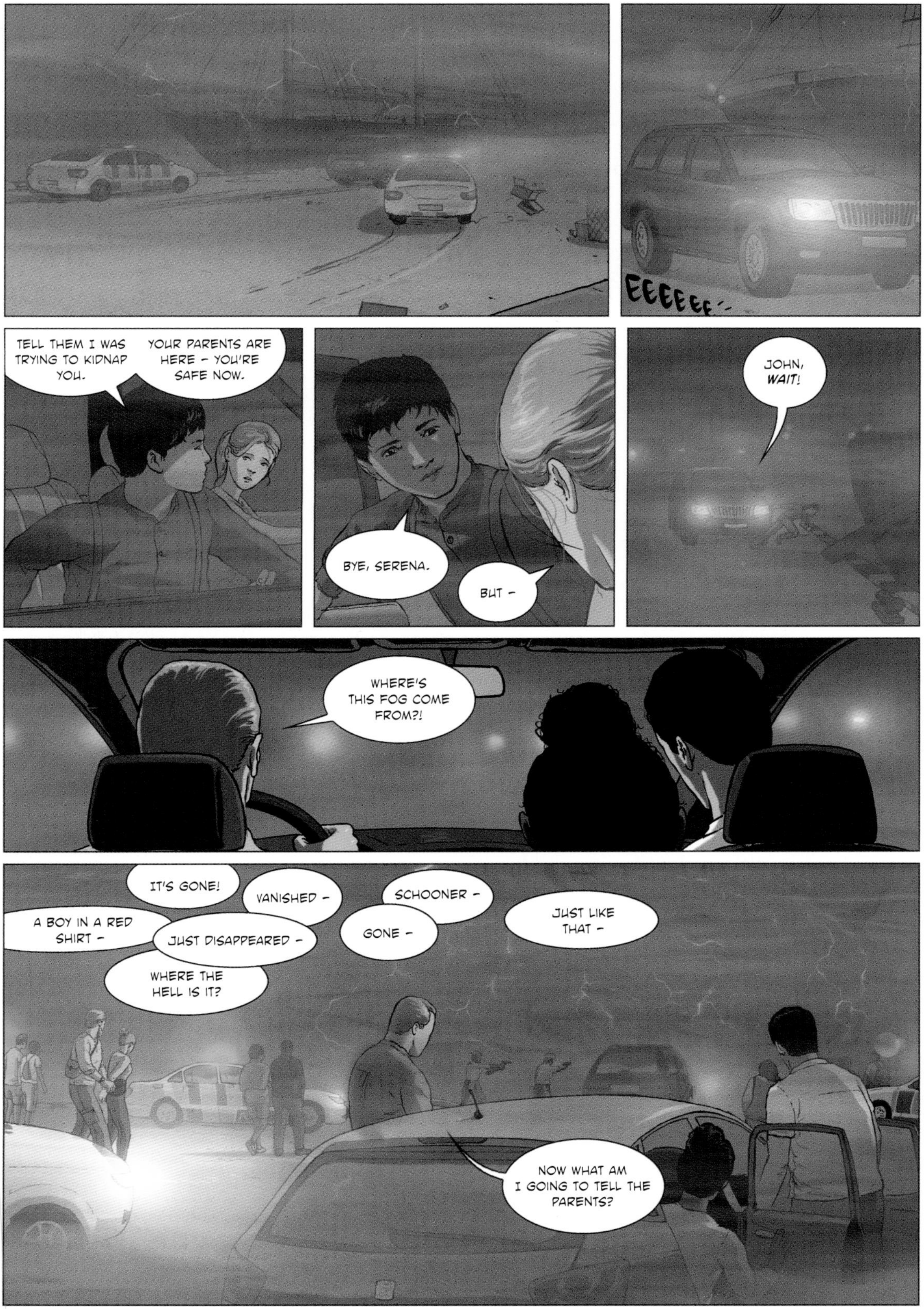
EEEEEE
TELL THEM I WAS TRYING TO KIDNAP YOU.
YOUR PARENTS ARE HERE – YOU'RE SAFE NOW.
BYE, SERENA.
BUT –
JOHN, WAIT!
WHERE'S THIS FOG COME FROM?!
IT'S GONE!
VANISHED –
SCHOONER –
A BOY IN A RED SHIRT –
JUST DISAPPEARED –
GONE –
JUST LIKE THAT –
WHERE THE HELL IS IT?
NOW WHAT AM I GOING TO TELL THE PARENTS?

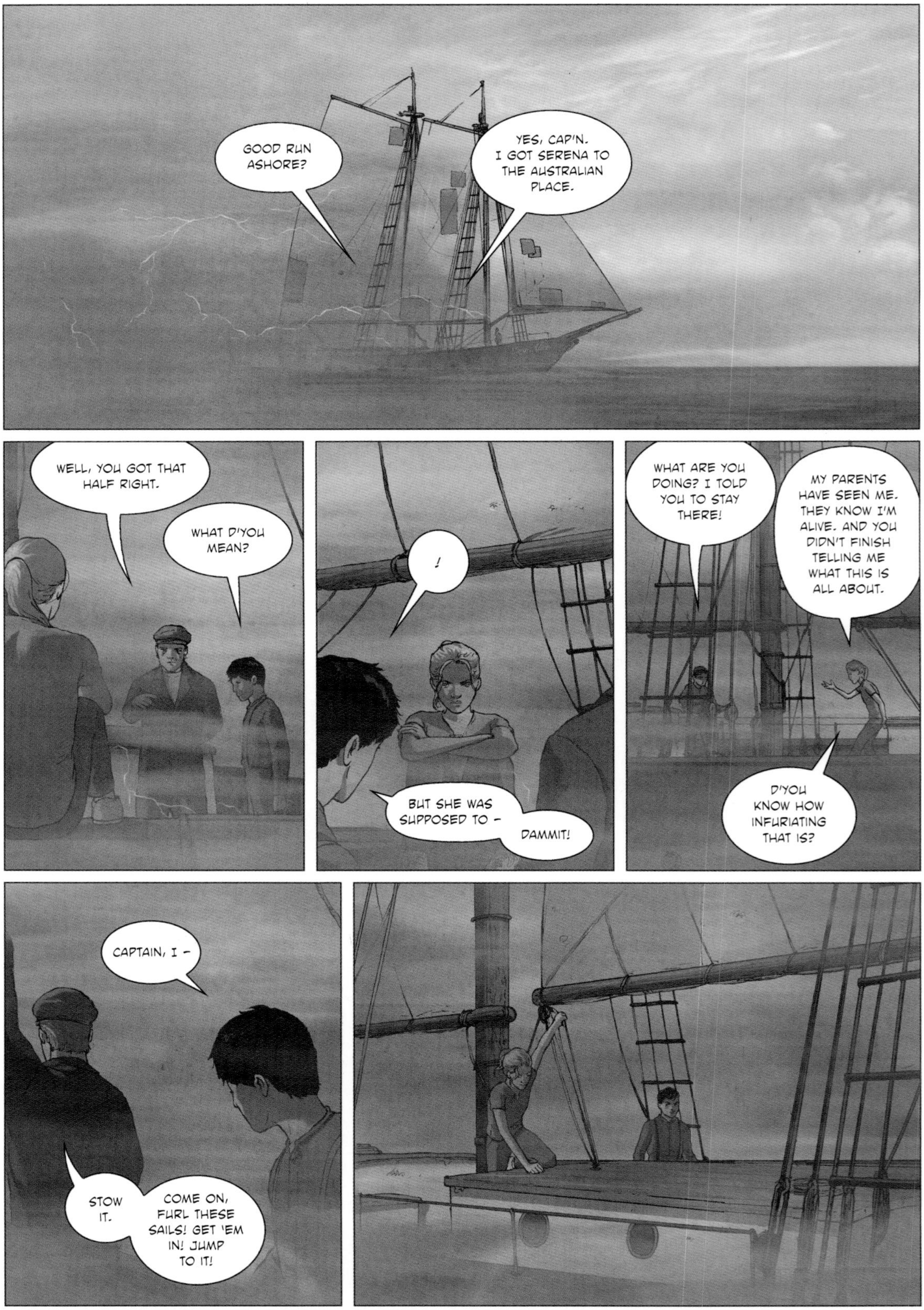
GOOD RUN ASHORE?
YES, CAP'N. I GOT SERENA TO THE AUSTRALIAN PLACE.
WELL, YOU GOT THAT HALF RIGHT.
WHAT D'YOU MEAN?
!
BUT SHE WAS SUPPOSED TO –
DAMMIT!
WHAT ARE YOU DOING? I TOLD YOU TO STAY THERE!
MY PARENTS HAVE SEEN ME. THEY KNOW I'M ALIVE. AND YOU DIDN'T FINISH TELLING ME WHAT THIS IS ALL ABOUT.
D'YOU KNOW HOW INFURIATING THAT IS?
CAPTAIN, I –
STOW IT.
COME ON, FURL THESE SAILS! GET 'EM IN! JUMP TO IT!

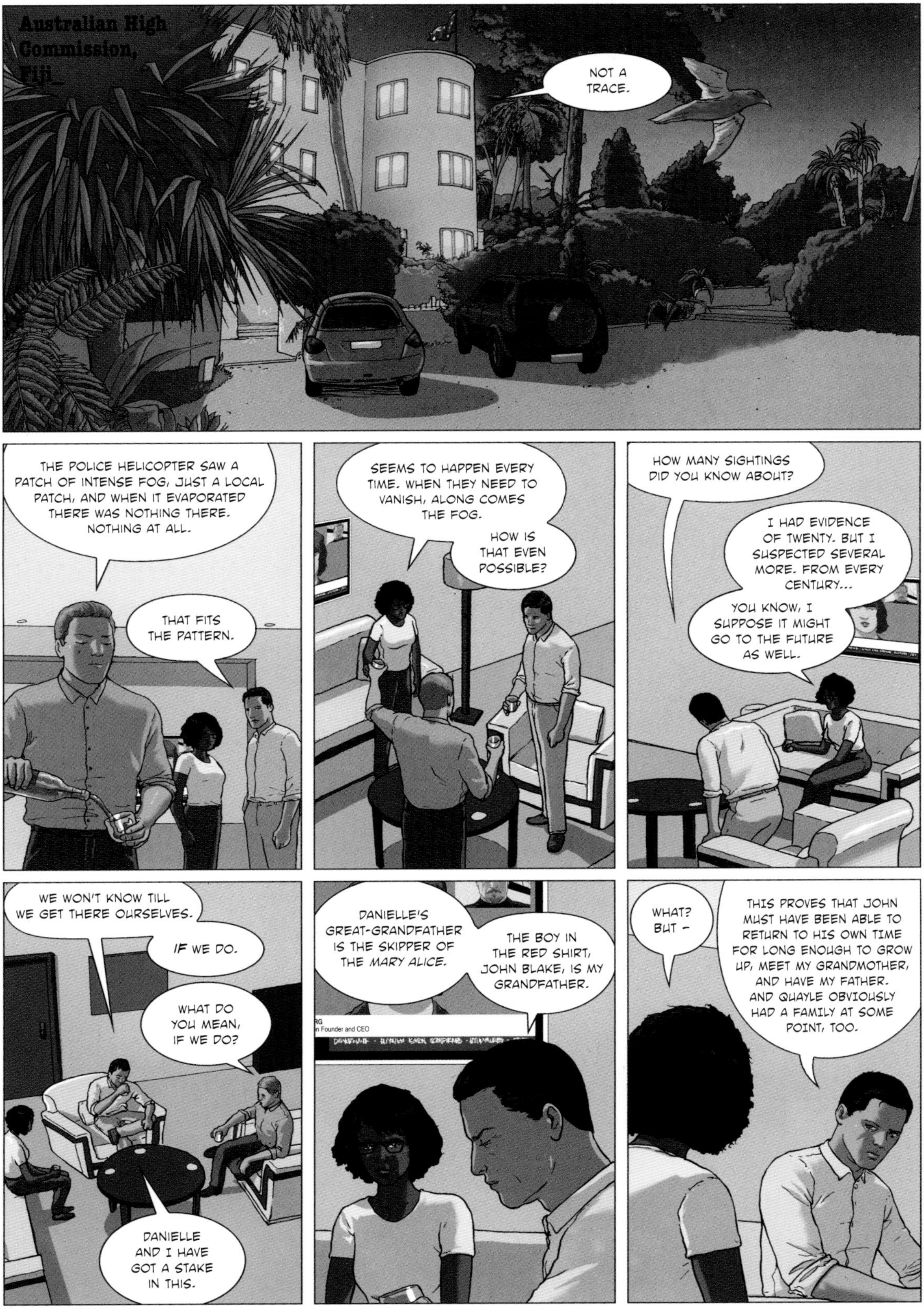
Australian High Commission, Fiji_
NOT A TRACE.
THE POLICE HELICOPTER SAW A PATCH OF INTENSE FOG, JUST A LOCAL PATCH, AND WHEN IT EVAPORATED THERE WAS NOTHING THERE. NOTHING AT ALL.
THAT FITS THE PATTERN.
SEEMS TO HAPPEN EVERY TIME. WHEN THEY NEED TO VANISH, ALONG COMES THE FOG.
HOW IS THAT EVEN POSSIBLE?
HOW MANY SIGHTINGS DID YOU KNOW ABOUT?
I HAD EVIDENCE OF TWENTY. BUT I SUSPECTED SEVERAL MORE. FROM EVERY CENTURY...
YOU KNOW, I SUPPOSE IT MIGHT GO TO THE FUTURE AS WELL.
WE WON'T KNOW TILL WE GET THERE OURSELVES.
IF WE DO.
WHAT DO YOU MEAN, IF WE DO?
DANIELLE AND I HAVE GOT A STAKE IN THIS.
DANIELLE'S GREAT-GRANDFATHER IS THE SKIPPER OF THE *MARY ALICE*.
THE BOY IN THE RED SHIRT, JOHN BLAKE, IS MY GRANDFATHER.
WHAT? BUT –
THIS PROVES THAT JOHN MUST HAVE BEEN ABLE TO RETURN TO HIS OWN TIME FOR LONG ENOUGH TO GROW UP, MEET MY GRANDMOTHER, AND HAVE MY FATHER. AND QUAYLE OBVIOUSLY HAD A FAMILY AT SOME POINT, TOO.

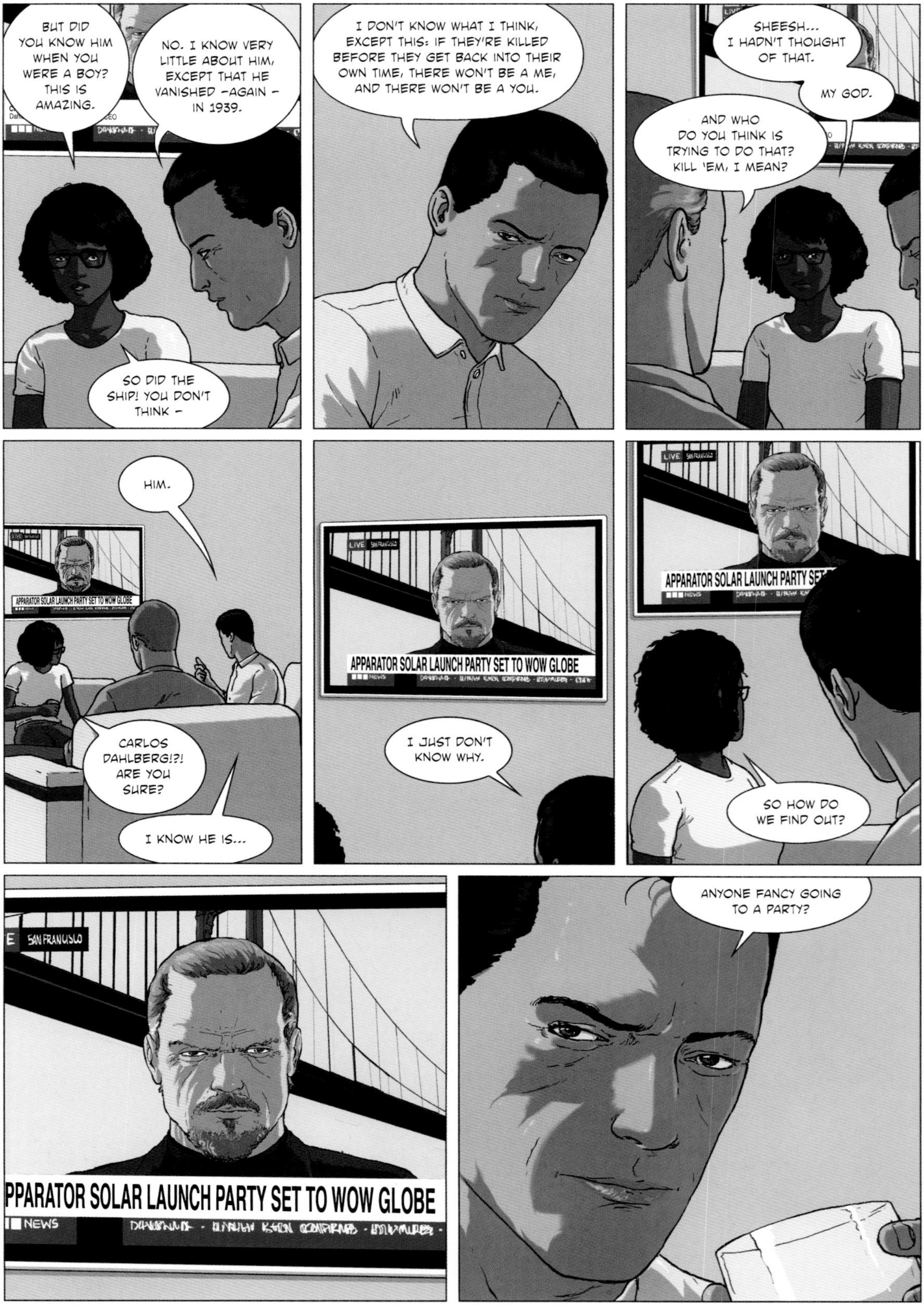
BUT DID YOU KNOW HIM WHEN YOU WERE A BOY? THIS IS AMAZING.
NO. I KNOW VERY LITTLE ABOUT HIM, EXCEPT THAT HE VANISHED -AGAIN - IN 1939.
SO DID THE SHIP! YOU DON'T THINK -
I DON'T KNOW WHAT I THINK, EXCEPT THIS: IF THEY'RE KILLED BEFORE THEY GET BACK INTO THEIR OWN TIME, THERE WON'T BE A ME, AND THERE WON'T BE A YOU.
SHEESH... I HADN'T THOUGHT OF THAT.
MY GOD.
AND WHO DO YOU THINK IS TRYING TO DO THAT? KILL 'EM, I MEAN?
HIM.
APPARATOR SOLAR LAUNCH PARTY SET TO WOW GLOBE
CARLOS DAHLBERG!?! ARE YOU SURE?
I KNOW HE IS...
LIVE SAN FRANCISCO
APPARATOR SOLAR LAUNCH PARTY SET TO WOW GLOBE
NEWS
I JUST DON'T KNOW WHY.
LIVE SAN FRANCISCO
APPARATOR SOLAR LAUNCH PARTY SET
NEWS
SO HOW DO WE FIND OUT?
SAN FRANCISCO
PPARATOR SOLAR LAUNCH PARTY SET TO WOW GLOBE
NEWS
ANYONE FANCY GOING TO A PARTY?

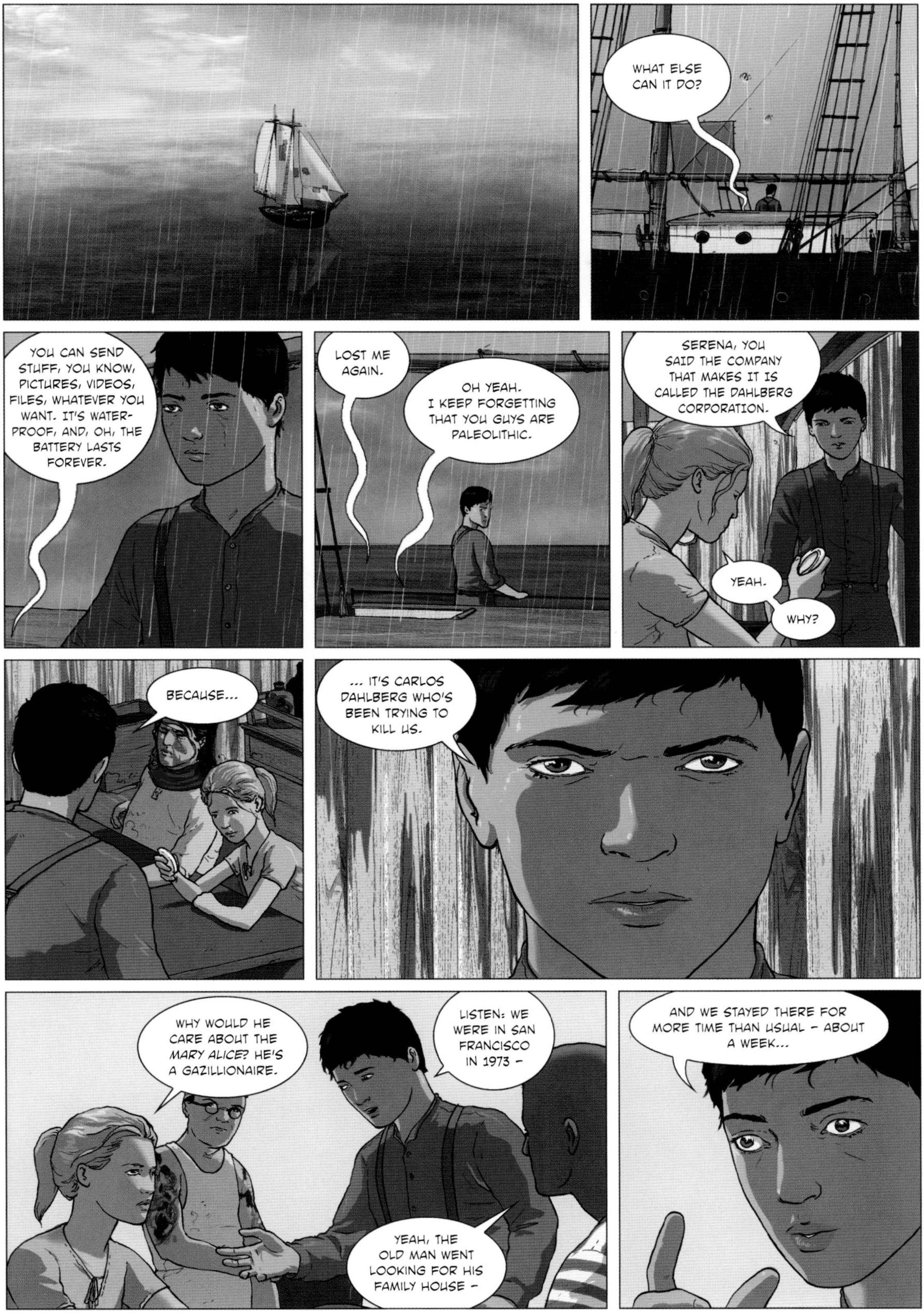
WHAT ELSE CAN IT DO?
YOU CAN SEND STUFF, YOU KNOW, PICTURES, VIDEOS, FILES, WHATEVER YOU WANT. IT'S WATER-PROOF, AND, OH, THE BATTERY LASTS FOREVER.
LOST ME AGAIN.
OH YEAH. I KEEP FORGETTING THAT YOU GUYS ARE PALEOLITHIC.
SERENA, YOU SAID THE COMPANY THAT MAKES IT IS CALLED THE DAHLBERG CORPORATION.
YEAH.
WHY?
BECAUSE...
... IT'S CARLOS DAHLBERG WHO'S BEEN TRYING TO KILL US.
WHY WOULD HE CARE ABOUT THE *MARY ALICE*? HE'S A GAZILLIONAIRE.
LISTEN: WE WERE IN SAN FRANCISCO IN 1973 –
YEAH, THE OLD MAN WENT LOOKING FOR HIS FAMILY HOUSE –
AND WE STAYED THERE FOR MORE TIME THAN USUAL – ABOUT A WEEK...

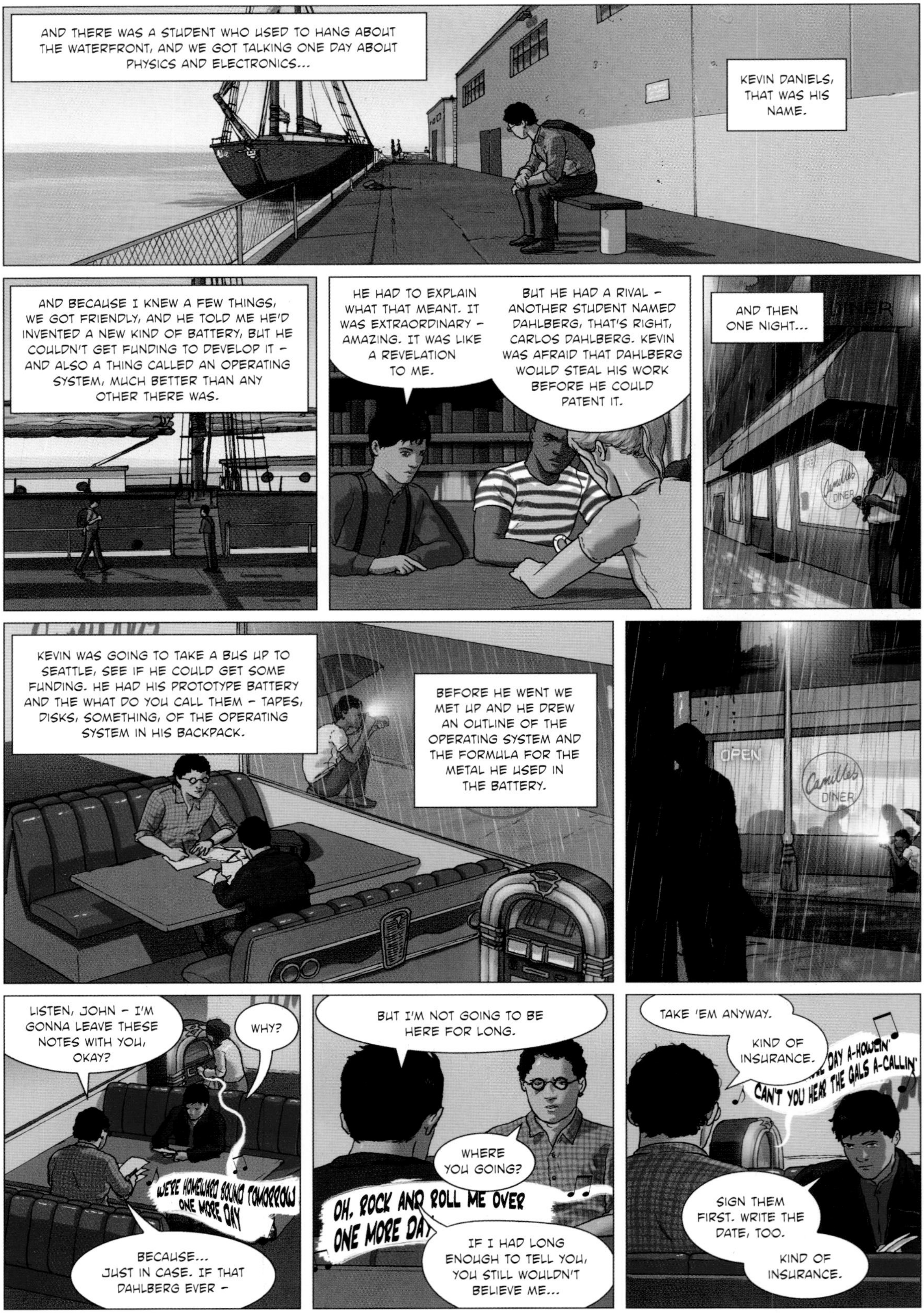
AND THERE WAS A STUDENT WHO USED TO HANG ABOUT THE WATERFRONT, AND WE GOT TALKING ONE DAY ABOUT PHYSICS AND ELECTRONICS...
KEVIN DANIELS, THAT WAS HIS NAME.
AND BECAUSE I KNEW A FEW THINGS, WE GOT FRIENDLY, AND HE TOLD ME HE'D INVENTED A NEW KIND OF BATTERY, BUT HE COULDN'T GET FUNDING TO DEVELOP IT - AND ALSO A THING CALLED AN OPERATING SYSTEM, MUCH BETTER THAN ANY OTHER THERE WAS.
HE HAD TO EXPLAIN WHAT THAT MEANT. IT WAS EXTRAORDINARY - AMAZING. IT WAS LIKE A REVELATION TO ME.
BUT HE HAD A RIVAL - ANOTHER STUDENT NAMED DAHLBERG, THAT'S RIGHT, CARLOS DAHLBERG. KEVIN WAS AFRAID THAT DAHLBERG WOULD STEAL HIS WORK BEFORE HE COULD PATENT IT.
AND THEN ONE NIGHT...
DINER
Camille's DINER
KEVIN WAS GOING TO TAKE A BUS UP TO SEATTLE, SEE IF HE COULD GET SOME FUNDING. HE HAD HIS PROTOTYPE BATTERY AND THE WHAT DO YOU CALL THEM - TAPES, DISKS, SOMETHING, OF THE OPERATING SYSTEM IN HIS BACKPACK.
BEFORE HE WENT WE MET UP AND HE DREW AN OUTLINE OF THE OPERATING SYSTEM AND THE FORMULA FOR THE METAL HE USED IN THE BATTERY.
OPEN
Camille's DINER
LISTEN, JOHN - I'M GONNA LEAVE THESE NOTES WITH YOU, OKAY?
WHY?
WE'RE HOMEWARD BOUND TOMORROW ONE MORE DAY
BECAUSE... JUST IN CASE. IF THAT DAHLBERG EVER -
BUT I'M NOT GOING TO BE HERE FOR LONG.
WHERE YOU GOING?
OH, ROCK AND ROLL ME OVER ONE MORE DAY
IF I HAD LONG ENOUGH TO TELL YOU, YOU STILL WOULDN'T BELIEVE ME...
TAKE 'EM ANYWAY.
KIND OF INSURANCE.
CAN'T YOU HEAR THE GALS A-CALLIN'
SIGN THEM FIRST. WRITE THE DATE, TOO.
KIND OF INSURANCE.

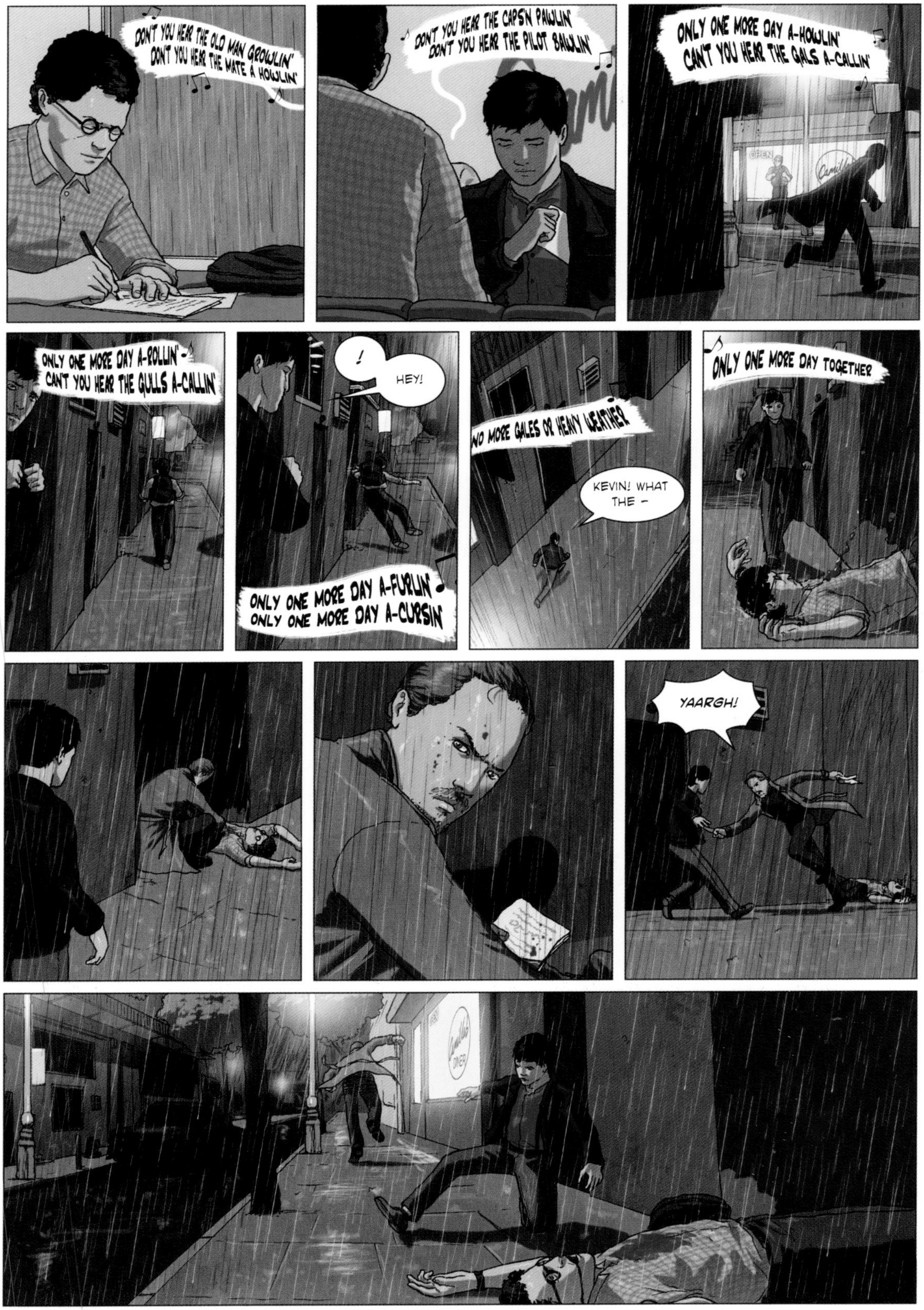
DON'T YOU HEAR THE OLD MAN GROWLIN'
DON'T YOU HEAR THE MATE A-HOWLIN'
DON'T YOU HEAR THE CAPS'N PAWLIN'
DON'T YOU HEAR THE PILOT BAWLIN'
ONLY ONE MORE DAY A-HOWLIN'
CAN'T YOU HEAR THE GALS A-CALLIN'
ONLY ONE MORE DAY A-ROLLIN'
CAN'T YOU HEAR THE GULLS A-CALLIN'
!
HEY!
ONLY ONE MORE DAY A-FURLIN'
ONLY ONE MORE DAY A-CURSIN'
NO MORE GALES OR HEAVY WEATHER
KEVIN! WHAT THE –
ONLY ONE MORE DAY TOGETHER
YAARGH!
DINER

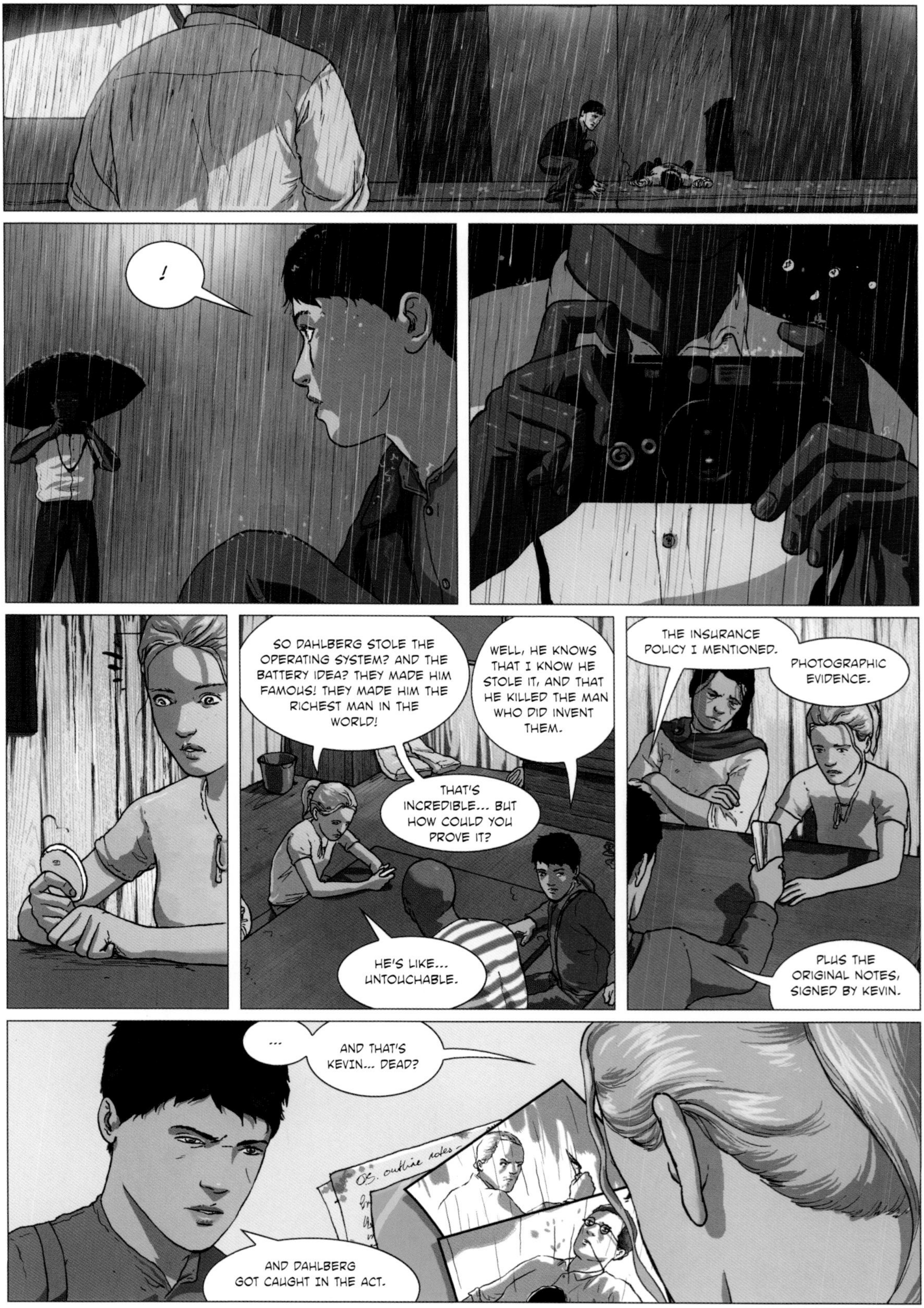
!
SO DAHLBERG STOLE THE OPERATING SYSTEM? AND THE BATTERY IDEA? THEY MADE HIM FAMOUS! THEY MADE HIM THE RICHEST MAN IN THE WORLD!
THAT'S INCREDIBLE... BUT HOW COULD YOU PROVE IT?
WELL, HE KNOWS THAT I KNOW HE STOLE IT, AND THAT HE KILLED THE MAN WHO DID INVENT THEM.
HE'S LIKE... UNTOUCHABLE.
THE INSURANCE POLICY I MENTIONED.
PHOTOGRAPHIC EVIDENCE.
PLUS THE ORIGINAL NOTES, SIGNED BY KEVIN.
...
AND THAT'S KEVIN... DEAD?
AND DAHLBERG GOT CAUGHT IN THE ACT.

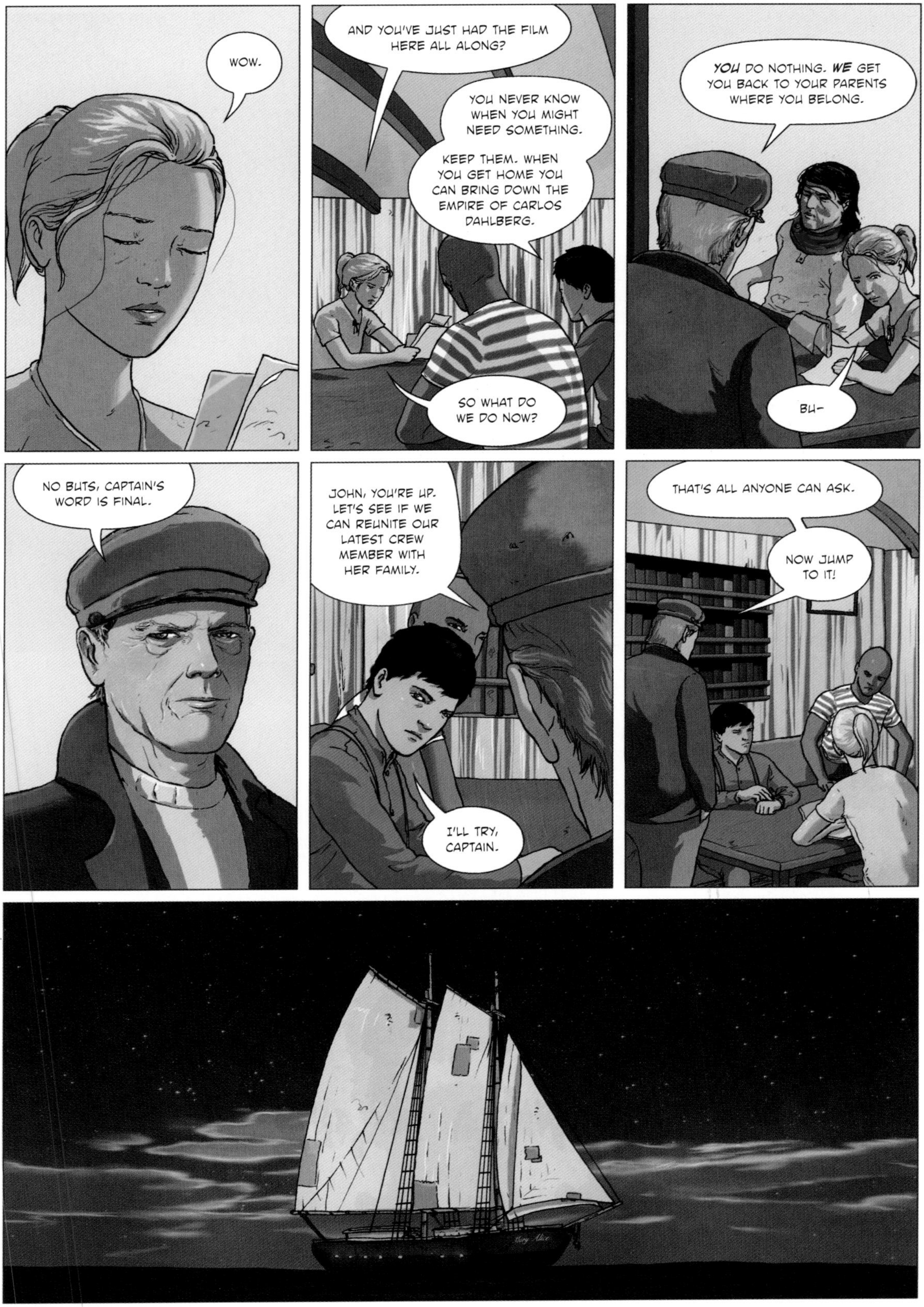
WOW.
AND YOU'VE JUST HAD THE FILM HERE ALL ALONG?
YOU NEVER KNOW WHEN YOU MIGHT NEED SOMETHING.
KEEP THEM. WHEN YOU GET HOME YOU CAN BRING DOWN THE EMPIRE OF CARLOS DAHLBERG.
SO WHAT DO WE DO NOW?
YOU DO NOTHING. *WE* GET YOU BACK TO YOUR PARENTS WHERE YOU BELONG.
BU–
NO BUTS, CAPTAIN'S WORD IS FINAL.
JOHN, YOU'RE UP. LET'S SEE IF WE CAN REUNITE OUR LATEST CREW MEMBER WITH HER FAMILY.
I'LL TRY, CAPTAIN.
THAT'S ALL ANYONE CAN ASK.
NOW JUMP TO IT!

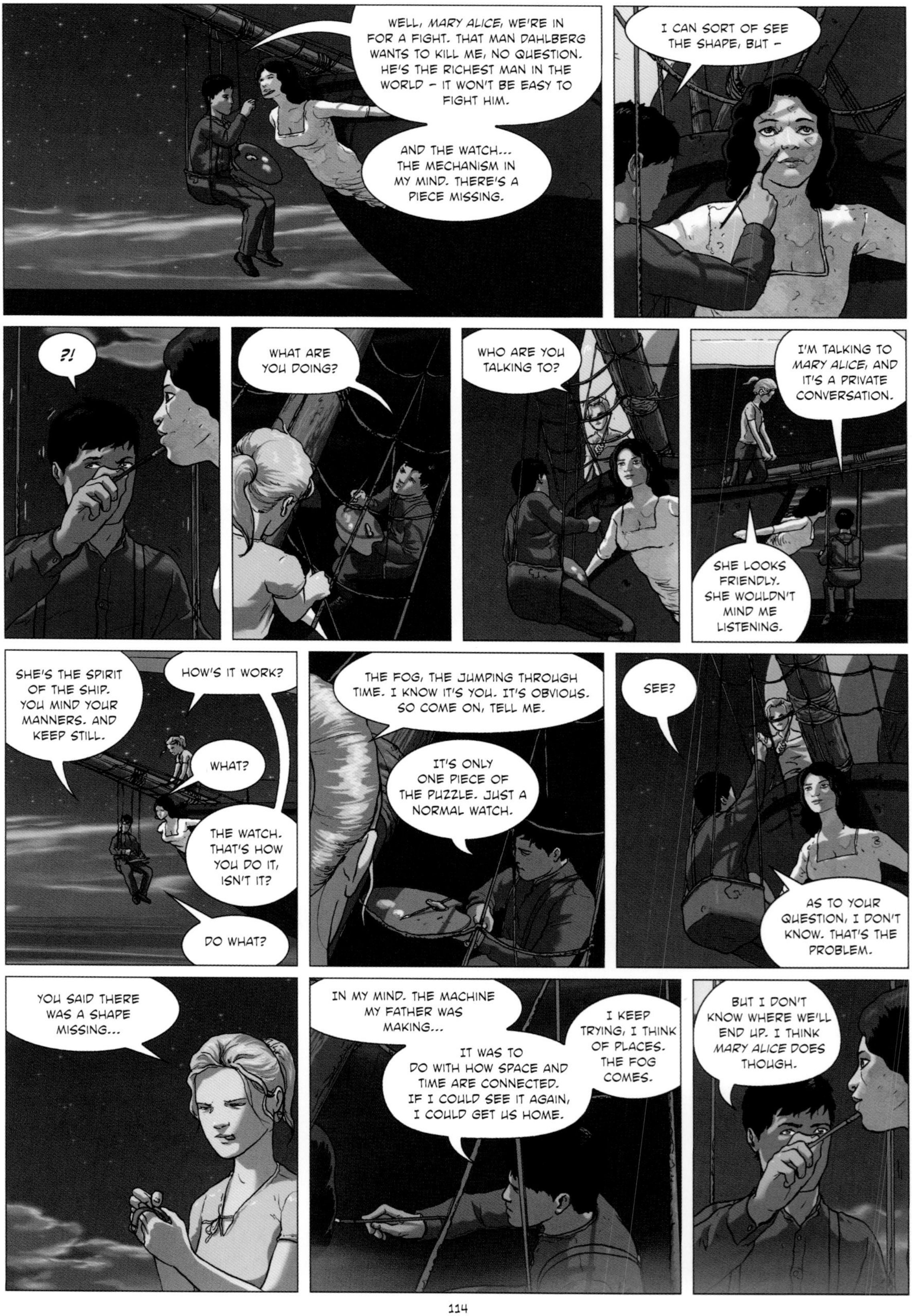
WELL, *MARY ALICE*, WE'RE IN FOR A FIGHT. THAT MAN DAHLBERG WANTS TO KILL ME, NO QUESTION. HE'S THE RICHEST MAN IN THE WORLD – IT WON'T BE EASY TO FIGHT HIM.
AND THE WATCH... THE MECHANISM IN MY MIND. THERE'S A PIECE MISSING.
I CAN SORT OF SEE THE SHAPE, BUT –
?!
WHAT ARE YOU DOING?
WHO ARE YOU TALKING TO?
I'M TALKING TO *MARY ALICE*, AND IT'S A PRIVATE CONVERSATION.
SHE LOOKS FRIENDLY. SHE WOULDN'T MIND ME LISTENING.
SHE'S THE SPIRIT OF THE SHIP. YOU MIND YOUR MANNERS. AND KEEP STILL.
HOW'S IT WORK?
WHAT?
THE WATCH. THAT'S HOW YOU DO IT, ISN'T IT?
DO WHAT?
THE FOG, THE JUMPING THROUGH TIME. I KNOW IT'S YOU. IT'S OBVIOUS. SO COME ON, TELL ME.
IT'S ONLY ONE PIECE OF THE PUZZLE. JUST A NORMAL WATCH.
SEE?
AS TO YOUR QUESTION, I DON'T KNOW. THAT'S THE PROBLEM.
YOU SAID THERE WAS A SHAPE MISSING...
IN MY MIND. THE MACHINE MY FATHER WAS MAKING...
IT WAS TO DO WITH HOW SPACE AND TIME ARE CONNECTED. IF I COULD SEE IT AGAIN, I COULD GET US HOME.
I KEEP TRYING, I THINK OF PLACES. THE FOG COMES.
BUT I DON'T KNOW WHERE WE'LL END UP. I THINK *MARY ALICE* DOES THOUGH.

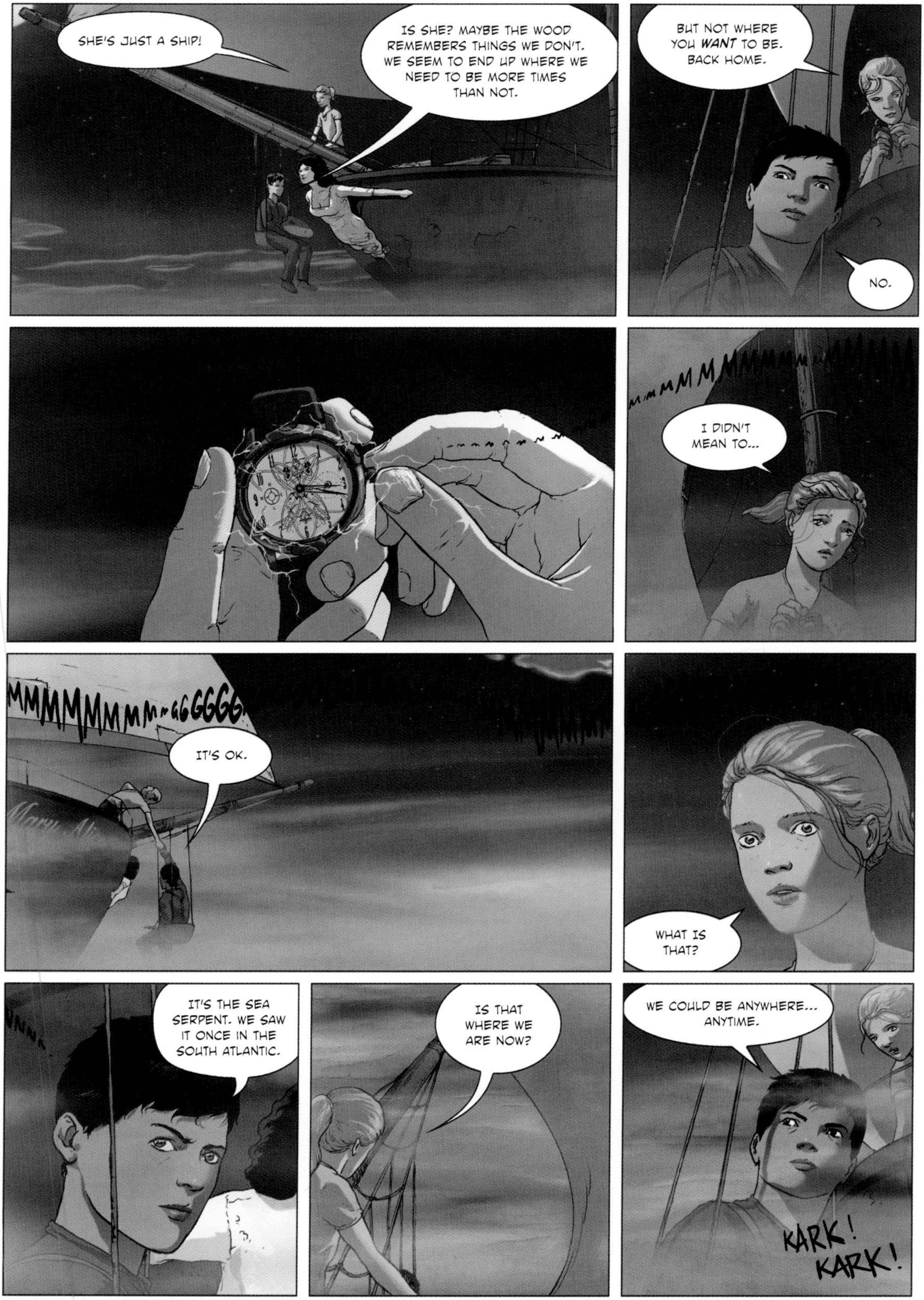
SHE'S JUST A SHIP!
IS SHE? MAYBE THE WOOD REMEMBERS THINGS WE DON'T. WE SEEM TO END UP WHERE WE NEED TO BE MORE TIMES THAN NOT.
BUT NOT WHERE YOU *WANT* TO BE. BACK HOME.
NO.
I DIDN'T MEAN TO...
IT'S OK.
WHAT IS THAT?
IT'S THE SEA SERPENT. WE SAW IT ONCE IN THE SOUTH ATLANTIC.
IS THAT WHERE WE ARE NOW?
WE COULD BE ANYWHERE... ANYTIME.
KARK! KARK!

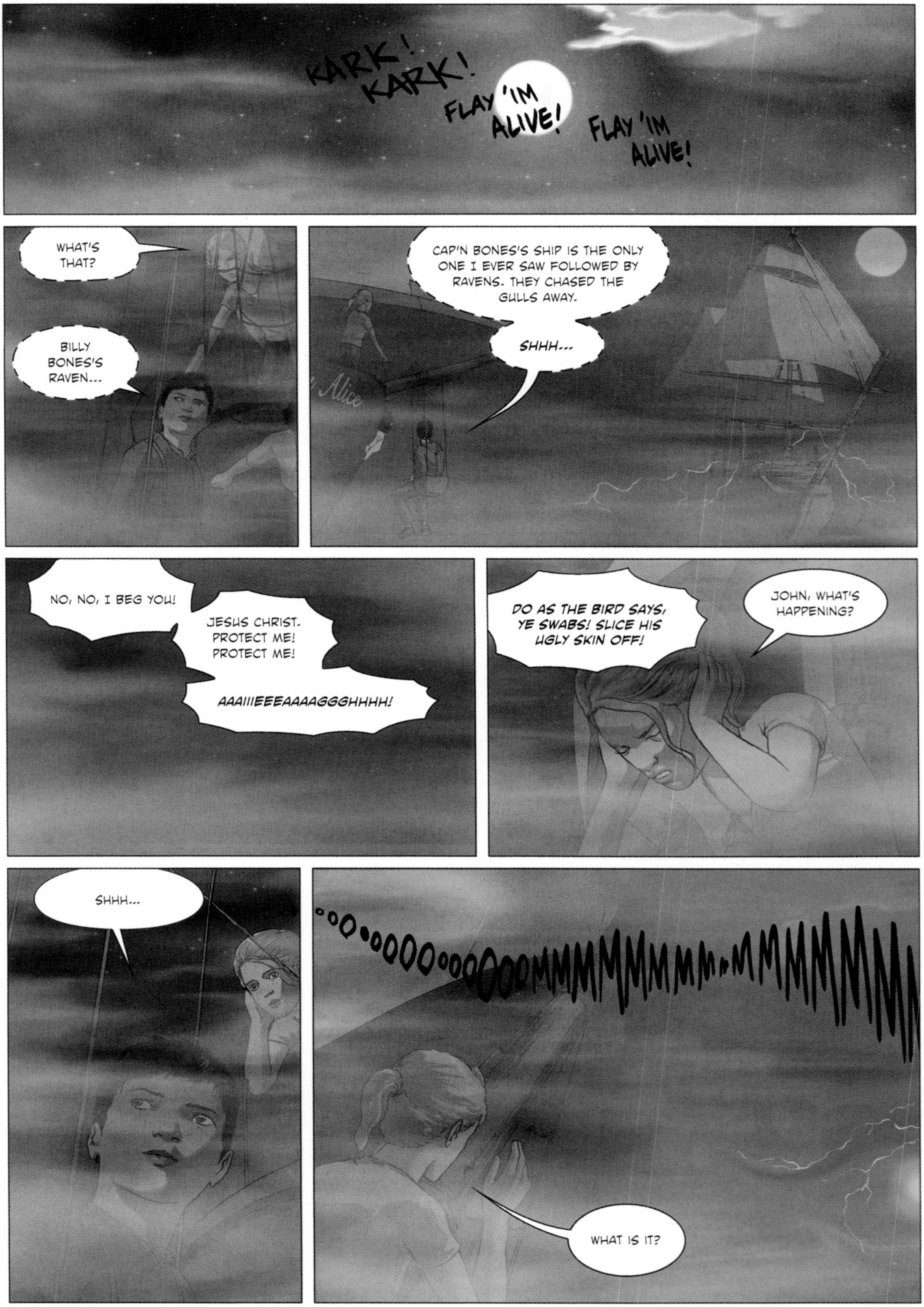
KARK! KARK!
FLAY 'IM ALIVE!
FLAY 'IM ALIVE!
WHAT'S THAT?
BILLY BONES'S RAVEN...
CAP'N BONES'S SHIP IS THE ONLY ONE I EVER SAW FOLLOWED BY RAVENS. THEY CHASED THE GULLS AWAY.
SHHH...
NO, NO, I BEG YOU!
JESUS CHRIST. PROTECT ME! PROTECT ME!
AAAIIIEEEAAAAGGGHHHH!
DO AS THE BIRD SAYS, YE SWABS! SLICE HIS UGLY SKIN OFF!
JOHN, WHAT'S HAPPENING?
SHHH...
ooOooOOOooOOOOMMMMMMMMMMMmmMMMMMM
WHAT IS IT?

IT'S BEAUTIFUL...

YOU EVER HEAR THE STORY OF ODYSSEUS AND THE SIRENS?

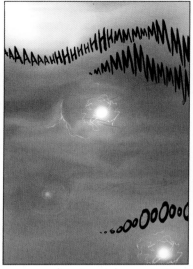

COVER YOUR EARS...

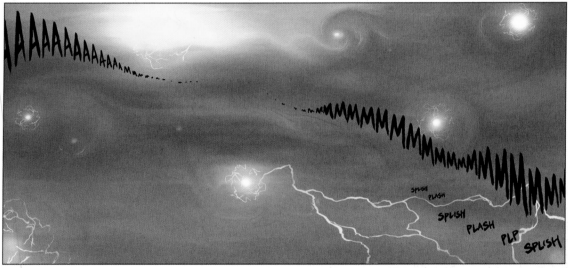

SPLISH

PLASH

SPLISH

PLASH

PLP

SPLISH

IT'S STOPPED BUT, IT WAS SO BEAUTIFUL...

OH, I WANT TO HEAR MORE OF IT... I CAN'T BELIEVE HOW MUCH I WANTED TO JUST... GO TO THEM...

WE HEARD THEM ONCE BEFORE, AND LOST TWO CREWMEN. THEY JUST JUMPED OVERBOARD AND WE NEVER SAW THEM AGAIN.

LISTEN –

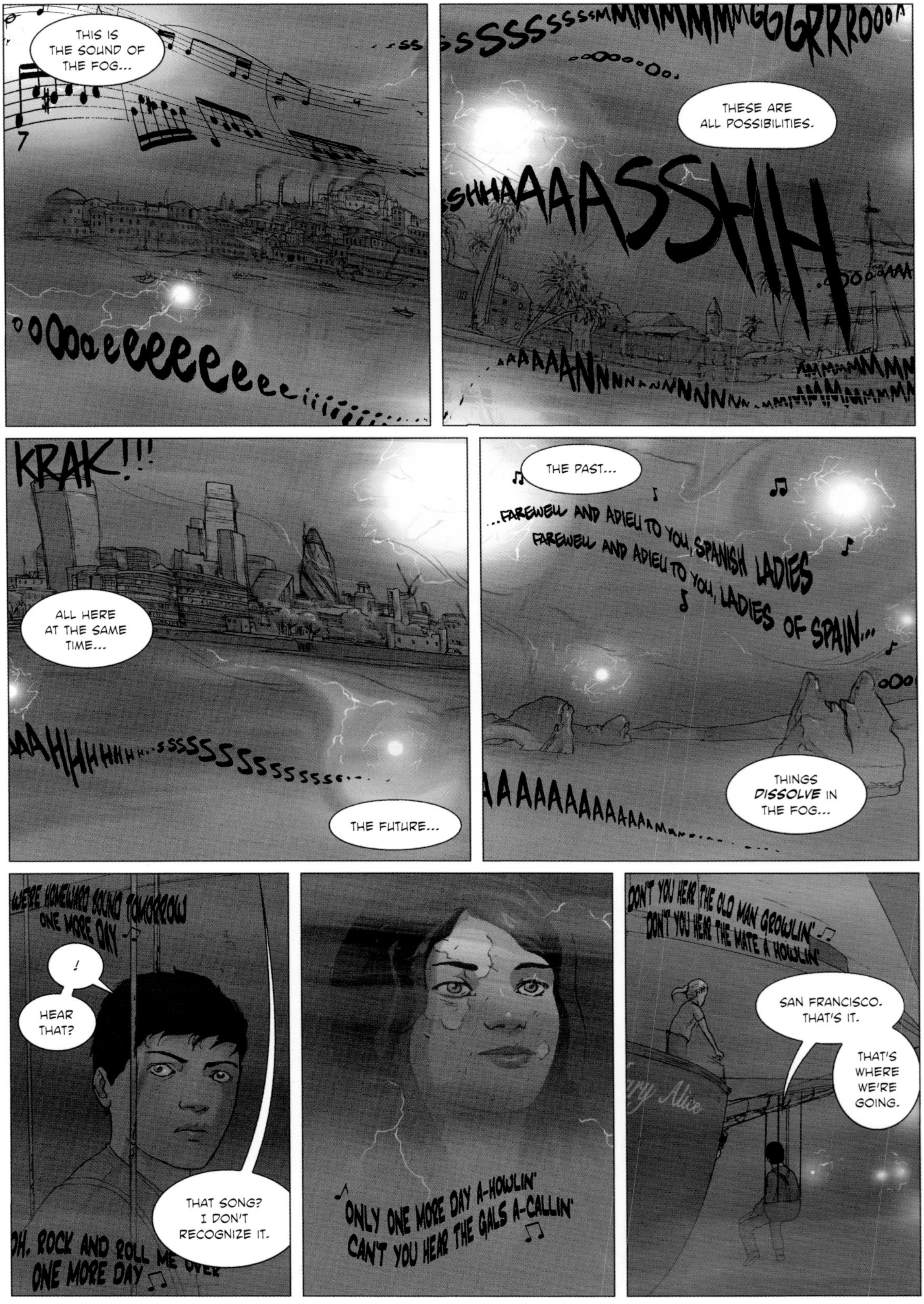
THIS IS THE SOUND OF THE FOG...
OOOaeeeeeeeeiiiiii
...SSSSSSSSSSMMMMMMMMGGRRROOOA
THESE ARE ALL POSSIBILITIES.
SHHAAAASSHH
..OOOOAAA
AAAANNNNNNNNN..MMMMMMMMMM
KRAK!!!
ALL HERE AT THE SAME TIME...
AAHHHHHH...SSSSSSSSSSSSSSS...
THE FUTURE...
THE PAST...
...FAREWELL AND ADIEU TO YOU, SPANISH LADIES
FAREWELL AND ADIEU TO YOU, LADIES OF SPAIN...
THINGS *DISSOLVE* IN THE FOG...
AAAAAAAAAAAAAAAAA...
WE'RE HOMEWARD BOUND TOMORROW
ONE MORE DAY
!
HEAR THAT?
THAT SONG? I DON'T RECOGNIZE IT.
OH, ROCK AND ROLL ME OVER
ONE MORE DAY
ONLY ONE MORE DAY A-HOWLIN'
CAN'T YOU HEAR THE GALS A-CALLIN'
DON'T YOU HEAR THE OLD MAN GROWLIN'
DON'T YOU HEAR THE MATE A HOWLIN'
SAN FRANCISCO. THAT'S IT.
THAT'S WHERE WE'RE GOING.

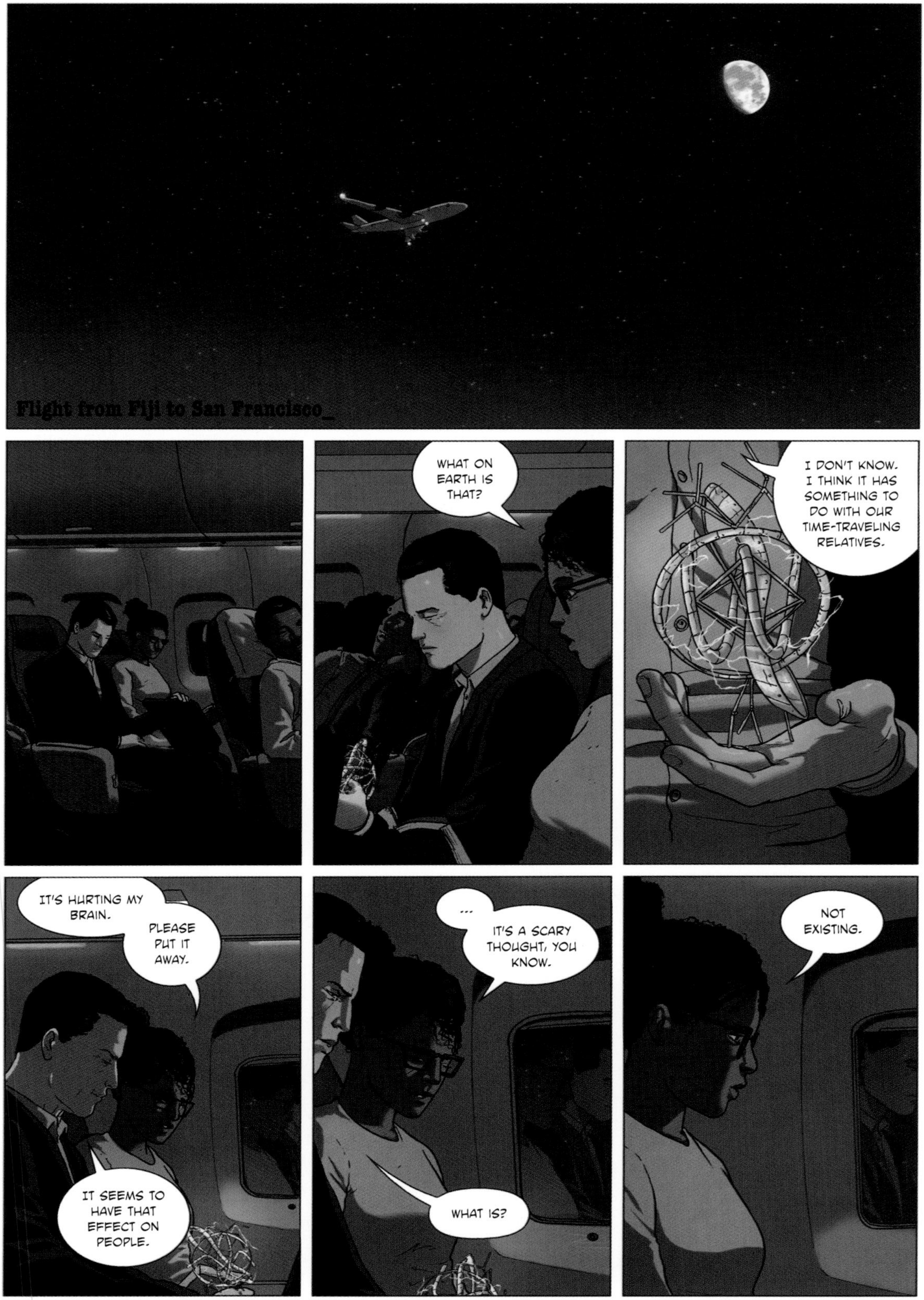
Flight from Fiji to San Francisco_
WHAT ON EARTH IS THAT?
I DON'T KNOW. I THINK IT HAS SOMETHING TO DO WITH OUR TIME-TRAVELING RELATIVES.
IT'S HURTING MY BRAIN.
PLEASE PUT IT AWAY.
IT SEEMS TO HAVE THAT EFFECT ON PEOPLE.
...
IT'S A SCARY THOUGHT, YOU KNOW.
WHAT IS?
NOT EXISTING.

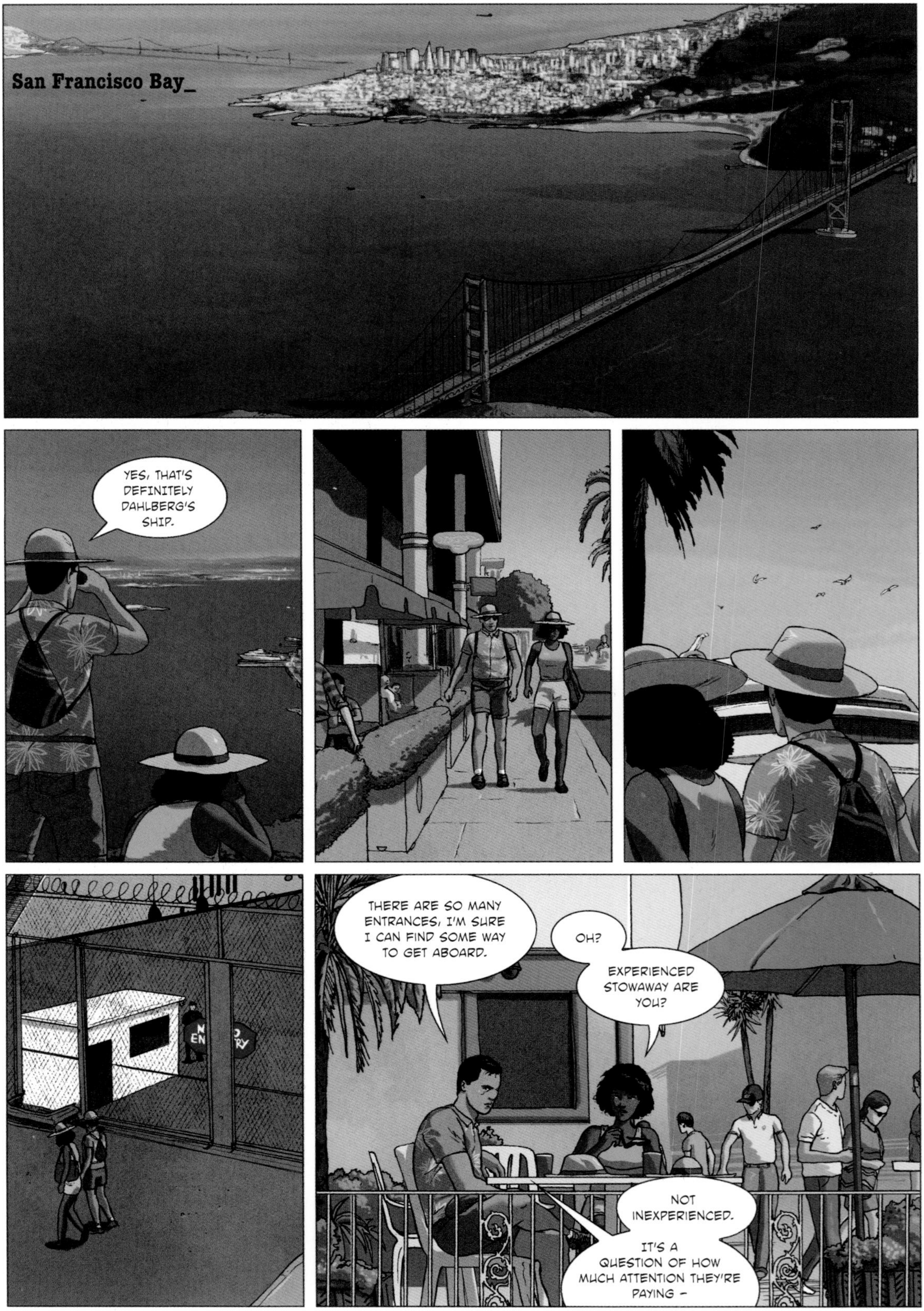
San Francisco Bay_
YES, THAT'S DEFINITELY DAHLBERG'S SHIP.
THERE ARE SO MANY ENTRANCES, I'M SURE I CAN FIND SOME WAY TO GET ABOARD.
OH?
EXPERIENCED STOWAWAY ARE YOU?
NOT INEXPERIENCED.
IT'S A QUESTION OF HOW MUCH ATTENTION THEY'RE PAYING –

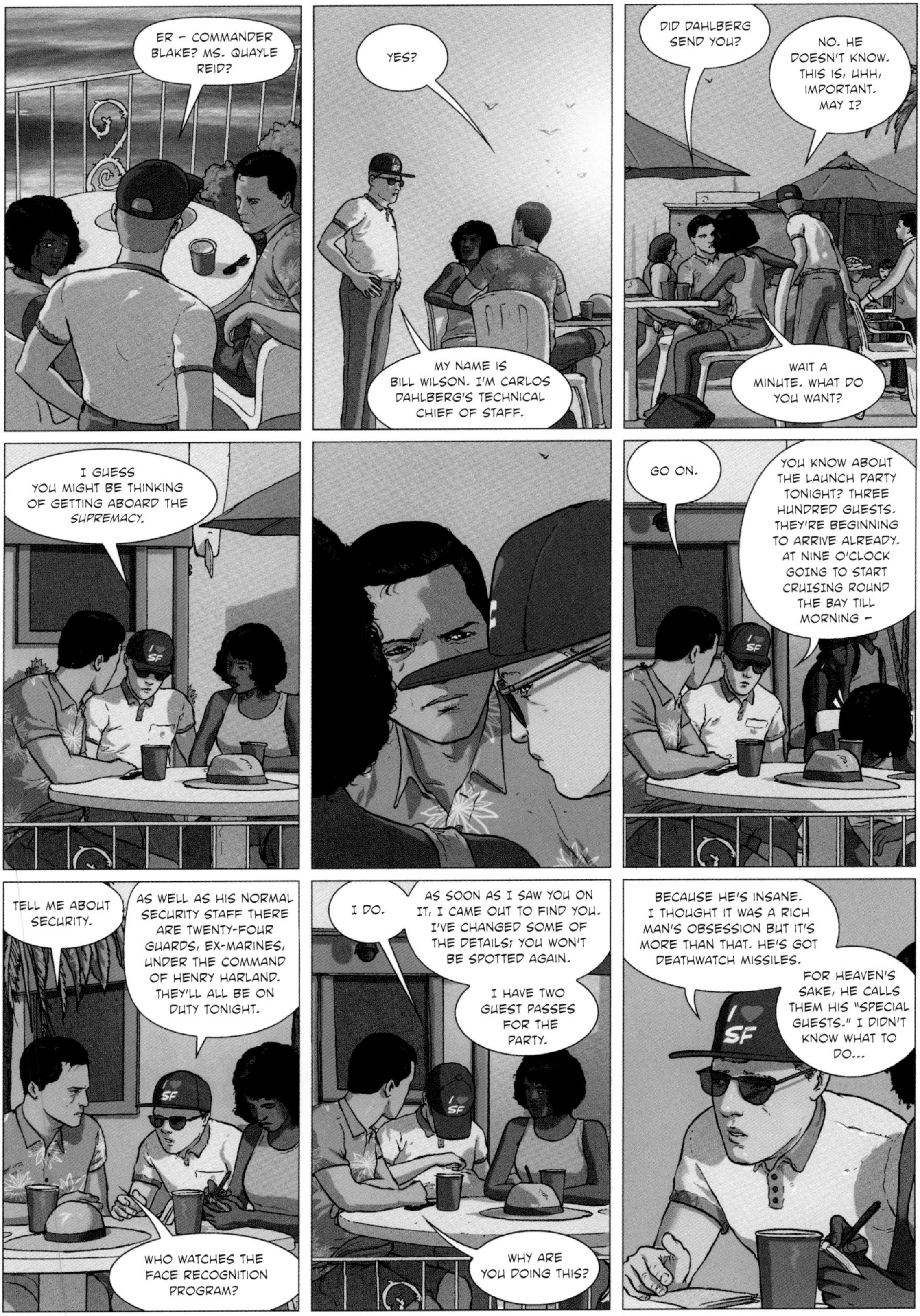
ER – COMMANDER BLAKE? MS. QUAYLE REID?
YES?
MY NAME IS BILL WILSON. I'M CARLOS DAHLBERG'S TECHNICAL CHIEF OF STAFF.
DID DAHLBERG SEND YOU?
NO. HE DOESN'T KNOW. THIS IS, UHH, IMPORTANT. MAY I?
WAIT A MINUTE. WHAT DO YOU WANT?
I GUESS YOU MIGHT BE THINKING OF GETTING ABOARD THE *SUPREMACY*.
GO ON.
YOU KNOW ABOUT THE LAUNCH PARTY TONIGHT? THREE HUNDRED GUESTS. THEY'RE BEGINNING TO ARRIVE ALREADY. AT NINE O'CLOCK GOING TO START CRUISING ROUND THE BAY TILL MORNING –
TELL ME ABOUT SECURITY.
AS WELL AS HIS NORMAL SECURITY STAFF THERE ARE TWENTY-FOUR GUARDS, EX-MARINES, UNDER THE COMMAND OF HENRY HARLAND. THEY'LL ALL BE ON DUTY TONIGHT.
WHO WATCHES THE FACE RECOGNITION PROGRAM?
I DO.
AS SOON AS I SAW YOU ON IT, I CAME OUT TO FIND YOU. I'VE CHANGED SOME OF THE DETAILS; YOU WON'T BE SPOTTED AGAIN.
I HAVE TWO GUEST PASSES FOR THE PARTY.
WHY ARE YOU DOING THIS?
BECAUSE HE'S INSANE. I THOUGHT IT WAS A RICH MAN'S OBSESSION BUT IT'S MORE THAN THAT. HE'S GOT DEATHWATCH MISSILES.
FOR HEAVEN'S SAKE, HE CALLS THEM HIS "SPECIAL GUESTS." I DIDN'T KNOW WHAT TO DO...

THERE ARE THREE TENDER DOCKS, A DOCK FOR THE SUBMARINE, AND TWO JET SKI DOCKS. IS THAT RIGHT?

YEAH, THAT'S IT.

WE'LL ARRIVE AT THE TENDER DOCK ON THE PORT SIDE AT NINE THIRTY. CAN YOU MAKE SURE IT'S OPEN FOR BUSINESS?

SURE, ABSOLUTELY.

WE KNOW NOTHING ABOUT YOU. YOU COULD BE SETTING A TRAP.

IF YOU DON'T TRUST ME, THEN I SUGGEST YOU GET AS FAR AWAY FROM HERE AS POSSIBLE. THAT'S WHAT'S I'M GOING TO DO.

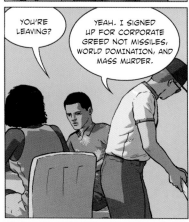

YOU'RE LEAVING?

YEAH. I SIGNED UP FOR CORPORATE GREED NOT MISSILES, WORLD DOMINATION, AND MASS MURDER.

DO YOU TRUST HIM? REALLY?

NOT REALLY, BUT THIS IS WHERE WE HAVE TO START TAKING RISKS.

LET'S GO AND RENT A BOAT.

AREN'T HER FOLKS IN FIJI?

THIS DON'T LOOK LIKE FIJI.

SEEMS OUR DEAR MARY ALICE HAS OTHER PLANS.

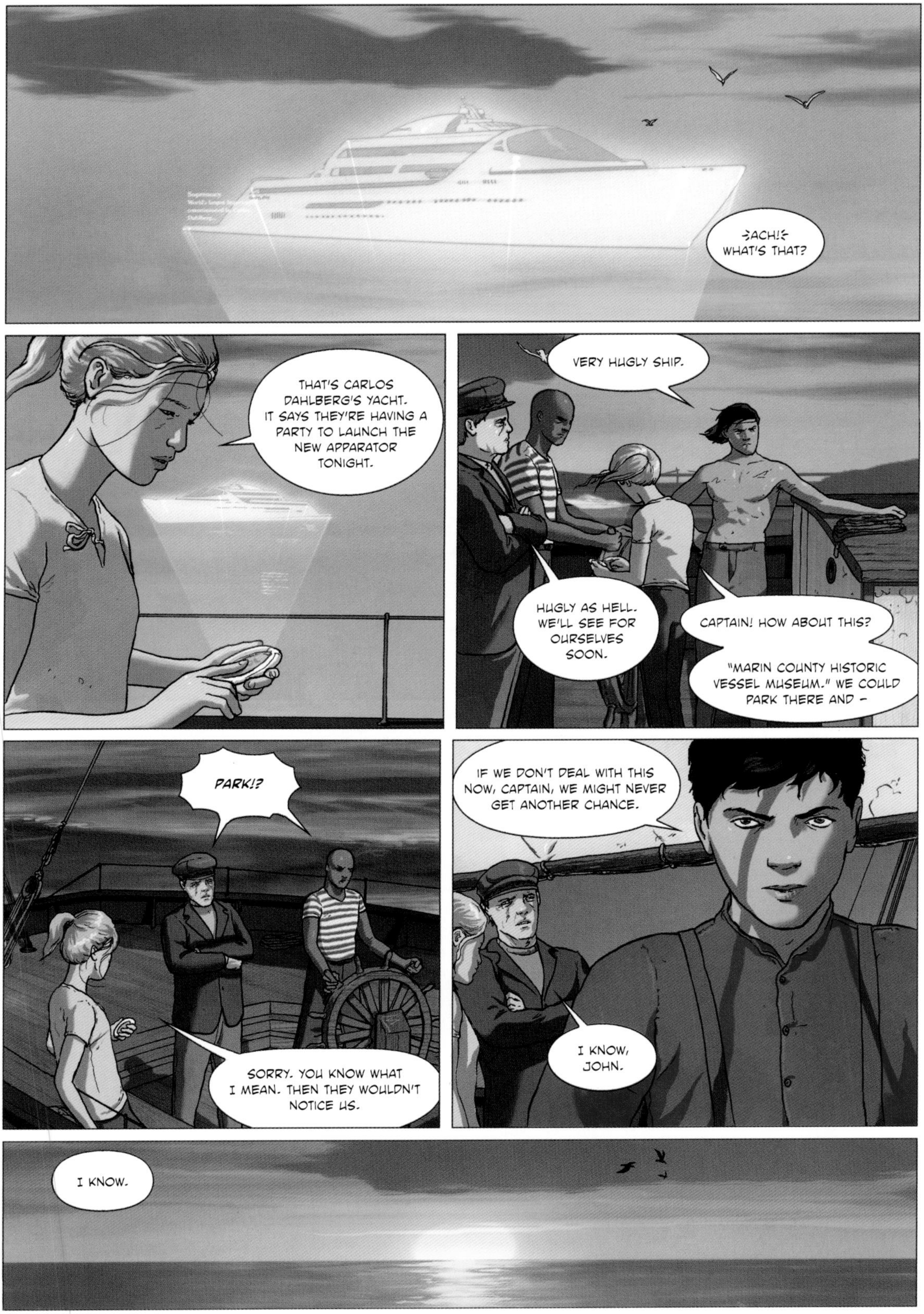

ACH!
WHAT'S THAT?
THAT'S CARLOS DAHLBERG'S YACHT. IT SAYS THEY'RE HAVING A PARTY TO LAUNCH THE NEW APPARATOR TONIGHT.
VERY HUGLY SHIP.
HUGLY AS HELL. WE'LL SEE FOR OURSELVES SOON.
CAPTAIN! HOW ABOUT THIS?
"MARIN COUNTY HISTORIC VESSEL MUSEUM." WE COULD PARK THERE AND –
PARK!?
SORRY. YOU KNOW WHAT I MEAN. THEN THEY WOULDN'T NOTICE US.
IF WE DON'T DEAL WITH THIS NOW, CAPTAIN, WE MIGHT NEVER GET ANOTHER CHANCE.
I KNOW, JOHN.
I KNOW.

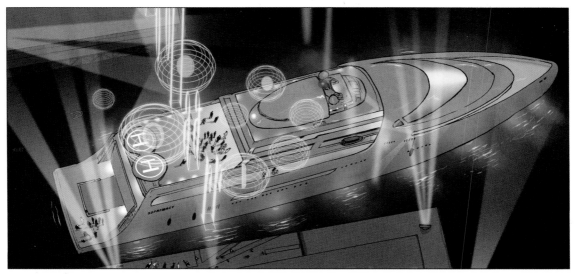

THE APPARATOR SOLAR IS THE MOST ADVANCED SMART DEVICE IN THE WORLD.

WITH FOUR TIMES THE POWER OF ITS PREDECESSORS, AND THE LATEST VERSION OF OUR AWARD-WINNING DAHLBERG OPERATING SYSTEM, THE SOLAR WILL BE THE CENTER OF YOUR LIFE.

BOOP BOOP BOOP

YES?

SIR, WE'VE GOT SOMETHING.

IT HAD BETTER BE GOOD.

APPARATOR 45378GAMMA REGISTERED TO SERENA HENDERSON HAS JUST SYNCED WITH THE NETWORK.

AND WHERE ARE THEY?

THEY'RE RIGHT HERE, SIR.

IN SAN FRANCISCO BAY.

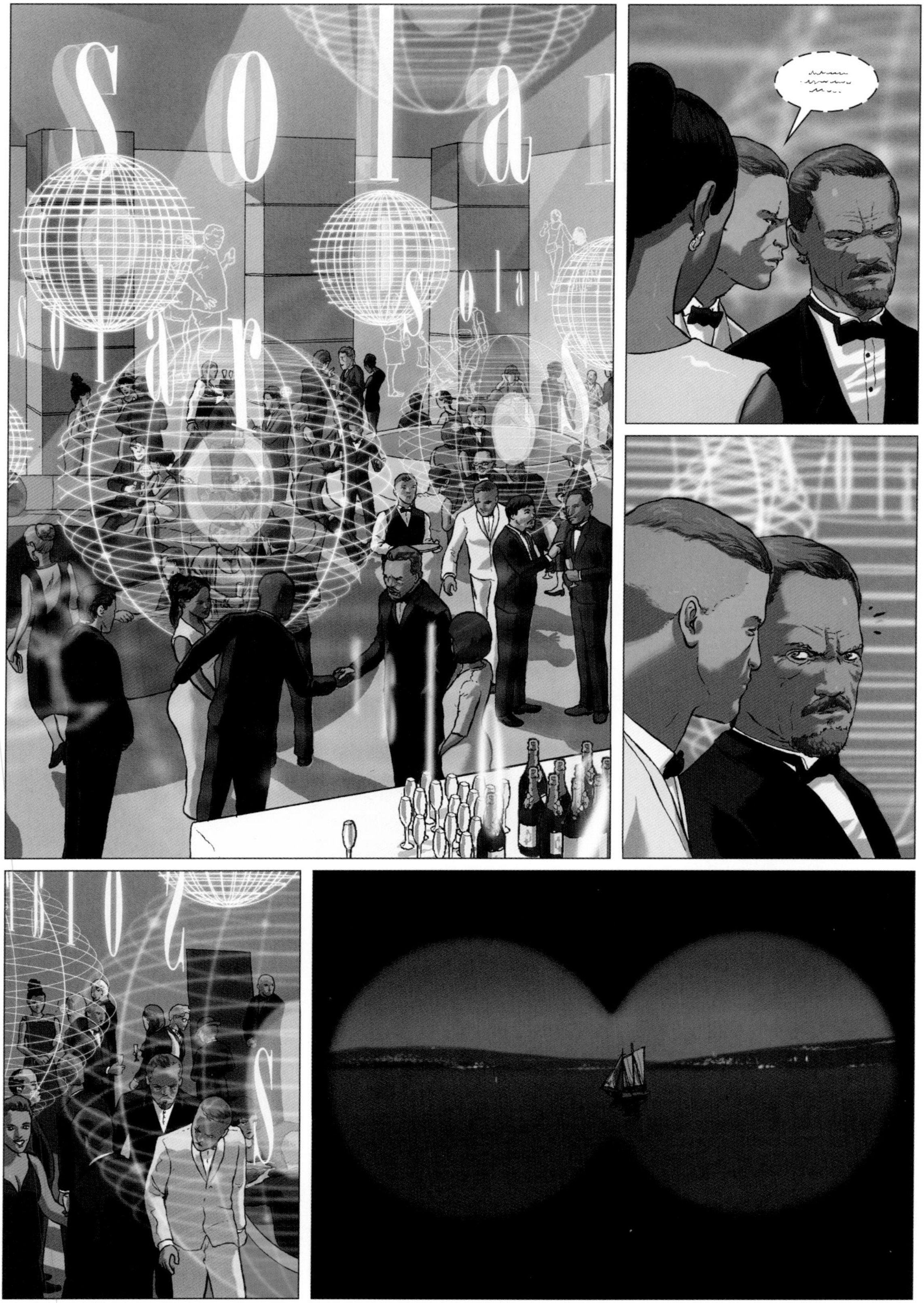

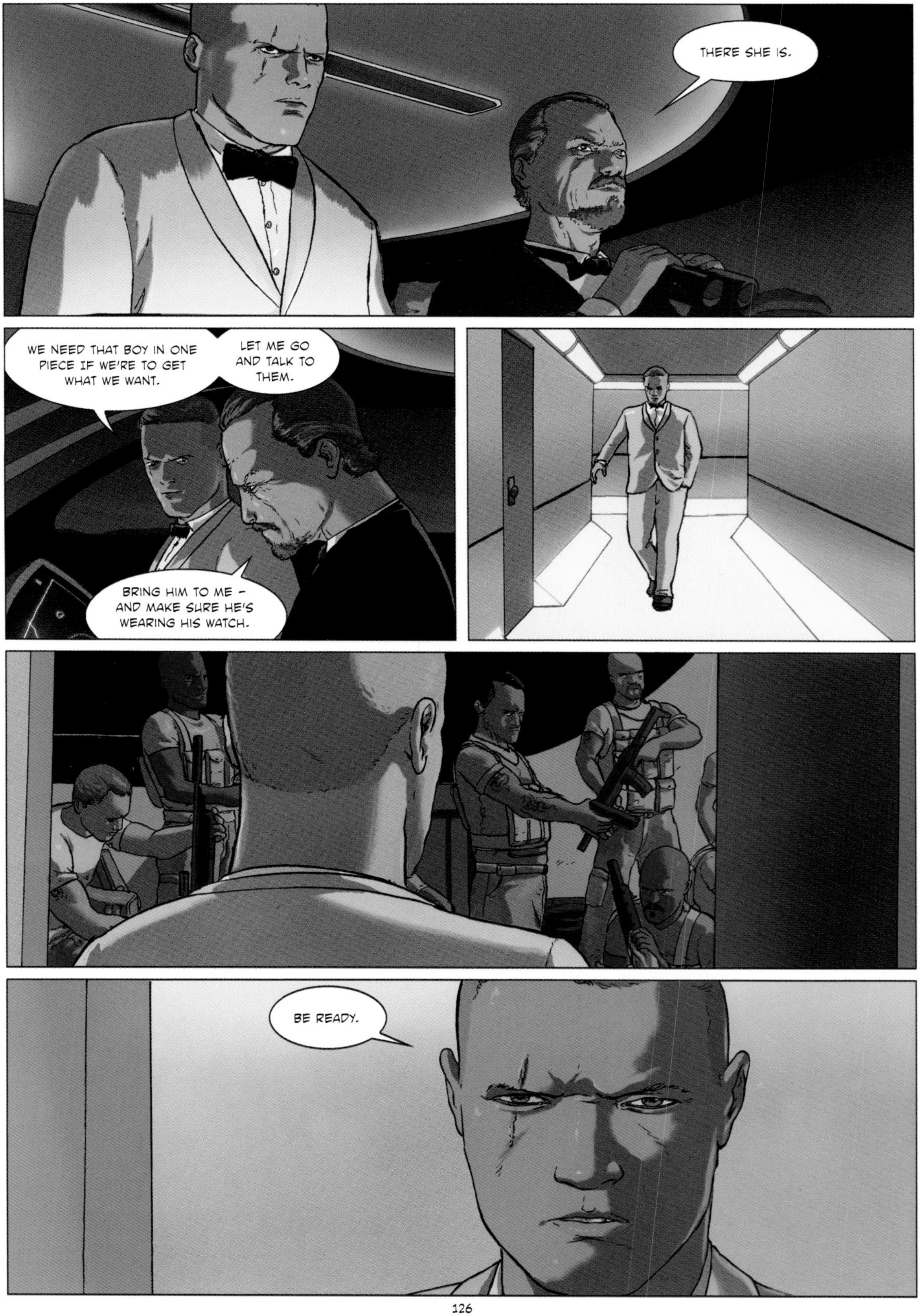
THERE SHE IS.
WE NEED THAT BOY IN ONE PIECE IF WE'RE TO GET WHAT WE WANT.
LET ME GO AND TALK TO THEM.
BRING HIM TO ME – AND MAKE SURE HE'S WEARING HIS WATCH.
BE READY.

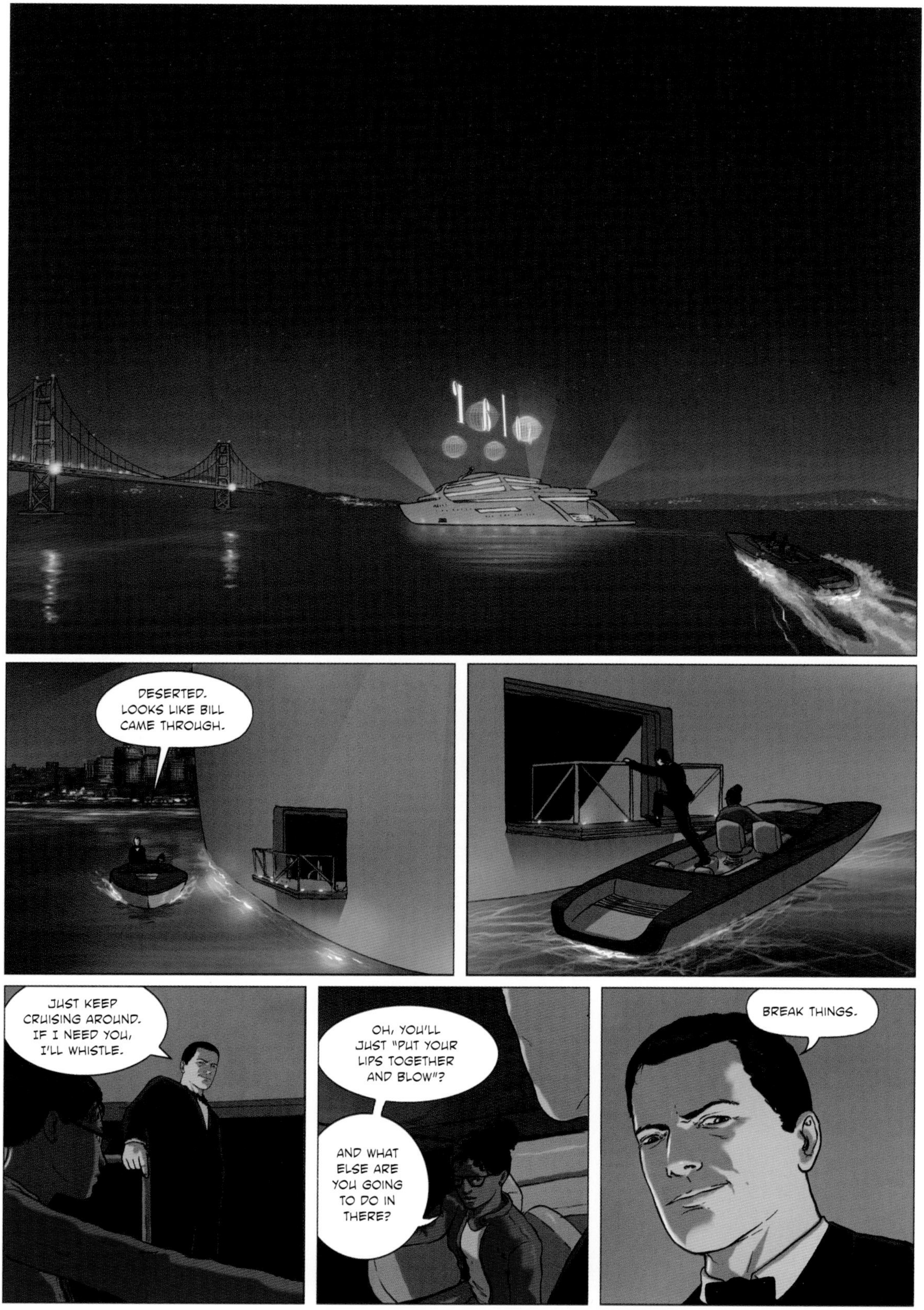
DESERTED. LOOKS LIKE BILL CAME THROUGH.
JUST KEEP CRUISING AROUND. IF I NEED YOU, I'LL WHISTLE.
OH, YOU'LL JUST "PUT YOUR LIPS TOGETHER AND BLOW"?
AND WHAT ELSE ARE YOU GOING TO DO IN THERE?
BREAK THINGS.

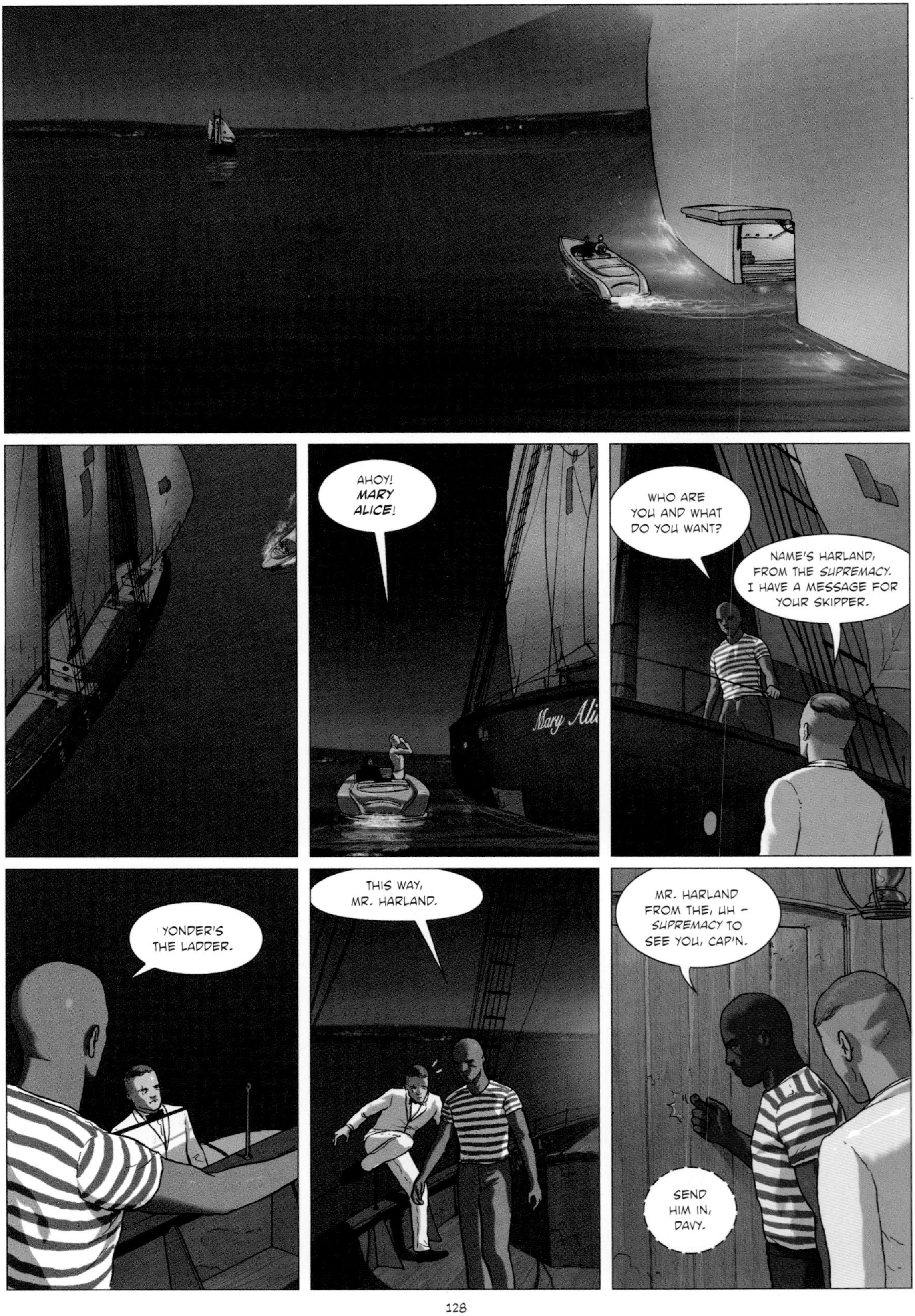
AHOY! *MARY ALICE*!
Mary Alice
WHO ARE YOU AND WHAT DO YOU WANT?
NAME'S HARLAND, FROM THE *SUPREMACY*. I HAVE A MESSAGE FOR YOUR SKIPPER.
YONDER'S THE LADDER.
THIS WAY, MR. HARLAND.
MR. HARLAND FROM THE, UH – *SUPREMACY* TO SEE YOU, CAP'N.
SEND HIM IN, DAVY.

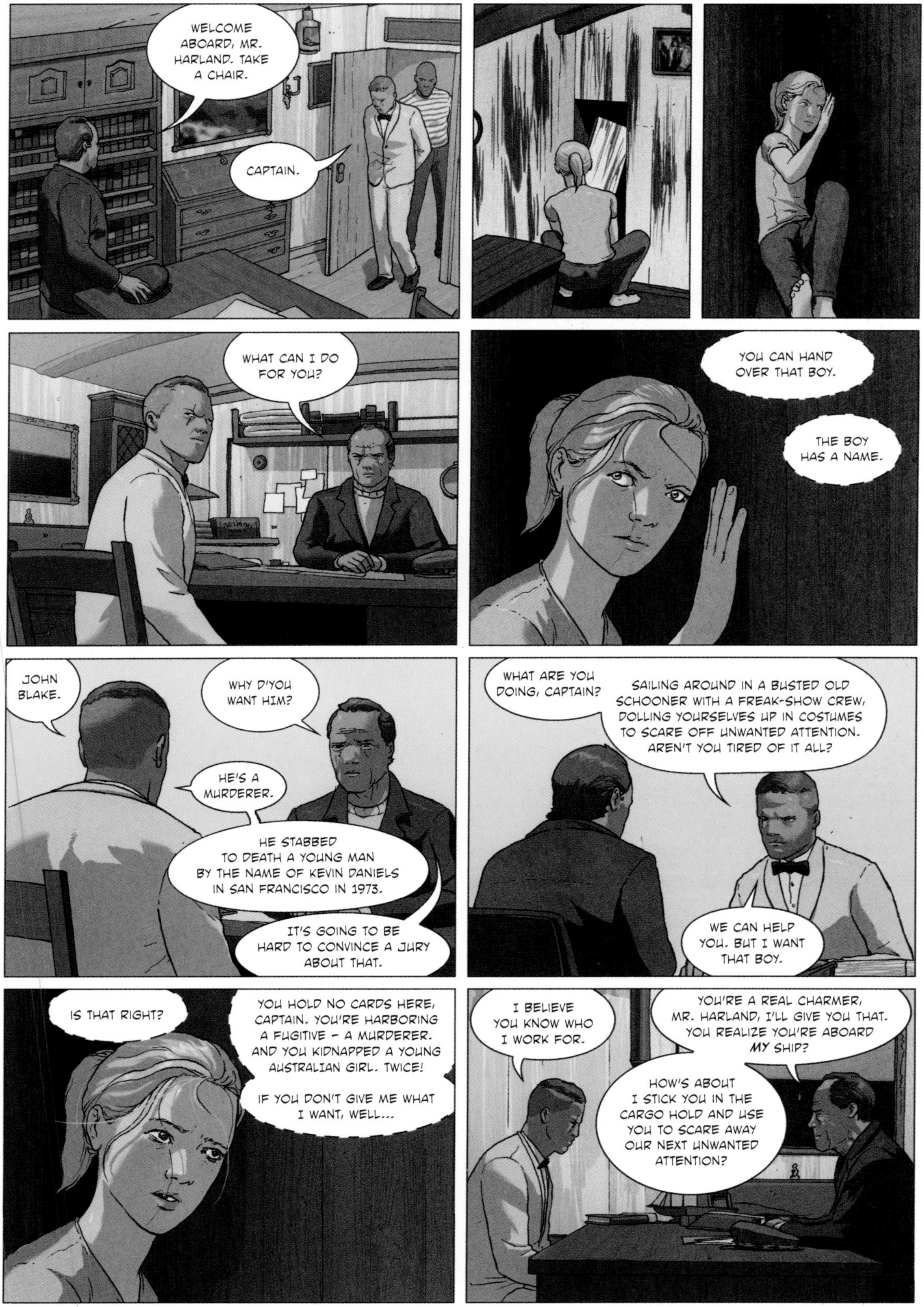
WELCOME ABOARD, MR. HARLAND. TAKE A CHAIR.
CAPTAIN.
WHAT CAN I DO FOR YOU?
YOU CAN HAND OVER THAT BOY.
THE BOY HAS A NAME.
JOHN BLAKE.
WHY D'YOU WANT HIM?
HE'S A MURDERER.
HE STABBED TO DEATH A YOUNG MAN BY THE NAME OF KEVIN DANIELS IN SAN FRANCISCO IN 1973.
IT'S GOING TO BE HARD TO CONVINCE A JURY ABOUT THAT.
WHAT ARE YOU DOING, CAPTAIN?
SAILING AROUND IN A BUSTED OLD SCHOONER WITH A FREAK-SHOW CREW, DOLLING YOURSELVES UP IN COSTUMES TO SCARE OFF UNWANTED ATTENTION. AREN'T YOU TIRED OF IT ALL?
WE CAN HELP YOU. BUT I WANT THAT BOY.
IS THAT RIGHT?
YOU HOLD NO CARDS HERE, CAPTAIN. YOU'RE HARBORING A FUGITIVE – A MURDERER. AND YOU KIDNAPPED A YOUNG AUSTRALIAN GIRL. TWICE!
IF YOU DON'T GIVE ME WHAT I WANT, WELL...
I BELIEVE YOU KNOW WHO I WORK FOR.
YOU'RE A REAL CHARMER, MR. HARLAND, I'LL GIVE YOU THAT. YOU REALIZE YOU'RE ABOARD MY SHIP?
HOW'S ABOUT I STICK YOU IN THE CARGO HOLD AND USE YOU TO SCARE AWAY OUR NEXT UNWANTED ATTENTION?

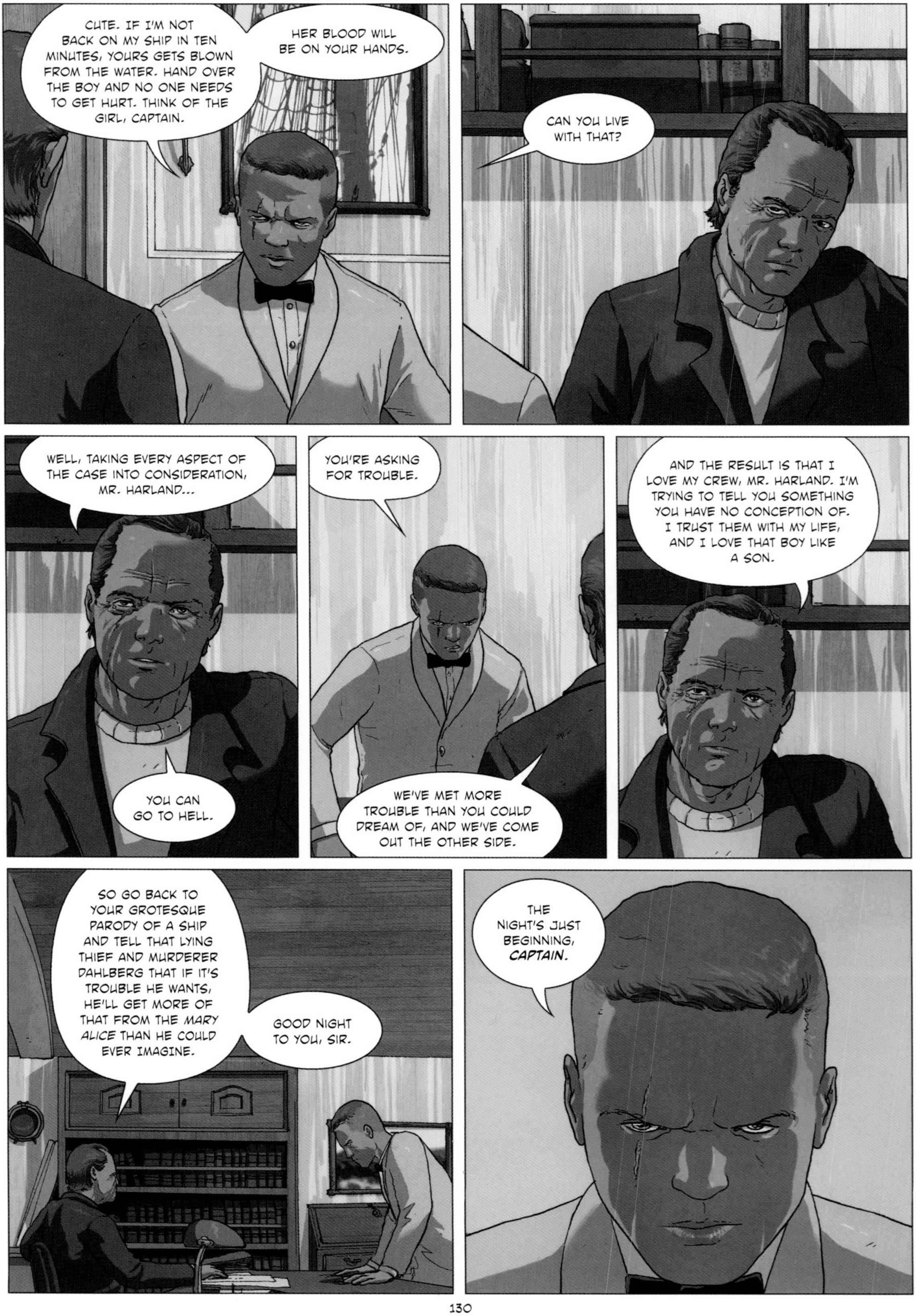
CUTE. IF I'M NOT BACK ON MY SHIP IN TEN MINUTES, YOURS GETS BLOWN FROM THE WATER. HAND OVER THE BOY AND NO ONE NEEDS TO GET HURT. THINK OF THE GIRL, CAPTAIN.
HER BLOOD WILL BE ON YOUR HANDS.
CAN YOU LIVE WITH THAT?
WELL, TAKING EVERY ASPECT OF THE CASE INTO CONSIDERATION, MR. HARLAND...
YOU CAN GO TO HELL.
YOU'RE ASKING FOR TROUBLE.
WE'VE MET MORE TROUBLE THAN YOU COULD DREAM OF, AND WE'VE COME OUT THE OTHER SIDE.
AND THE RESULT IS THAT I LOVE MY CREW, MR. HARLAND. I'M TRYING TO TELL YOU SOMETHING YOU HAVE NO CONCEPTION OF. I TRUST THEM WITH MY LIFE, AND I LOVE THAT BOY LIKE A SON.
SO GO BACK TO YOUR GROTESQUE PARODY OF A SHIP AND TELL THAT LYING THIEF AND MURDERER DAHLBERG THAT IF IT'S TROUBLE HE WANTS, HE'LL GET MORE OF THAT FROM THE *MARY ALICE* THAN HE COULD EVER IMAGINE.
GOOD NIGHT TO YOU, SIR.
THE NIGHT'S JUST BEGINNING, ***CAPTAIN.***

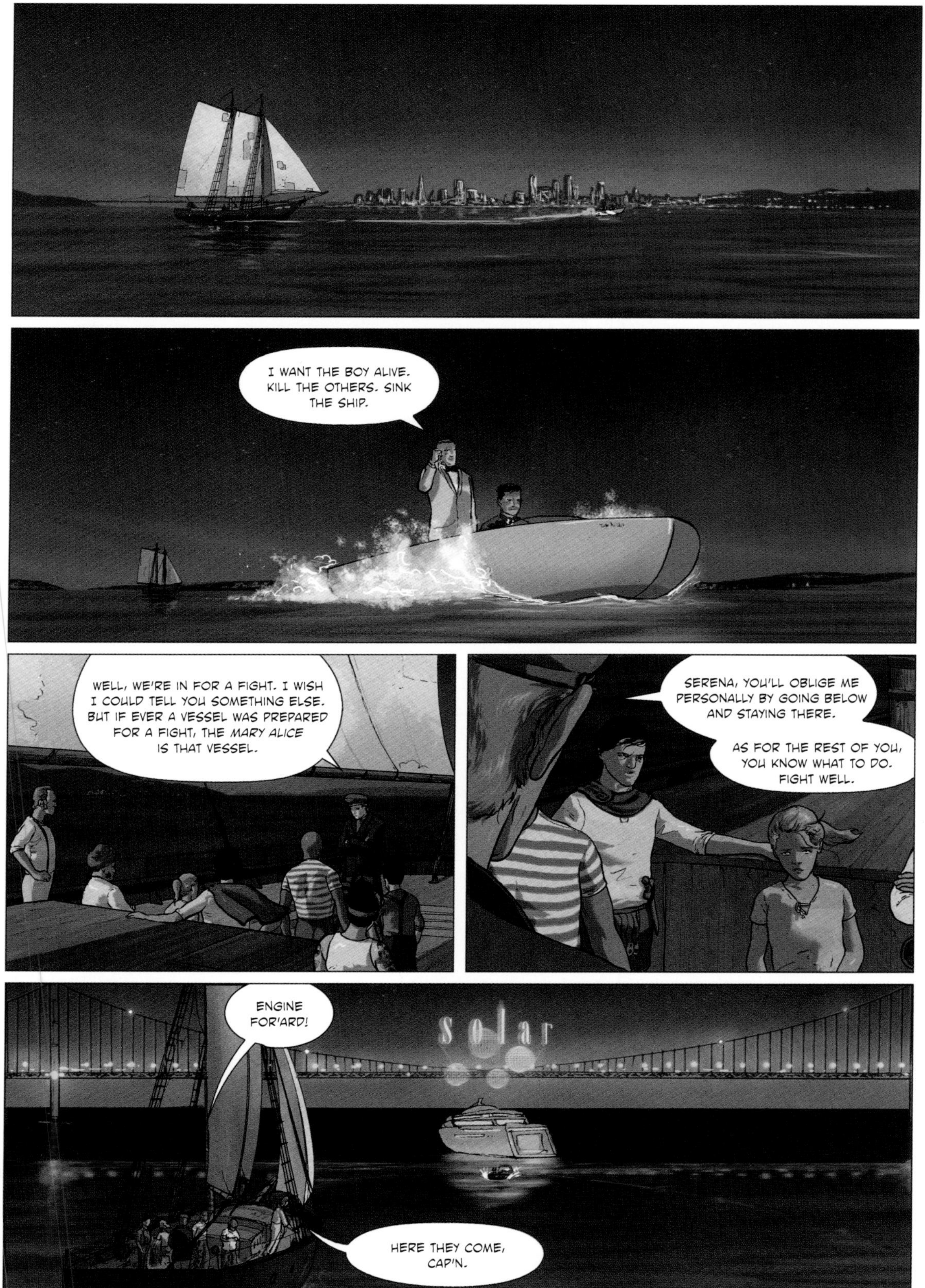
I WANT THE BOY ALIVE. KILL THE OTHERS. SINK THE SHIP.
WELL, WE'RE IN FOR A FIGHT. I WISH I COULD TELL YOU SOMETHING ELSE. BUT IF EVER A VESSEL WAS PREPARED FOR A FIGHT, THE *MARY ALICE* IS THAT VESSEL.
SERENA, YOU'LL OBLIGE ME PERSONALLY BY GOING BELOW AND STAYING THERE.
AS FOR THE REST OF YOU, YOU KNOW WHAT TO DO. FIGHT WELL.
solar
ENGINE FOR'ARD!
HERE THEY COME, CAP'N.

CAN'T SEE ANY CREW, SIR —

THIS IS THE HAUNTED SHIP, AIN'T IT?

STOW THAT. GET ABOARD.

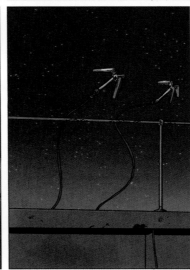

WHAT THE... MY HANDS ARE STUCK!

THE RAIL'S BEEN GLUED!

UH-OH —

BBLLBB-HHLLPP-BBLLBB —

SARGE! UP THIS WAY!

LOOKS CLEAR.

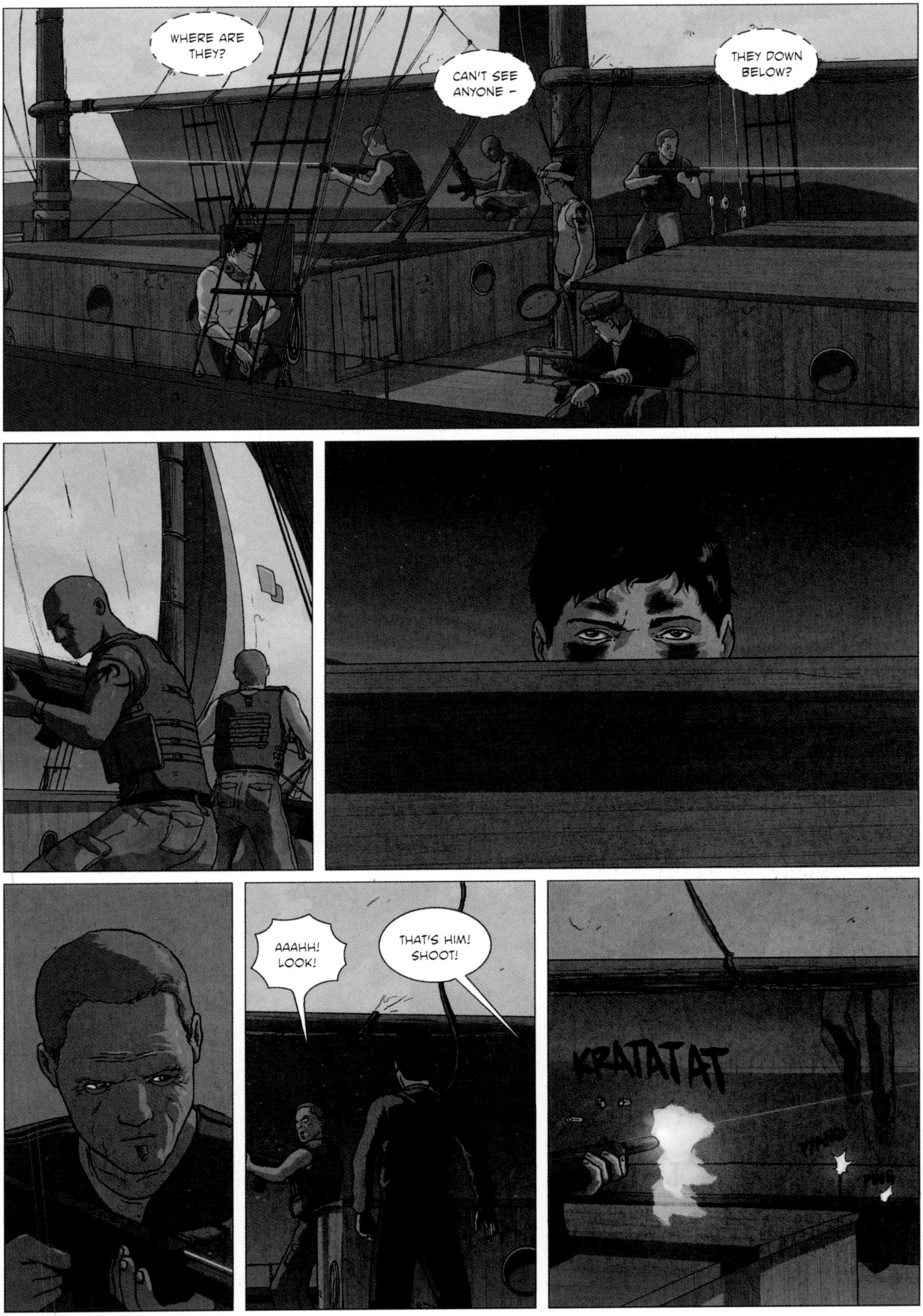
WHERE ARE THEY?
CAN'T SEE ANYONE –
THEY DOWN BELOW?
AAAHH! LOOK!
THAT'S HIM! SHOOT!
KRATATAT

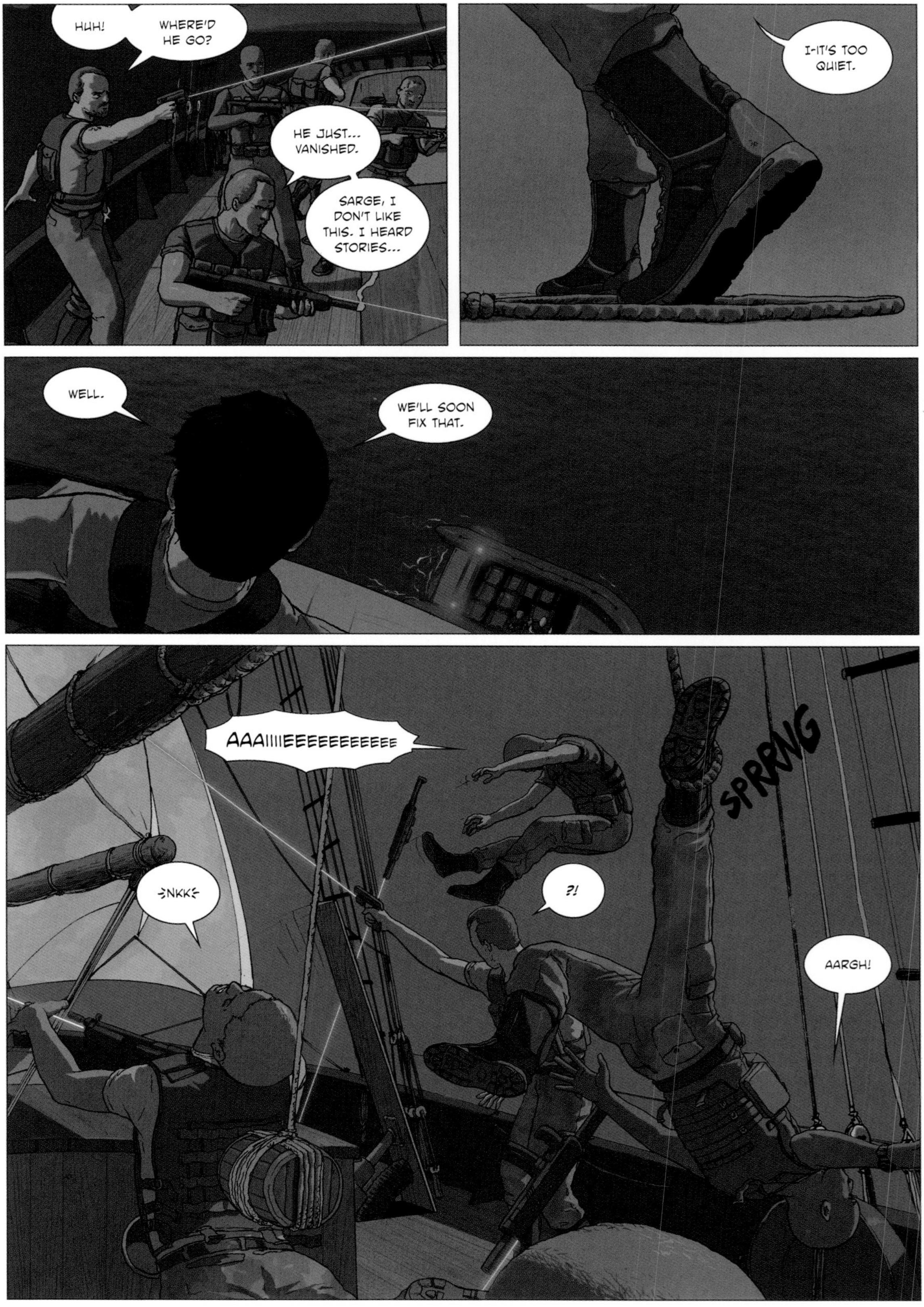
HUH!
WHERE'D HE GO?
HE JUST... VANISHED.
SARGE, I DON'T LIKE THIS. I HEARD STORIES...
I-IT'S TOO QUIET.
WELL.
WE'LL SOON FIX THAT.
AAAIIIIIEEEEEEEEEEEE
SPRRNG
NKK
?!
AARGH!

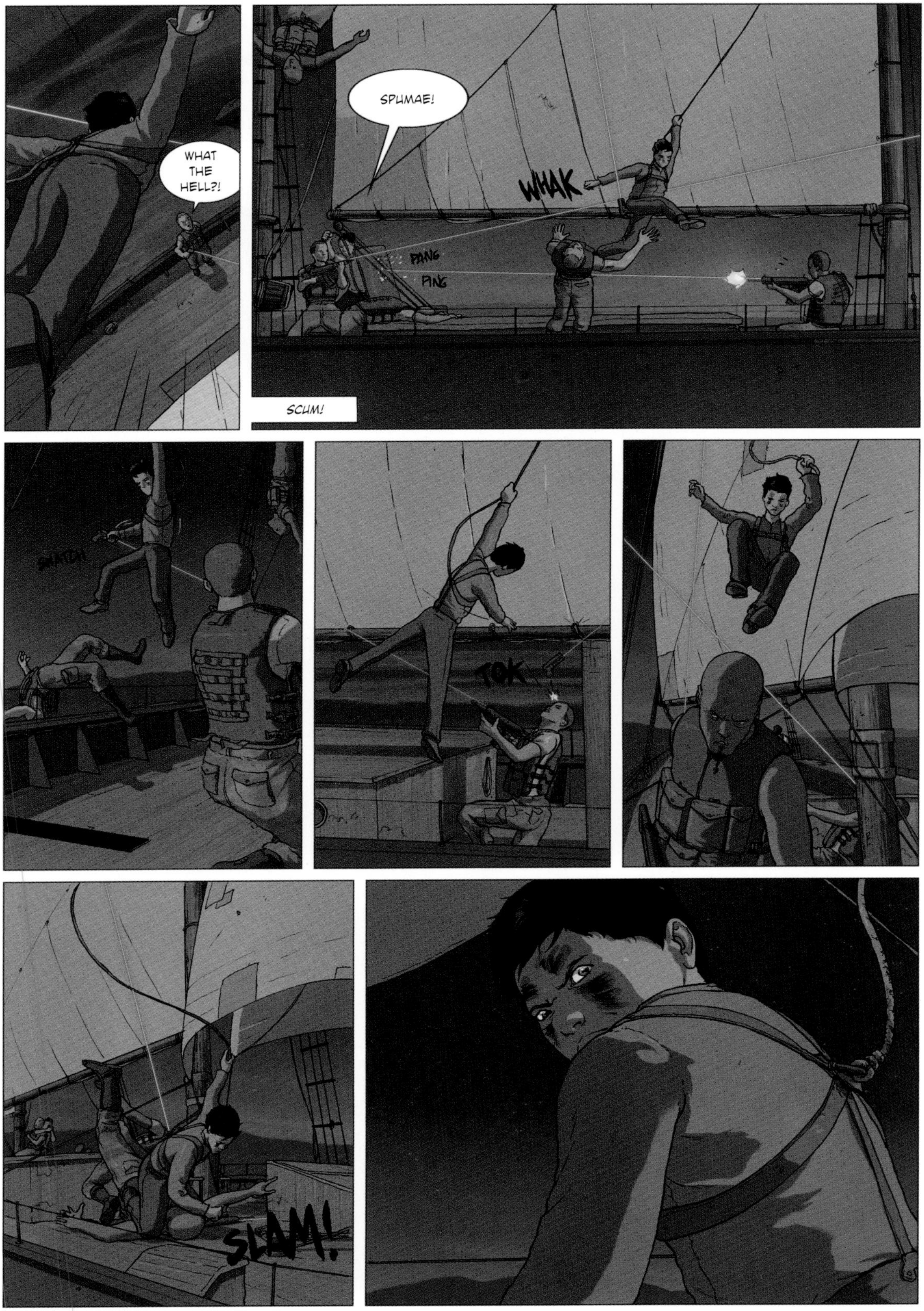
WHAT THE HELL?!
SPUMAE!
WHAK
PANG
PING
SCUM!
TOK
SLAM!

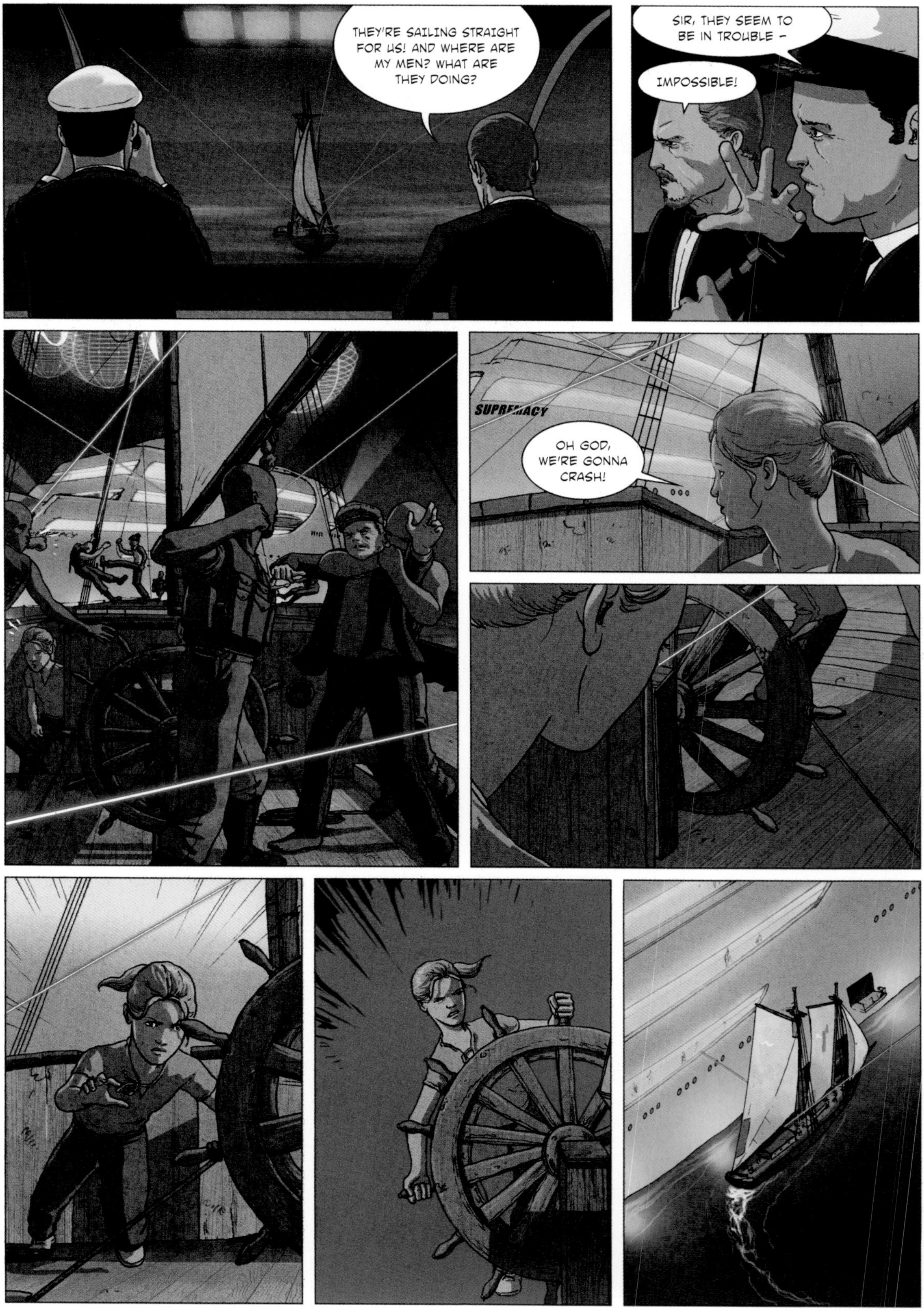
THEY'RE SAILING STRAIGHT FOR US! AND WHERE ARE MY MEN? WHAT ARE THEY DOING?
SIR, THEY SEEM TO BE IN TROUBLE –
IMPOSSIBLE!
SUPREMACY
OH GOD, WE'RE GONNA CRASH!

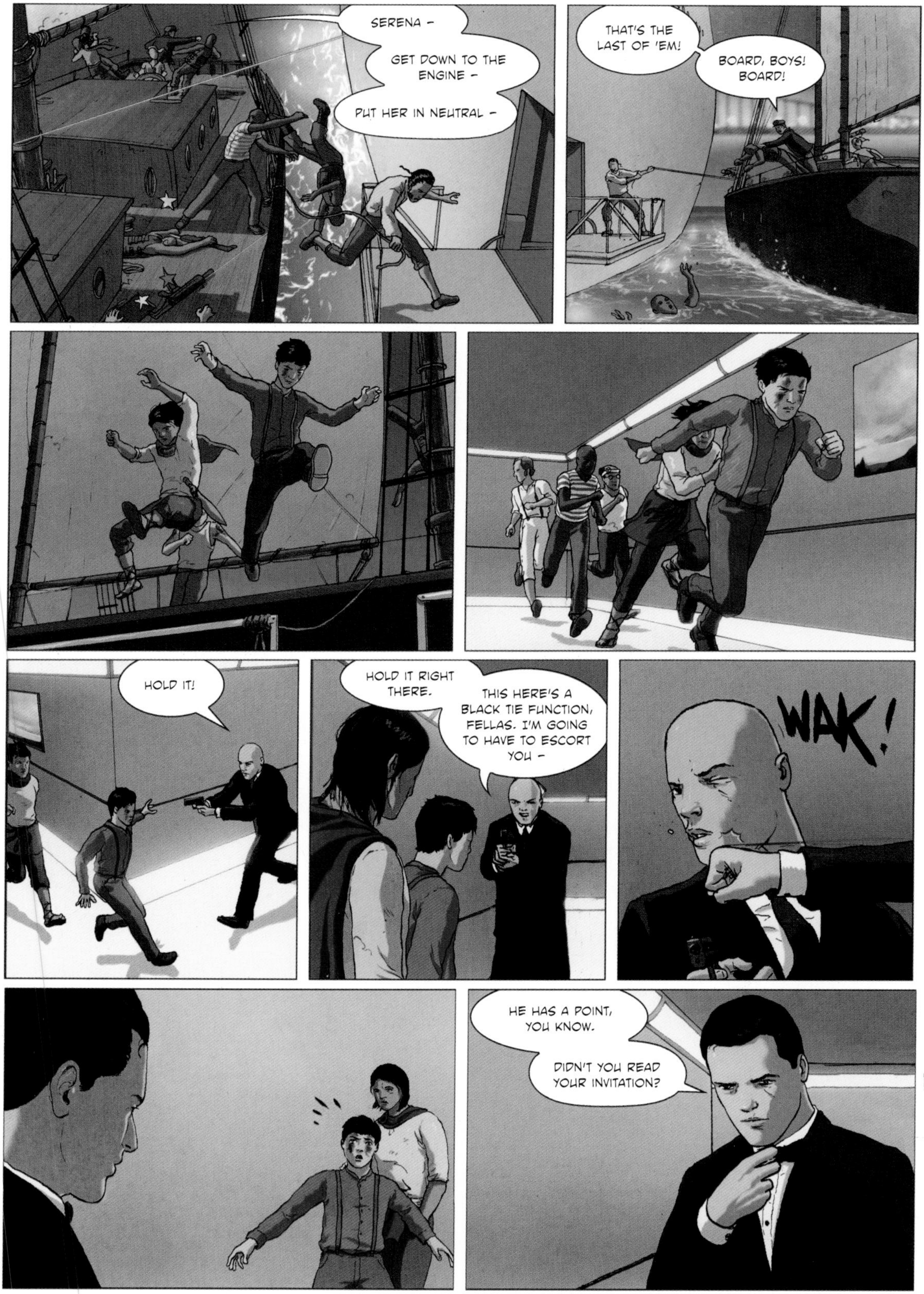
SERENA –
GET DOWN TO THE ENGINE –
PUT HER IN NEUTRAL –
THAT'S THE LAST OF 'EM!
BOARD, BOYS! BOARD!
HOLD IT!
HOLD IT RIGHT THERE.
THIS HERE'S A BLACK TIE FUNCTION, FELLAS. I'M GOING TO HAVE TO ESCORT YOU –
WAK!
HE HAS A POINT, YOU KNOW.
DIDN'T YOU READ YOUR INVITATION?

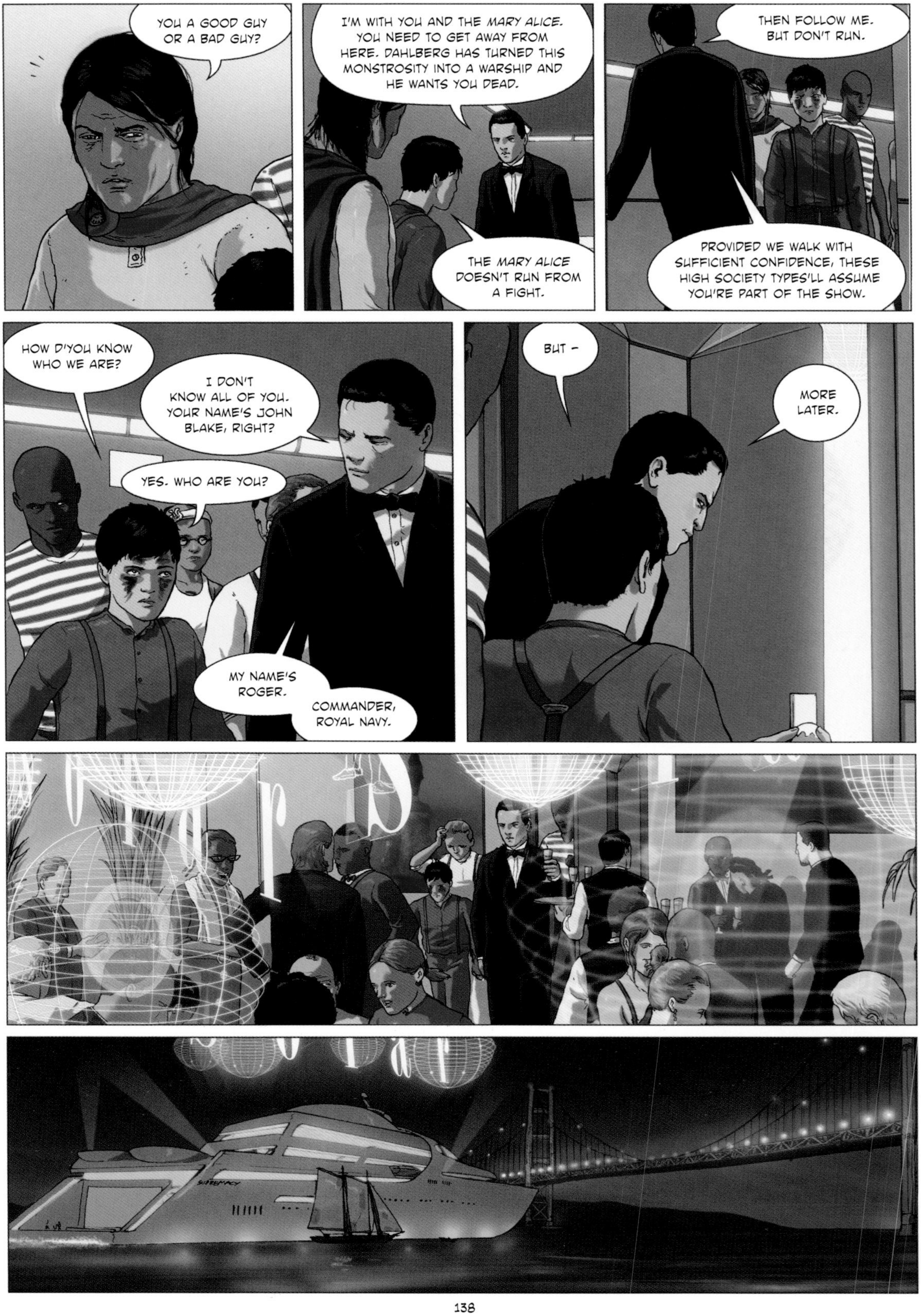
YOU A GOOD GUY OR A BAD GUY?
I'M WITH YOU AND THE *MARY ALICE*. YOU NEED TO GET AWAY FROM HERE. DAHLBERG HAS TURNED THIS MONSTROSITY INTO A WARSHIP AND HE WANTS YOU DEAD.
THE *MARY ALICE* DOESN'T RUN FROM A FIGHT.
THEN FOLLOW ME. BUT DON'T RUN.
PROVIDED WE WALK WITH SUFFICIENT CONFIDENCE, THESE HIGH SOCIETY TYPES'LL ASSUME YOU'RE PART OF THE SHOW.
HOW D'YOU KNOW WHO WE ARE?
I DON'T KNOW ALL OF YOU. YOUR NAME'S JOHN BLAKE, RIGHT?
YES. WHO ARE YOU?
MY NAME'S ROGER.
COMMANDER, ROYAL NAVY.
BUT –
MORE LATER.

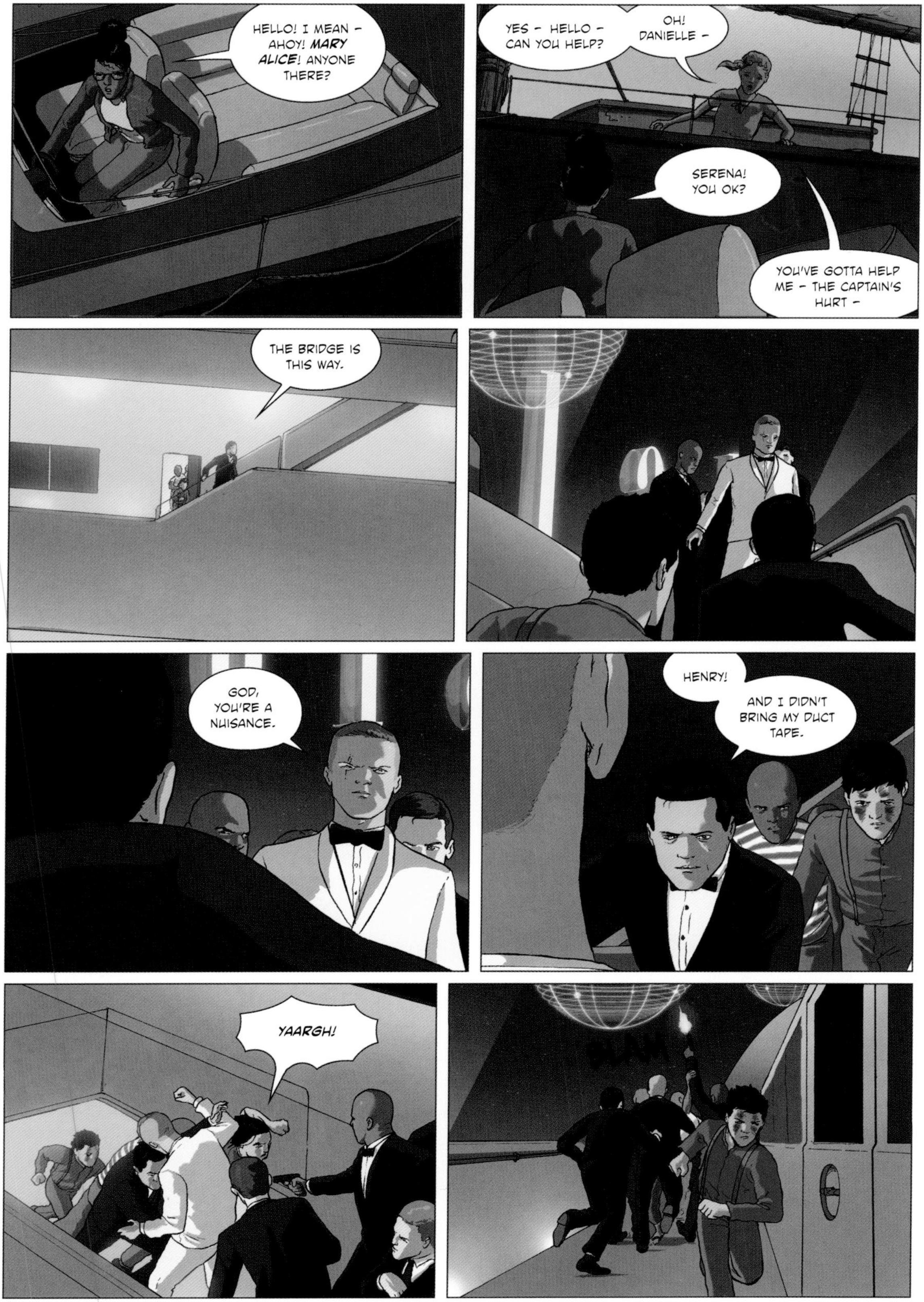
HELLO! I MEAN – AHOY! **MARY ALICE**! ANYONE THERE?
YES – HELLO – CAN YOU HELP?
OH! DANIELLE –
SERENA! YOU OK?
YOU'VE GOTTA HELP ME – THE CAPTAIN'S HURT –
THE BRIDGE IS THIS WAY.
GOD, YOU'RE A NUISANCE.
HENRY!
AND I DIDN'T BRING MY DUCT TAPE.
YAARGH!

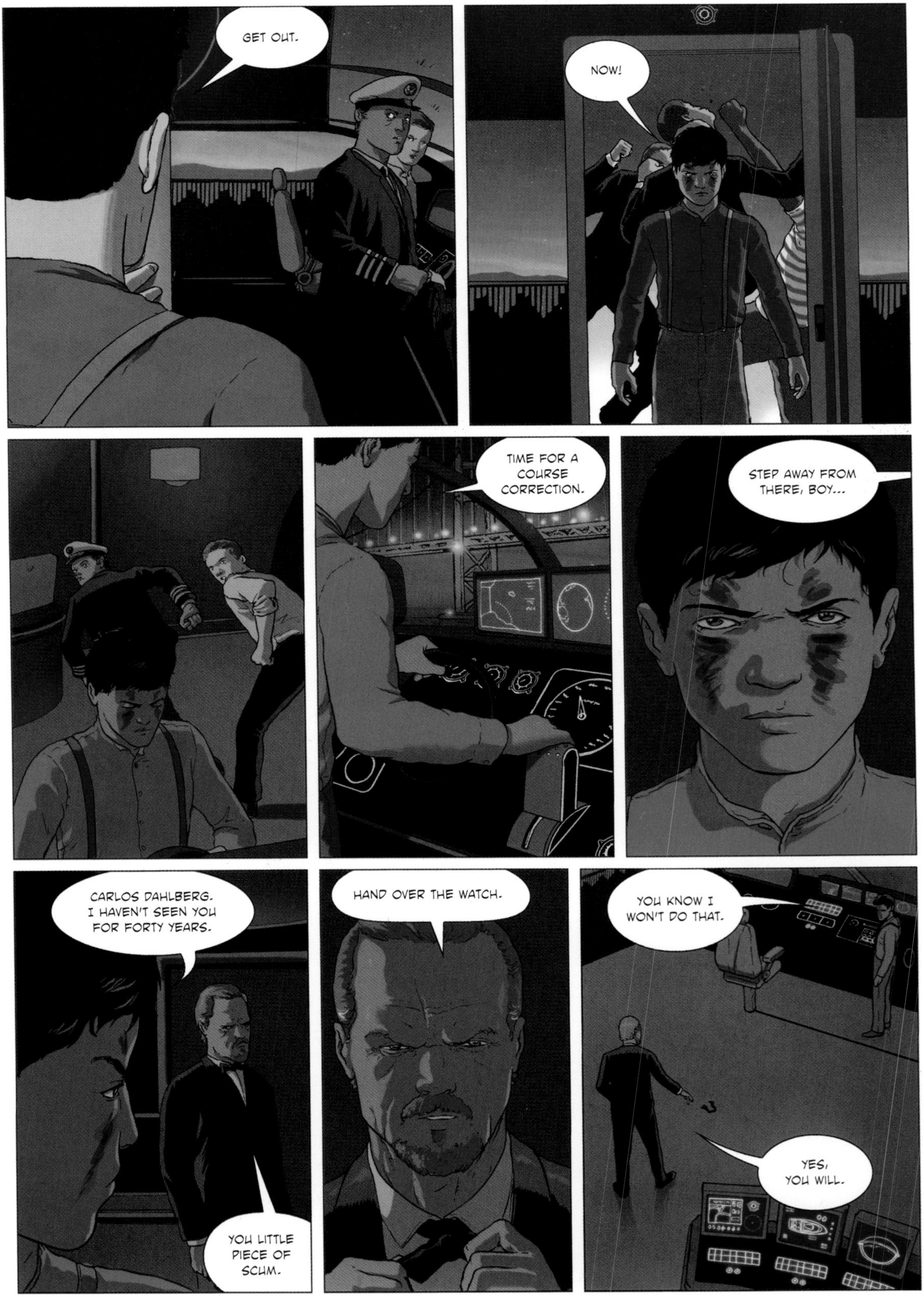
GET OUT.
NOW!
TIME FOR A COURSE CORRECTION.
STEP AWAY FROM THERE, BOY...
CARLOS DAHLBERG. I HAVEN'T SEEN YOU FOR FORTY YEARS.
YOU LITTLE PIECE OF SCUM.
HAND OVER THE WATCH.
YOU KNOW I WON'T DO THAT.
YES, YOU WILL.

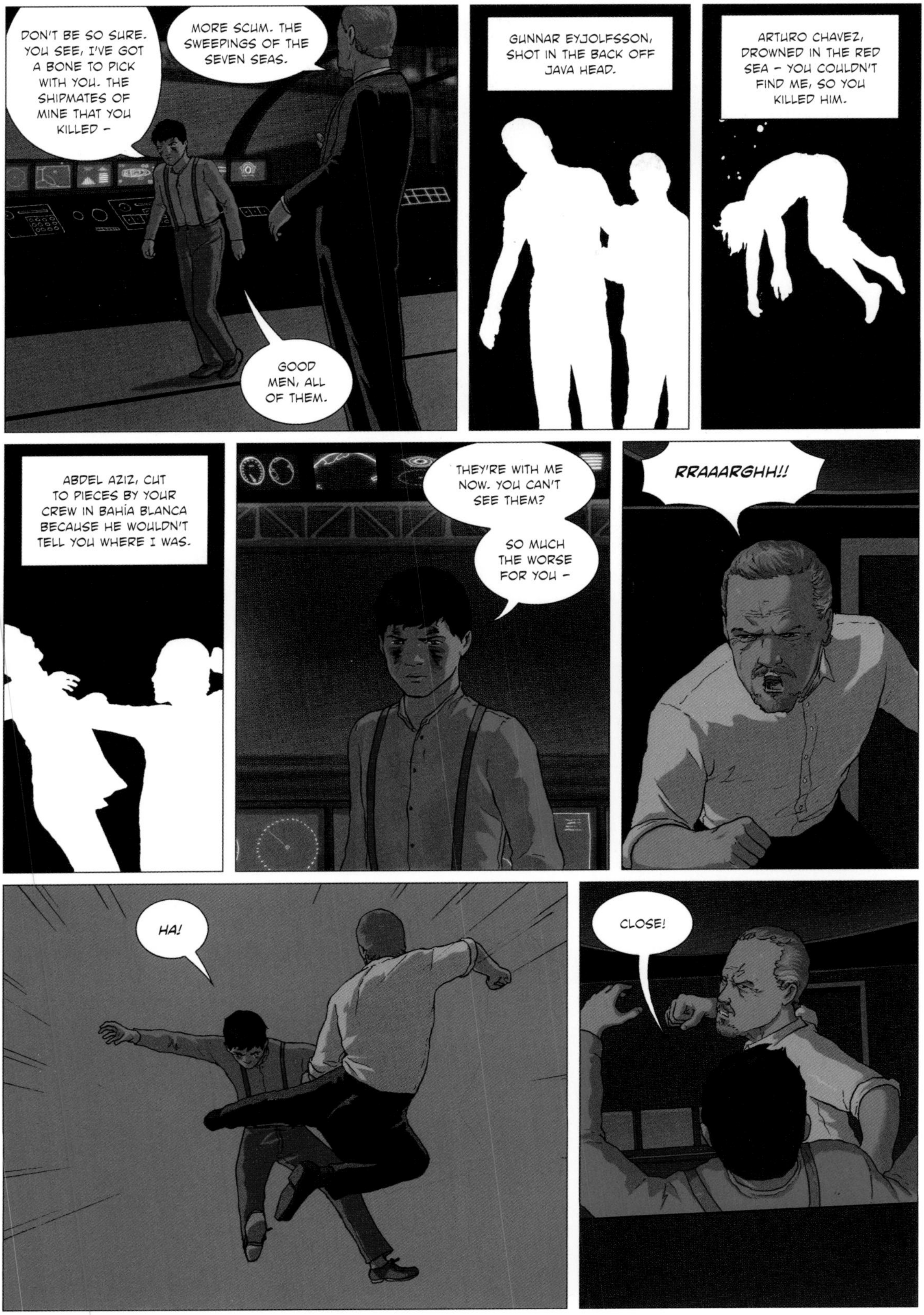
DON'T BE SO SURE. YOU SEE, I'VE GOT A BONE TO PICK WITH YOU. THE SHIPMATES OF MINE THAT YOU KILLED –
MORE SCUM. THE SWEEPINGS OF THE SEVEN SEAS.
GOOD MEN, ALL OF THEM.
GUNNAR EYJOLFSSON, SHOT IN THE BACK OFF JAVA HEAD.
ARTURO CHAVEZ, DROWNED IN THE RED SEA – YOU COULDN'T FIND ME, SO YOU KILLED HIM.
ABDEL AZIZ, CUT TO PIECES BY YOUR CREW IN BAHÍA BLANCA BECAUSE HE WOULDN'T TELL YOU WHERE I WAS.
THEY'RE WITH ME NOW. YOU CAN'T SEE THEM?
SO MUCH THE WORSE FOR YOU –
RRAAARGHH!!
HA!
CLOSE!

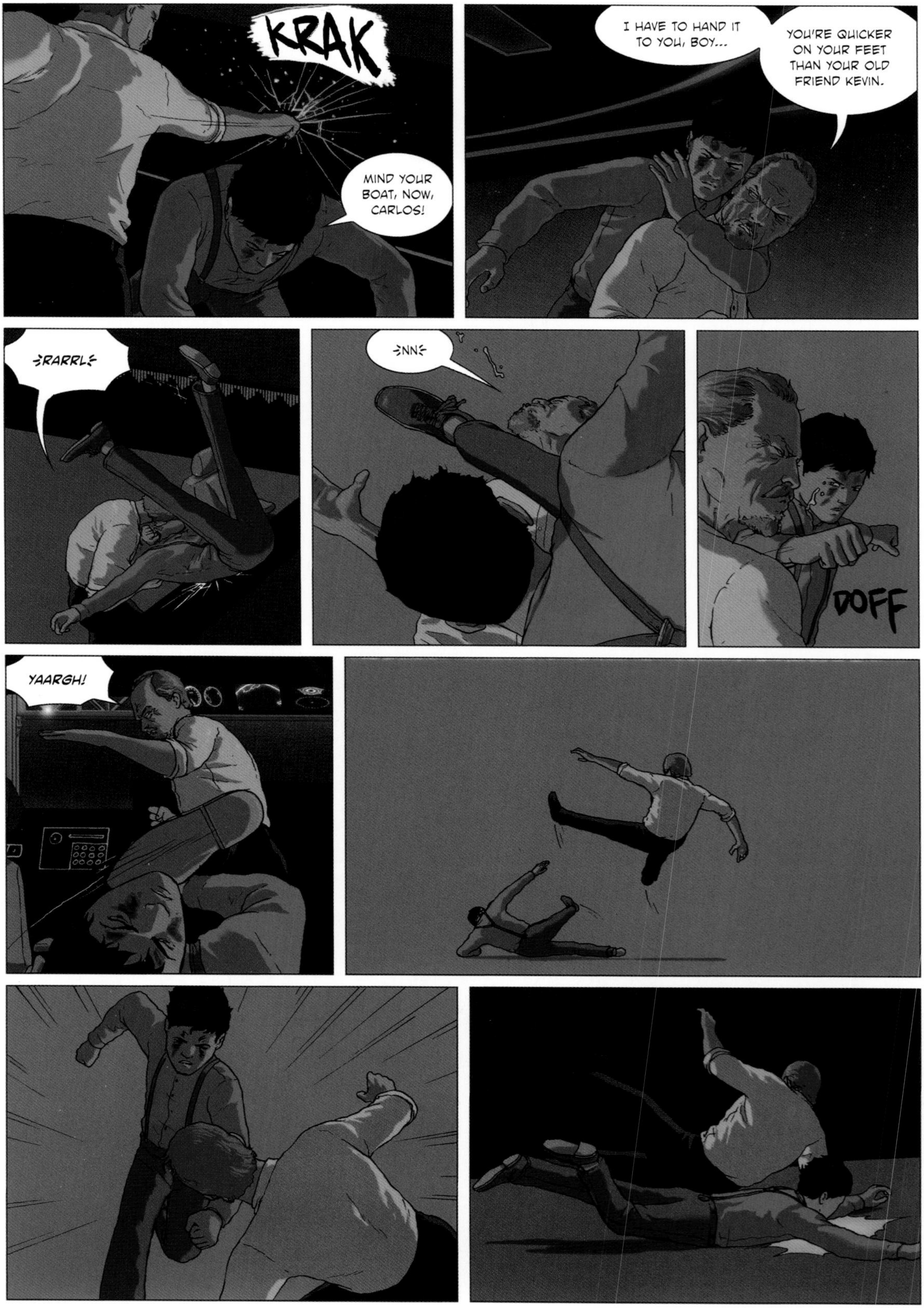
KRAK
MIND YOUR BOAT, NOW, CARLOS!
I HAVE TO HAND IT TO YOU, BOY...
YOU'RE QUICKER ON YOUR FEET THAN YOUR OLD FRIEND KEVIN.
RARRL
NN
DOFF
YAARGH!

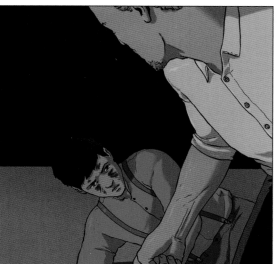

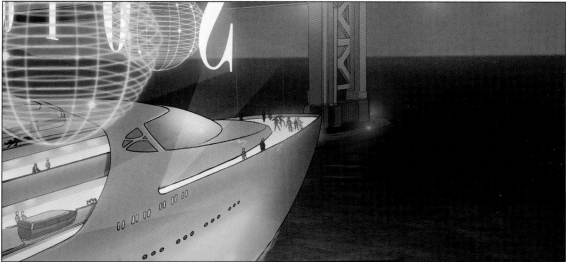

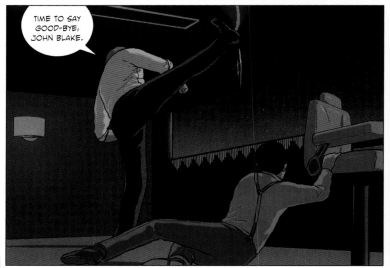

TIME TO SAY GOOD-BYE, JOHN BLAKE.

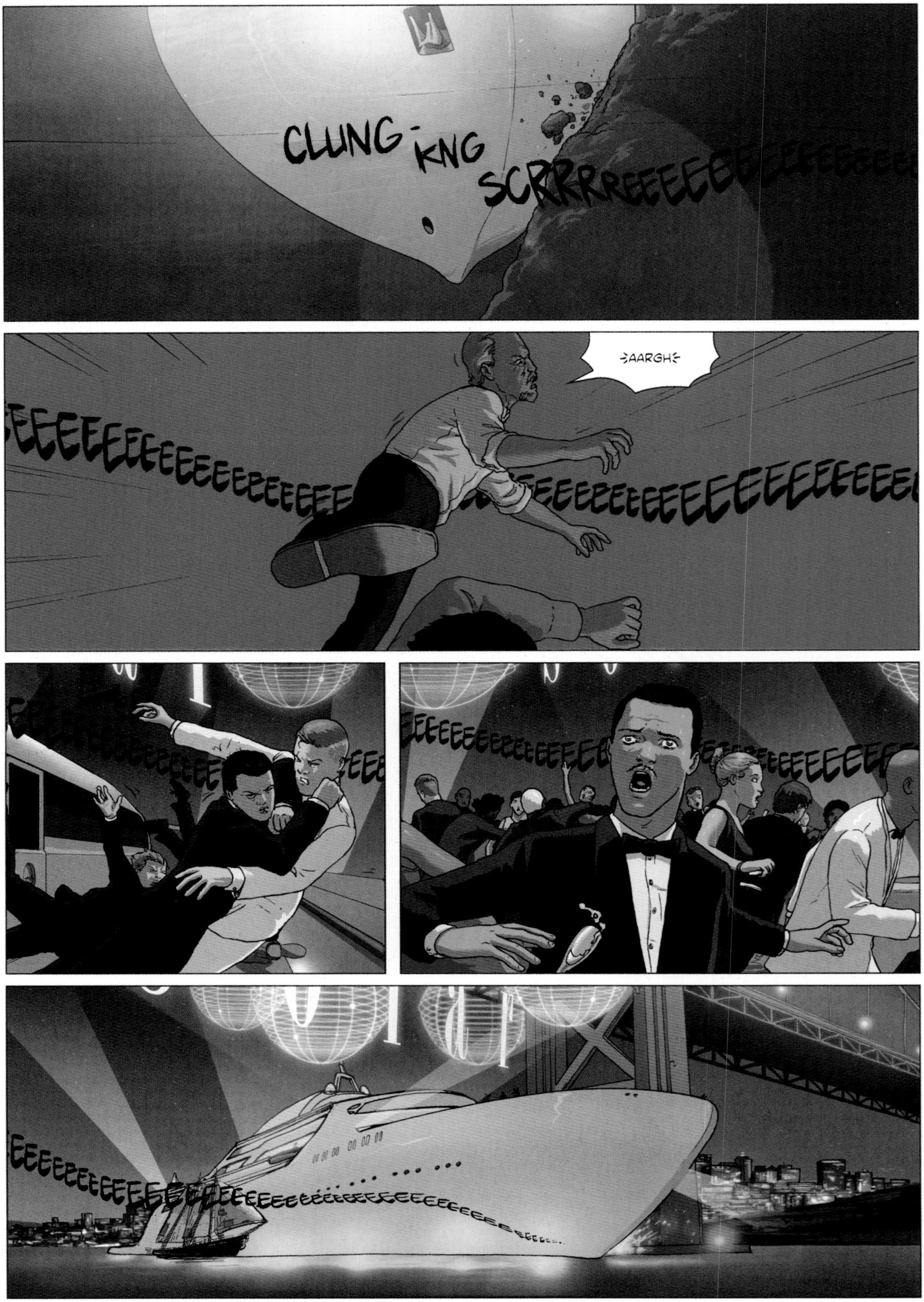
CLUNG-KNG
SCRRRREEEEEEEEEEEEEE
AARGH

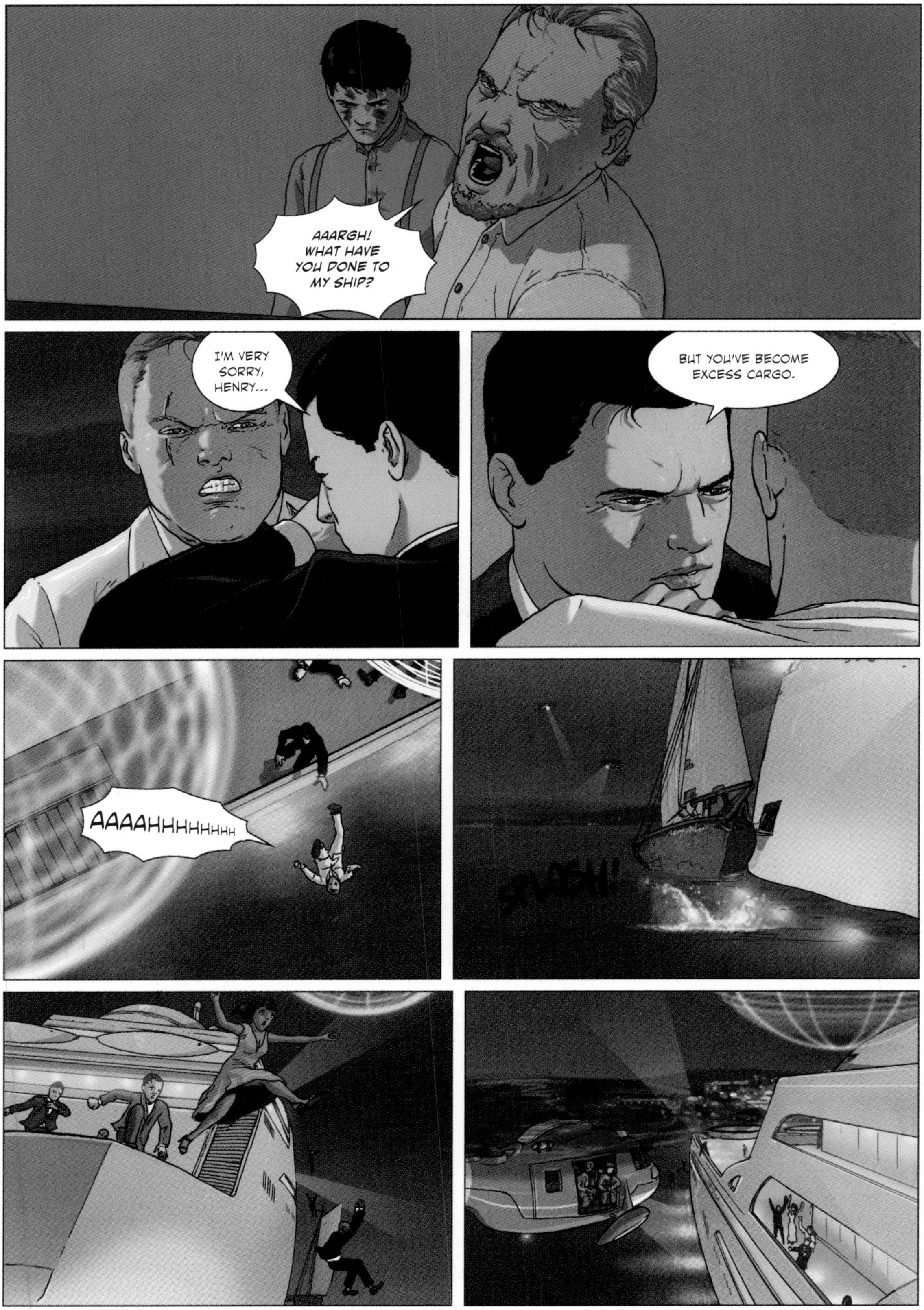
AAARGH! WHAT HAVE YOU DONE TO MY SHIP?
I'M VERY SORRY, HENRY...
BUT YOU'VE BECOME EXCESS CARGO.
AAAAHHHHHHHH
SPLOSH!

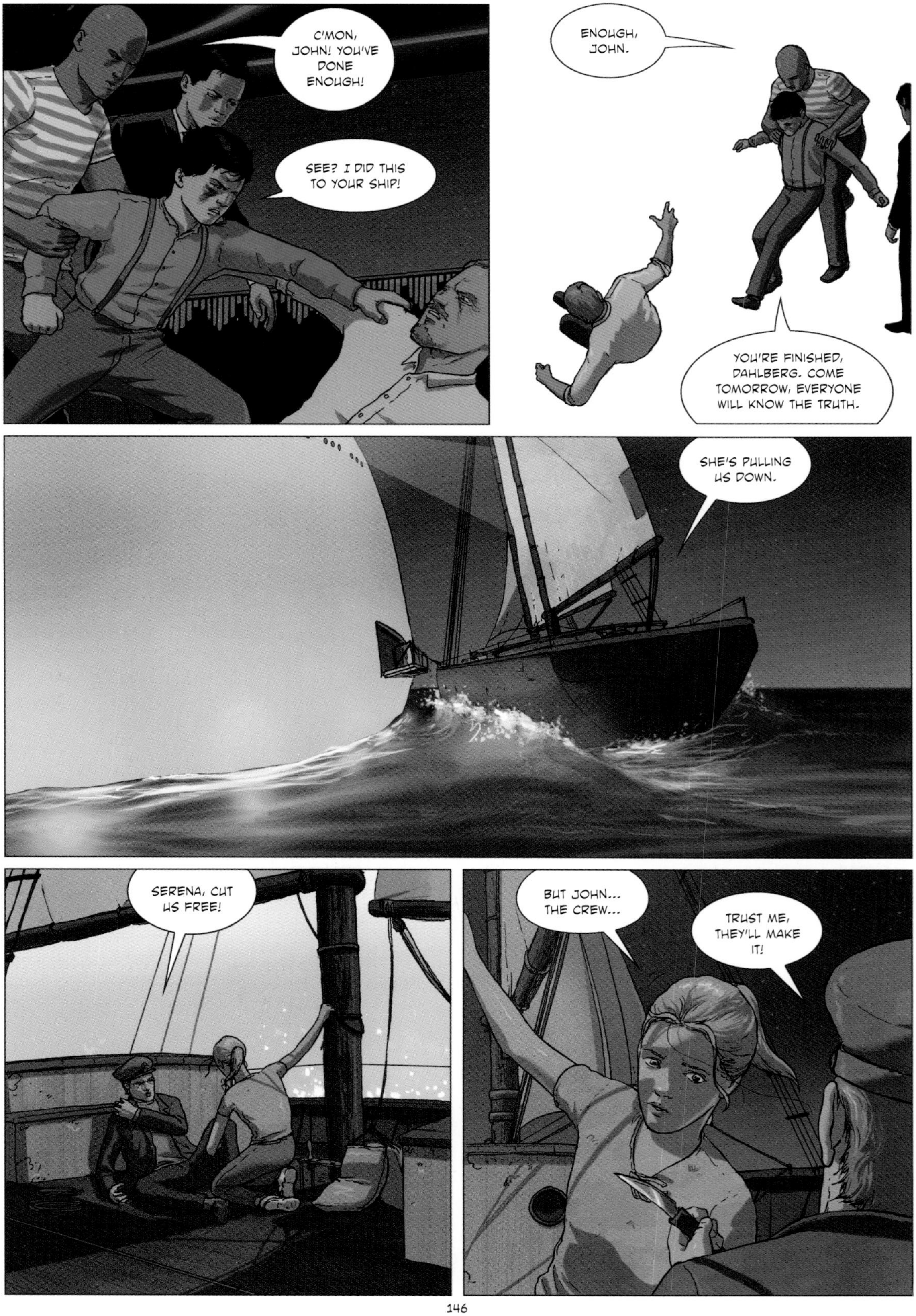
C'MON, JOHN! YOU'VE DONE ENOUGH!
SEE? I DID THIS TO YOUR SHIP!
ENOUGH, JOHN.
YOU'RE FINISHED, DAHLBERG. COME TOMORROW, EVERYONE WILL KNOW THE TRUTH.
SHE'S PULLING US DOWN.
SERENA, CUT US FREE!
BUT JOHN... THE CREW...
TRUST ME, THEY'LL MAKE IT!

ENGINE! FOR'ARD!

CLANG
SHNG
GNG
RRRMMMD
BBBBBB

RRRBBBB

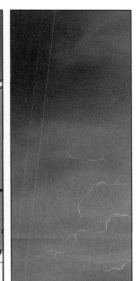

FWEEET

...BBBRRRM

GET IN! IT'LL
TAKE US ALL,
BUT *GET IN!*

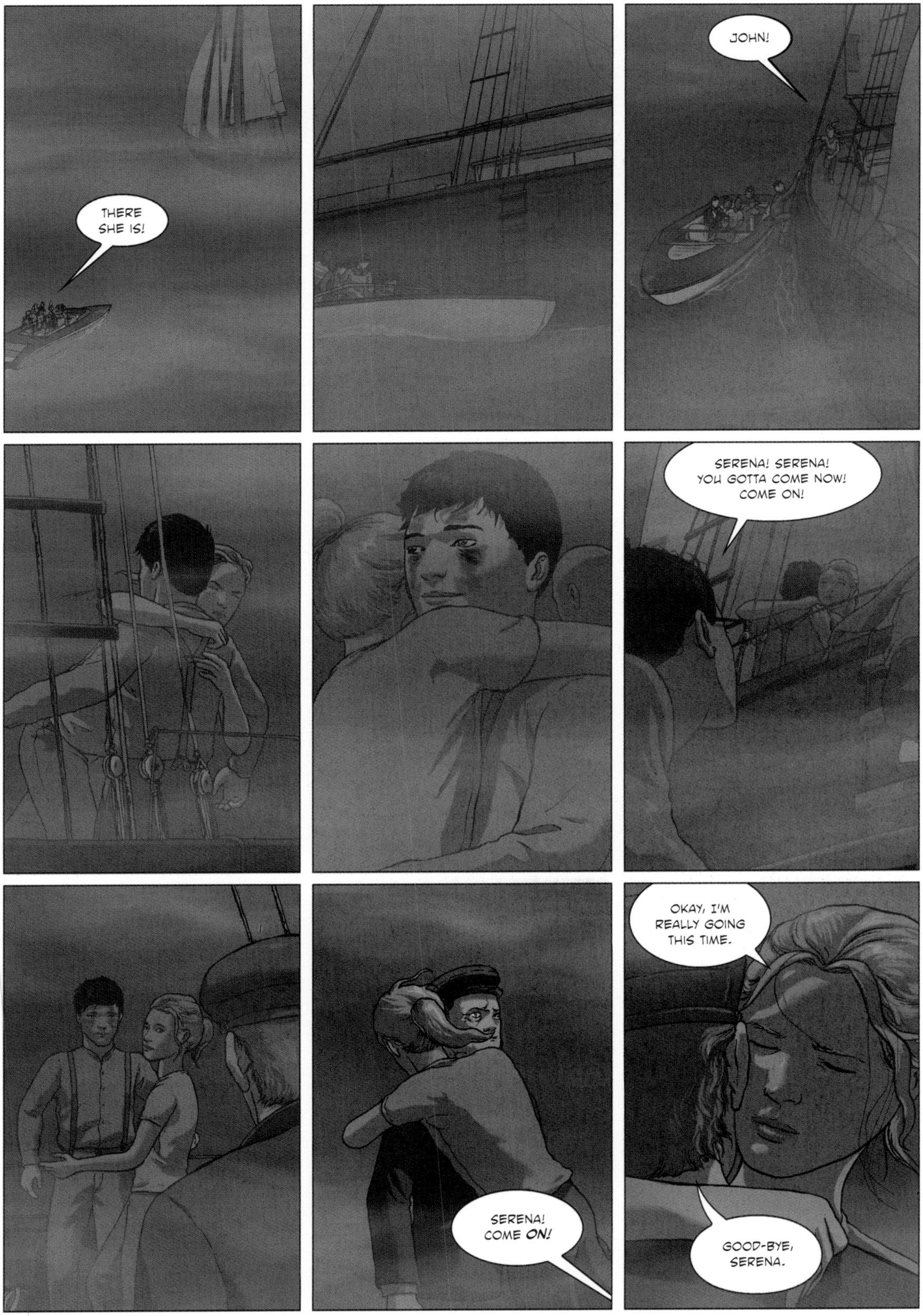
THERE SHE IS!
JOHN!
SERENA! SERENA! YOU GOTTA COME NOW! COME ON!
SERENA! COME ON!
OKAY, I'M REALLY GOING THIS TIME.
GOOD-BYE, SERENA.

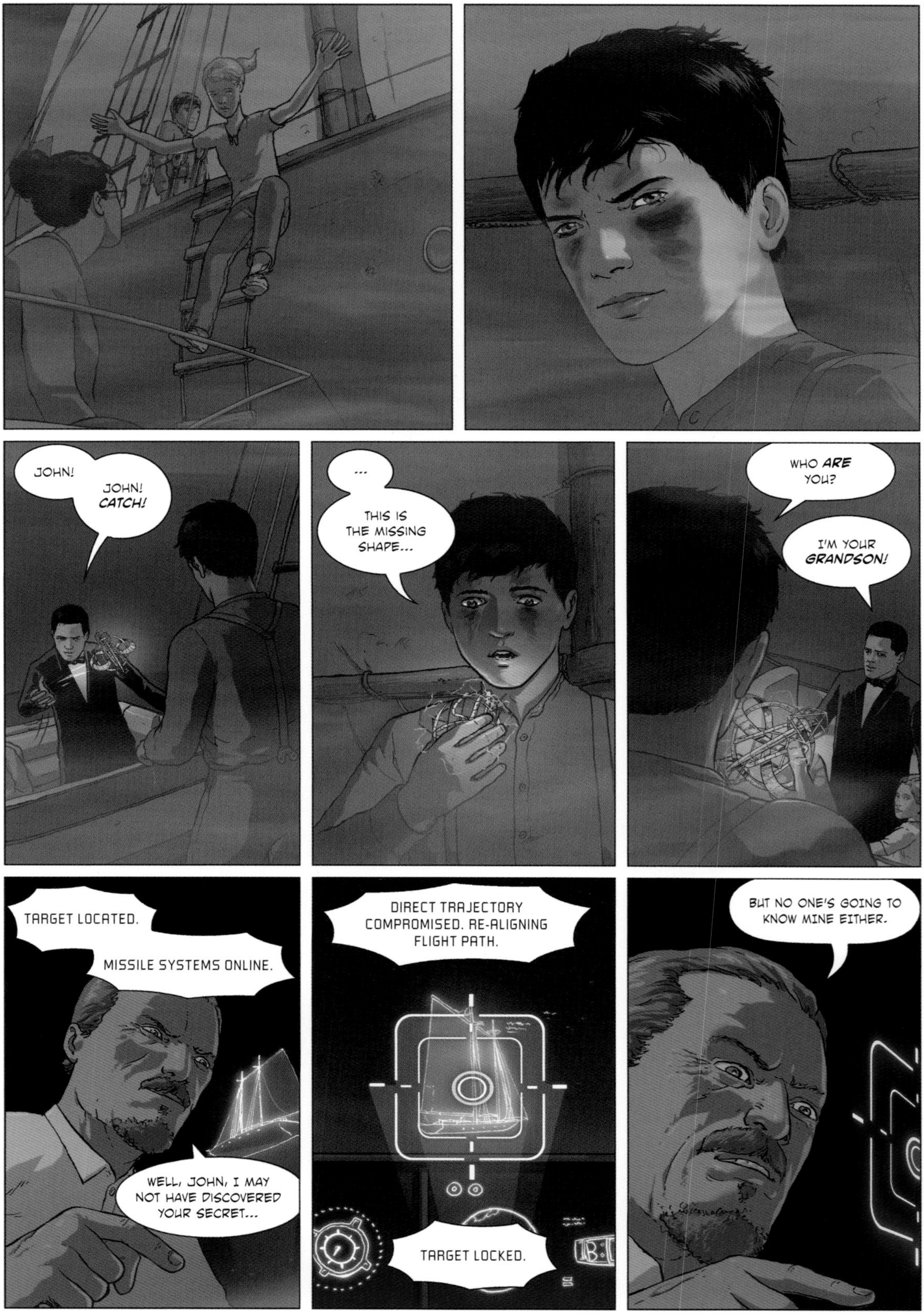
JOHN!
JOHN! CATCH!
...
THIS IS THE MISSING SHAPE...
WHO ARE YOU?
I'M YOUR GRANDSON!
TARGET LOCATED.
MISSILE SYSTEMS ONLINE.
WELL, JOHN, I MAY NOT HAVE DISCOVERED YOUR SECRET...
DIRECT TRAJECTORY COMPROMISED. RE-ALIGNING FLIGHT PATH.
TARGET LOCKED.
BUT NO ONE'S GOING TO KNOW MINE EITHER.

SSSHAAAAASSHHHH

WHAT THE HELL WAS THAT?

THEY'VE LAUNCHED A DAMN MISSILE!

IT'S ARCING AROUND!

JOHN, GET US OUTTA HERE!

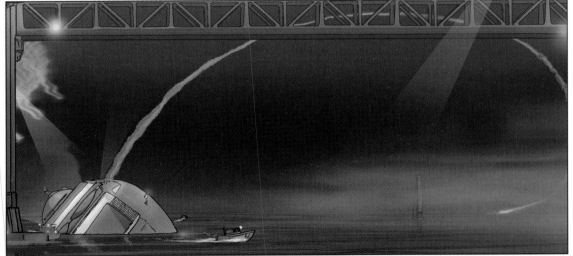

JOHN!!

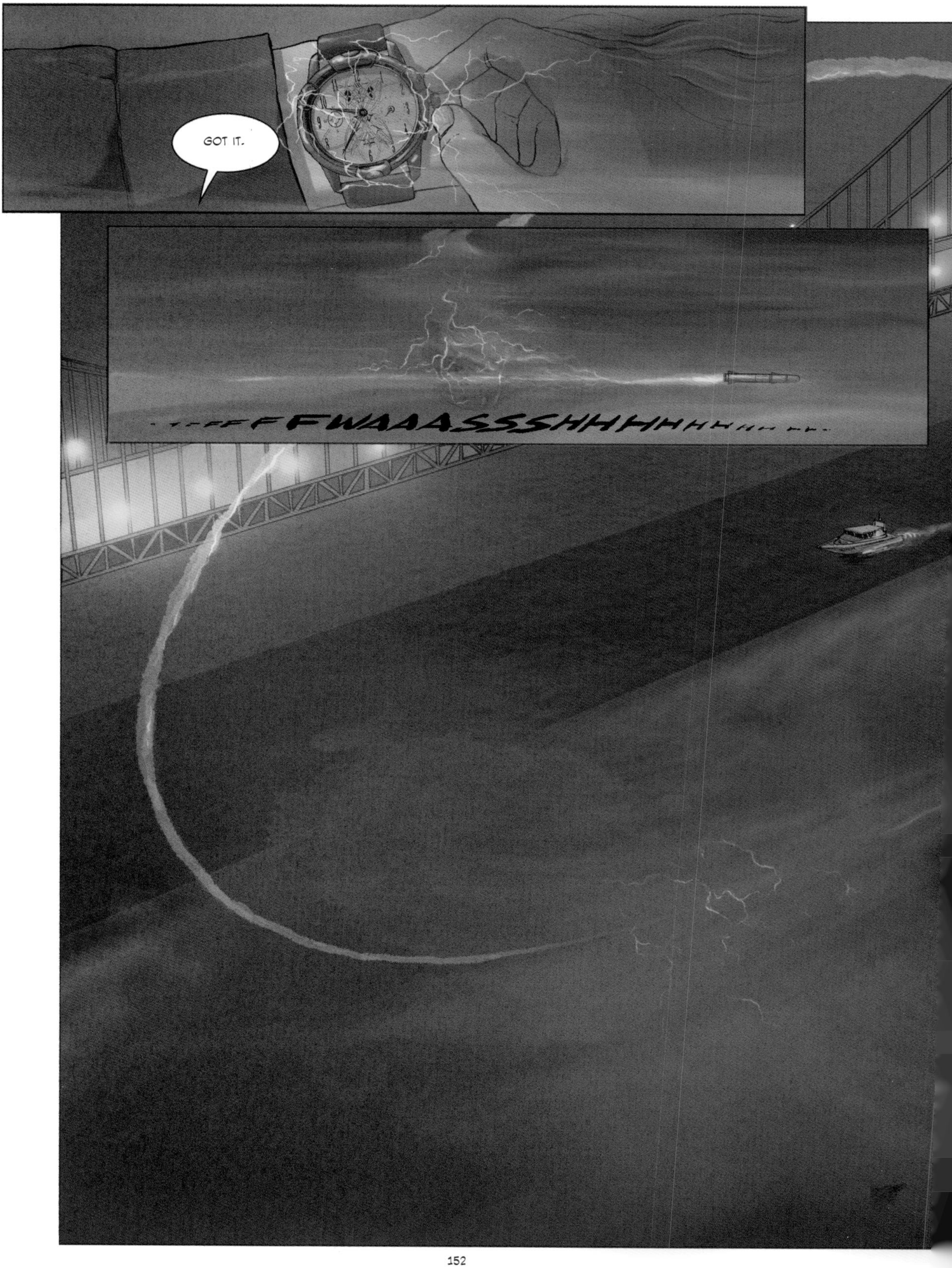
GOT IT.
FWAAASSSHHHHHHH

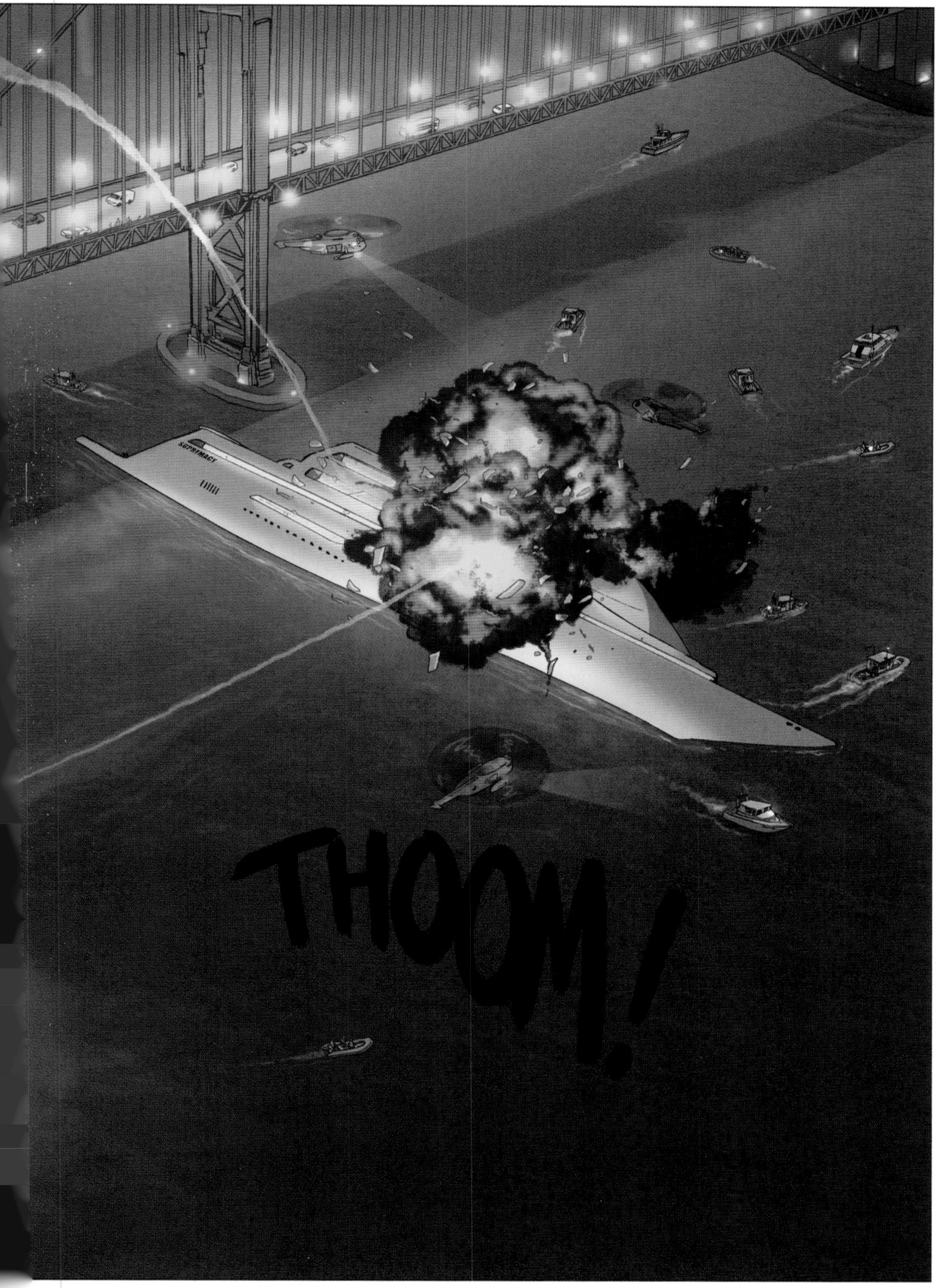
SUPREMACY
THOOM!

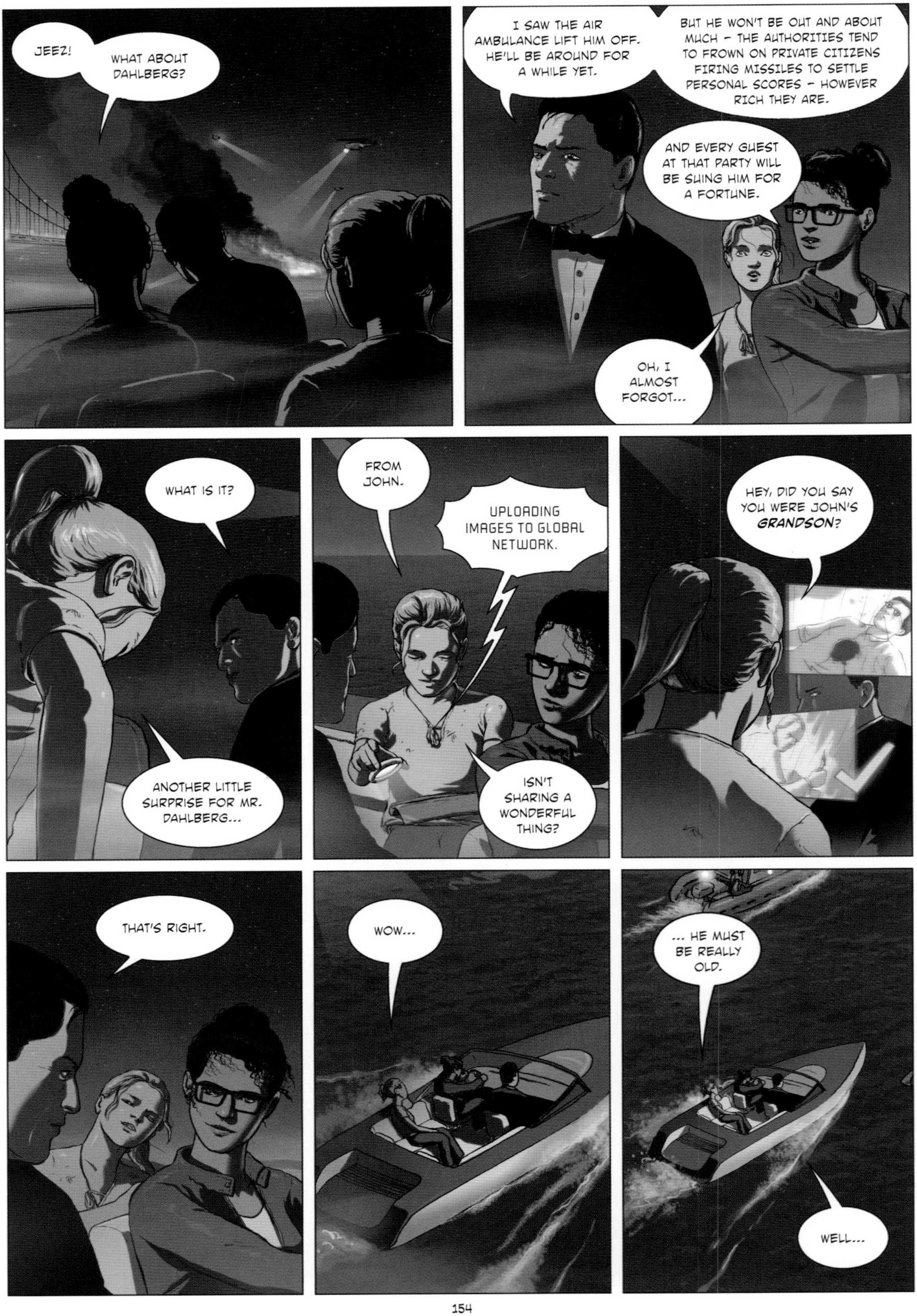
JEEZ!
WHAT ABOUT DAHLBERG?
I SAW THE AIR AMBULANCE LIFT HIM OFF. HE'LL BE AROUND FOR A WHILE YET.
BUT HE WON'T BE OUT AND ABOUT MUCH – THE AUTHORITIES TEND TO FROWN ON PRIVATE CITIZENS FIRING MISSILES TO SETTLE PERSONAL SCORES – HOWEVER RICH THEY ARE.
AND EVERY GUEST AT THAT PARTY WILL BE SUING HIM FOR A FORTUNE.
OH, I ALMOST FORGOT...
WHAT IS IT?
ANOTHER LITTLE SURPRISE FOR MR. DAHLBERG...
FROM JOHN.
UPLOADING IMAGES TO GLOBAL NETWORK.
ISN'T SHARING A WONDERFUL THING?
HEY, DID YOU SAY YOU WERE JOHN'S **GRANDSON**?
THAT'S RIGHT.
WOW...
... HE MUST BE REALLY OLD.
WELL...

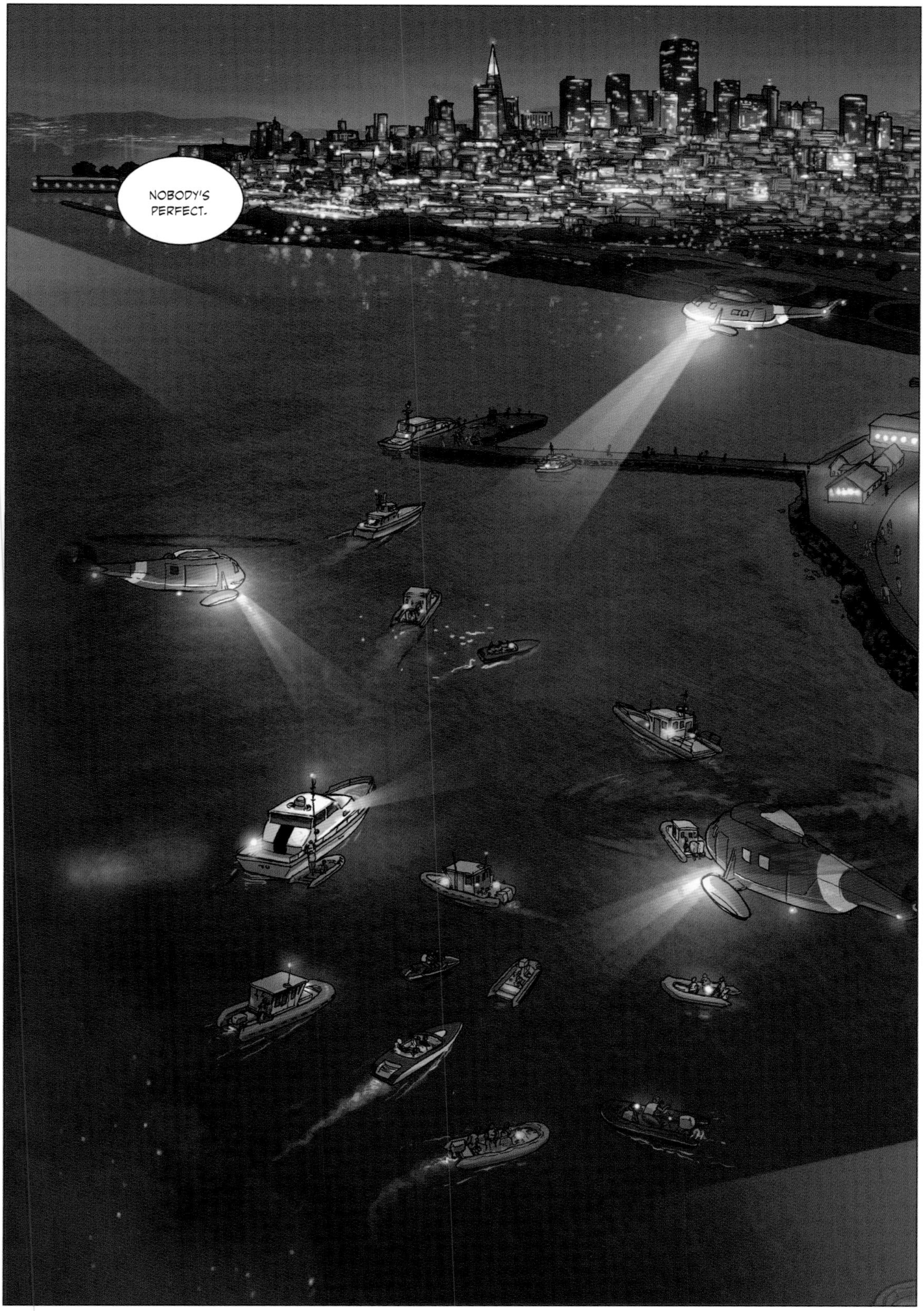
NOBODY'S PERFECT.

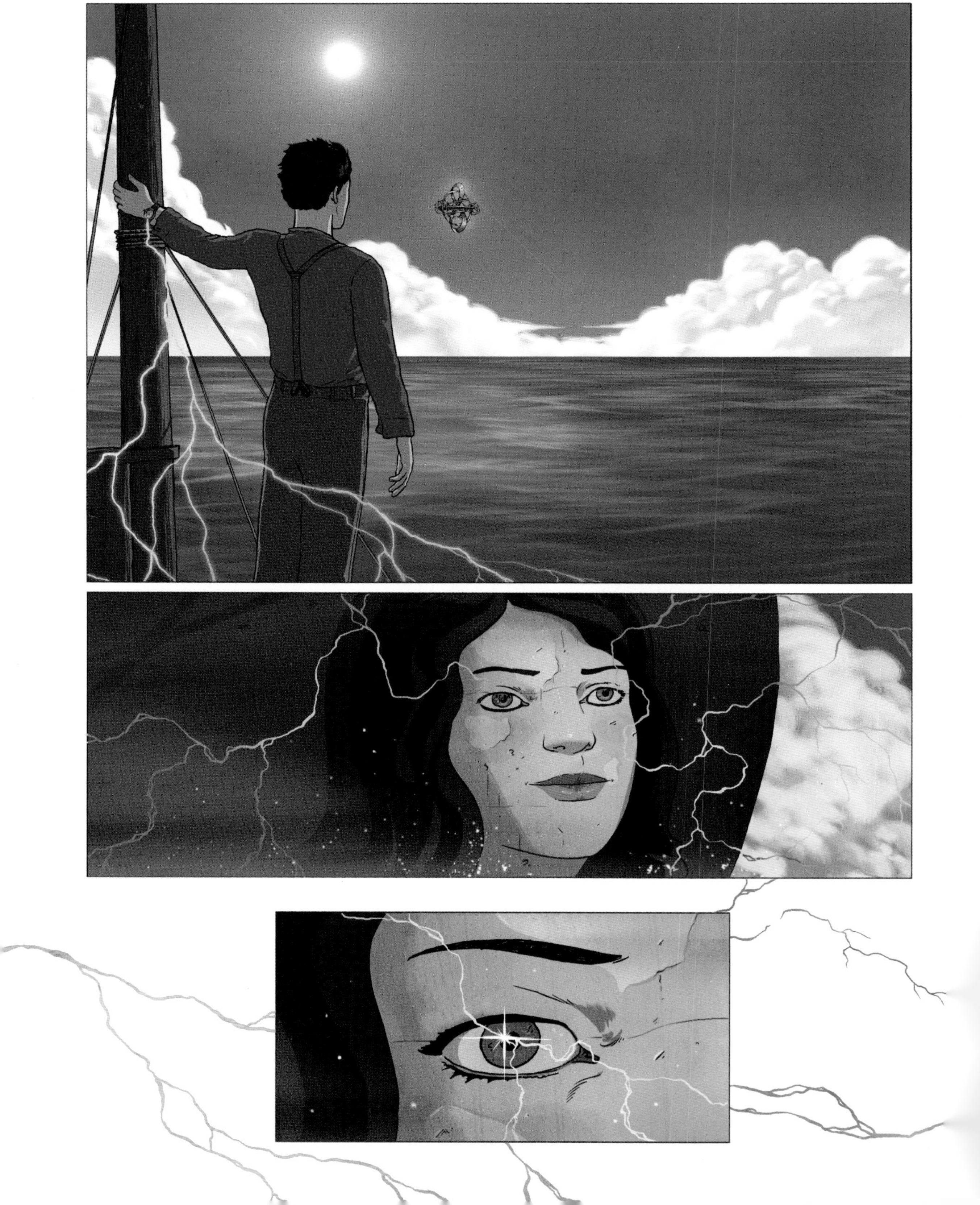

THE ADVENTURES OF
JOHN BLAKE

THE CREW

CAPTAIN QUAYLE has a checkered and colorful past. A sailor and leader right down to his bones, Quayle is a man who finds the rolling waves of the ocean a comfort and dry land a prison. Though he has made many a promise to settle down, the call of the open sea has always proved too strong. Along the way he has been a husband, a father, a merchant, a navy man, a smuggler, and everything in between. Whatever he does he is firm, steady, and resolute.

JOHN BLAKE'S father was involved in a top secret weapons program. He hitched a ride on Einstein's scientific voyage to test out one of his weapons experiments, taking John with him. But the experiment went horribly wrong. John was caught in the blast and thrown overboard. Luckily the *Mary Alice* was nearby. Quayle's crew hauled John from the sea, but it soon became clear that much more than just the bedraggled boy had come aboard. Strange energies soon engulfed the *Mary Alice* and her journey through time began.

SERENA HENDERSON is a schoolgirl from Sydney and is addicted to her Apparator. Her parents have taken her and her younger brother out of school for a year to sail around the world, which Serena thinks is pretty cool. It gets even more incredible when she finds herself a temporary member of the crew of the *Mary Alice*, traveling through space and time, after being washed overboard during an epic storm. John Blake rescues her and thus begins the adventure of a lifetime!

SAMMY WU is from a wealthy family who made their fortune in the silk trade during the 1890s. But just as Sammy was set to take over the family business, a freak storm in the South China Sea left his junk wrecked. Sammy survived for a month - and fought off anything that wanted to eat him - before the *Mary Alice* hauled him to safety. While he enjoys the excitement that life aboard the *Mary Alice* offers him, he regrets missing out on the life of luxury that would have been his destiny.

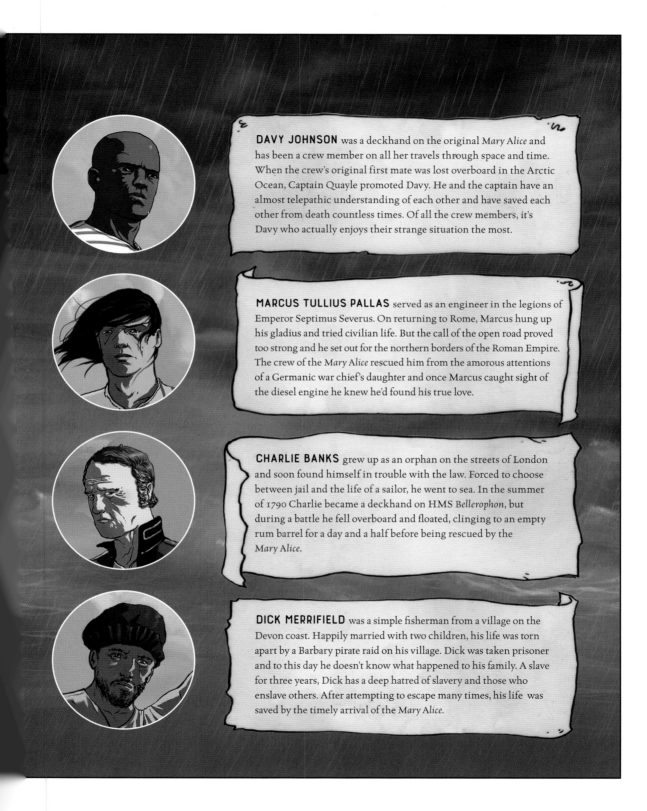

DAVY JOHNSON was a deckhand on the original *Mary Alice* and has been a crew member on all her travels through space and time. When the crew's original first mate was lost overboard in the Arctic Ocean, Captain Quayle promoted Davy. He and the captain have an almost telepathic understanding of each other and have saved each other from death countless times. Of all the crew members, it's Davy who actually enjoys their strange situation the most.

MARCUS TULLIUS PALLAS served as an engineer in the legions of Emperor Septimus Severus. On returning to Rome, Marcus hung up his gladius and tried civilian life. But the call of the open road proved too strong and he set out for the northern borders of the Roman Empire. The crew of the *Mary Alice* rescued him from the amorous attentions of a Germanic war chief's daughter and once Marcus caught sight of the diesel engine he knew he'd found his true love.

CHARLIE BANKS grew up as an orphan on the streets of London and soon found himself in trouble with the law. Forced to choose between jail and the life of a sailor, he went to sea. In the summer of 1790 Charlie became a deckhand on HMS *Bellerophon*, but during a battle he fell overboard and floated, clinging to an empty rum barrel for a day and a half before being rescued by the *Mary Alice*.

DICK MERRIFIELD was a simple fisherman from a village on the Devon coast. Happily married with two children, his life was torn apart by a Barbary pirate raid on his village. Dick was taken prisoner and to this day he doesn't know what happened to his family. A slave for three years, Dick has a deep hatred of slavery and those who enslave others. After attempting to escape many times, his life was saved by the timely arrival of the *Mary Alice*.

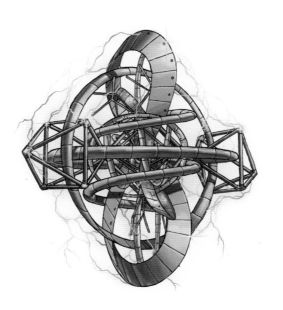

Freshwater Habitats
Life in Freshwater Ecosystems

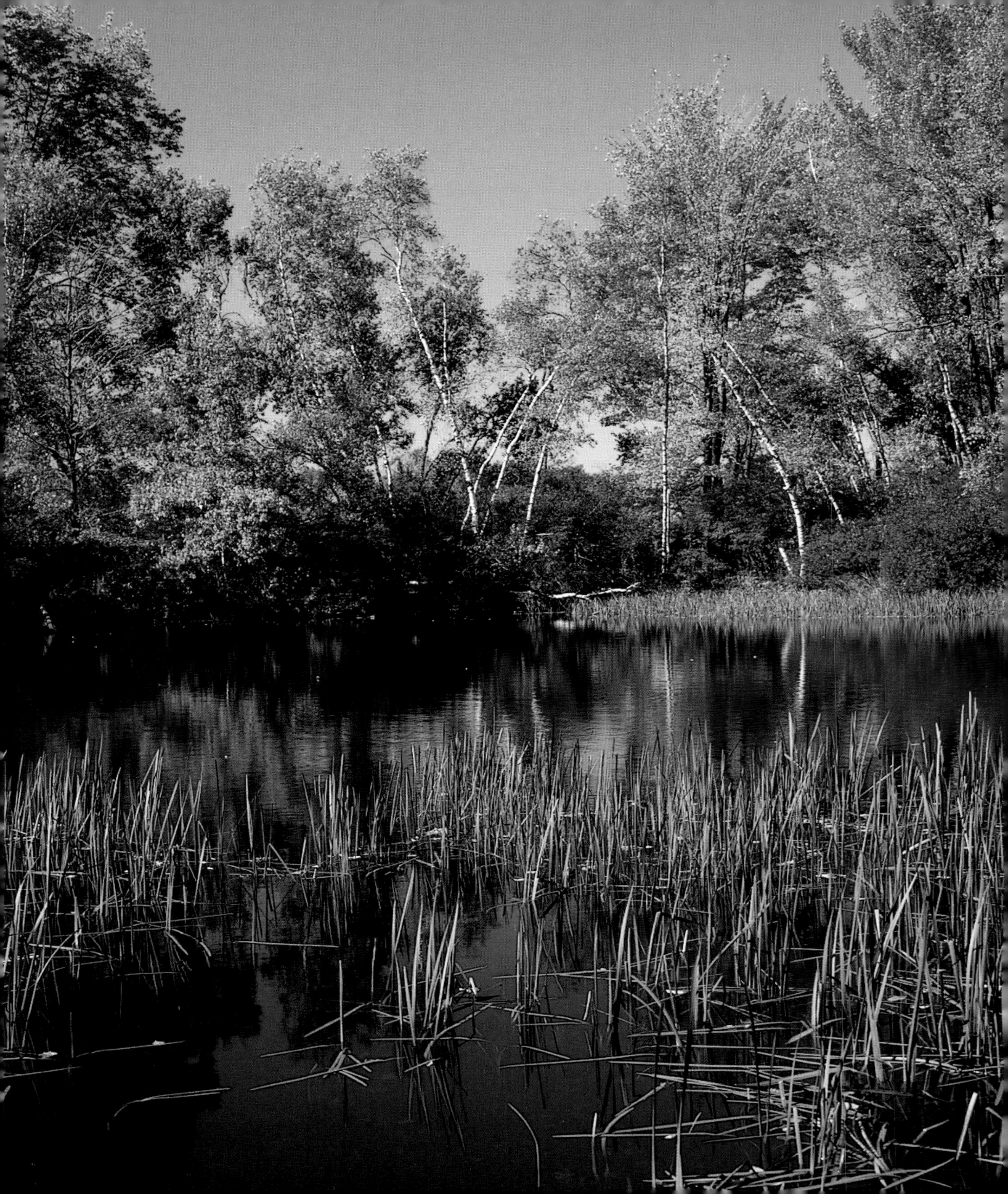

Freshwater Habitats
Life in Freshwater Ecosystems

Laurie Toupin

Franklin Watts
A Division of Scholastic Inc.
New York • Toronto • London • Auckland • Sydney
Mexico City • New Delhi • Hong Kong
Danbury, Connecticut

To my husband, David—my canoeing partner through life as well as through all of New England's freshwater!

Note to readers: Definitions for words in **bold** can be found in the Glossary at the back of this book.

Photographs © 2004: Dembinsky Photo Assoc./NASA: 16; Dwight R. Kuhn Photography: 20, 23, 38, 39; George Steinmetz: 6, 12; Photo Researchers, NY: 24 top (John M. Coffman), 40 (Suzanne L. & Joseph T. Collins), 45 left (Tim Davis), 25, 26, 37, 41 (E.R. Degginger), 10 (Aaron Ferster), 48 (Simon Fraser/SPL), cover, 2, 5 left, 18 (Michael P. Gadomski), 5 right, 32 (Jacques Jangoux), 40, 42 (Tom & Pat Leeson), 45 bottom center (Jeff Lepore), 45 right (C.K. Lorenz), 29 (Maslowski), 36 (Gary Meszaros), 31 (William H. Mullins), 45 top center (Wm. Munoz), 35 (Carl Purcell), 50 (Jim Steinberg), 24 bottom (David Weintraub), 46 (Jim Zipp).

The photograph on the cover shows a river in Audra State Park in West Virginia. The photograph opposite the title page shows Brady's Lake in Pennsylvania.

Library of Congress Cataloging-in-Publication Data

Toupin, Laurie Peach.
Freshwater habitats : life in freshwater ecosystems / Laurie Peach Toupin.
p. cm. — (Watts library)
Summary: A look at the plants, animals, locations, and various habitats that make up the freshwater ecosystems of the world.
Includes bibliographical references (p.).
ISBN 0-531-12305-7 (lib. bdg.) 0-531-16675-9 (pbk.)
1. Freshwater ecology—Juvenile literature. 2. Freshwater organisms—Juvenile literature. [1. Freshwater ecology. 2. Freshwater organisms. 3. Ecology.] I. Title. II. Series.
QH541.5.F7T68 2003
577.6—dc22

2003016572

Printed in the United States of America.
2 3 4 5 6 7 8 9 10 R 13 12 11 10 09 08 07 06

Contents

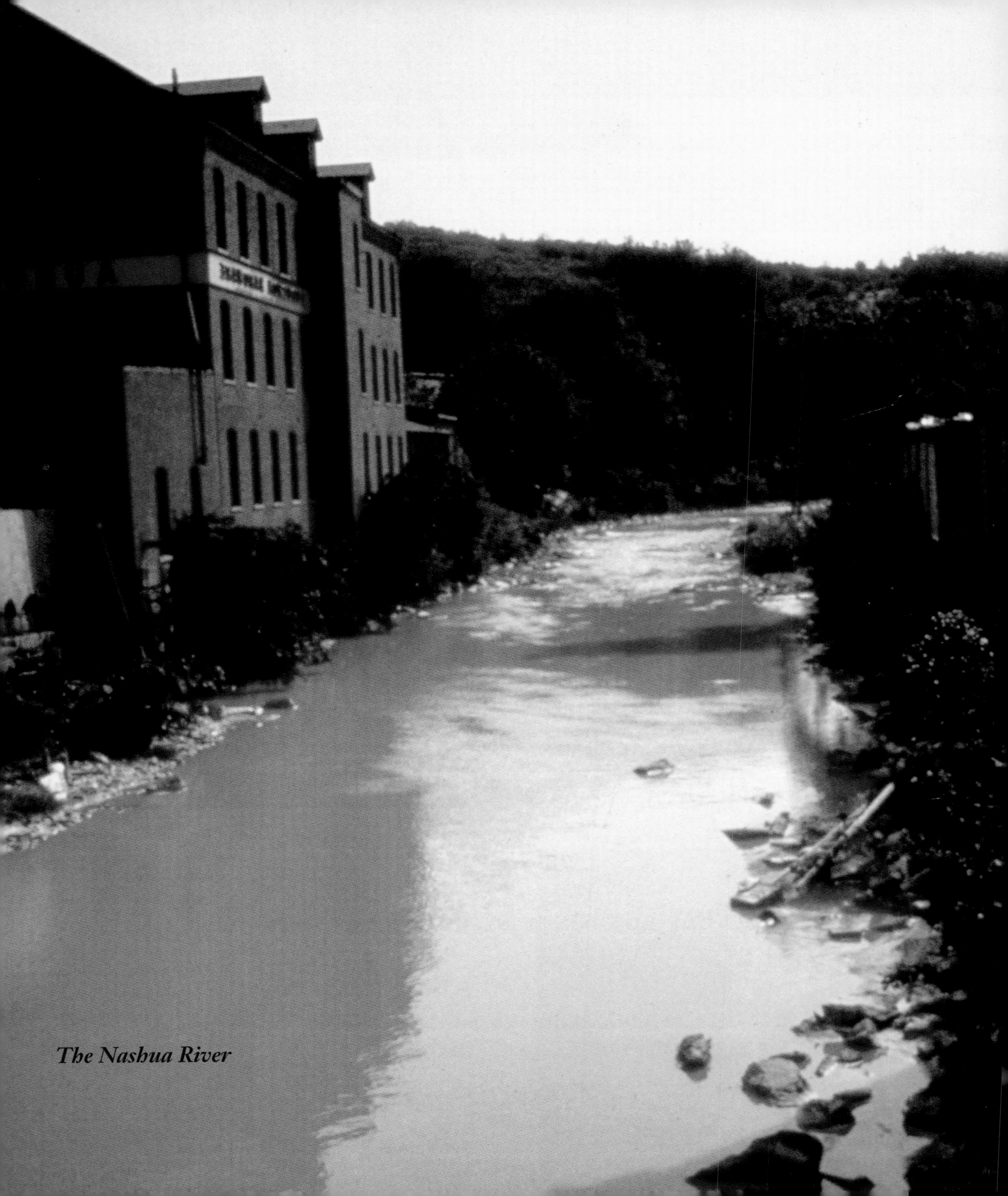

The Nashua River

Chapter One

Saving a Dying River

On some days, the Nashua River ran red. On others, it ran blue or yellow. It depended on what color dye the paper mills were using that day. The waters were so full of pollution that, occasionally, a person would spot a squirrel or chipmunk running across the scum on the river's surface to get to the other side.

But no fish swam in the river. No plants grew along its bottom. No birds lived in the trees on its banks. No people wanted to live along its smelly shores.

The river was "ecologically" dead. When Marion Stoddart moved to Groton, Massachusetts, in 1962, she took one look at the condition of the Nashua River and decided to do something about it.

Stoddart organized other people who cared about the river into a group called the Nashua River Cleanup Committee. These people signed petitions. They sent letters to local politicians asking for new laws to be passed that would protect all rivers. They even gave legislators bottles of dirty Nashua River water.

In the Top Ten

The U.S. Federal Water Quality Administration considered the Nashua River to be one of the top ten most polluted rivers in the country.

Their efforts paid off. Three years later, paper companies along the Nashua joined together to build a treatment plant. Seventeen years later, bass, pickerel, trout, bald eagles, osprey, and great blue heron returned to the river.

A Precious Resource

Stoddart knew her efforts were important. She understood how little **freshwater** there is in the world. Although three-quarters of Earth is covered by water, the majority of it is salt water. Only 3 percent is freshwater. This fresh water is found in lakes, rivers, streams, ponds, and underground. It is also frozen in glaciers, ice caps, ice floes, and icebergs. A small amount exists as vapor in the atmosphere.

Setting a Precedent

In 1965, wastewater treatment operators in Massachusetts organized the first nonprofit Water Pollution Control Association.

One Spoonful

Fill a large canoe with water. This represents all the water on Earth and in our atmosphere. Take one bucket of water out of the canoe. This represents all the freshwater on the planet. Now, take 1 teaspoon (5 milliliters) of water out of the bucket. This represents all the usable freshwater available to humans and wildlife in the form of ponds, lake, streams, and rivers.

Because frozen freshwater and water vapor are inaccessible, only about 1 percent of the total amount of freshwater found on Earth can be used by people, plants, and animals. For a resource so vital to our survival, that isn't very much!

The average American uses approximately 70 gallons (265 liters) of water per day for drinking, bathing, washing dishes, and washing laundry. Industry and agriculture require millions of gallons more. For example, one small paper mill located along the Squannacook River in Massachusetts, a tributary of the Nashua River, uses up to 2.5 million gallons (9.5 million l) per day. That equals about one million flushes of an average toilet!

The Freshwater Community

Stoddart knew that wildlife depends on freshwater habitats such as the Nashua River. Most of the wildlife that lives in this environment could not live anywhere else. Not only do birds, animals, and fish depend on the water; they also rely on one another. This type of interdependency creates a community, or **biome**.

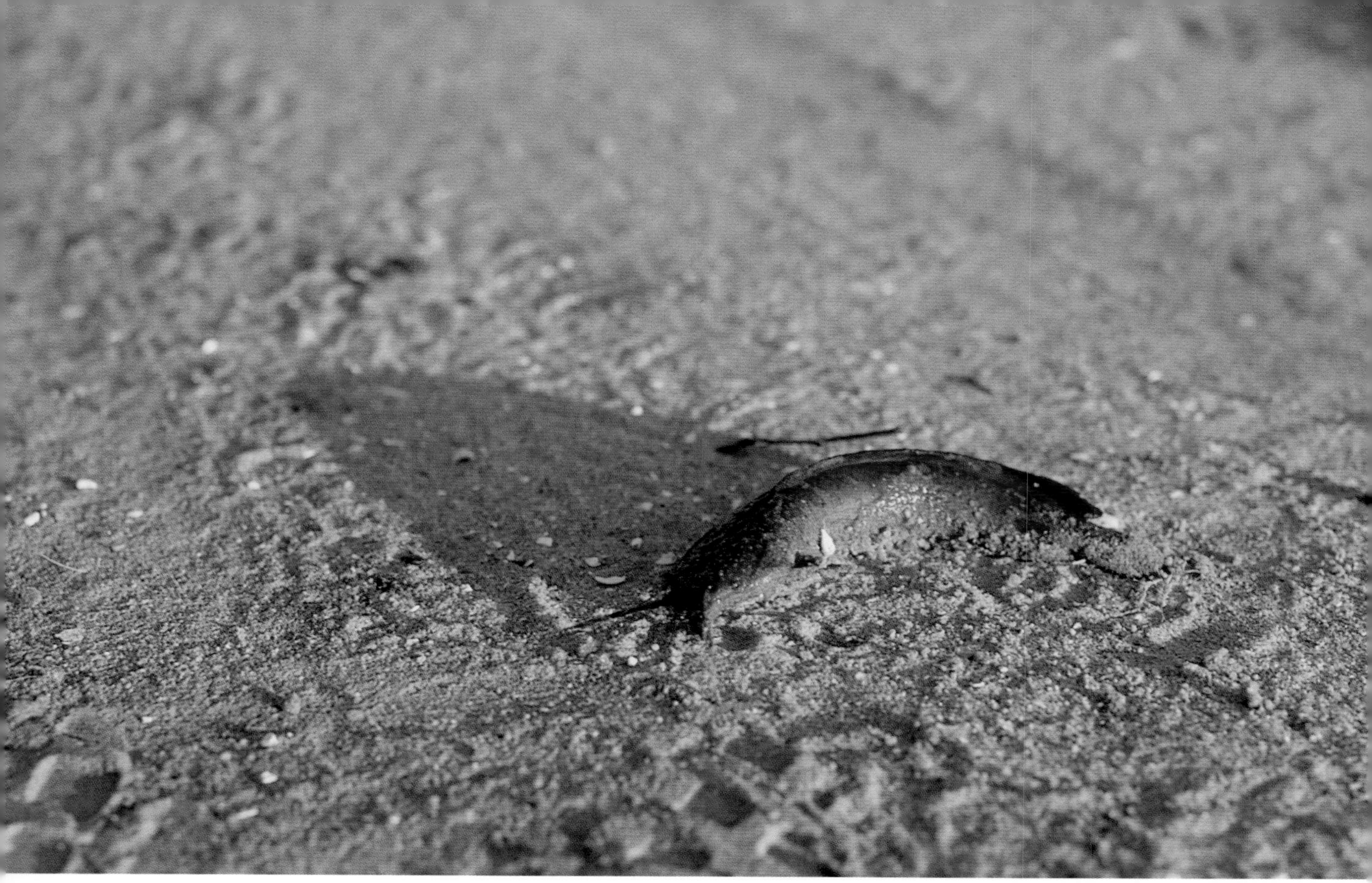

This walking catfish is crossing a dirt road in Florida.

Most biomes are defined by climate, such as the polar regions or rain forests. A freshwater biome is unique because it intersects every other biome in the world. Ponds, lakes, streams, and rivers exist in just about every climatic zone.

Living organisms that make their homes in water have to adapt to moving or still water. They also must survive rainfall changes, temperature fluctuations, human impact, and geological features. All of these factors determine what kind of plants, insects, fish, mammals, and birds will survive in a particular body of water.

This wide range of conditions makes freshwater habitats home to many different types of freshwater fish—from the walking catfish of the Everglades in Florida to the piranha of the Amazon River. Freshwater amphibians range from the red-spotted salamander of North America to the South American false-eyed frog. Mammals include everything from the beaver to the hippopotamus.

The one thing these creatures have in common is that they need some portion of that 1 percent of usable freshwater to survive. But where does this precious resource come from and how can we protect it?

No Salt

Water is considered fresh if it has less than a 1 percent salt concentration.

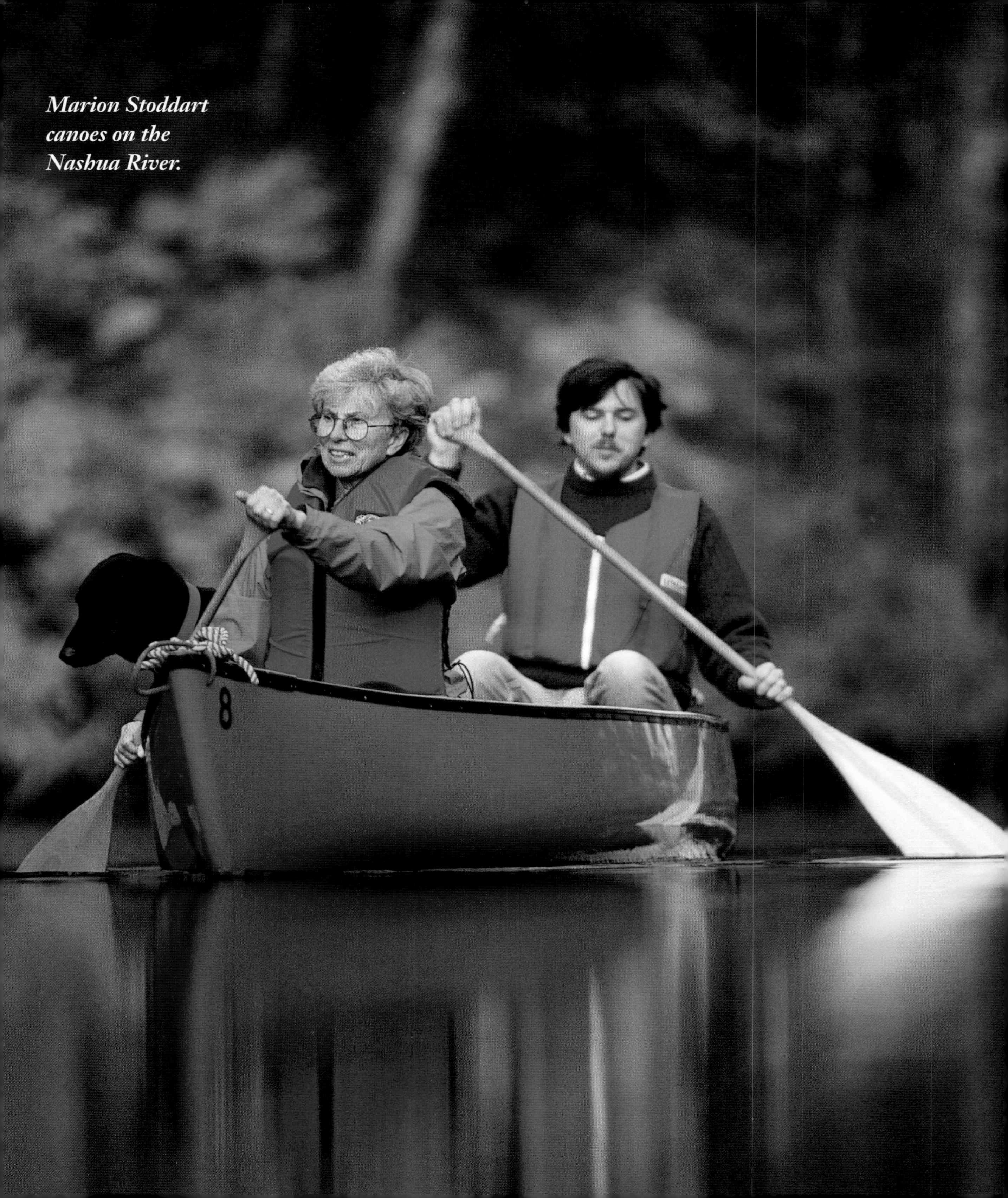

Marion Stoddart canoes on the Nashua River.

Chapter Two

Watery Homes

When Stoddart's group decided to clean up the Nashua River, they looked at more than just the river. They determined every piece of land through which rain and snowmelt flowed before it reached the river. They considered every puddle, stream, and wetland whose water would eventually drain into the Nashua River. This wide drainage area was the Nashua River's **watershed**. Every watershed is made up of ponds, lakes, wetlands, streams, and rivers.

An Enclosed Water World

Becky loves to visit the pond near her house. During the summer, she comes home with buckets full of tadpoles, crayfish, turtles, and an occasional snake. She keeps them overnight and then takes them back to the pond the next day and releases them. She finds something new almost every day because thousands of plants and animals thrive in a pond environment.

A pond is an independent **ecosystem**. Ponds can be either natural or man-made. If natural, they could have been formed by glaciers, rivers, landslides, or such animals as beavers. The pond by Becky's house was made many years ago by a farmer who dug a large hole and lined it with clay.

Biologists consider any contained body of water to be a pond. More commonly, a pond is a body of water that has a muddy or silty bottom. It is shallow enough that sunlight reaches the bottom of the deepest part of the pond, allowing plants to grow from shore to shore.

No two ponds are exactly alike. Living conditions and water quality in each pond depend on the pond's size, depth, and shape. The local climate and surrounding land features

The Water Cycle

Water moves constantly whether it looks like it is or not. Waters from lakes and ponds flow into streams. Streams flow into rivers. Rivers flow into seas. Puddles evaporate. Icicles melt. Water continuously travels back and forth between Earth and the atmosphere in various forms: gas, liquid, and solid. This movement is called the water cycle. This cycle replenishes the freshwater on Earth.

Spring Pools

Vernal ponds are temporary pools. They usually exist only during heavy spring and autumn rains. They evaporate during dry spells. For this reason, fish don't live in them. However, vernal ponds are breeding grounds for many insects and amphibians. Endangered marbled salamanders, for example, lay their eggs in places that normally fill with water in the autumn. After laying their eggs, they guard them until the site becomes flooded and the eggs hatch.

also impact this enclosed body of water. Pond conditions can change daily, depending on the time of day, weather, and season.

Ponds may be small, but they are mighty. They are miniature agricultural power plants that, when exposed to plenty of sunshine, can produce more plant life than many farm fields or natural grasslands.

Still Waters Run Deep

Lakes are often considered "still waters," but their surfaces constantly move. Even without the effects of boats and wind, the heating and cooling of surface water causes movement.

When surface waters are colder than the water beneath, the cold water sinks. This causes warmer water from the lower layers of the lake to rise. This movement of warmer and colder waters, called **thermal stratification**, helps to mix everything that organisms living in the lake need to survive—nutrients, carbon dioxide, and oxygen dissolved in water.

Many lakes were formed when glaciers scooped out land

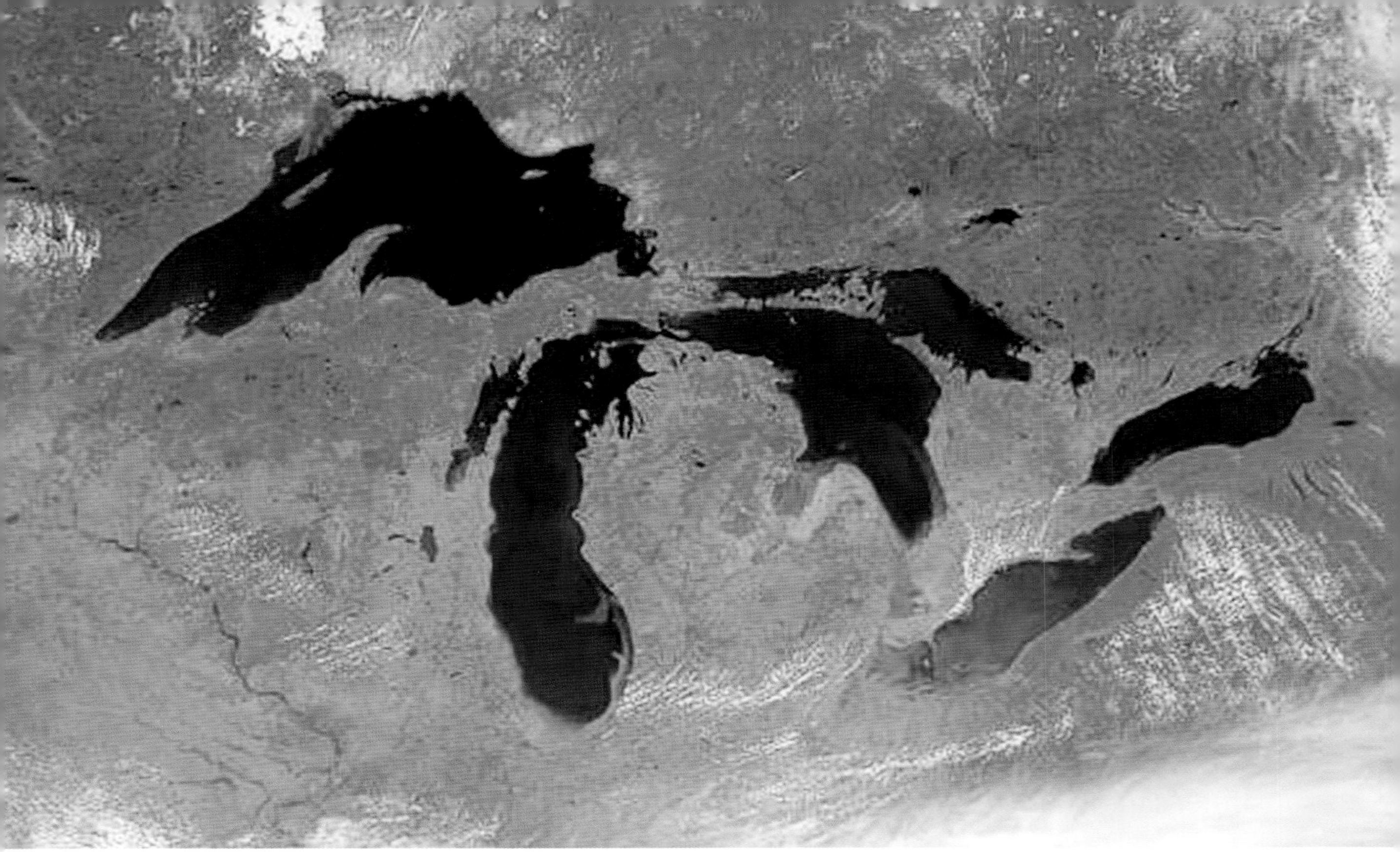

This photo of the Great Lakes was taken from space.

during the last Ice Age and the remaining depressions filled with meltwater from glacial ice. The Great Lakes in North America were formed when the weight of one ice sheet caused the land beneath it to sink and form a basin. People make lakes by building reservoirs to collect water for drinking, recreation, or to reduce the likelihood of flooding. Most lakes have a deep bottom where sunlight does not reach and plants cannot grow.

Sometimes a river will create an **oxbow lake**. When a river straightens its course from a curve to a straighter one, the old channel is blocked off from the main part of the river. The shape of the channel that is left behind resembles the

U-shaped piece of wood used by farmers on an ox yoke, hence the name "oxbow."

Like living organisms, a lake can age. When this happens, its water becomes shallow, and resident organisms die and fill in the bottom. Over time, dying lakes become bogs, marshes, swamps, or wetlands.

Home to Many, Appreciated by Few

Wetlands are areas of slow-moving, shallow water, typically not more than 6 feet (1.8 meters) deep. At one time, wetlands were considered a nuisance. They were breeding places for mosquitoes and other types of insects that were viewed as pests. Wetlands appeared to serve little or no use. As a result, people filled them in and sometimes built on that land. Huge areas of Boston, Mexico City, and Venice, Italy, were built on former wetlands.

However, scientists understand how important these habitats are to a healthy environment. Wetlands act as natural water regulators, helping to hold back floods in the wet season and gradually releasing the water in times of droughts. They filter out pollutants and sediments from waters that pass through them. Additionally, they sustain a great deal of wildlife. Numerous ducks, wading birds, and shorebirds breed or stop in wetlands to feed while migrating.

Wetlands form where flat, poorly drained land collects enough water for the surface to be submerged or saturated

Not a Small Chunk

Wetlands cover 15 percent of Canada and 3.5 percent of the continental United States.

Wetlands, once considered a nuisance, are an important part of a healthy environment.

much or all of the time. Land does not have to be constantly full of water to be considered a wetland. It only has to be wet enough to support typical wetland vegetation.

Hang On Tight

Unlike wetlands, some freshwater habitats are fast-moving. Living in a fast-flowing mountain stream is like living in a constant hurricane. Organisms that live in streams are equipped with special features that allow them to anchor themselves so that they are not swept away.

Take **diatoms**, for example. If you've tried crossing a stream, you may have had trouble keeping your footing because the rocks were slippery. Diatoms, a type of algae, keep themselves from being washed downstream by attaching to rocks with slimy secretions. This coating makes the rocks very slippery.

Streams are formed from such sources as rainwater, groundwater moving through the soil, springs, and snowmelt flowing down a mountain.

Rivers form when several streams converge, or flow together. Definitions vary as to when a stream actually becomes a river. One description says a stream becomes a river when it is 4 yards (3.66 meters) wide.

Rivers are made up of three distinct sections. The upper portion, which is close to the water's source, is called the head-waters. This section is usually quick-flowing and contains few fish. In the middle section, where the river becomes wider, the water moves more slowly. In this section, the river contains soil particles that have washed into it from the banks. Many fish and plants call this portion of the river home. At its mouth, the river flows either into a larger river or into the ocean. Rivers that run into the ocean or another large body of water usually fan out into smaller channels before reaching their final destination. All sorts of wildlife depend on these areas, which are called **deltas**.

Source of Civilization

The first cities were built more than five thousand years ago on the Tigris and Euphrates rivers in Mesopotamia, or what is known today as Iraq.

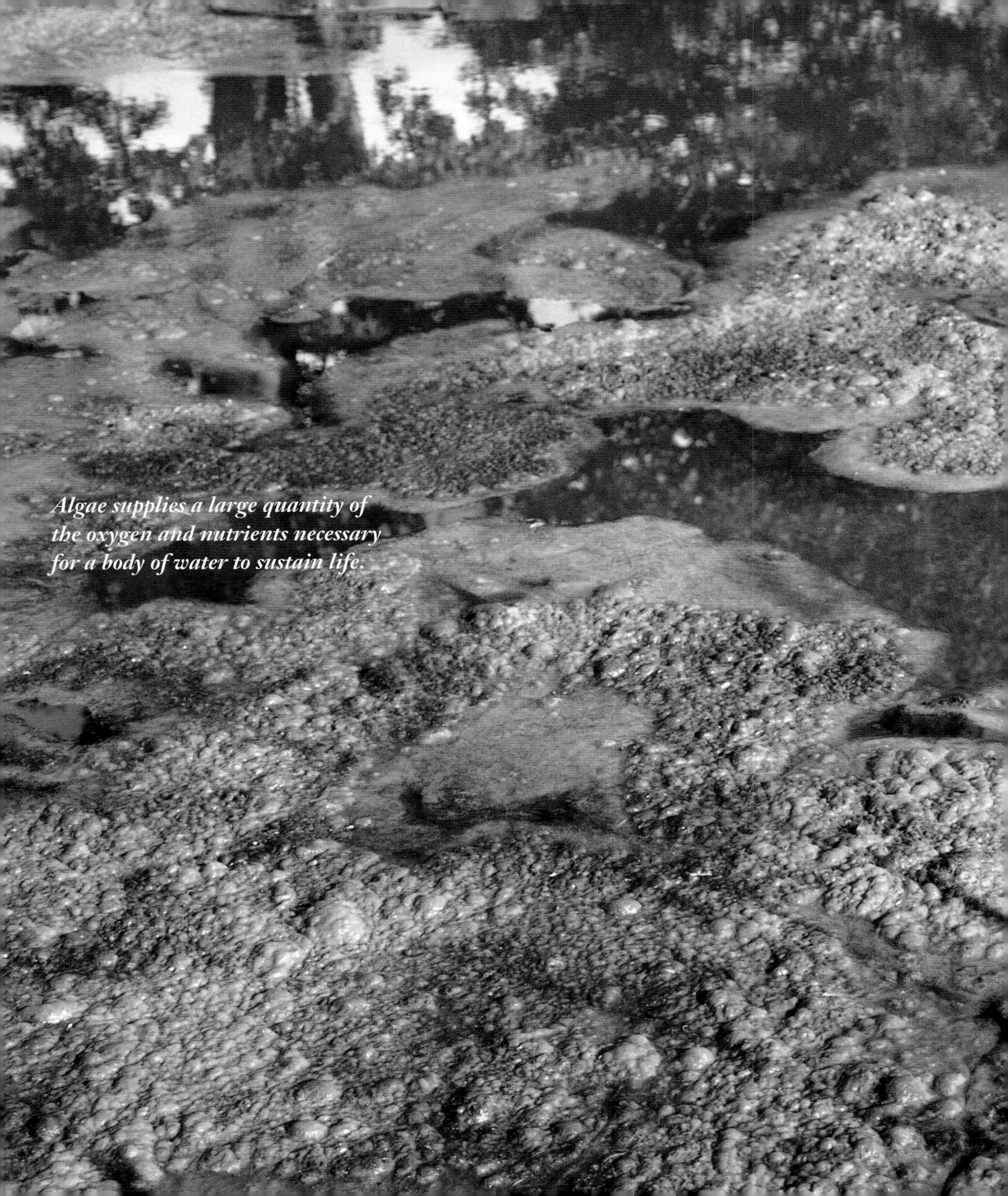

Algae supplies a large quantity of the oxygen and nutrients necessary for a body of water to sustain life.

Chapter Three

It's Good to Be Green

Plants and algae are essential for supporting other life in freshwater habitats. Not only are they at the bottom of every **food chain**, they also supply a large quantity of the oxygen and nutrients necessary for a body of water to sustain life. In addition, they offer protection and nesting sites to a variety of fish and other animals.

Just as plants do on land, algae and aquatic plants produce their own food through **photosynthesis**. During photosynthesis, green plants use sunlight to

The Aquatic Food Chain

Algae and aquatic plants, such as water lilies, are considered **producers** because they manufacture their own food. This "food" is consumed throughout the food chain, supplying every living thing with energy. **Herbivores,** or grazers, such as turtles, minnows, and ducks, eat aquatic plants and algae. **Carnivores,** such as dragonfly nymphs, bass, and alligators, feed on the herbivores. Otters and bears are **omnivores** and eat both producers and grazers. Bacteria and other **detrivores** consume dead and decayed plant and animal material.

change hydrogen from water (H_2O) and carbon and oxygen from carbon dioxide (CO_2) into sugar, or **organic matter**. The plants then release extra oxygen as waste.

When algae and plants die, bacteria and other detrivores consume them. These **decomposers** break down the leaves and stems, releasing the component chemicals back into the water as nutrients and carbon dioxide.

Aquatic producers are typically divided into five categories. Those categories include algae, floating-leafed plants, free floating plants, emergent plants, and submerged plants.

Microscopic Producers

"Algae is as important to a pond, lake, or stream as grass is to a field of grazing cows," writes Michael J. Caduto in his book *Pond and Brook: A Guide to Nature in Freshwater Environments*.

Just about every living thing depends on algae, either directly or indirectly. Not only do algae add oxygen to the water, they also serve as a major source of organic matter at the base of the food chain.

Algae are mostly microscopic organisms that contain chlorophyll and grow by using energy they create through photosynthesis. They don't have roots, stems, or leaves. Instead, the cells absorb nutrients directly from water or sediments.

Although they are green, algae are not plants. Nor are they animals or fungi. Algae are **protists**, members of the kingdom Protista, which is a group of predominantly single-celled microorganisms with a nucleus. Fossil records suggest that the

Too Much of a Good Thing

Algae require nutrients, such as nitrogen and phosphorus, to grow. They use nitrogen for tissue growth and phosphorus for reproduction. Waters containing high concentrations of these nutrients can usually support a great deal of algae, plant, and animal life. However, too many nutrients may cause an **algae bloom**, or an overabundance of algae. As the algae die, bacteria use oxygen to decompose them. Because there are so many decomposing algae, the bacteria use almost all of the oxygen available in the water, suffocating other living creatures in this environment.

first green algae appeared 500 to 600 million years ago. Scientists believe algae paved the way for the evolution of early plants, animals, and fungi.

Floating-Leafed Plants

If you've ever seen a picture of a pond, you've probably seen a lily pad. These flat, semi-circular leaves rest on the water's surface and connect to a huge root system at the bottom of the pond. This foundation makes water lilies so stable that small aquatic animals often lay their eggs on their leaves and stems.

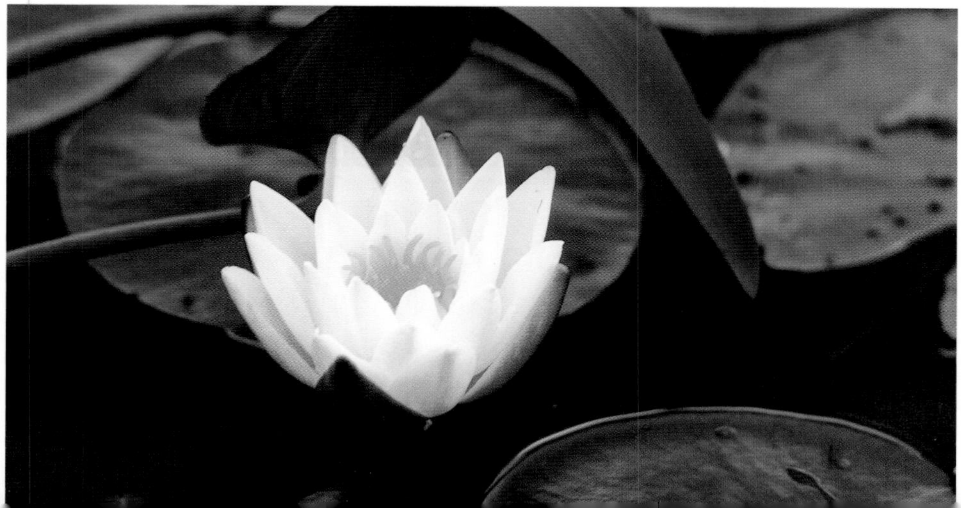

Water lilies rest on the water's surface.

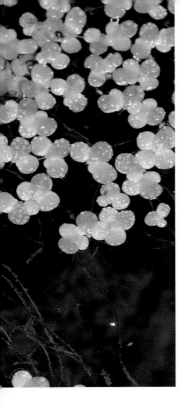

Duckweeds have one to three roots that dangle below the surface of the water.

The biggest lily pad ever recorded was 10 feet (3 m) across, though most are just a few inches.

Free-Floating Plants

Along with water lilies, one may see duckweed or very small floating plants that sometimes form dense mats in ponds, lakes, and slow-moving streams and rivers. Duckweeds don't have stems. Each duckweed has just a tiny leaf with one to three roots that dangle below the water's surface. The roots may be up to 1 inch (2.54 centimeters) long, but the plant is only about 0.1 inch (2.5 millimeters) wide.

Even smaller than duckweed is water meal, or *Wolffia*. This plant, no larger than a pinhead, is the smallest flowering plant in the world. It is often mistaken for duckweed, but *Wolffia* has no roots.

Emergent Plants

Cattails grow just about anyplace where there is shallow, standing water for at least part of the year. They are a perfect example of an emergent—a plant that is rooted in the soil and

Cattails are made of thousands of tiny brown flowers.

grows near shore. Emergents can tolerate having their roots flooded, but they do not like being submerged for an extended period of time.

Cattails are easily recognized by their flower—the long, thin, brown mass on top of the stem. This mass is actually thousands of tiny, tightly compressed brown flowers.

Coontails grow completely underwater.

Submerged Plants

Submerged plants grow totally under-water. Fishers have often reeled in a "really big fish," only to find a coontail on the end of their fishing line. Coon-tails grow beneath the surface in quiet waters throughout North America. Their slender, branched leaves crowd around a skinny stem, making it look bushy—just like the raccoon tail for which coontail is named.

Bladderwort, another variety of sub-merged plant, is carnivorous. It gets its name from the special hair-covered "bladders" on its underwater leaves. These sacks remain deflated until a crea-ture touches the hairs surrounding it. Then the bladder inflates suddenly and sucks in the prey.

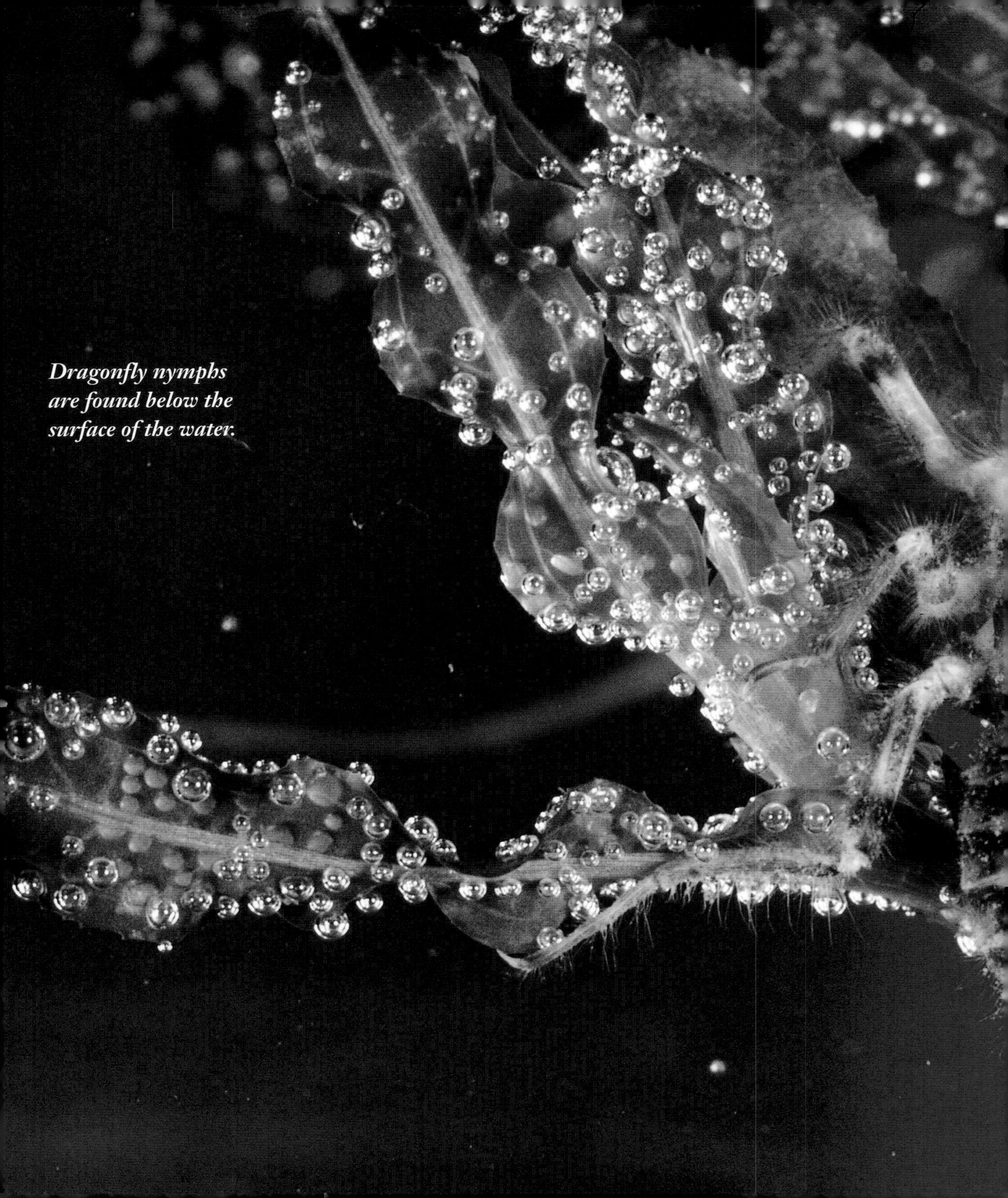

Dragonfly nymphs are found below the surface of the water.

Chapter Four

Small but Mighty

The bottom of a river or stream literally crawls with life. Baby mosquitoes, dragonflies, damselflies, mayflies, worms, and beetles all live in the mud and muck. You will rarely see these animals simply by looking at the surface of the water. If you take a scoop of sediment and carefully poke through it, though, you will find some interesting-looking bugs.

Although odd in appearance, these aquatic insects are some of the most important inhabitants of freshwater

Living Fossils

Dragonfly nymphs, a common macroinvertebrate, have been around for 300 million years. They predate dinosaurs by more than 100 million years.

habitats. After plants, **macroinvertebrates**—small aquatic animals with no backbones—are the next step in the freshwater food chain. Many of these animals are nymphs and **larvae**, insects that are in an early stage of their life cycles. They live in the **benthos**, or the bottom of a body of water where dead organisms decay.

How Clean Is It?

Besides being an important food source, macroinvertebrates are indicators of the health of a watershed because they live in the water for all or most of their lives. They cannot survive if the water does not have enough oxygen or if it has too many pollutants. They also only inhabit areas suitable for their survival. If the water is contaminated, the adults will lay their eggs elsewhere.

When the Nashua River was "ecologically dead," the only organism that lived in the water was the sludge worm, or tubifex worm. Tubifex worms make a tube in the mud and eat the muck. These worms are commonly sold in pet shops as food for tropical fish.

As the river water became cleaner, other organisms, such as leeches, were able to live in it again. These animals can survive in fairly polluted water. Leeches range in length from minute to about 8 inches (20 cm) or even longer. The giant Amazon leech can grow to 18 inches (45.7 cm) in length. Some leech species eat decaying plant and animal matter. Other species feed on blood, which is why they sometimes attach themselves to people who swim in freshwater. If a leech sticks to you, either pull it off and throw it back into the water, or sprinkle it with salt, and it will immediately let go.

It's Getting Better

When the water became even cleaner, crayfish and mosquito larvae could be found in it. They rely on good or fair water quality. Crayfish resemble miniature lobsters. In fact, many people in the southeastern United States eat a species of crayfish. Crayfish can be brown, green, reddish, or black and can grow to be up to 6 inches (15 cm) in length. Being omnivores, they use their pair of strong pincers to tear plants and animals into bite-size chunks.

Crayfish are able to live in fair water quality.

How Clean Is the Water Near You?

Biologists like to use macroinvertebrates as water-quality indicators because they are easy to collect and identify. You can do your own macroinvertebrate study with a few "scientific" tools found around the house. You need a net or strainer, a bucket, a magnifying glass, a spoon or turkey baster, and an ice cube tray or a foam or plastic egg carton.

With adult supervision, take your equipment to the edge of a pond or river.

Fill your bucket with an inch or two of water. Use the top of the net to stir the pond or river bottom. Then scoop up a portion of the bottom with the net and dump it into your bucket.

Use the magnifying glass to see if you can locate anything that is moving. When you find a bug, fish it out with the spoon or turkey baster and put it into one of the squares of the ice cube tray or egg carton. Try to keep different insects separated, or else they may eat one another!

Now identify the organisms and see how many are found in poor water, in fair water, and in good water.

When finished, put the bugs back in the water where you found them.

Although most people don't appreciate the mosquito, it is an important link in the food chain. Its larvae are an important food source for aquatic organisms.

It's Clean!

Today, the Nashua River is clean enough for biologists to find caddis fly larvae. These animals are pollution-sensitive and need very clean water to survive. The caddis fly larvae are macroinvertebrate architects. They protect their soft, wormlike bodies by constructing hollow cases from sand, twigs, small stones, crushed shells, rolled leaves, and pieces of bark. They feed on algae, plant material, and animals. Some species build cone-shaped nets and attach them to rocks so that they can catch drifting food. The caddis fly also uses its case for **pupation**—a stage in an insect's life when it encloses itself to undergo major physical changes before emerging as an adult. This is similar to a caterpillar building a cocoon in order to change into a butterfly.

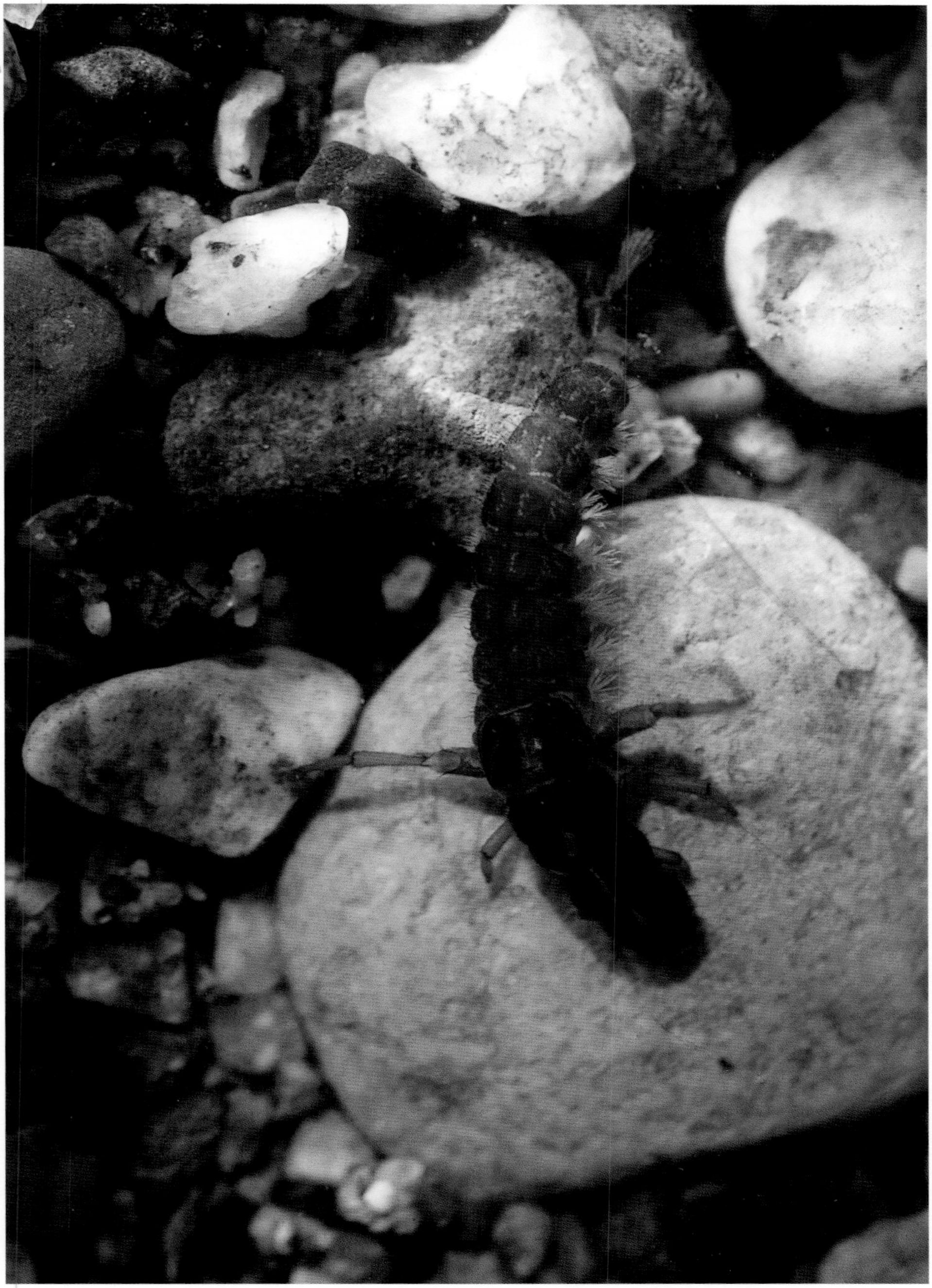

The caddis fly can only live in clean water.

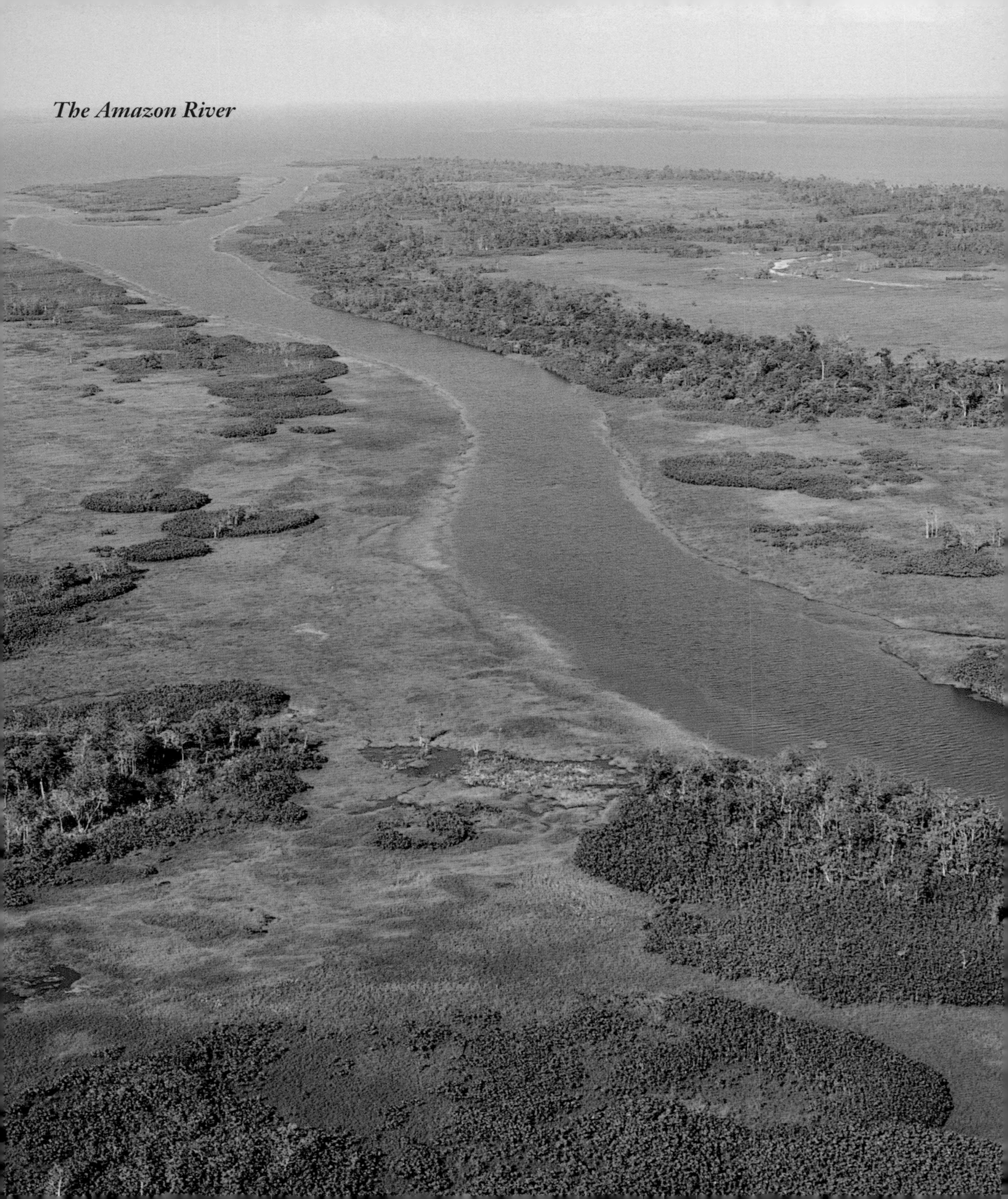

The Amazon River

Chapter Five

Slick and Slithery

Scientists estimate that there are about twenty thousand species of fish. Some species are found throughout the world; some are limited to a single lake or stream. The Amazon River alone contains an estimated three thousand species of fish.

Freshwater fish are adapted to the low salt content and would not be able to survive in areas of high salt concentration, such as those found in the ocean. However, some fish, like the salmon and the

A Scaly Situation

Fish have no scales when hatched, but most develop them during the first year of life. Scales are formed from bone and grow out of the skin. One can determine a fish's age by counting the number of rings or lines on a scale, similar to counting the growth rings of a tree.

alewife, return from the ocean to lay their eggs in freshwater rivers. The American eel does just the opposite. It lives its life in freshwater and returns to the ocean to lay its eggs.

Many fish build nests. The male bass, for example, uses his tail to fan away debris and form a circular depression in the soft dirt bottom of ponds and lakes. After the female bass lays her eggs, the male sprays them with his sperm. The male stays with the eggs and protects them until they hatch. The male will protect the baby fish, called fry, from frogs, turtles, and other fish, until they mature.

A New Home

Many fish that are common in the Nashua River today did not live there one hundred years ago. This is because people have transfered fish from one river or lake to another.

State fish and wildlife departments routinely do this with sport fish. Biologists release, or stock, thousands of trout and pike from fish hatcheries into streams and rivers so people can enjoy fishing. Not all of these fish are caught. Those that survive reproduce, or spawn, and become part of the fish community.

State fish and wildlife departments release fish from fish hatcheries into streams and rivers so people can enjoy fishing.

Normally, introducing a new species to an area is bad news for the organisms that already live there. A new species often has no natural predators and will compete with native animals for food and places to raise their young. But in some rivers and ponds, stocking provides stability to the fish community's structure, says Charles Bell, a fisheries biologist for the Massachusetts Division of Fisheries and Wildlife.

Today, introduced species take the place of many of the fish that once swam in rivers and lakes. Many years ago, salmon swam up the Nashua River to spawn. When people built dams too large for the salmon to jump over, the salmon stopped coming. Stocked trout and bass have taken the place of salmon in the food chain.

Long and Skinny or Short and Flat

Because humans have introduced fish to just about every freshwater habitat, you will find similar species living in ponds, lakes, and rivers. However, some fish survive better in certain habitats than in others.

Where Are the Fish?

Scientists estimate that one-third of North American freshwater fish species qualify for threatened or endangered status because of loss of habitat.

Now You See Them . . .

Sometimes introducing fish can have a dramatic affect on the populations of native animals. Every spring for fifty years, the California Department of Fish and Game (CF&G) dropped trout from planes into high-altitude lakes in the Sierra Nevada. Trout don't normally live there because these lakes are too cold for the fish to breed. Biologists noticed that native amphibians started disappearing. The biologists knew that trout ate frog eggs and tadpoles. So the CF&G decided to stop stocking certain high-altitude lakes to see what happened. What do you think was the result? The amphibian population started rebounding.

The pumpkin seed fish, for example, has the perfect body for living in a pond, lake, or quiet river. This tiny relative of the black bass prefers still waters where it can wait in the weeds for insects to swim by for it to eat. The pumpkin seed's flat body allows it to stay in one spot. To breathe, it uses its muscular fins to fan water over its gills.

Trout, on the other hand, thrives best in clean, fast-moving water with lots of oxygen. This fish can't move its fins to fan oxygen-rich water over its gills, but instead relies on the flow

Pumpkin Seed Fish

of water. It swims to get enough oxygen flowing over its gills. *Brook Trout*
Its body is long and narrow, like a canoe. This shape allows it
to move easily through the flowing water.

If a pumpkin seed lived in a trout stream and turned side-
ways for even a second, its big, flat body would act like a sail
and the water would push it downstream.

Amphibians Tell Tales

Amphibians include frogs and toads, newts and salamanders,
and a legless variety known as caecilians. This last type of animal looks more like an earthworm than a frog. There are
about five thousand known species of amphibians, and new
ones are discovered frequently, particularly in tropical rain
forests. Amphibians are natural pest controllers because they
eat many insects, such as mosquitoes. In turn, they serve as a
food source for snakes, birds, and small mammals.

Salamanders live on land, but return to water to lay their eggs.

Frog Life Cycle

The eggs of frogs hatch into larvae, or tadpoles, that have a tail and gills. As they grow, they lose their gills and develop lungs so they can live on land. Frogs often stay in the tadpole stage for more than a year. Bullfrogs take as long as two years to mature into full-sized adults.

Although amphibians were the first animals with backbones, or **vertebrates**, to live on land, they return to water to lay their eggs. They have lungs, but they absorb much of the oxygen they need through their skin, which must be kept moist in order for it to function properly.

Many scientists use amphibians as indicators of a habitat's health. "They are great indicators of what is going on in ponds, forests, the soil, and even the air," says Dr. Richard Wyman, executive director of the Edmund Niles Huyck Preserve in Rensselaerville, New York. Amphibians are more sensitive to the degradation of their environment than other animals are because their thin, porous skin absorbs pollutants directly into their bodies.

What are they telling us? Amphibian populations are declining rapidly. Scientists are concerned because no one can point to one reason why this is the case. They believe there are multiple causes, including global warming, pollution, loss of habitat due to urban and suburban sprawl, and acid rain.

Reptiles Rule

If you are paddling on a lake or a pond on a summer afternoon, you are likely to see turtles sunning themselves on a log. They need to warm their bodies in the sun because all reptiles are **cold-blooded**—they have no natural way to keep themselves warm because their body temperature is not internally regulated.

The three major groups of reptiles that live in freshwater habitats are turtles, snakes, and crocodilians. All of these animals are protected by scales or horny plates, and most lay eggs that are covered by a leathery shell.

While there are many types of turtles, snapping turtles are unique because they cannot retract their heads into their shells to protect themselves. Instead, they have sharp beaks and spiny tails so they can fight back if something attacks. Snapping turtles leave their water habitat to bury their eggs along the sandy shores of ponds, lakes, or slow-moving rivers. When the young hatch, they instinctively move toward the water, where they are safer than they would be on land.

Most snakes found near the water are harmless, although

This turtle suns itself on a fallen log to get warm.

Most freshwater snakes are harmless, but don't get too close. Some snakes will bite if provoked.

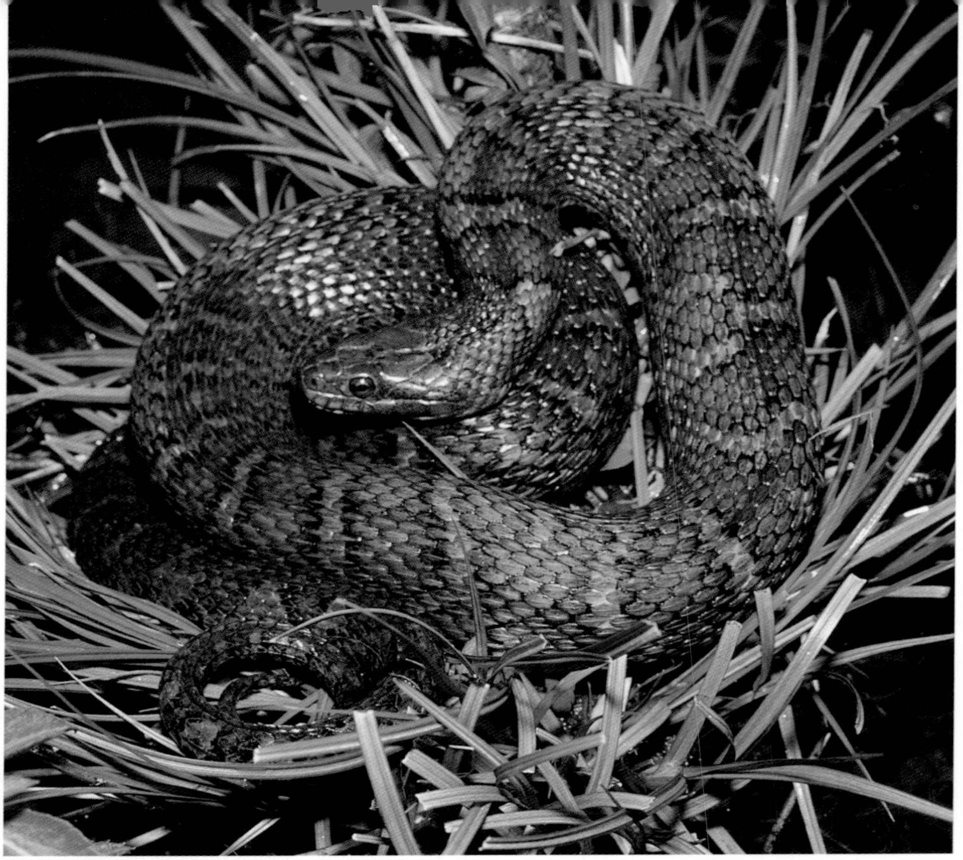

Crocodilians are survivors. They outlived the dinosaurs and appeared on Earth 200 million years ago.

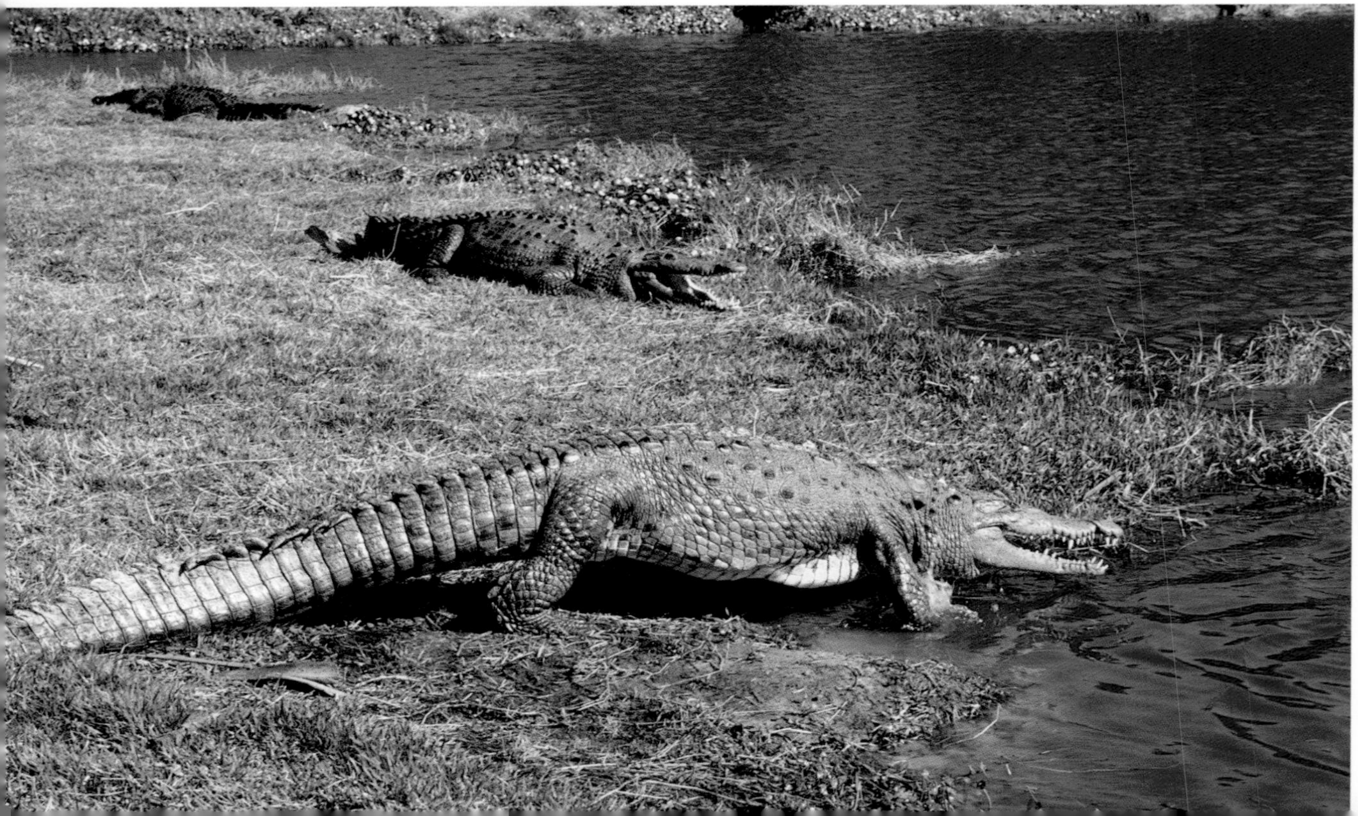

some will bite if provoked. They live under rocks or in debris along the shore. Some snakes lay eggs, while others, such as the common water snake and garter snake, give birth to live young.

The cottonmouth water moccasin is one of the few poisonous water snakes in North America. This thick-bodied snake lives in the southeastern United States and can grow to be as long as 5 feet (1.5 m). If startled, it raises its head and shows the white interior of its mouth, earning it the name cotton-mouth.

Alligators are an important predator in the tropics and subtropics. At one time, they were close to becoming extinct because hunters had killed so many for their skins. Thanks to efforts to protect the alligator, they are no longer endangered. A female lays about fifty eggs in the spring. After hatching, the young will stay with their mother for up to two years.

The poisonous cottonmouth water moccasin gets its name from the white interior of its mouth.

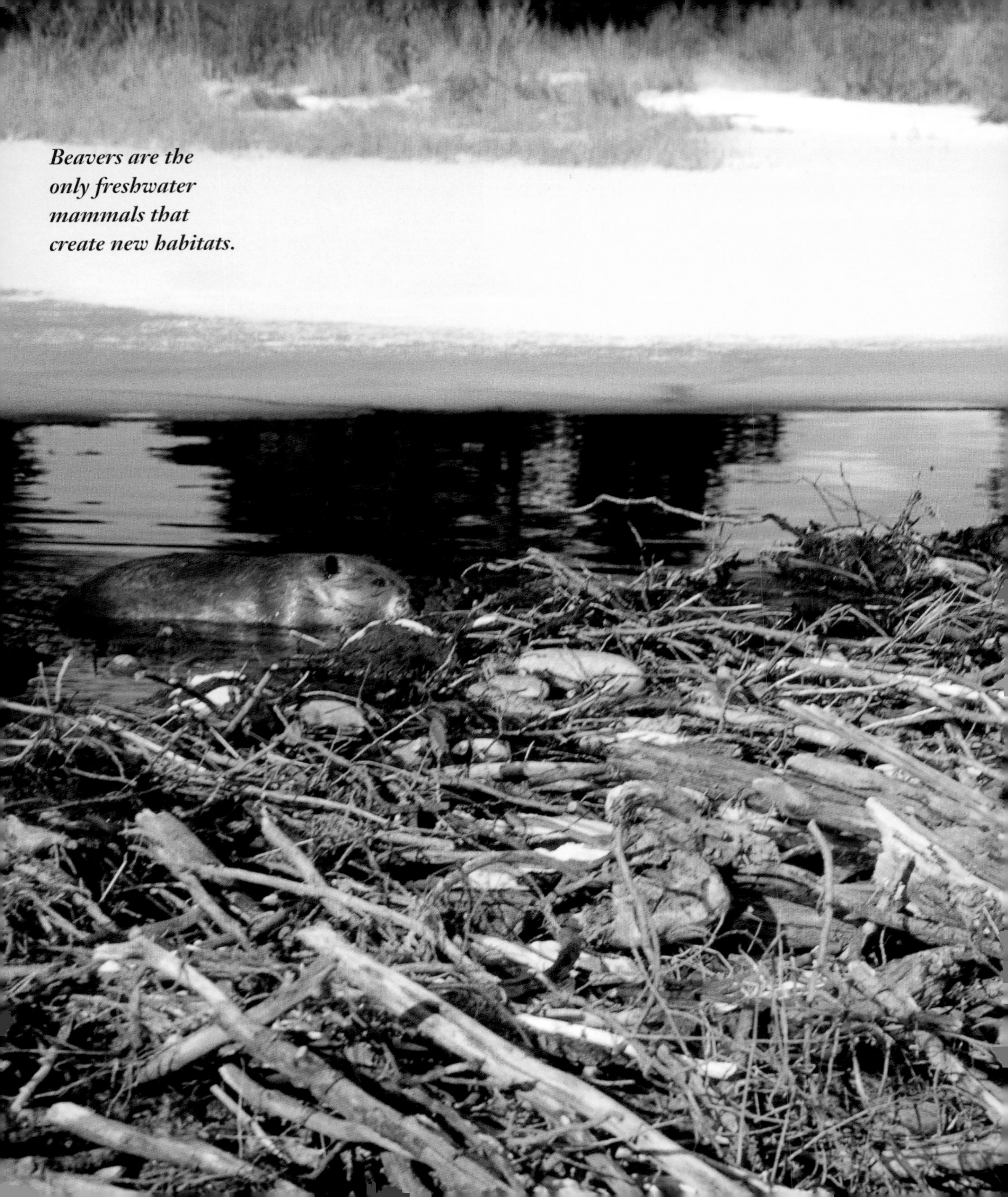

Beavers are the only freshwater mammals that create new habitats.

Chapter Six

Furry and Feathered

Aquatic mammals and birds were among some of the last inhabitants to return to the Nashua River. These animals depend on the plant, fish, and amphibian populations already established in a habitat.

Mammals have backbones and feed their young with milk that comes from the mammary glands of the mother. All mammals are **warm-blooded**. This means their body temperature remains constant, whatever the temperature of their surroundings.

An Active Builder

Beavers are the only freshwater mammals that create new habitats by damming rivers and streams. "Beavers are restoring the wetlands that we once ruined," says Chrissie Henner, wildlife biologist from the Massachusetts Division of Fisheries and Wildlife. "Because of beavers, we now have wetlands in places where they did not exist even ten years ago."

To beavers, the sound of running water seems to be a stimulus for building dams. Even in captivity, beavers have built dams when they heard a recording of rushing water.

Beavers are strictly herbivores. They use their large front teeth to gnaw down trees so they can feed on the leaves and the cambium, or inner bark, of the tree's upper branches. They also use the branches for constructing dams and lodges.

Beavers are not the great lumberjacks they are made out to be. They never know how a tree is going to fall. Instead, they chew around the tree in a circle. When a beaver starts to feel the tree fiber snapping, it chews a little, runs away, and waits. If the tree doesn't fall, it chews a bit more and runs away again. This continues until the tree is finally down—sometimes even falling on the beaver!

Let's Have Some Fun!

Otters, members of the weasel family, are probably the most playful of all freshwater mammals. If you sneak up on a pair, you may see them jumping over each other and chasing each other as if they were playing a game of tag.

Tracks and Signs

Although fish and macroinvertebrates are often hard to spot, birds and mammals leave their mark on their surroundings. You just need to know what to look for.

To help, here are some signs and tracks made by some of the more common birds and mammals you are likely to see in freshwater habitats.

Beaver

Muskrat

Otter

Great blue heron

One sign that otters live in an area is the mud slides they make that lead down the sides of the riverbanks into the water. Otters don't slide just for fun. They make these slides as a quick way to travel over land—uphill as well as downhill.

An adult otter can grow to be 4 feet (1.2 m) long, not including the tail, and weigh anywhere from 10 to 30 pounds (4 to 14 kilograms). It uses its sharp teeth to catch crayfish, frogs, and snakes.

Just as human children need to learn to swim, so do otter babies. They have to practice keeping their heads above water before they become skilled swimmers like their parents.

Great Blue

If you've seen a large bird that looks a bit like a pterodactyl when it flies, you've seen a great blue heron. The great blue is one of the most common birds seen in freshwater habitats. It

This great blue heron has captured a catfish.

is also the largest heron in North America, with a wingspan of 6 feet (2 m). It has a blue-gray back and a gray-and-white-striped belly. The great blue is known as a still hunter. It stands as motionless as a statue, waiting for a fish to swim by. Then it strikes like lightning with its long, slender, pointed bill.

A Bird That Swims

One of the more unusual birds that has adapted especially well to freshwater life is the American dipper. This robin-sized bird can swim underwater and can even walk on the bottom of a stream as it searches for insects and other small creatures. The female dipper makes a domed nest of moss and grass in a crevice in a stream bank, where she lays three to six eggs.

He's the King

The belted kingfisher is a fierce fisher. This bird, with its large head and crested feathers, stalks its prey from perches along clear streams. When it sees a fish, it dives from the tree branch with its eyes closed, capturing its prey in its beak. Kingfisher babies have big appetites. A baby kingfisher can eat up to eighteen fish a day!

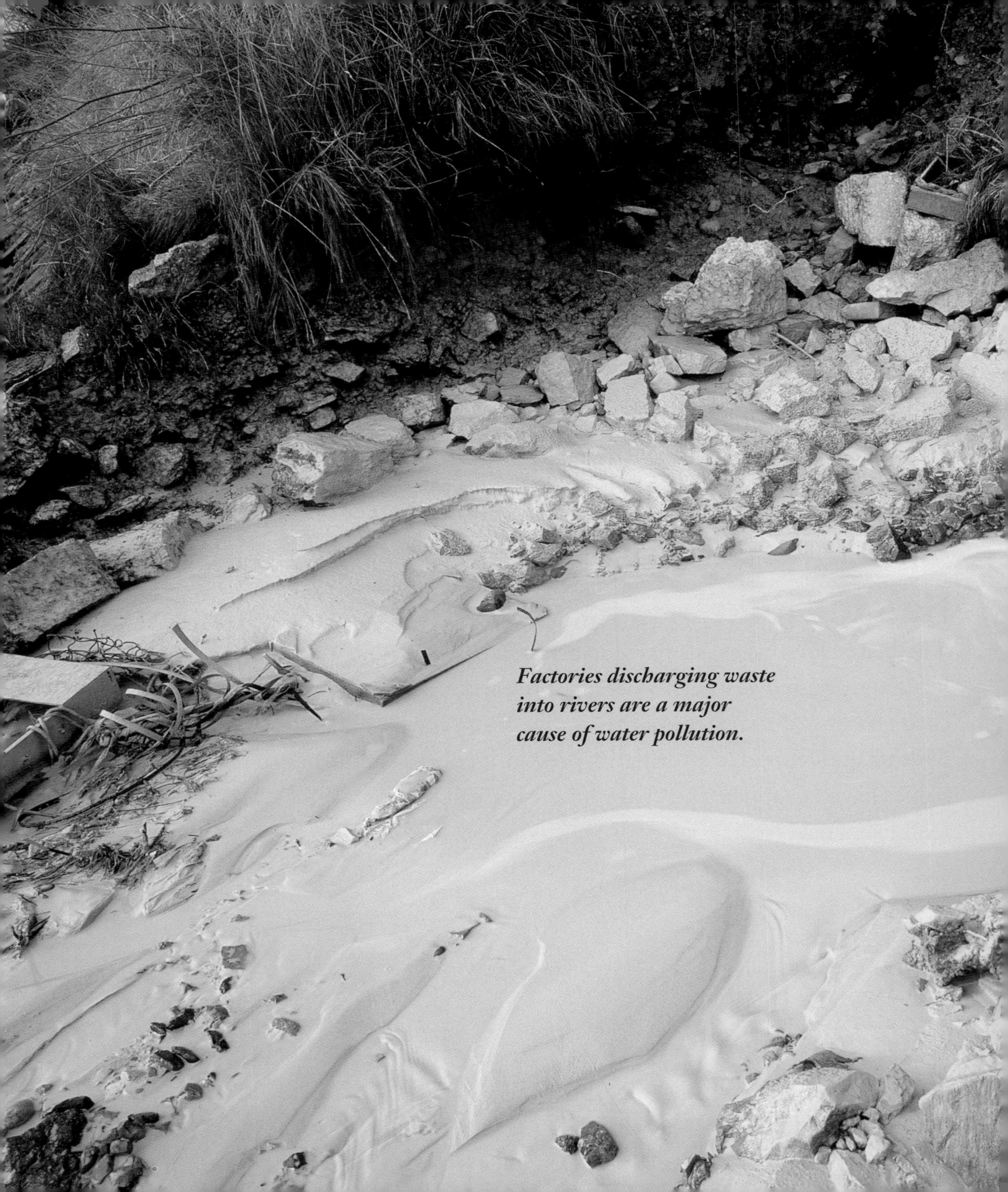

Factories discharging waste into rivers are a major cause of water pollution.

Chapter Seven

Protecting Our Freshwater

Before there were people like Marion Stoddart who took an interest in the environment, many people considered rivers and streams to be bottomless garbage barges that conveniently carried away whatever trash they threw in. These people did not think about the consequences of continual polluting.

As Stoddart's group influenced legislators to pass laws to clean up the Nashua River, factories stopped polluting and built wastewater treatment plants. This took care of what is called **point-source pollution**, in which waste enters a river from a pipe or some other known source.

But the cleanup work for the Nashua River and other freshwater habitats is far from complete. Chemicals continue to enter the water through **non-point source pollution**, which comes from sources that cannot be narrowed down to one place. For example, fertilizer washes into rivers from such places as lawns, golf courses, and agricultural fields. In addition, rainwater carries motor oil and gasoline from streets into storm drains, which then flows into rivers.

Clean Water For All

In 1972, the U.S. Congress passed the first Clean Water Act, which regulated the chemicals that could be discharged into the waters of the United States.

The Way Is Green

There are several ways people can reduce non-point source pollution. They can use organic fertilizers on lawns and golf courses, as these types of fertilizers break down quickly. They can also take measures to prevent oil leaks and gasoline spills.

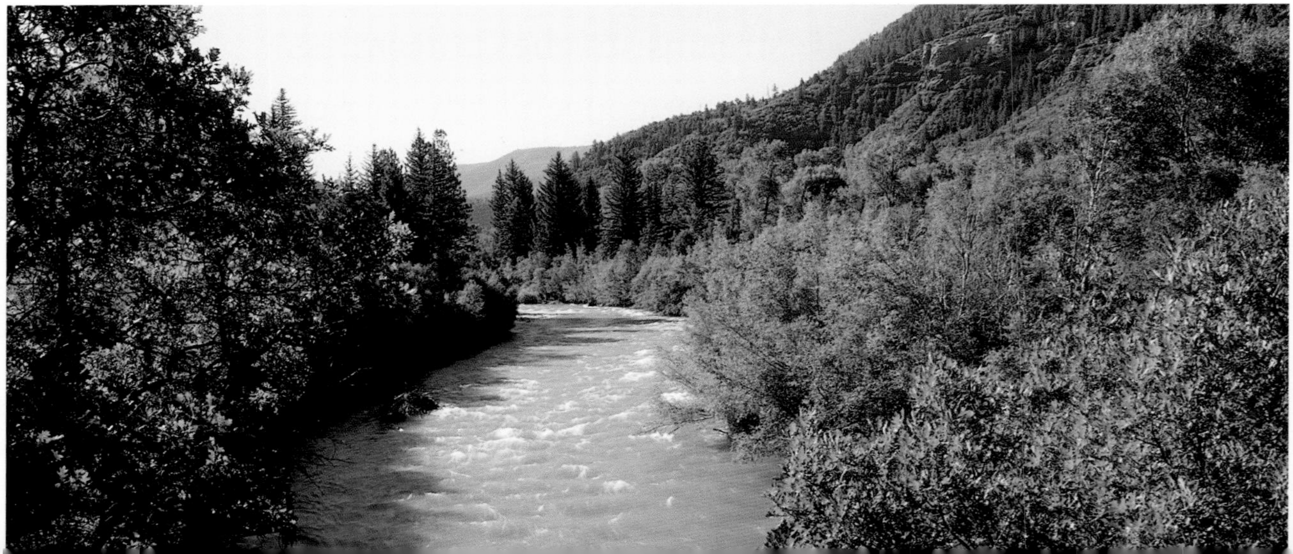

Greenways help keep rivers healthy.

Most importantly, they can maintain corridors of natural vegetation, such as trees, shrubs, and ground cover, along all waterways. This zone of green is called a **greenway** or a **riparian corridor**.

Greenways offer many benefits to rivers and lakes. Such vegetation as trees and brush keeps the water temperature cool. The leaves that fall into the water provide a source of nutrients. The roots keep riverbank soil from eroding. Finally, the vegetation acts as a filter by helping to keep non-point source pollution from reaching the water.

Mining Water

Nature's water cycle keeps freshwater in the environment. But humans can interrupt the water cycle. JoAnne Carr, the Massachusetts Watershed Initiative team leader for the Nashua River, says, "In some parts of Massachusetts, we are using more water than the water cycle can create."

Many towns and cities pump water from one river's watershed to use as drinking water. Then instead of returning treated wastewater to the same system, these towns redirect the treated water to an entirely different river's watershed. "It is like mining water," says Carr, "and it results in a net loss." Rivers, lakes, and wetlands in that watershed could eventually dry up.

What You Can Do

Beginning with the efforts of just one person, the Nashua River was cleaned up. Just think what you can do! You can get involved with local groups that are working to protect the environment. Organizations like the Nashua River Watershed Association, which Stoddart formed in 1969, exist almost everywhere. They always need volunteers to help sample water or check for sources of pollution.

With adult supervision, you can organize a group of your friends to help remove bottles, tires, fast-food containers, and other trash from the waters. "Young adults can also have a big influence on families," says Stoddart. "They can ask their parents not to use excess fertilizers on their lawn. They can help educate their friends and family to pick up trash."

You can also keep a nature journal in which you record all the organisms you see in an area over a period of time. As you keep notes, you might notice changes in the wildlife that could indicate a problem. If you see lots of frogs in a pond one year and very few the next, you may want to report the situation to the local conservation commission.

Today, otters play along the Nashua's banks. Ospreys (fish hawks) fish in its waters. Deer and fox drink from it. People swim, fish, and canoe in it. The cleanup has been such an amazing success that only pictures remain to remind everyone of how polluted the river once was.

But this one river is only a tiny fraction of all freshwater habitats in the world. The same efforts to protect our rivers, streams, ponds, and lakes must continue everywhere. That effort can start with you.

Glossary

algae bloom—when too many nutrients are present in the water, algae growth increases rapidly. As the algae die, bacteria deplete the dissolved oxygen in the water in an attempt to decompose them

benthos—the bottom of a body of water where dead organisms decay and macroinvertebrates live

biome—community of living organisms in a single ecological region

carnivore—organism that eats other animals

cold-blooded—animals that do not have an internal way of regulating body temperature. To compensate, reptiles, for example, use the sun to warm up and the water to cool down

decomposer—organism such as a bacterium that breaks down plant and animal remains into forms that are usable by producers

53

delta—deposit of soil, sand, and clay at the mouth of a river, where swiftly moving water enters a slow-moving body of water and drops its sediment. Deltas are usually triangular in shape, with the triangle pointing upstream, toward the source of swifter water

detrivore—organism such as a bacterium that eats dead plants and animals

diatom—single-celled alga that is one of the main plants in first link of the food chain

ecosystem—all living and nonliving things found in a given area, such as plants, animals, insects, water, and soil

emergent plants—plants that are rooted in the ground and can tolerate flooded soil but not for extended periods of time. Their stems and leaves emerge above the water surface

floating-leafed plants—plants whose underwater roots grow in the ground and whose leaves and flowers float on top of the water

food chain—flow of energy through an ecosystem, moving from producers to the top-level consumers

free-floating plants—plants that are not rooted in the ground

freshwater—water that contains less than 1 percent salt concentration

greenway—buffer zone of natural vegetation that grows alongside waterways

herbivore—organism that eats only plants

larvae—immature stage of development of insects that undergo major changes before taking their adult form

macroinvertebrate—small aquatic animal with no backbone

non-point source pollution—broad areas that are sources of pollution, such as lawns and parking lots

nymph—interim stage of development between the egg stage and adulthood in insects that undergo incomplete metamorphosis

omnivore—organism that eats both plants and animals

organic matter—material containing carbon, a basic component of all living things

oxbow lake—crescent-shaped body of water formed as a meandering river gradually changes direction and cuts this body of water off from the main channel

photosynthesis—process in which green plants use chlorophyll, sunlight, water, and carbon dioxide to create water, oxygen, and carbohydrates, such as sugars. Photosynthesis is the primary source of energy in the global ecosystem

point-source pollution—pollution or waste that comes from a known, specific source

producer—organism, such as green plants, that is capable of changing inorganic elements into organic tissues

protist—member of the kingdom Protista, a group of predominantly single-celled microorganisms with a nucleus

pupation—process through which insects that undergo complete metamorphosis will enclose themselves into a protective case such as a cocoon, where they will undergo major physical changes before emerging as adults

riparian corridor—corridor of natural vegetation, such as trees, shrubs, and ground cover, along a waterway

submerged plants—plants that grow and reproduce completely underwater

thermal stratification—formation of vertical temperature zones in a lake or pond

vernal pond—temporary pool that exists only during the wet season

vertebrate—animal with a backbone

warm-blooded—organisms whose body temperature remains constant

watershed—area that drains into a river system

To Find Out More

Books

Allaby, Michael. *Wetlands*. Vol. 4, *Biomes of the World*. Danbury, Conn: Scholastic Library, 1999.

Caduto, Michael J. *Pond and Brook*. Hanover and London: University Press of New England, 1990.

Cherry, Lynne. *A River Ran Wild*. New York: Harcourt Brace & Company, 1992.

Haslam, Andrew. *Make It Work! Rivers*. Chicago: World Book Inc., 1996.

National Geographic Animal Encyclopedia. Washington, D.C.: National Geographic Society, 1999, 2000.

Reid, George K., Jonathan P. Nolting, and Herbert S. Zim Latimer (eds.) *Pond Life: A Guide to Common Plants and Animals of North American Ponds and Lakes.* New York: St. Martin's Press, 2001.

Stokes, Donald, and Lillian Stokes. *Stokes Guide to Animal Tracking and Behavior.* Boston: Little, Brown and Company, 1987.

Videos

Eyewitness Nature Pond & River. BBC Worldwide American and DK Vision in association with Oregon Public Broadcasting. Copyright 1996.

Fresh Water Animals, Animals in Action Series, Eastman Kodak Company. Copyright 1988.

Online Sites

Water on the Web
www.nrri.umn.edu/wow

World Resources Institute (WRI)
www.wri.org/wri/biodiv/b03-gbs.html

Organizations

The Conservation Fund
Freshwater Institute
1098 Turner Road
Shepherdstown, WV 25443
304-876-2815
www.freshwaterinstitute.org

U.S. Environmental Protection Agency
Office of Ground Water & Drinking Water
Ariel Rios Building
1200 Pennsylvania Avenue, NW
Washington, DC 20460-0003
202-564-3750
www.epa.gov/kids
www.epa.gov/OGWDW/kids

U.S. Fish & Wildlife Service
1849 C Street, NW
Washington, DC 20240
www.fws.gov/kids

A Note on Sources

I started my research by reading other books about freshwater habitats, such as Michael Caduto's *Pond and Brook* and E.C. Pielou's *Fresh Water*. I read related magazine and newspaper articles. I scoured the Internet. For the story of the Nashua River and its biology, I interviewed people such as Marion Stoddart and Neal Menschel and others involved with River Classroom, a local environmental education program. For current research and conservation issues, I contacted the Massachusetts Division of Fisheries and Wildlife and the Massachusetts Watershed Initiative for the Nashua River, as well as the U.S. Environmental Protection Agency. Many thanks to all my sources!

Laurie Peach Toupin

Index

Numbers in *italics* indicate illustrations.

About the Author

Laurie Toupin loves nature and enjoys helping others uncover its mysteries through writing and teaching. She has written about nature and the environment for publications such as *The Missouri Conservationist*; *Odyssey*, a science magazine for children; and *The Christian Science Monitor*.

Laurie has been teaching environmental education with River Classroom since its inception. She also led an environmental afterschool program called the Monoosnoc Brook Patrol for middle schools in Leominster, Massachusetts.

She has an undergraduate degree in environmental engineering from the University of Pittsburgh. While getting her master's degree in journalism from the University of Missouri, Laurie worked at the Missouri Department of Conservation.

In her free time, she enjoys canoeing in freshwater with her husband and two dogs.

Today, she is a freelance writer. This is her first book.